D1598284

JILL P. BACHMAN

CALLED TO
CARE

Called to Care

Author website: www.jpbachman.com

Dedication

To the memory of my mother,

who introduced me to the world of books and libraries and the pleasures of reading.

Because of you, I fell in love with words and their power to transform.

I feel your hands on my shoulders.

CONTENTS

Part One: Sarah

Change of Heart

October 10, 1861
Greeneville, Tennessee

Swooshing blood sounds filled her ears; her heart pounded as if her body consisted of only that organ. "Why? Why now, Evan?" she demanded, springing up from the loveseat. Tears threatened to fail her will. Her lips quivered. She hated for him to see her cry, she looked so unappealing. Some women could cry beautifully, but she was not among them. "We had our wedding planned out and ready to announce. What happened? Don't you love me?"

"Sarah, I do love you, more than I can say, and that is why we should not marry … at least not now. With war closer every day. I cannot in good conscience—"

She interrupted. "That makes no sense at all to me, Evan! If you loved me more than you can say, why would you be leaving me? Especially now! In good conscience?"

"Sarah, I cannot stand by and do nothing. You know that, you know me. It will be over soon, everyone says so, so I need to join now, now when it can make a difference. I truly believe I will survive, but what if I am wrong and leave you a widow, or worse, a widow with a child? Maybe I would return with an injury that you would have to take care of for the rest of our lives. That is no life for you."

Her cheeks flamed hot.

"It is *my* life to decide for myself, Evan, not yours!" she shouted. "And yes, have you considered this? If you survive, but are wounded for life, what kind of life is that for either of us, married or not? Why put yourself at such a risk? Is love, our love, not more important than your whim to fight?"

Now it was his turn to be stunned. Evan had never heard Sarah speak to him like this. His voice rose to match her power. "Whim, Sarah, you call this a whim? We are fighting for our values, and if we are not willing to stand behind them, what are our lives really worth? Would you truly wish to be married to a man who is a coward?"

"Coward? You think choosing a life with me over joining a regiment of men anxious to go out and fight—evidence of *cowardice*? I call it love." Sarah took one breath, then sighed out another. "Evan, I am not opposed to your joining the Union fight. I believe in it, I really do. But join them after we marry, not before, so that I may know that you truly love me …." Her words began to falter as she heard her argument weaken. She took another breath and pressed on.

"Evan, there are other ways to stand for the Union and against slavery. It doesn't have to be you on a battlefield. You could help with the efforts to move slaves to freedom. You could pass on information. You could collect money. And you write so passionately!"

He raised his right eyebrow. "Sarah, those are efforts that others would look on in disgust. Why am I not fighting, they would wonder. My writing is read only by those who agree with me—no hearts have been moved by it. Only bullets will work now. I must do something! I am strong and healthy. Besides, I thought you said you were for me joining the fight." He stared hard at her, his gaze as intense as his words. He waited as he ran his long fingers through his hair, slowing his breath.

She was silent. Could he see through her that easily? Had her anger at his resistance carelessly revealed her deepest motivation—that once married, he would change his mind and not leave her? Did he know that he had become her whole life?

"So you are letting your worries about others' opinions carry more weight than my desires?"

Her words hung in the air, unanswered. He moved closer to her and tried to wrap her in an embrace. She pulled away in stony silence, her jaw hard, her face averted. Neither spoke until he broke the quiet.

"Sarah, let's not leave the conversation like this. Let's stop now. I will return tomorrow afternoon, after both of us have had a chance to consider my decision."

"*Your* decision? Your decision for *our* life? Your decision for *my* life? Come back later if you wish, or not. We shall see then what *I* have decided!"

Her words echoed in the silence as Evan strode out of her parents' parlor, closing the door quietly behind him.

Five long minutes later, she left the house to clear her head. She could not face her parents. At the corner, she met George, youngest of her four siblings, walking home from his day at the family's dry goods store. "Hello, there, Sister, is it not a beautiful fall afternoon? I love it when the leaves begin to reveal their changing colors, don't you?"

Always affable, what a fool, Sarah thought, *he has not a care in the world while mine crumbles around me.* "George, I am not feeling well at all. I thought a little walk would do me good, but I see I was mistaken. I'll walk back with you. If I do not come down for supper, please tell Mother and Father that I am feeling poorly and need to sleep. I may be having one of those awful headaches of Aunt Louisa's." *A headache is most certainly true.*

She woke late the next morning, dull and listless. She knew she needed to move, but had no heart for it. Her mother's gentle knock interrupted her thoughts. "Sarah, are you all right, my dear? May I come in?"

"Yes, Mother, come in," she sighed, as she put on her dressing gown and went to the door. "I'm some better."

"You don't look better, my dear." Jane Anne held her daughter at arm's length and studied her closely. "Do you have a fever? George said it might have been one of Louisa's headaches. Shall I fetch a doctor for you?"

"Um … no, Mother," she said slowly, rubbing her face. She regarded her mother's clear gray eyes, full of concern. "The problem is one of my heart, not my body. Evan … Evan wants to go with the Union Army almost immediately. That is not what we were planning." She felt the tears gathering. Sarah sat down, resignedly, on the corner of the bed. Jane Anne joined her, arm around Sarah's shoulders.

"Sarah, what were you planning? A wedding?"

She nodded. "Evan was getting ready to talk with Father yesterday when he came to see me. We had discussed it before and I was so full of joy, Mother. Then he stole it all with just a few words." She told her mother about their argument. A long silence filled the room, broken only by the chatter of busy squirrels in the oaks outside.

Sarah started to speak, but Jane Anne held up her palm. "Wait my dear. Let us think about this." *Is Mother against me, too?*

Sarah's sudden sullen expression made Jane Anne hesitate. She cleared her throat, reached for her daughter's unlined hand, looked thoughtfully at it, and then at Sarah's face as she continued. "Hear me out, my dear, please. Is it possible that Evan is right, that his truest concern is for you and the life that you will have, hopefully with him, happily, for many years? It is no way to begin a marriage with just a few days together, and then send your husband off to the battlefield, no matter how short the war. Why the haste, Sarah? I know you feel like you are an old spinster, as you say, but you are merely twenty-two."

Sarah looked at her hand in her mother's. "I suppose I hoped, deep in my heart, that once we were married, once we were truly man and wife," her cheeks flushing, "that he would have cause to change his mind and not join the army."

Her mother nodded her head slowly, the situation clearer now. "Oh my dear girl, I have known other women who wished similar things in their marriages, but sadly, almost no one has found that a husband's deepest yearnings can be overturned by his wife's affection, no matter how new and passionate."

Sarah had no words against her mother's wisdom. Jane Anne got up to leave, and at the door she added, "So many forms of love exist, Sarah. The love between a man and a woman early in marriage is a sweet and wonderful blooming, but it is a prelude to something much more solid and stable. You will see."

Jane Anne Morrison Dunlap, born at the turn of the century, didn't know what to make of her daughter's struggles. She saw a spark in Sarah that needed kindling, but she wasn't sure how it should catch flame. Her younger daughter had a restless spirit. For a time she had wanted to become a teacher. Then she wanted to study art and poetry. Then languages. Jane Anne saw these as temporary, trivial pursuits that Sarah would follow until she married. None of her suitors had proposed marriage, and Sarah worried that there must be something wrong with her. No one seemed to want her.

Her older daughter Caroline, whom everyone called Cara, was happily settled as a minister's wife in western Tennessee. Jane Anne and Wilson had three sons, Philip, James, and George, who gave them little cause to worry. A sixth child, Leah, died when she was two years old.

Jane Anne, a quiet and thoughtful woman, was committed to equality for all. She joined Wilson in his abolitionist crusading, as well as standing for women's rights and suffrage. She was happy that Cara seemed fulfilled as a minister's wife and mother to Bethanne and Eddie. But she was skeptical that marriage alone would satisfy her younger daughter's intelligence and curiosity. However, Sarah was young and time would tell.

As the day wore on, Sarah tried to occupy herself with the usual home chores, but they gave her too much opportunity to think and prepare her arguments. When not planning her appeal, her thoughts kept returning to the evening nearly two years ago when she and Evan met.

She had never laid eyes on a man so handsome or charming as Evan Winslow Rule. He commanded any room he entered, and people were drawn to him like a magnet. With ramrod-straight posture and a fluid grace of movement, he knew the power of his presence. He spoke in a slow, deep, melodious voice. Evan's nearly black hair was thick and wavy, and long enough so that he had to finger-brush it off his forehead, which he did habitually. He had a way of looking someone in the eye with more intensity just before breaking it off, as if to remind the other, "You must remember this. Fix it forever in your mind." *Those eyes,* Sarah remembered thinking.

She was not given to swooning or preoccupation until she met Evan. She loved the look of his strong and graceful hands, fingers long and elegant, ink stains between the index and middle finger of his right hand. He practiced law with his uncle, and when not drafting contracts and arguments, those beautiful hands wrote impassioned letters to the newspapers about the evils of slavery. Sometimes she let herself imagine his hands on her skin, his fingers combing through her thick brown curls to tenderly hold her head while he kissed her.

She could not help smiling as she recalled their first meeting. Her older brother James had met Evan a few weeks prior, and a friendship developed. Her mother urged James to invite him to dinner, probably hoping for him to meet Sarah without being obvious. When Evan walked through the door, Sarah's natural ease with strangers drifted away like smoke. Throughout the evening she stumbled over her words, or spoke silly things, so unlike her. Most unsettling was how her attention was riveted on him and his speech. She did not notice her family, nor could she recall the table talk or what was served for dinner. She only remembered his look on her.

As Evan said farewell, Sarah positioned herself at the end of the little group, hoping to be his last, *what,* she wondered … *memory? Impression?* He took her hand in his warm one, and she watched, spellbound, as he slowly raised it to his full lips, the custom of southern gentlemen. "Miss

Sarah, it has been a most delightful evening. James has spoken of you often, and it is my misfortune that I did not seek an introduction earlier. It would be my honor to call on you. May I?" And then he fixed her with his green-eyed gaze.

As promised, Evan arrived mid-afternoon. His expression so sober, Sarah knew he had not changed his mind. The house was quiet, and she directed him to the parlor. Sarah sat and indicated that he should, too, but across from her, instead of beside her on the loveseat.

She began, hands pressed down on her lap, hoping he couldn't see them shaking. "What I need to know is this, Evan. For me, this is at the core of our—" she hesitated for the right word … *argument, disagreement, quarrel?*

"Situation," he supplied. *Oh my, situation is much larger than a disagreement. Such a dry word.*

"Our situation," she echoed, swallowing. "What happened to change your mind about our plan, Evan? Did someone advise you against our marrying, your aunt or uncle perhaps?"

"None of that, Sarah. My change of heart—"

A thud hit her chest. *A change of heart? Is that not more serious than a change of plan?*

"—came from visiting Patrick last week. He had been seriously wounded in those skirmishes near here, and we had a long discussion. He could not return to the fight. He was clearly needing to unburden himself, and after the usual pleasantries, it came pouring out of him. He returned to his family deeply changed from the man he was before the war, Sarah."

He leaned forward with his hands clasped, elbows on knees, earnestly searching her face. "I fear something like that could happen to me." He shook his head slowly in thought. "He has nightmares and pain. His thoughts are difficult to control, and he can no longer take charge of a classroom. You know he was a teacher? Like me, he felt compelled to serve,

Change of Heart

he felt called. He pretends to, but takes no joy in the prattling about of his two little ones. They are a bother to him now."

Evan stopped and looked away. "Sarah, my dearest, can you not see my confusion and difficulty with these choices? I am torn between my deepest values and my love for you. It will be just a short time to wait, and when I return, you will know that I am home for good. And ..." he halted, "and, you will be able to judge for yourself if I am still the man you want to marry."

Evan, the boulder, would not be moved.

To Help, to War

Sarah's Diary: October 23, 1861

I awoke this morning after our farewell, taken by surprise that I could easily move ... when anticipating this day, I thought I would most likely be indescribably sad, moored to my bed by an invisible, iron-like emotional tether. But the truth is—I was primarily fearful. Partly for Evan and the hardships he would surely face, but most of it was for me. The fear that I might never marry the man I feel such love for. The fear that things will change between us, or have already, unable to be mended. The fear of not being useful to anyone or not knowing how to fill my hours. It can't all be spent in waiting. How do I shape this life of mine after our goodbye?

Sarah's Diary: October 30, 1861

Evan has been gone a week. I have not received a letter yet, but I wait, confident the mail will come. Evan is a good writer and has made me many poems during our courtship. He is so intelligent and witty, and knows just how to amuse me. My anger at him has softened a small amount, and I am not worried much about him, yet, because he and James had to travel to join their Union regiment up in Kentucky. The men will require time to learn everything they need to be trained on, so I do not worry that he is in the midst of fighting, yet. The day will come, I expect, when the lack of news will cause me much consternation, but not today.

Before our last farewell, I was absolutely certain that Evan would resist the idea of me coming with him. He did, the stubborn man. Other women have accompanied their men, hoping to help in any way, including nursing them if they become injured or sick.

Yesterday I was at a sewing circle in town, and my friend Clarissa brought a copy of the popular book written by Miss Nightingale from England on how to take the best care of those who need nursing. "Notes on Nursing," it is called. She promised to let me read it in a day or two as it is not too long and I am a fast reader. In the meantime, I am sewing uniforms, trousers to be exact, just as fast and as hard as I can. I am not very good at it, but it is a way I can help, and maybe help Evan. Though the soldiers are promised all sorts of supplies and equipment, it is said they always need more.

Sarah's Diary: December 28, 1861

Christmas was a sad day, though we tried to enjoy ourselves and make merry. We all had hoped, Union and Confederate alike, that the war would have been over by Christmas. It is getting cold here in Greeneville, and Confederates are all around. Some have taken to stealing our food, others to asking for it, but no money ever changes hands. I am surprised that so many of our neighbors support Lee. I thought they were for the Union and abolition, just like us.

The sewing circle lately has taken to meeting in different places each time, and yesterday we decided to sew privately at our homes, perhaps with one other lady present to while away the time with chatter and companionship. It is getting more dangerous for us to be so open about our leanings and work.

I am so down of heart that Tennessee seceded from the Union. Though most of our neighbors and friends in east Tennessee are firmly for the Union, we still find ourselves in the midst of Confederate sympathizers. The tensions and increasing divisiveness make me yearn for the days when we didn't know that our opponents were so against us.

Sewing has never been of interest to me, and since reading Miss Nightingale's book I have talked with Mother and Father about leaving to help nurse our sick and wounded soldiers. I am hearing of any number of places I could volunteer. They are against it, they say, because they are worried for my safety. Besides, Mother asks,"Did you not wish for your role to be here, for when Evan returns? What will he think, when he finds you in the same battles that he has fought to rid himself of the memories? He will need you to be his sanctuary." I see her point, but the outcome she foresees is just one possibility ... there are many, some very fearful ... and here I sit with willing heart and hands. May I not be used in such a noble calling, not to do battle, but to care for and help heal our soldiers? And if not to heal, to be a comfort as they face their pain or their Maker?

I need a distraction from my constant imaginings about Evan.

Sarah's Diary: January 23, 1862

Yesterday I received two letters, one day after my 23rd birthday, spinster that I am, and oh! my heart was lifted, and my prayer, my eagerness to be useful somehow, was answered, at least in a small way. And I finally received a letter from Evan. I read and reread it many times over, sure that my handling of it would erase his words, but they are now so impressed upon my heart that they cannot go missing, even if the paper does! Evan assures me that he is well, and that he and James are keeping safe and warm in spite of being in the dead of winter. They are eager for the war to be over, but they want to be of some use, like me, and some of his regiment say they would hate it if they never had any fight with the Rebels. That may be the common thought of men preparing for battle, bolstering each other up, showing each one an outward bravado. But is it their deepest wish? Evan assures me of his love for me, and his desire to make a home for us the very instant that the war is over and he is back in our beloved Greeneville.

The other was from Cara. She is with child again, expecting the baby sometime in late spring, middle of May she thinks. Bethanne is almost six years old now, and Edward, who just turned three, is a little slow. Cara is hopeful it is just a period of adjustment he must get over. Although her pregnancies went well, she had difficult births with each. Knowing no one in the little area of Pittsburg Landing where they moved, she asked if I might come and stay a while, helping with the children and the new baby—and doing whatever she might need. She is nearly ten years older than I am, but we have always had a sweet and kind sisterly bond. And I like her husband very *much. He seems to be a true man of God, anxious to help the people of his church. I prayed to help our soldiers somehow, but this request from Cara makes me feel most needed, and I immediately wrote her a letter saying YES.*

Is this of God, answering my prayer to be useful?

To Cara's Side

February 21, 1862
Greeneville, Tennessee

She could stay idle at home no longer—it was time. The weather was beginning to improve, and recently, the Union won battles at Forts Henry and Donelson. Travel to Cara and Samuel's would be easier and safer now.

Sarah didn't worry much about her parents and George. They seemed able to avoid suspicion even though they were strict abolitionists. They had decided to remain quiet, her father told her, "for the long duration ahead. This war is just the beginning. The fight to abolish slavery will have many fronts, in many forms, for years to come. It is best not to be targeted now. And besides," her father continued, "we know several important abolitionists who have connections with the rebels, and they seem safe enough. Look at my friend Judge Temple. He is getting along fine."

The weather was sunny and cold the day she left Greeneville. Sarah stood at the corner, waiting for the wagon to take her to Knoxville, where she would stay with her brother Philip and his family for a day or two. Then she would travel by train halfway across the state to Nashville, and then finally by steamboat on to Pittsburg Landing, a few miles from Cara and Samuel and their little Shiloh Chapel. After their defeat at Fort Donelson, it was rumored that the Confederate army was now amassing more strength to respond. But the ardent hope on both sides was still that war would soon be over. Clarissa had urged Sarah to join in her effort to collect supplies needed for the wounded. But Sarah declined. She needed to get to Cara's side.

The wagon appeared, and Sarah climbed aboard, relieved she was wearing extra layers of clothing for the air was cold in the open wagon.

March 10, 1862

When she arrived, sun was filtering through leafing-out trees, dappling the ground. She smiled in relief at finally seeing Samuel after her long journey. *Home,* she thought, *where my people are, that is my home. I must lay my worries for Evan and James aside, and turn my attention to Cara and her growing family.*

Samuel greeted her warmly at the dock. He was noticeably thinner than on their visit to Greeneville two years ago. But his eyes, big and warm and brown as ever, even over dark circles, looked directly into her, trying to say something that she couldn't decipher.

"How is it with Cara?" she asked after they were settled into the wagon.

He watched the horse and road while he spoke, avoiding Sarah's eyes. "She finds it most difficult to keep nourishment. She should be getting bigger by now, seven months into her pregnancy, but she is growing only in the belly, the baby. Cara is tired all the time, I think withdrawn, too, and has not had the period of increased energy before the birth that she had with Bethanne and Eddie."

"You will see for yourself, Sister," he continued. "Do not let it surprise you—oh, I am so grateful you are here! A local midwife, Mrs. Abell, will help Cara when the time comes, but Pittsburg Landing is very small, and the people are divided in their devotion to Lee or to the Union. We find it hard to make the acquaintance of friends. She is lonely, too, without any women she feels affection for, and I am not much help since I have my ministerial duties. You are a godsend, Sarah, thank you a thousand times over for coming to us."

Sarah smiled and put her gloved hand out to squeeze his. "Samuel, Brother, the letter from Cara was like a call from God to me. I have been so worried about Evan and James, and everyone back home. I have wanted to help the Union in some way, and Mother and Father have not taken kindly to the idea of me helping to care for our injured men. But this appeal from

Cara has given me a direction and a place to be of real service. I know it is of God, answering my prayer. It is not what I had been asking for, but we are told God does answer prayer, though not always in the way one thinks. Isn't that right?" She smiled at him.

"Yes, Sister, that is right."

When they entered the little cabin, Sarah hid her surprise at Cara's appearance. Their sisterly embrace was warm and long, but in spite of her obvious belly, Cara's arms and shoulders and face were thin, much too thin. Her eyes, gray like Jane Anne's, were sunken.

"Oh, Sarah! I am so glad to see you!" Cara cried out. Cara's hold on her was fierce, but Sarah said nothing. She could tell from the shudder of her sister's shoulders that Cara was sobbing. After another minute Cara released her.

Seeing her wide-eyed niece and nephew in the corner which served as kitchen, she could not hold herself back. "Oh, there you are, my sweet-ies—come to Aunt Sarah!"

Bethanne, who did not have much recollection of her aunt, moved slowly into Sarah's arms as she bent down to hug them. Eddie, never one to be shy, boldly bounded into his aunt's embrace, piling on top of his sister. "Oh you children, I am so glad to see you! We will have a grand time together while I am here."

Sarah backed herself onto a wooden stool and pulled a small rag doll from the top of her traveling bag. Ceremoniously she presented the doll to Bethanne, straightening its dress and adjusting the little bonnet. "This is your baby now, Bethie. She has journeyed all the way from Greeneville just to be yours."

Turning to Eddie, who had suddenly found his thumb at his mouth, Sarah handed him a little wooden horse. "This is from your Grandfather Dunlap, Eddie. He made this from an old tree just for you. He says you are to name it yourself and take very good care of it. And if you do, you will be that much closer to having a real horse of your own someday to ride and enjoy."

The boy's thumb came out of his mouth as he clutched the toy to his little chest. "His name is Horsey," he declared.

"Is that right?" Sarah smiled. "Then Horsey it is."

Cara took her younger sister by the hand. "Let me show you where you will stay while you're here. Here is your bed, in this corner with the bigger one. Neighbors gave it to us for the children to share. The space is tiny, but we hope it will be cozy. When the baby comes, he or she will sleep in the little cradle next to us."

"It is fine, Cara. It will be good for the children and me to get used to each other. You know I barely know them, Eddie especially. They are beautiful children."

While the children were occupied with their toys, Sarah sat on the edge of her bed and patted a spot for Cara. With one hand on Cara's shoulder, she sought out her dull gray eyes. "Tell me truly, dear Sister, how is it with you?"

Sarah listened. She nodded and squeezed Cara's hand, remaining silent as her sister unburdened her weary self. She talked of tiredness, Samuel's frequent absences tending his church, and the constant demands of her children. She told of her fears for the Union, and of the neighbors who hated President Lincoln and wanted slavery to continue.

"They depend on those slaves for their very livelihood," she explained, "and it is so hard for them to see a different way. I am afraid to talk to anyone about my beliefs, though our little church knows how we stand.

"And Samuel! He is so deeply troubled about how to respond. We have the Union Army close to us on the North, and Lee's men all around. Both Eddie and Bethanne are curious about the men, and the horses they see when they are outside. Bethanne has become quite the little worrier.

Whenever she sees soldiers from the window, she quickly entices Eddie into a game or some other diversion."

Cara stopped to draw breath before continuing. "Last week she asked me if Samuel will have to go to war, and if he did, would he die."

Sarah couldn't speak and just shook her head.

"But most of all, Sarah," Cara said, tears rolling slowly down her cheeks, "I am lonely. So very lonely, and tired deep into my soul."

Sarah reached out to her sister and held her close for a long time. Then she pulled away and searched her face. "Cara, I am here now. I'm here to help with the children, and the chores, and the meals. I have been longing for a way to offer my help, and you have given me the wonderful gift of using my service. And," she continued conspiratorially, "we shall talk as sisters about all sorts of things. I have so much to tell you, particularly about Evan, the man I will marry when this war is over. But before we do one more thing, tell me what you had planned for supper, and I will get it started. You," she ordered, "will take a little nap."

The hearty meal of ham slices, bean soup with cornbread, jam, and butter was over. After the children had said their prayers and gone to bed, Cara retired next. Samuel and Sarah sat at the hearth in front of the fading fire, she in her sister's rocking chair, he in his.

Samuel asked, "What do you think, Sarah? How do you see your sister?"

"I am a little fearful, Samuel, about many things …. Her health, her involvement with the children, and you," she said, directing her focus on him pointedly, "but mostly I am concerned for her mood and her state of mind. What difficult times these are, even if one wasn't facing the trials of another birth and another babe to care for. And I am not very experienced in these matters myself. I am just twenty-three." After a moment's pause she added, "I think I shall call upon Mrs. Abell soon, and see if she has knowledge of how we can best help Cara. Perhaps it is a womanly thing, and some herbs or a concoction could help. I wonder, does she spend any time out of doors?"

"Well, she does love the out of doors as do Bethanne and Eddie. The best we can do right now is to spend a little time outside in the garden area, when the earth gets warmer and the soil can be worked. She enjoyed our garden in east Tennessee. But with war looming all around us, it seems dangerous to spend time too far from our cabin. I think her feeling house-bound contributes quite a lot to her current state. We have talked about leaving here and moving north, but we both feel we have been called here for a reason ... and, it is not a good time ..." he trailed off.

Two weeks passed, and Sarah fell into a contented routine that used up all her energy. She woke early before the children and Cara. While Samuel tended to the fire, she looked through the pantry to see what was available for breakfast fixings. Most mornings it was oatmeal, with bread and butter, and milk. Some days they had scrambled eggs, a style everyone agreed upon, even Eddie. Besides a little garden, they kept chickens, and the children were delighted to show their aunt how to safely gather eggs.

Crocuses pushed up through newly cleared soil, hinting of spring. The scent of warming breezes over matted leaves replaced the smell of old snow and melting ice. Trees began to bud out a ripening green. Cara sat on the little bench on the porch, shawl around her shoulders, taking in the sun. A smile graced the corners of her mouth, and she closed her eyes. *She is actually doing some better,* Sarah thought. *Her cheeks are pinker, and I've seen her smile more often.*

"Cara," Sarah said, getting up from the porch step, "while Eddie and Horsey are down for a nap, I'd like to take Bethie on a little walk, stretch our legs. Maybe we'll explore a bit, or visit Mrs. Abell. It's been two days since we've seen soldiers on the road. Could be that the threat of war here has lessened. We'll be back shortly, sooner if there's trouble."

Eyes still closed, Cara smiled toward her sister. "A wonderful idea."

Bethanne worked hard to keep pace with her aunt. Sometimes she had to skip to make up the gap. The attention she received from Sarah was life-giving, and she'd begun to favor her aunt over her mother. Sarah did not miss Cara's wistful look as Bethanne addressed more and more conversation to her. Now the girl reached for her aunt's hand and hummed a little tune as they walked.

"Soon, Bethie, your mother will give birth to another baby, and things will change around your little cabin. What do you think about all that?"

Bethanne was unusually silent.

"It looks like you've been giving some thought to the situation, haven't you?"

"Yes, ma'am," her eyes at the ground.

"I would like to know what a person your age thinks about these things. Will you tell me some of them? What is most important to you?"

"I'm worried."

"Worried? What worries you, dear girl?"

"The soldiers."

Of course! Not the baby, the war. "What is it about them?"

"They look mean. Sometimes when they see me and Mama and Eddie, they laugh at us, or smile—but it's not a nice smile. Sometimes there's a lot of them. Sometimes they come to the gate and talk to Papa. Why are they here?"

"That is a very big question, Bethie. What do you know about why they are here?"

"Papa says slavery, and he says slavery is wrong. Mama says people in different towns don't agree, and so they are fighting over it. Although we don't like slavery, most people here do, and the Union men are coming to beat the Rebs here and make them give up their slaves. Is that right?"

"Yes, that's most of it, Bethie, and it is surely a sad thing for our country. But, it's not a thing for you to worry about. Your Mama and Papa and I are here to make sure that nothing bad happens to you and Eddie and the new baby. Are you hoping for a brother or a sister?"

"I want a sister, Aunt Sarah, I already have a brother. Eddie is nice enough, but he does not like dolls. He likes screaming loud and running instead. Not me. I want a girl so we can play alike."

"Have you met children to play with at your Papa's church?"

She nodded.

"Are there children you like there?"

Bethanne nodded again. "Especially Abigail. She has pretty hair, all braided nice. I wish Mama would fix my hair like that."

"We'll see what we can do about that, Bethie, I think your mother and I remember how." Sarah gave her niece's hand a little squeeze. "How would that be?"

Nodding again, Bethanne returned the squeeze and grinned at Sarah.

They walked on along the road until sounds in the distance stopped them. Men's voices, lots of men's voices. Bethanne gripped her aunt's hand more tightly. Sarah looked down at her frowning face, and gently suggested they turn back, going by Shiloh Chapel. *Maybe we can find Samuel there.* "Let's stop and say a little prayer, and perhaps there will be some other children around to play with for a time this afternoon. What do you think?"

"Yes, please." Beth's hand had become clammy.

———

Samuel sat at a little desk in the doorless closet that served as his office, writing furiously.

She tapped gently on the door frame. "Samuel," she said, "I don't want to interrupt, but can we speak for a minute? I'm wondering about the commotion we heard on the road ahead."

He nodded. Sarah looked over her shoulder to Bethanne, who was settled on a pew helping her doll read the hymnal. She turned back to Samuel. "We heard men's voices, lots of them, and they seemed to be getting clearer, and um, closer, I suspect. Soldiers?" Her worried expression needed no clarification.

"I think so, Sister, yes, that is what the neighbors told me earlier today. Apparently the Rebels are amassing for an attack by Grant and his men, not sure when or where, but now it appears to be soon. We need to make sure we have the food and wood that we need. And bullets and guns, just in case. It is a good thing we are not Quakers who would not fight a lick to save their souls," he offered feebly.

"That is not a bad idea, I think—although the Quakers were left alone in Greeneville and no one on either side harassed them. And we are family of a man of God, with your wife nearing delivery, AND with young children? Surely we will be safe here if we stay inside the cabin, with the windows covered and the doors bolted?"

"That is what we are hoping, Sarah, but we need to be ready for worse. I'm making a list for a trip to Corinth to purchase as much as we can."

Missing Evan

March 25, 1862
Pittsburg Landing, Tennessee

Dearest Evan,

Oh, how I miss talking with you and feeling the comfort of your presence and your arms, and of your calming words. You have no idea! I arrived at Pittsburg Landing where Cara and Samuel live 2 weeks ago, after the long journey from Greeneville. This time period seems like an eternity as I think back upon it. The travel, the wonderful though much too short visit with Philip and his family, the sights of varying geography from our lovely mountains, through the winter fields readying for spring and the bleak areas destroyed by battle. My heart breaks at the insanity and destruction. But then, I am telling you things that you have likely already witnessed, several times over!

If I had the time and energy to write more letters, I would have, I sincerely tell you, but I have been fully used up at the end of the day with the chores of child care, and cooking most of the meals, and looking after Cara. Oh, yes, she does help, and she directs me, but she is so poor of appetite, and tired all the time. When I first arrived, she seemed despondent; she is lonely, she says. I know that I have cheered her somewhat. But I am most fearful about what will happen after this baby is delivered.

Yesterday, I went to visit the midwife that Samuel has found to help Cara when her time comes, but was prevented in doing so, using my best judgment while walking with Bethanne. We heard soldiers on the road, a far distance I would estimate, but not a sight I would want to encounter with a girl of six in my care. So I did not have the opportunity to inquire of Mrs.

Abell if she knew of help or potions or actions we could take to assist Cara. Cara and Samuel, being new here, have not had time to make friends.

But now that I think of it, dear Evan, I can hear your good counsel at my ear. You would say to me, "Find another woman, Sarah, she does not need to be a friend. She needs only to have the experience of birthing children to understand Cara's dilemma. What woman would refuse another woman this kind of help and advice? Friend? Enemy? Hogwash. Concern yourself only with Cara's welfare." There, Evan, have I captured truly your sentiments to me? And yes, I have received two letters from you, one at home, and one here at Cara's. I look at them every day, though I do not need to for I have committed to memory every word you have written to me.

I am tired, Dear One, and the children I share this little corner with are enjoying a deep and untroubled slumber. I am anxious to join them soon. Know that I think of you, and say my prayers for you, unceasingly. I pray for your safety, your health, your good cheer, and for a quick end to this awful war that has separated us so painfully. I long to be your wife.

Love,

Your Sarah

PS. This time with Cara's children has given me a clearer picture of family life. It is a good thing that one does not normally welcome children fully developed at three and six years of age. Living through infancy on helps one get used to them!

S.

Shiloh

April 6, 1862
Pittsburg Landing, Tennessee

The bullet pierced his right thigh, powering its way through muscle, slowed down by bone. He had been taking aim just as he was shot, so he missed his chance to kill another Reb. He was getting used to the process of battle, and fortunately the uncontrollable shaking came only after the fighting was over. Then, all he could do was shake.

But this time was different. The searing hot stabbing surprised him—but not as much as the shocking awareness that he was hurt, seriously. He knew automatically that he could not stand. "Shot, I've been shot!" he heard his shaky scream. "Help me!" A desperate plea to no one in particular, but to anyone or anything who could lift him from the panic of this nightmare.

Thomas was nineteen years old.

He had fallen on his back. Trying to protect his heart, he scuttled around onto his stomach to face the enemy line. As he maneuvered to his left side, the horror of seeing bone fragments in his blood-soaked trousers caused bile to rise in his throat, and he vomited. The pain and fear were too intense. He hollered out again, and again. And then he lay there in frightened and frustrated tears. When the screaming ceased because it did nothing to stop the pain and the fear, he did the only thing left that might help.

He prayed.

April 8, 1862
Pittsburg Landing, Tennessee

The sudden pounding sounded like thunder to Sarah, still dreaming. It was barely dawn. Samuel shuffled from sleep and moved awkwardly to the door.

"Open up, open up!" loud voices called. More pounding. "Union soldiers, open up!"

Sarah and Cara dressed hastily and joined Samuel. The five occupants of the minister's cabin had barely slept the past two days. War raged all about them. The unpredictable boom of cannon fire, shots of rifles, horses screaming, flames and smoke from fires all around, and worst of all, the human sounds—men raging at each other, and the crying and pleading of the injured. Cara and Samuel had resorted to medicinal whiskey to lull the children into something resembling sleep. Exhausted, the adults had found some respite at night when the worst of the war noises settled.

The first day's fighting was terrifying, and the Confederates seemed to be winning, at least by the occasional shouts of Lee's men, and glimpses Sarah could get by lifting the curtain and wedging the window open when gunfire ceased. Secluded in their cabin, none of them realized Grant's army began to turn the tide on the second day. The newspapers would later report the Union victory as an early turning point in the war. Staggering, however, was the loss of life on both sides, more than 20,000 in the two-day Battle of Shiloh alone.

Battle sounds ceased as the third day dawned. Union soldiers were now rousting area residents for any supplies and aid they could command. When they came to Samuel's cabin, they found nothing to confiscate, only people—one man, two women, one in the last month of pregnancy, and two young children.

"Friendly, we are friendly, Sergeant. My name is Samuel Beale. I am the minister here at Shiloh Chapel," Samuel declared, opening the door, and inviting the two soldiers inside. The young soldier accompanying the sergeant carried himself as if sleepwalking, slumped, unable to focus on anything, his eyes barely open. "What is the outcome of this battle of the last two days? Is the fighting over?"

"Reverend Beale, I am sorry to disturb you at such an early hour. We need food, anything would be helpful. The Rebs burned many of our supply wagons on the first day. But more than anything, sir, we desperately need people to help tend our wounded. Yes, we were victorious, but our loss of life and injuries is so much more than we expected. We need help with burial, Christian burial," he nodded at Samuel, "if at all possible. Is your young woman there," looking pointedly at Sarah, "able to help us care for our wounded?"

At that question blood suddenly pulsed in Sarah's ears. Pressure in her neck and chest ballooned so fast she was afraid she might burst. *This is something I have wanted for months,* she thought, *to be of service to the Union, but I had no idea that war would sound and feel as horrific as it did the past two days. A hospital, Miss Nightingale's hospital is what I imagined, tidy with beds and white sheets and windows, but I have seen no hospital around here. Where would I go to help? Am I even free to go? What about Cara through the rest of her pregnancy, and the new baby, and Bethanne and Eddie?*

"You are sorely needed, Miss. Please come. Please come with us."

Sarah frowned at Cara and Samuel, torn between her loyalty to them, and her desire to go with this sergeant. "I cannot, sir, I am needed here to help my sister and her family. As you can see there will soon be another child to care for. And my—"

"Miss," he interrupted, "I implore you, having a child is a part of nature and a part of life, but what has happened to our men is not a natural thing. I know—I have a family of my own. What these men suffer is so far beyond what your sister will face, and she will have a reward. Many of my men will have no reward, in this life at least. Please, I am *begging* you, come with us. Our hospital tents are close by, and you can come back here later to check on your family. We need you now. Your sister will need you … when?" he asked.

Cara reached out to take Sarah's hand. "Sister, you have been such a blessing to us for this short time, and I agree with the sergeant. I am stronger now than when you came a few weeks ago. With the disruption all around us, Samuel's usual occupations won't be needed for some time. He will have time to help me with chores and children, and I can still make the meals for us."

She straightened and took a deep breath. "You see, Sarah, I too have been called to be of greater use in all this awful war. It is good for me to have a bigger purpose, the one of releasing you to do what needs to be done for these injured men. Go. Go, and come back here when you can."

Samuel stood behind Cara, his hands on her thin shoulders, nodding as she spoke. "Go help," he said quietly. "We will make do."

Sarah paused. *This is my opportunity,* she thought.

Turning back to the sergeant, she said, "Then give me a little time to collect the things I need to bring with me, and to change into garments that will be serviceable." She added, "Samuel, why don't you make some tea for the sergeant and his man here?" and to the two weary men, "You should sit. I won't be long."

The sergeant carried her traveling bag as they made their way from the cabin. The new day should have begun clear and crisp, but it dawned eerily smoky and foggy. Instead of sweet birdsong, she heard the sounds of soldiers, some injured and crying out, others who labored to haul bodies and bury the dead.

As they approached the hospital tents, Sarah saw exhausted soldiers scurrying around, setting up more shelters. These men were nothing like the uniformed men she had seen in parades and posters and magazines. Their uniforms were muddy and in disrepair; some men with large areas of their bodies bandaged and blood-soaked.

The sergeant spoke to her for the first time since they'd left. "Miss—" he paused.

"Dunlap," she replied.

"Miss Dunlap," he repeated. "I am Sergeant Michael Crane of the Army of the Potomac, and this is Private Wilkie. You may not see me much or at all while you are helping tend the men, but if you need me, please let the officer in charge of the field hospital know, and someone will be dispatched to locate me. When you are ready to go back to your sister's, the officer will find a man to escort you. You should not travel the distance, short though it is, unaccompanied. There are many dangers surrounding a recent battlefield."

She stood at the entrance of the first tent she came to, Sergeant Crane ahead of her. He spoke to a soldier who appeared to be in charge, and pointed to her. Sarah was sure she must have looked like a frightened little rabbit, her eyes quickly dashing here and there, but her feet were leaden. Outside the tent a soldier lay on a table, held down by three men, while a fourth, apparently a doctor wearing the bloody apron of surgery, reached toward the ground for a saw.

They are taking off that soldier's leg! Right there, in front of me—without anesthetic? Or cleaning the blade?

Sarah was terrified but knew she had to force herself stay and witness. She swallowed hard. She swallowed again to push back the nausea that threatened her. *I don't want to see this—I cannot look!* She turned away. The man screamed, a ragged, soul-clutching scream, and screamed again— one long, drawn out pitiful cry, and she forced herself to look as the saw blade bit through skin, the surgeon using both arms and all his might to saw the leg through. The grating of saw teeth on bone was a sound she had never heard before. She never wanted to again.

She thought she would vomit, but something like curiosity held her back. *Interesting—why doesn't the blood spurt and pool the way I'd expect?* Higher up on the man's leg Sarah noticed a belt, cinched tight, cutting off

Shiloh

circulation to the lower part of the leg. *So that's how it's done, the wasted part of his leg has no more need of its blood.*

Sarah would never forget the shock and horror and brutality of her first amputation. In the years to come she would help with more than she could recall. Usually the soldier was unaware of her presence, whether from injury or whiskey or fear and stress. Sometimes, if they were lucky, they had chloroform for anesthesia. A pile of grisly limbs on the ground under a window or in a wagon was an image she could never shake.

And it wasn't just the physical pain—it was also the man's anguish at the loss of part of his body, the stark brutality of the choice, the impossible choice, to give up part of himself. Nothing she could say would make the choice any easier. Sarah's best was to be a witness to the soldier's suffering, to be present, to offer him part of her strength while he went through it, to be part of his strength as he recovered. If he did. If he shunned what she had to offer and refused to fight for his life, she found it difficult to avoid taking offense. *I'm fighting for your life,* she would think, *how can you not?*

Thomas

April 8, 1862
Pittsburg Landing, Tennessee

At first, Thomas wondered if he'd woken up in heaven. But, no, not with screams and moans, and smells so bad—rarely had he ever smelled anything that bad in his life, even on the farm.

Two people stood at his side; one a woman, the other a man he took to be some kind of doctor. Somehow, blessedly, they had managed to get pieces of the leg bone back in where they belonged, sort of, but by the way they fretted over him, Thomas guessed his condition was not good. He had lain in the filth of the battlefield for a day and a half before he was carried off to the arrangement of tents serving as the field hospital. He was surprised to discover he had a shoulder wound, too. A second bullet had found his left arm, plowing through the fleshy part of the muscle but missing the artery and bones of the upper arm and shoulder. Still, the muscle was badly damaged.

"Clean this leg as best you can, then dress it," the doctor directed Sarah, "and check for pus, so we can tell if it's getting better. The arm is not nearly as dirty, but it still needs tending." He lifted a hand to brush back his hair, and closed his eyes with a deep sigh.

Out of Thomas's hearing he whispered to her, "I am really concerned about the leg. I'm thinking we will have to take it."

He looks exhausted, Sarah thought. *How distressing to see so many of our boys at death's door, or over the threshold, and be saying the same things over and over: clean, dress, watch, amputate. And pray.*

"Yes, Doctor," she replied, as they moved off to the next boy.

When she returned to Thomas, she touched him lightly on his good shoulder. "Soldier, I need to clean your wounds. It might hurt some, are you ready?"

Thomas peered out his good eye, free of the dried mud, and decided surely heaven wouldn't have so much suffering. He was probably in hell.

Sarah's basin of water started out clear, but a few dips of the cleaning cloth turned the water to bloody rust. Some areas she had to soften to remove the caked-on crust to discover what was underneath. Thomas stirred fretfully.

"What's your name, soldier? Mine's Sarah."

"Thomas, ma'am," he answered, softly. "Thomas Swain. From Greenville, Kentucky. Such a pretty place. Specially from the hilltops."

"Is that so, Thomas? You're the first soldier I've met from Kentucky." She caught herself just before she said "boy," guessing that these wounded, if they had nothing left, still held on to the pride of manhood even if they were too young to know much about it.

She thought of asking him about Evan. *Maybe Thomas is from that same regiment Evan joined in Kentucky and they met?* She decided it would be wrong to ask about her own personal matter when the boy before her suffered so and needed her full attention. Deeper still, she wondered if she was afraid to find out bad news. She knew that news, especially bad news, would find her; she didn't have to seek it out. "I'm from Greeneville, too, but the one in Tennessee. What a coincidence."

She finished with his leg and arm wounds. The leg was swollen tight and hot to the touch. The smell that she would come to know as gangrene signaled an awful fate. Sarah wondered when they would decide whether to take it off.

After less than a day, she found that talking to the men, helping the doctors and the nurses, and doing whatever she could do at the bedside, brought out something good in her.

Perhaps it's a sense of purpose?

Sarah's Diary: April 12, 1862, dawn

I have had a brief stay of two nights' rest at Cara and Samuel's. I will leave the respite of their little sanctuary after breakfast, and return to the hospital. Samuel will accompany me. He has been asked to help the men with their dying pleas. And burials.

What a blessing to manage a brief glimpse of family life again, though for every moment I am here, part of me is back at the hospital, wondering just how many more soldiers who, taken for dead, have been brought in from the battlefield, how many more have died, and how many have been transferred by steamship to the established hospitals in the east. They can barely spare me, but I must check on Cara. And if I say that I am back in normal family life again, well, that is simply a pretense. The children are agitated, Eddie being impossibly loud at times, and wanting nothing of the food that is before him. Cara sits alone by herself, answering us in only one or two words. She does not ask questions or reach out to her children, and she has not attempted a spit bath or even combing her hair since the day before the battle began. Dare I say that Samuel is a rock, but one with deep dark circles under his eyes and shrouded with sadness every time he looks at Cara. What is to become of her?

Samuel's log church suffered much damage during the two days of fighting, and the Union soldiers tore it down to use the wood. It is a miracle that their little home was spared, and we are all grateful for small mercies. S. seems as if he has no direction, but I am hopeful he will come back to himself soon. In a way, we are all dull of spirit.

My little niece has been the tiniest ray of sunshine in this dark period. She has asked all kinds of questions. Some have surprised me. "What are you eating? What is it like there? How are the linens washed? Could I come help you? Have you seen any Rebels? Are you helping the men, Aunt Sarah? Are our Union boys brave as they say?" She is so curious, as was I, until the end of my first day, when I was, like many, brokenhearted. But I have watched the surgeons and the nurses and the helpers, and even the soldiers cooking, as

Thomas

they survey a scene of the most dreadful suffering. I have witnessed them tak-
ing it all in, and then as if a silent order is given, they straighten their backs,
put a better look on their faces, a smile even sometimes, and step back into the
work they have been called to do. It is hard, much, much harder than I could
have prepared myself for.

    And I have heard no news of Evan.

Letter to Greenville

April 14, 1862
Pittsburg Landing, Tennessee

Sarah picked up the button from under his bed. It was the last thing of his she touched, and she would keep it with her nearly to the end of her days.

She had tended Thomas for a week and watched him slip away, sometimes faltering with a glimpse of improvement, sometimes plummeting. Sometimes she became excited thinking he would get better, but most days she knew she was looking at the wrong signs. The others would tell her that the glimmer of life in his eyes or him asking for more broth was just a delusion of the moment, not a true sign of recovery. They could not be sure that the amount of pus was a sign of worsening or improvement.

But in the end his leg wound was too grievous, even after the amputation. Gangrene had taken hold and infection had spread through his blood. The smell that immediately made her want to vomit was something she could dredge up from memory at a moment's notice. She compared it to the worst rotten smells she knew, and gangrene was always the worst.

Why, she often wondered, did Thomas hold her heart like he did? He was from Kentucky, she from Tennessee. He was younger than her, she guessed, maybe seventeen or eighteen. He had those golden eyes that reminded her of the barn cat she loved at home, and early on when he was mostly conscious, those eyes regarded her deeply, sometimes pleading, sometimes telling, but always looking at her as if he knew who she really was.

She had learned he had a family at home. He had gone off to fight for the Union with two of his four brothers in early 1862. His ma and pa, two sisters and the other brothers stayed at home to tend the family farm. He knew it was a hardship on the family for three of the five boys to be gone to fight, but it was important, his pa had said, to fight for your deepest beliefs. There was never going to be another time in their lives to help right the wrongs of slavery.

Thomas's sweetheart, Suzanne, promised to wait for him, even though they had just started getting to know each other. She was twenty, pretty, and very smart—a teacher. Thomas liked that about her the most, he said, she could help open the world for him in books and learning, and he wanted to know more of this world.

Sarah held the sadness in her heart in a walled-off place, watching and guessing that the world he longed to explore with Suzanne was rapidly shrinking. What was he seeing, really, she wondered, behind his fevered eyes?

Yesterday, when it seemed like Thomas's life had only hours left, Sarah asked if he wanted her to help him write a letter home. "Oh yes," he said, "would you do that for me? I been thinking what I need to be sure they know ..." as his words drifted into silence, a place that neither wanted to acknowledge.

Sarah finished for him, "—about how you're doing, and where you are?" as if words could steer the reality to a better place. He wanted to write two letters, he said, and thought it best to begin with one to his family, warming to what he wanted to say to Suzanne.

April 13, 1862

Dearest Ma and Pa, Brothers and Sisters,

I am rightly pleased to be sending you my thoughts because Miss Sarah, who has been keeping care of me while I am in this place called Pittsburg Landing, Tennessee, is writing for me. Do not fret, dear family, I know you haven't had word from me for some time now, but I am being well taken care of. I have taken a bullet to my right leg, and another in my left shoulder which is not so bad. The leg, just above my knee, could not be saved and had to be removed. I am hopeful that it is getting better. It is kindly hard for me to get around right now, but I pray to be joining the boys soon as I can, even on a crutch I can help somewhere.

How is you all doing at home? I think with great happiness of the vision in my head of you all around the table at supper. Ma's cornbread and jam, ham hocks and beans, and those pickles. You know, Ma, I miss them pickles most. Funny, ain't it?

I got to tell you the truth, it is hard to be here. They's lots of boys hurt worse than me, and they's suffering a lot. It is an agony to hear them at night especially, when I can see the beauty of a night sky and all the stars from an opening in the tent, and to know the injustice and unfairness for the others inside here.

Oh dear family, know in your deepest hearts that I miss you all and our happy times together, and cannot wait for that joyous day when I will be able to look directly upon your smiling faces, and feel your loving arms holding me close once again. I will do all I can to make that day come soon. And if that time is in the hereafter, know with all your sure strength that I will wait faithfully for you all and Suzanne. What a joy it has been to have you as my family.

Your loving and devoted son and brother,

Thomas

PS. Hello, I am adding this note of mine to let you know what a fine young man your Thomas is. He is being cared for at the field hospital near Pittsburg Landing. He has talked about his family with much affection. I learned he is from Greenville, Kentucky, and I am from another Greeneville, in the state of Tennessee. I wish your boy and you the best of luck in these grievous conditions that this war has brought upon us. I am enclosing a lock of his beautiful curls because I am told that so many families are comforted by receiving a favored remembrance of their loved ones.

Sarah L. Dunlap

Jane Plants a Seed

April 1862
Pittsburg Landing, Tennessee

Sarah's days fell into a strange routine. When she could, she slept fitfully at the back of a tent on a cot, some part of her always listening for a sound that might mean "wake up, help!" Or for a spoken word, "Ma'am?", or a hand on her shoulder, "Miss Dunlap, you are needed." During the next two weeks, she was able to get away to Cara and Samuel's twice more for a brief stay.

No more soldiers arrived for treatment, but the remaining ones still needed care. Though their injuries may have stabilized, more forbidding dangers lurked, the causes of which could not be easily seen, so different from the damage caused by the minie ball or bayonets. Typhus, diarrhea, pneumonia, and yellow fever all fought to claim the wounded if injuries didn't.

Sarah watched every aspect of the camp intently: the cooks, the soldiers who were assigned to be nurses or assistants, the high-ranking officers who barked off commands, the women like her with little or no training who helped wherever they could. In her sheltered life in eastern Tennessee she had never been a part of anything dedicated to such an important mission.

Sarah was amazed by the calmness and practicality of an older woman who befriended her, a recent widow, Jane Howard. *How can Jane be so self-assured in the midst of this storm? I am a jumble of nerves and anxiety at the sound of any strange noise.* "Well, my dear, when you have lost the one thing that really matters to you, you learn that circumstances that usually frighten you no longer have their hold. I am not shaken like I used to be. I have very little concern for my own safety now—worry seems to have retreated into the past. I do not need things to be a certain way anymore."

During a break in their work, Jane told Sarah about her plans when the field hospital closed. "I think I might like to apply to work on a hospital ship until I am no longer needed. Or maybe one of the Union hospitals near Washington where I can try to prevent one more wife from becoming a widow. When this war is over, I shall take an accounting of my life and seek its purpose anew. Maybe there is a special place for me."

"A hospital ship? There is such a thing?"

"Yes, the first one, I believe, is called the Red Rover. My brother has written me about its outfitting in St. Louis. It was a Confederate ship, recently damaged and confiscated by the Union, who plans to transfer it to the Navy, he says. It will be running on the Mississippi River."

Hmm—if I was helping aboard a ship with lots of exposure to different people, maybe I could learn news of Evan sooner?

"Your plans, Sarah? I know you hope to marry your Evan as soon as you can."

As Sarah's eyes filled with tears, Jane reached out to grab her hand. "It is normal to fret and stew, dear, and I am not one to tell you that everything will be all right. My own life as a new widow is a testament to the unpredictability of life, and of war. But I do know this—if you have an anchor of some sort, you will make it through whatever appears. It is hard to believe at the time—" Sarah's silence spoke doubt and worry.

"Oh, Jane, I am ever hopeful that we will be reunited soon, and that Evan will not have suffered injury or illness as so many of our men. That is all I pray about. Oh, yes, and for my sister Cara, who should deliver her baby any time now. If all goes well, I expect to return home to Greeneville where we'll raise a family of our own."

"But in the meantime?"

"Well, these days here have shown me that I have a gift I never knew of, an ability to be with someone, who may be even in his last moments, and not shirk, but stay and accompany him on his journey out of this life. I have so much to learn about caring for the sick and injured. And, I wonder how we could possibly put into place more of Miss Nightingale's recommendations?"

Jane looked at her quizzically, eyebrows raised.

"This time of caring for the men makes me remarkably sad, wondering how many more could have survived if they had early responses to their wounds on the battlefield. How horrible it must have been for those who lay for a day or more in the muck and rain with nothing but their injuries and dying fellows as company."

Jane nodded. "I know. I see it, too."

Sarah continued, "I ask myself, why have I been put here and shown this part of war, if not to use my talents and determination to make things better? It is so strange, but, as awful as the war is, I feel a great sense of belonging."

Jane smiled at her young friend. "Perhaps that is your anchor, Sarah," she said, arching her back and rolling her shoulders, "belonging to the work. Maybe not to the place, but to the work. Speaking of which, let us get back. My teacup is empty."

As she performed her duties, Sarah began to imagine working aboard a hospital ship herself, perhaps with Jane. *Surely it would be better supplied than this place, with more organization and room than with these tents on uneven ground.* Remembering her friend, she smiled at the thought of Clarissa's efforts to collect items for wartime relief. *Hooray for you! Maybe our hands have touched the same bandages.*

Cara

April 27, 1862
Pittsburg Landing, Tennessee

Sarah was brought up short from her thoughts as she finished a dressing and turned from a soldier's bedside. "Samuel, is it time? Oh, my, is everything—"

"Oh, Sister," he closed his heavy eyes and breathed a weary sigh. "It is over. Cara and the baby are fine. We have a son, and the delivery was surprisingly fast. There was no time to fetch you, barely time for the midwife. Cara is tired of course, and Mrs. Abell is with her and the children until I can return. I wanted you to know, and to see whether you would be able to get release from your work here. I see lots fewer men to tend now. Can they spare you?"

May 6, 1862
Pittsburg Landing, Tenn.

Dear Evan,

By now, dearest, you must have had news about the Union victory at Pittsburg Landing, or Shiloh as it is often called. We celebrate this victory though with a heavy heart for all the men lost to the effort, but a victory nonetheless. Can the end of this war be far away, and, dear Evan, the time when we will be married? I feel as if I can now breathe fully. There is so much to tell you, and I want to weep with sadness and despair, and as well with joy and happiness. My feelings are such a confused jumble, I feel some of the shock that the soldiers speak of. But before I go on, know that I am so grateful for your last letter, and that I am fine.

We have a new baby in our family! Cara delivered a healthy boy nine days ago, and she blessedly had no complications. I was deep down surprised because the last weeks until his birth were very hard ones for her. They have named him Michael, for Samuel's uncle, and Wilson, for Cara's and my father. How surprising that Eddie has shown such an interest in this sweet little one, but predictable that Bethie is disappointed that Michael is not a little sister. I am needed here more intensely than at the field hospital, and so I have asked the officers in charge if I may be spared. I may, they reply, but if I have a change, I should see if I am still needed.

I had no idea that so many of our soldiers would succumb to illnesses not brought on by their injuries. Caring for them in such primitive conditions is bound to cause additional problems to appear, as they have. It is a blessing and a mercy that I have been spared any illness myself from caring for them. I am mainly tired all the time, and I have lost weight. The food is sparse, generally most unappetizing.

It is my daily prayer, dear Evan, that you have avoided such injuries or illnesses yourself. Miss Nightingale says fresh air, good food, and maintenance of a positive attitude are key to maintaining one's health. I hope that you have been able to have all three of these conditions for your own dear self. I am hopeful that this war will end post haste, and that we can reunite soon to become husband and wife. I long to have our own family of little ones to care for.

Because we have no certainty of when this dreaded war will be over, I have taken it upon myself to apply to work for the time being on a hospital ship that travels the Mississippi River, transporting soldiers from battlefields to Union hospitals. I am not sure of the likelihood of my acceptance, partly due to Miss Dix's edict that Army nurses be over thirty years of age, which I am not. But I meet her other requirement of being plain-looking. Perhaps that will win her over. I sent her a photograph to prove that, as well as the information that I am betrothed to you, so she can be convinced that I am not in the business of attempting to locate an unsuspecting soldier to become my husband.

And the business about no hoop skirts—my stars, that is such a ridiculous rule! One hour in a field hospital, or a regular hospital, would have one out of such a contraption in minutes, modesty be damned. Never would I show up in a hoop skirt today, and on a ship? I daresay where would the room be to accommodate me, AND my clothes?

It is time for me to sleep. The entire cabin is quiet, and now it is my turn to join those in slumber. Know, dearest, that you are in my prayers for safekeeping by God's mercies. Please send me a letter to tell me you are well. I long for some word to settle my worries.

With utmost love and affection, I am,

Your Dear Sarah

July 29, 1862
Pittsburg Landing, Tennessee

On a sweltering late afternoon with no breeze for a little relief, baby Michael was listless. He lay covered with wet cloths to reduce his fever. His mother tried to get him to take a drink of water, dropped onto his lips from a clean cloth, but he did not respond. He had been that way for two days, disinterested in the breast and with watery stools most of the time.

Cara was anxious, as was Samuel. Bethanne and Eddie had experienced robust early infancies, having their share of sicknesses later, but nothing so early in their lives. Life in the Beale cabin now had a central eight-pound focus, and even the children knew that something was seriously wrong with their baby brother.

Sarah tried her best to distract them from the sad little scene, while Cara alternately picked Michael up to cuddle, perhaps nurse, then laid him back to cool off a bit. His skin was hot, and his breath came very quickly. "Get well, my little sweetling. We love you and want you with us so much," she crooned to him over and over.

Samuel attempted to take the baby, and urged Cara to rest, but she would have none of it. "It is not so much that I am the only one who can comfort him and get him to take water. It is that I can do nothing *but* this. If I am occupied with something else, my thoughts are constantly about what I can do to help him, and Samuel—" she said, her voice catching as tears overflowed her pleading gray eyes, "what if this is the last day we can hold him at all? I cannot pass this moment by, I cannot."

Samuel and Sarah stood nearby, impotent to change the direction of the baby's suffering, or of Cara's. Sarah recognized that Samuel ached too and had as much care for Michael as did her sister, but she dared not interfere with these hours, likely to be the last, for Cara with her baby. Sarah had heard and read about the high rate of infant death called cholera infantum, summer diarrhea in infants.

It was dark, nearly 11 p.m., when Michael Wilson Beale took his last silent breath. His heart stopped shortly thereafter.

Sarah's Diary: October 1, 1862

How can the sky hold its magnificent blue, and the brilliant orange and red leaves show every nuance of color, while inside this little cabin four bleak hearts have broken? It is impossibly unfair. I can barely bring myself to write these words, that my Cara has died. The only consolation is that she has followed her precious babe, Michael, into the next life.

I do so pray that there is a God who understands the power of sadness to pull one to the other side. And a God of mercy and forgiveness who understands when a life no longer seems worth living, it is within His power to welcome one across—even if that death be by one's own hand? I have cried the saddest of tears till I am sure there are none left, and forced myself to think of the welfare of Bethanne and Eddie, and of Samuel, too, and try to keep some routine after the first few days of Cara's passing.

Oh, that dark day, that awful day when it happened. Cara said she was going to walk to Pittsburg Landing, to meet a supply ship when it docked in hopes that she could fetch some flour and tea. The walk, she said, would help to clear her head; it would do her good to be with the trees and sky, and think of God. Those were her actual words to me. She seemed unusually cheerful, and my heart gave a little leap of happiness to see her so.

She asked me to walk with Bethanne and Eddie to a neighbor's in the other direction. They too have young children, and she was sure they all might occupy themselves for a lovely afternoon outdoors. The children were so excited to go. I had a nice chat with Mrs. Florence and a soothing cup of tea with honey. She shared some quick bread with us, and we all enjoyed the surprising little treat. What an afternoon it was, fun for the children, warm sun on the porch, and the chance for many deep breaths after the difficult times we've just had. As we walked home, ignoring the devastation all around, we chattered like squirrels about what stories we would share with Cara and Samuel. We had even been pressed to bring some of the sweet bread back home.

The sun was lowering in the west and cool was coming on when I opened the cabin door. I knew instantly that something was wrong—very wrong. Samuel sat in his rocking chair staring at an empty fireplace, tears streaming from his eyes. Before saying a word to him, I asked Bethanne to take Eddie into the bedroom so we could have time for grownup talk. The pair of them were still occupied with thoughts of the yard cat.

"What is it Samuel? Where is Cara? Has something happened?" He only looked through me, his weeping eyes addressing my fearful heart.

Finally, he swallowed with difficulty and said, "Cara is gone, Sarah. Your dear sister, my sweet wife … she has left us. She has died, Sarah."

"Died, Samuel, what are you talking about!? She was perfectly fine earlier this afternoon. Did she have an accident? An animal? A snake? What happened? Soldiers?" I was searching for a logical answer.

"None of that, Sarah. Oh, I am so sick, Sister. She drowned. She drowned at the river. She—she—made it happen. Herself."

My heart stopped and I nearly fell to the chair.

Cara

"She took her apron and filled it with stones and tied it around her. Then she walked to the dock and stepped off. Two soldiers who were offloading the steamboat noticed her action at the last and tried to save her. It took them too long to locate her body and bring her to the surface. She left this envelope addressed to me at the dock." He sat still as a stone for a minute, then gathered himself and stood. "I must go now to collect her body at the river. They have a wagon for me to bring her back to bury." The unopened envelope fell from Samuel's lap.

Such ended our perfect little afternoon! After the hardships of two days of the most terrifying battle, and the loss of the Shiloh Chapel, and Michael … after all that we had been through, it seemed as if Fortune was finally on our side again, and we would all have an easier time. And now Cara—and by her own hand!

There are many, many hard things about this, and I wish I could talk with her one more time. If I could, this is what I would say.

What I find most difficult to reconcile is this: Cara, what about the four people here, your family who love you? What will Bethanne take from this as she grows to womanhood? What about the hardships she will face … will she give in to them? How will Eddie remember his mother and his mother's disregard for her little children? What motherly thought did you give to them? And Samuel … had you no feeling, Sister, for what you left your husband, the man that you loved, who loved you dearly, to manage for the rest of his life?

Was our love not enough to hold you and buffer you from the storms of this sadness? I think these thoughts with the deepest sorrow as well as an anger which I hope is righteous. And yet, Cara, a very small part of me can understand that your actions must have seemed like the only option you had, a natural progression of everything that led up to your demise. I believe this because I watched you suffer. So I end my rambling with one thought only—I only think I know what you were going through. I cannot know exactly.

USS Red Rover

December 27, 1862
Cairo, Illinois

Sarah fingered the button in her pocket, its familiar surfaces an ever-present companion, reminder of a vital call. When she felt it, she thought of Evan, the soldier, and Thomas, her patient.

Sarah and Jane had met in Cairo three days ago, finding lodging until they could board the USS *Red Rover* and begin their assignments. Both had written letters of application to Miss Dorothea Dix, appointed by President Lincoln to head the Sanitary Commission, which was responsible for the care of wounded and ill Union soldiers. Miss Dix indicated she would work aboard the *Red Rover* as an assistant under the direction of the Sisters of the Holy Cross. For her work, she would now receive forty cents a day, her first paid work. She smiled to herself, marveling at the idea.

She had written her parents and Evan about this development. Her mother and father wished she would come back home to Greeneville. They grieved so for Cara and the grandson they had never held. Sarah knew they feared losing her, too. She did her best to assure them that her life working aboard a hospital ship would be much safer and more predictable than the field hospital at Pittsburg Landing.

"We know that, dear Sarah," they wrote, "however the reports we have received about the conditions aboard ship are much too difficult for a young educated woman. Established hospitals exist already in the cities around Washington. You could work there and not always be on the move, or in harm's way."

But something about being on the move kindled a spark in her. She wanted to see as much of the country as she could, even if it was ravaged by war and destruction. Until now she had only known Greeneville and Pittsburg Landing. *While I'm waiting for Evan to return and I'm free from the business of a home and children, why shouldn't I satisfy my curiosity about what lies beyond Tennessee?*

When Sarah left Pittsburg Landing, Samuel and the children accompanied her as far as Cairo, Illinois. They were going to stay with his sister, Margaret, in Chicago. Margaret had been urging him and Cara to get out of that "awful place" the entire time he had been in Tennessee. He had naively thought that his ministry could help sway Southern hearts. *Chicago would be much more to his liking,* Sarah thought. *Margaret is a warm and welcoming woman, with five children near Bethanne and Eddie's ages. Getting the little family to Chicago and away from the sad reminders would be a blessing for everyone.*

The final goodbye was painful. Samuel's emotions had been dulled by the deaths of Michael and Cara, but Bethanne and Eddie cried and pleaded for their aunt to come with them. Though the family had lived through horrible times in a few intense months, their tears had no effect.

The USS *Red Rover* was a 650-ton side-wheel steamer nearly 300 feet long. Built in 1859, she had been purchased by the Confederate States of America in November 1861, but was seized by Union forces in April 1862. When the *Red Rover* was converted to a fully functioning floating hospital, she was transferred to the Department of the Navy. Her transformation included a steam boiler for laundry, an elevator, a separate kitchen for patient and staff meals, many bathrooms, and gauze window blinds to keep cinders and smoke away from patients. *Rover* was outfitted with two operating rooms, one reserved just for amputations.

Sarah and Jane carried their bags to the top of the boarding ramp where they showed their acceptance letters to the officer in charge. The open entry deck was covered with a large canvas shade for protection from sun and weather. People hurried about, carrying supplies and food, talking, checking details. Windows on all sides surrounded both levels of the hospital decks, with small rooms at the back for the crew and workers. Patient beds were arranged in tidy rows nearer the front of the ship, to take in more fresh air.

A young officer, Lieutenant Gregg, directed them to find Sister Veronica somewhere on the hospital decks. *He seems kind*, Sarah thought, *but not battle hardened. I wonder if he knows what lies ahead of him.* She was glad no patients had boarded yet because she had never been in a real hospital. The hospital tents at Pittsburg Landing did not prepare her for this new version, and she wanted to get her gawking over first. The *Rover* was scheduled to take on her first patients tomorrow at dawn, so she had a little time to get her bearings and meet the staff.

They found Sister Veronica on the upper deck, directing a black man to open all the windows. "Mr. William, it is insufferably cold outside, but the air is fresh, and since we are not underway, no breeze can move smoke or cinders. Tomorrow will be different. Please, we need to have all the good air that we can, now, and anytime that conditions permit." She stopped and regarded him thoughtfully, "So, Mr. William, I am appointing you to be in charge of the air on the *Rover*. Please see to it that it is as fresh as you would want for yourself."

"Yes, Sister," he nodded, and the man Sarah assumed to be William Something-or-other headed to the back of the deck to start opening windows.

Sister Veronica turned toward Sarah and Jane as they held out their acceptance letters. She was of slight build and medium height. Only her olive-toned face and hands were visible under her habit and head coverings. But her smile was warm and welcoming, and her brown eyes had a depth to them that Sarah found unusual. She liked Sister Veronica immediately and felt a kinship she couldn't explain. Sister studied their letters carefully. "Well, ladies, you are most certainly a godsend. We Sisters are grateful that you found your way here to us. It may seem like there are too many workers aboard and that we are full in each other's way today. But tomorrow? It will all be different."

She showed them where they would sleep in the back, a little room with four cots. Two were already claimed, and the two available were nearest the door. *I wonder if my sleep will be interrupted by the comings and goings of the cot owners in the back.* A window in the outer wall let in light and fresh air, and hooks hung on three walls for clothing and gear. Between two cots on each side was a small cabinet topped with a lantern. Two lanterns were also suspended from hooks in the ceiling. Sarah found an empty drawer in the cabinet and put her Bible, letters, and writing things in it. *How long will Red Rover be my home?*

She and Jane spent the rest of the day getting acquainted with the *Rover's* layout, following Sister Veronica and listening to her directions to others. The sister asked many questions about Jane's and Sarah's experience, more interested in the soldier's illnesses than their injuries.

Sarah learned that the Keeper of the Fresh Air, Mr. William, was "contraband," an escaped Negro slave. She overheard him declare that he was happy to be put to work on the *Rover*. His duties and his bosses were better and kinder than those he had in Mississippi—and he would be paid. She met several other contrabands including a man from Tennessee the soldiers called Big Art, and Alice, a woman she guessed to be about thirty, who would be working alongside her and Jane. Alice had made her way along the Underground Railroad to Cincinnati, then traveled to Illinois where she found work in Cairo.

The supper bell rang promptly at 6 p.m., and almost immediately nearly forty people made their way to the eating area. The medical crew would eat first, the sailor crew later. Dr. George Bixby, the Chief Medical Officer, stood somewhat formally and welcomed everyone briefly. Sister Veronica led them in the usual Catholic grace, "Bless us, O Lord, and these thy gifts...." The food and drink were simple, the table setting basic. Sarah hoped she would meet Dr. Bixby's expectations. He handled his eating utensils with careful precision, and when speaking, he had a kindly way of looking her in the eye, but without a shred of humor or joviality.

The table was cleared, and the Sisters left for prayers. "I suppose we should take our leave as well," Sarah said to Jane, "but I have too many thoughts rushing about in my head. They won't let me get tired, and I'm afraid sleep won't come." She stared off into the wintry darkness.

Jane put a hand on Sarah's shoulder. "Come, Sarah," she smiled, "let us at least rest our bodies even if sleep is elusive. We cannot imagine what tomorrow has in store. But I know one thing: Whatever you have or can give, you will be enough. This is an imperfect life, and we humans are meant to suffer, I suppose. But we are called to do what we can, and I have watched you, Sarah. You have a natural talent for healing. You will be fine. And those you care for will be as fine as possible. You'll see."

The next morning, with barely enough time to finish breakfast, the scrambling and shouting began in earnest. Able-bodied men carried the sick and injured to the beds directed by Sister Adella. "Sarah, see what these four need before Dr. Bixby can get to them. He should be here with me overseeing their placement, but he has been detained on the second deck."

Sarah nodded and got to work.

Except for the effects of the bitter cold weather, the condition of these men was similar to those at Pittsburg Landing. She saw men with frostbitten noses, ears, fingers, and toes. *Those contraptions they call boots are worthless,* she thought. Sounds of rattling, hacking coughs made her cringe. The men with coughs and likely fevers were carried up to the second deck, where fewer people would be exposed to them. Those with minie bullet wounds, falls, amputations, and every other sort of battlefield injury were assigned to the first deck.

Almost every bed was filled by the time Captain McDaniel gave the order to untie and head downstream to join the Western flotilla above Vicksburg. They were finally under way. Sarah watched the moving

USS Red Rover

shoreline in the gray first light of day. *Goodbye, Cairo and Pittsburg Landing. Rest in peace, Cara and Michael and Thomas. May angels watch over Samuel and Eddie and Bethanne, and most of all, my beloved Evan. And dear God, please, please help me.*

Life on the River

May 3, 1864
Aboard the Red Rover, Memphis, Tennessee

Dear Mother and Family,

What a delight to receive your last letter! I have a short time while we are docked to answer a few of your questions. First off, know that I am well and think of you all with love and longing. Signs of this terrible war's ending are all around, are they not? What do you hear from James—and Evan?

Yes, the work can be sporadic, especially as we take on new patients, which will happen again tomorrow. You would see such a flurry of assigning and yelling and trying to move without bumping into men being carried! I dread the approaching summer along the Mississippi as more and more are likely to be as ill with malaria and yellow fever as they were last summer. Besides the tropical diseases, summer brings hordes of mosquitoes and flies and other fierce, annoying insects.

We are lucky to be outfitted with easy access to water and bathrooms on every deck. And plenty of ice! Because we have so much ice, I have tried an experiment to see if mosquito-bitten skin can be relieved for more than a few minutes by applying ice. Some say it helps, others prefer a paste of baking soda and water. Jane has used vinegar, and when we have plenty, oatmeal. One soldier told me that urine works, but I find that too distasteful to try.

The Rover follows Union gunboats up and down the Miss. Riv., from Louisville to New Orleans, transporting men to friendly hospitals along our route. While they are with us, we care for them as in any hospital. I have learned so much from the Sisters here; they are excellent teachers. Besides Jane and myself, five other women, contraband slaves actually, are under the

Sisters' direction. It amazes me what they know, and I have witnessed, from all the contrabands aboard, how able and knowledgeable they are.

During my time here I see daily just how wrong it is to hold these black men and women as slaves. If we were blind and everyone's speech the same, could one really tell a difference? Almost 1/3 of the men aboard are contrabands, and they, along with the women, serve the Navy as "first class boys," a basic assistant position for which they are paid.

Almost forty people work as medical crew, including the surgeons. Forty more comprise the sailing and soldiering crew. We have capacity for nearly 200 men under our care. In addition to being a floating hospital, with our ice stores and secure locked hold, we also deliver ice, food, and other supplies to Union gunboats along our way.

When we are docked, we often offload able soldiers to help with burial detail after a battle. They leave the Rover grim-faced and determined; they return dispirited. Once they are back aboard, cooks usually prepare a heartier meal, with wine or spirits, and always double portions of dessert. No food can erase the awful images the men see, but it is the gesture of "welcome back" that makes a sort of difference, a family sort of welcome. I sense a greater kindness in the air.

The Union defeat at Fort Pillow last month caused a great stir among the crew here. I am sure you have seen many of the newspaper accounts about the intentional "massacre, the slaughter," especially high of the Negro troops, as the Union, who refused to surrender, was overrun with Confederates. I heard that more than 2/3 of the black men were murdered outright, about 1/3 of the white soldiers. Not taken as prisoners of war! We are all heartsick, and grateful that the mutterings of "no quarter, no quarter—" have died away a little every day. Do you know, though, that the Rover took aboard, for a brief time, injured Confederates, and stabilized their injuries until they could be offloaded? I suppose even in a war about the fight for justice, justice might not prevail. It makes me sick.

And yes, it can be very exciting on the river. The fighting is usually ahead of us, and we are not in the direct line of fire. Often at night we creep along, all lights out, well behind the gunboats trying to advance the Union position, praying that no noise such as patient's shout of pain or nightmare, will alert the Confederates on shore that we are passing. On wide stretches of the river it is not a problem, but when the channel narrows, we have to be extra cautious.

And yes, Mother, to answer your unanswered question, in spite of it all, I am grateful to be of use.

Much Love,

Your Sarah

November 10, 1864
Red Rover, Miss. Riv.

Dear Mother, Father and George,

I am coming home, I am coming home, I cannot believe it!!! The mercies of God have surely been with me these past two years, and with Evan as well. I pinch myself almost hourly to make sure that I am not imagining this good fortune. The Rover will dock at Memphis to deliver our last group of men to Hospital Pinckney on November 23, and I will leave with them, as will many of the medical crew. I expect to arrive in Greeneville in early December at the latest, God willing.

I have learned so much about the care of the sick and injured, and I am so grateful to the Sisters and the surgeons. You may find it hard to believe that I have changed so much from the questioning young woman, no, girl really, timid and unsure, to the woman I am now. I have been inspired every day by the kindness and compassion and bravery of the crew around me.

I decided that if Evan did not return to me, I would, nevertheless, continue in this nursing life. The Sisters have talked about schools to educate

Life on the River

women properly to become nurses, and that would be a wonderful thing for me ... to learn more and more about the best methods. Dr. Bixby has been most remarkable in directing us all here, and he has boasted, rightly so, that the patients on the Rover were in a safer and healthier environment than any place or hospital in the country. And by our witness, his boast is fact more than bragging.

I assume that you know of Evan's condition from James's letters to you? He was injured at the battle of Jonesborough in Georgia. His right arm had to be removed above the elbow, and to compound matters, he contracted malaria. Of course, those unsanitary conditions! I received a letter from James about him, in which he assures me that Evan will recover well as long as he is cared for properly. Oh, dear Family, that is my purpose! To help him in any way that I can to return to the man he was before, with all his faculties intact and happiness at being my husband.

I understand this will take some time and patience on my part, but I have been prepared to offer this and knowledgeable care. I know we will succeed. Evan has begun to use his left hand for writing, and he tells me that it is a small injury compared to many men. He assures me that he wishes to marry just as soon as he is fully recovered. So I have a new mission!

You will recognize me in outward appearances, though I have lost much weight and my hands are rough as any farmer's. Washing them so fre-quently, as we are required, takes its toll, but I am assured that with proper attention they will be beautiful again ... for my wedding ring.

As much as I am anxious to return to my happy life, and you, at Greeneville, I will surely miss the people who have become my friends here, Jane most of all. She has been a constant calming presence here on the Rover, everyone says so. When I have been distressed at the condition of a man, or the likelihood of an impending death for no good earthly reason, her counsel has always helped me get right again. She is so wise and knows exactly how to help those who are caring for the men so wasted and destroyed.

She is about your age, Mother, and I often think of her as an angel in human form that you have sent to guide me. I know that you would love her as much as I do. When I have been so sad and down of heart at the useless, worthless effort of war to win an argument, costing so many lives on both sides, Jane reminds me to take a breath and think only of <u>this</u> moment, the only one that I may affect. "Stay focused, Sarah, on this man and what you are doing just for him. Give all your attention to him."

The Sisters, too, and the surgeons all tell me that if I should ever choose to apply to a nursing school, they will write letters of recommendation for me. What kindnesses they offer.

It is late and I must close now. Know that I am so anxious to see every one of you again, counting the days until I am back in my old room, and dining at the table with you. I have missed you more than I can say.

Love,

Sarah

The Warmth of Home

December 1, 1864
Greeneville, Tennessee

"Wilson! Wilson, she's here! It's our Sarah! Come at once, hurry! *Hurry!*"

Before Jane Anne could open the door, tears of joy and relief streamed down her face. She had been on pins and needles for two days. "Oh my, you're here, you're really home!" She grabbed her daughter fiercely at the shoulders and pulled Sarah to her in a tight long embrace. Neither woman could speak words, only tears.

She pulled back to look at her daughter's face, streaked too with tears. "Oh my dear daughter, how I have prayed for this day, and for you and all that—" but more words would not come for the weeping. Wilson joined in their embrace on the cold porch.

Sarah's emotions were a confused jumble of happiness and grief and relief and a great, great sadness. Tennessee was second only to Virginia in the number of battles fought within its borders. The faces of people she saw mirrored the devastation of the towns and countryside, especially along the rivers and railroads. Although the war was coming to an end, strife was not. Tennessee was the geographic heart of the Confederacy and would continue to bear the brunt of many costs. *I wonder if the effort required to rebuild and heal could somehow transform combatants into peaceful neighbors. I hope so. But, whatever the case, I will still marry Evan, no matter what.*

Evan's last letter seemed more hopeful than the others since his injury. She expected him, and James, to arrive any day now and Sarah welcomed the time to readjust. Her clothing needed considerable attention, and her mother was delighted to have a happy project to occupy her mind. It had been over three years since Sarah's departure and Cara's death.

Samuel had written a few times from Chicago, and his family had acclimated to their new life, far from the memories of a violent war seen through a cabin window. When weather and travel ease permitted, he promised to come to Greeneville for a good visit. He liked Chicago well enough, being a sanctuary for Bethanne and Eddie. But his heart was in Tennessee. *Maybe they'll settle near Greeneville,* Sarah hoped.

"But," Samuel wrote, "keep these notions to yourself. I don't want your mother to raise her hopes unnecessarily." Sarah laughed aloud at those words. *As if my mother's mind was not already imagining that on her own!* Eddie had no memories of his grandmother, and hers of him as a toddler were dim. *Perhaps they'll be here for our wedding. What a happy reunion that would be!*

Seven days flew by. Sarah ate heartily and slept and woke when her body dictated. The days had shortened now that winter was coming on. Sleeping was a wonderful thing when she could sleep. But images haunted her. The men she had cared for, many who were so brave in their suffering. Their gratitude for the smallest favors. Those were the nice images. The ones that often startled her awake were of the Union soldiers when they first boarded the *Rover*. The sounds of battle from the gunboats as they held back from a blockade, or the tension on the entire ship as it silently crept by Confederate posts at midnight praying they wouldn't be noticed … those were the disturbing ones.

And in all her experiences, she never forgot Thomas.

Sarah's Diary: December 11, 1864

My world has taken a new turn. I am trying to keep a positive attitude for Evan. He and James returned to us three days ago, just as we were having supper. Words cannot describe my happiness and surprise at seeing both of them. Oh, blessed day, I thought, as I leapt from my chair to greet them. "Finally," I shouted, "you are both home and safe at last!"

Evan, a normally thin man, has lost much weight, and his gauntness makes his beautiful green eyes huge and haunting. He had recently bathed and shaved and donned fresh clothes. The right arm of his jacket was pinned to make for easier movement without his lower arm. As I held him, I knew right away something was amiss. His return of my greeting lacked the intensity I remembered, and as we embraced, I felt him shudder ... then his tears began. He gripped me as if I were the only tree in a flooded world. This is good, I thought, even though it is strange from him. I had witnessed that enough times when soldiers finally let down their guard and submitted to their fears and pain.

After our greetings and everyone had regained their composure somewhat, Mother insisted they sit and eat even though we had just started clearing the table. Father and George scurried about making sure James's room was in order, and prepared a pallet for Evan. We did not have an extra room for him, but he and James had shared all sorts of sleeping accommodations ... they are like brothers now. One room would suit them fine. We would sort it all out the next day and make plans.

I was surprised that both of them wanted to retire as soon as they had eaten. I must admit I imagined that Evan and I would sit before the fire in the parlor, delighting in each other's company and dreaming where we left off, but that was not the case. I was disappointed and tried not to let it show, but as I thought about it, I knew that soldiers often had trouble fitting back into the hole they left before battle. Time, I knew, I must give Evan the time he needs. I reminded myself that it was time for me to apply what I had learned caring for our men. It was a kind of schooling for me, and now comes the test to see if I can take my own advice.

The next morning Evan left to go to his Aunt Claire's and Uncle Alfred's, who raised him from the age of six after his parents died. Before he left, I asked to look at his arm and assess its level of healing. A three-month-old amputation should have healed well enough. As he rolled up his sleeve, he looked at me with a kind of shyness. I knew this look and smiled to myself. He

sees me as his woman who has not seen him undress, instead of a nurse who
is used to every view of the human body possible.

Although he seemed to be gaining weight, Evan's haunted appearance had not improved in the ten days he had been home. Claire Rule was known throughout Greeneville as an excellent cook, and she spared no expense in fattening him up. But he often seemed distant. He finally admitted that he was having a great deal of pain.

"I don't understand it, Sarah, my arm seems perfectly healed. I had no real complications from losing it, though the malaria slowed it down some. I don't know why this is happening. Maybe my healing is not as complete as it looks."

"What is it like, Evan? The pain."

"Burning and stabbing. There's tingling in the missing part of me." He rubbed at the end of his arm and added, "Sometimes it is so intense as to be almost unbearable."

"Do you mean at the end?"

"No, beyond it, as if I still have my arm—that's where the pain is. I have seen others with the same affliction, they call it 'phantom limb.' Most everyone I saw with an amputation had something like this. There must be something to it that we cannot see." He started to lift his right arm as if to run his fingers through his hair, and she caught his eye. "This, this—I don't know what, this motion, reminds me that I am missing my forearm and hand, and it brings the battle back again every damned time."

"Are you in pain all the time, Evan? Even now?"

"Not at the moment, but it is intermittent. I cannot know in advance when it is going to happen."

"What helps you? Anything?"

"The morphine powder gives me some relief. I still have some from my time in the hospital, and Dr. Libbert in town tells me if I need more to come and see him."

Sarah studied him thoughtfully. "And what is happening with your sleep?"

"I suppose that it is taking me some time to adjust ...."

"So your sleep is interrupted by the pain?"

He nodded. "The pain, and the—" He stopped, looking past her.

"Nightmares?" she offered. "Are you having nightmares about the war?"

He nodded at her, his green eyes seeking hers. "I know they are dreams, but they are so real and vivid. I see men, no, parts of men really, lying around me in all forms of battle injury—a hand, a leg, and—oh, God, Sarah, a head lying all by itself talking to me, asking me to reunite it with its body." He was trembling now.

"I know some of it, Evan, you can tell me, I have seen a battlefield, too. Tell me." Tears were welling in her eyes. Her own experience was not far from mind.

"When they took off my arm, I dreamt it was just the beginning. Next was my other arm, then both my legs, then more of my first arm. Oh, Sarah, it is as if there would be nothing left of me! I wake up shaking and screaming and sweating even in a cold room. Aunt Claire came running to me last night thinking I had seen a ghost." He looked away from her gaze. "I did. It was the ghost of the man I used to be."

"Evan, I have seen this before," she took his hand and emphasized her words with a squeeze, "and I have seen men get better. With the right amount of fresh air and exercise, good food, a return to work with your uncle, and me to help, you will get better. They say that talking helps, too, and you have taken an important step, telling me some of the things that haunt you."

But she offered these words as if they were written in a script. She was afraid.

"I am grateful, Sarah, to have your help, and your willingness to stay by my side until I am healed. But you should not have to bear it." He stopped, and kissed her hand. "You should be preoccupied with women things, and bustling about with plans for our wedding."

Her heart turned over. *Our wedding! He finally said it! He still wants to marry*, she thought, *he is still in love with me.*

"Oh, Evan, I didn't know if," she stumbled, "or whether—" she swallowed and stopped, the tears beginning. "I have so much to tell you, my letters couldn't possibly say it all … and I don't know where to begin, and things I never thought I could do, or live through …."

"Hush, Sarah, we will both have time to unburden our hearts—" He stood and pulled her to him in a long embrace, both thinking of all they had lost, and of their future.

Evan proposed formally on Christmas Day, 1864. He had met with her father earlier to ask for her hand in marriage. The meeting went well, and Wilson was impressed with Evan's return to lawyering work with his uncle. He was convinced that Evan would be a good provider and that he cared deeply for his daughter. Besides, he held no doubt that their determined Sarah would marry Evan Rule, with or without his blessing.

At the end of the gift-giving after Christmas dinner, Evan cleared his throat. "Oh, here is one for you Sarah, I almost forgot." He pulled a small green velvet box from his jacket pocket and held it out, his left hand trembling. "This is from me."

Sarah had her suspicions as she had witnessed Evan's leaving from his "secret" visit to her father. She held the box reverently in her hands for a few moments, then eagerly opened it. A big smile spread across her face. "Is this what I think it is?" she questioned, grinning at him. "Evan, really?"

He returned her smile and dropped to one knee. "Sarah Lydia Dunlap, will you do me the honor of becoming my wife? I want to live with you and raise a family with you, and—" Seldom at a loss for words, he fumbled, "oh, and I love you with all my heart."

She laughed at him. "Finally, Evan, yes. Yes, it is yes. Yes!" She put her arms around his shoulders and chastely kissed him. The onlookers applauded.

The elegant engagement ring had belonged to his mother. Aunt Claire had kept it tucked away for him to use when the time came. The single modest diamond sat in a nest of silver leaves. She put it on and smiled, thinking it was a good omen that the fit was perfect.

Evan pulled the wedding band from his pocket. It was as simple and elegant as the diamond, with a leaf positioned on either side where the engagement ring interlocked.

"They are perfect, Evan. I shall be so proud to wear them."

They set the wedding date for Saturday, April 15, to allow more time for Evan's healing and settling into a stable routine. The weather should allow for easy travel then, and Sarah hoped that Samuel and the children would come. She could finish her trousseau and collect the household items they needed. Evan would be busy with his law practice and finding them a house to call home.

She could breathe fully now. All was in order.

Sarah's Diary: April 12, 1865

Two more days, and then I will be a married woman—not the spinster I feared I might be for the rest of my life! So much needs doing, and Samuel and the children arrived yesterday. Oh, how good to see them! Bethanne and Eddie have grown so; she is now nine years old and so very intelligent. Eddie is six and inquisitive and mischievous and full of fun. Evan was drawn to them immediately and confided that he hoped our children would be just as enjoyable to be around as they are. I am not surprised. He has a feeling for children.

Evan has rented us a very nice house on Union Street, and we have visited it several times to plan where to put things, and to dream of our future. I am so eager to be with him all the time, and not have to say goodbye in the evening, and to enjoy "married bliss." In our moments alone we are so drawn to each other. Our kissing lasts longer each time and leads to other things. But we have both been able to hold back, though it has been more difficult now that our great day draws near. Sometimes I think a few days won't matter, but it seems important to both of us to keep ourselves for the other until we are truly married.

Evan's pain in his missing arm has not subsided, and I am fearful about his sleep. But he assures me that when we are married, the sleep problems will vanish. He has found new ways to distract himself with all our preparations. Work with his uncle, visits with friends in the evening discussing the war's end and what will happen next. I feel some sympathies now for the Confederate people … so much of their land destroyed, and the loss of life greater than the Union's. A full Union victory is the obvious outcome. But after victory is declared—what then?

April 15, 1865
Greeneville, Tennessee

Everyone remarked that the wedding was the most joyful they had attended in years. Sarah was as radiant as any bride should be. Though fine material was scarce and expensive, Jane Anne found a white muslin jacket and embellished it with ecru lace. She altered an ecru silk skirt of hers to fit Sarah's thin frame, and the effect was understated and classic. Evan, Sarah thought, looked more elegant and desirable than she had ever seen him. His green eyes often filled with happy tears, and it seemed to her that he had a "devouring look," a phrase they would use and laugh at in the coming months.

Their late morning wedding at Greeneville Presbyterian Church was officiated by Reverend Elliott, a kind man who had known the Dunlap family for years. They returned to her parents' home where a wedding luncheon waited. The Dunlaps did not usually drink alcohol because the occasion didn't warrant it with the war on, or it was so expensive or unavailable. But today her father spared no expense, and they enjoyed wine freely.

Sarah surveyed the tables filled with the people she and Evan loved—her parents and brothers George and James. Philip and his family made the trip from Knoxville; Samuel, Bethanne and Eddie from Chicago. Evan's Aunt Claire and Uncle Alfred, and his sister Mariah joined a table with Reverend and Mrs. Elliott and Evan's close friend Patrick and his wife.

After they had eaten, and toasts offered in honor of the couple, Samuel, unaccustomed to wine or spirits of any kind, stood and clinked on his empty glass with a knife edge. "I, too, would like to offer my congratulations and best wishes to Sarah and Evan. Evan, I hope you know how fortunate you are to have married sush—such—a fine woman. I alone have seen Sarah in the worst of circumstances, the very worst times for me and my children."

He stopped and held his mouth as if holding back something. "She was my rock. She is strong and capable ... and determined. She has a heart so full of compassion and caring, one that seems to carry her beyond earthly bonds. I do not know how we would have survived without Sarah by our side during that awful time. So, Evan, if she has accepted you as the man she loves, we do, too, wholesome—no, whole—heartedly, because we love her so much and trust in the wisdom of her judgment. May God smile on you both and your children, and grant you every god blessing, um, *good* blessing."

The only cloud on their wedding happiness was the terrible news that President Lincoln had died in the early morning hours, the victim of an assassin's bullet. Jane Anne declared, "We will find time for political talk

The Warmth of Home

and sadness tomorrow. Nothing will cause my daughter distress or distraction on this blessed day. It is time for the sun to shine in her life."

Gray Days

Married life was not unfolding as Sarah had imagined.

Their wedding night had been awkward. She had hoped to finally enjoy being truly intimate with Evan and was disappointed. She knew that the first time was often painful for women, so she wasn't surprised. She had heard that for a man's first time it was often quick and over too soon. But that was not the case for Evan. He became aroused easily and seemed eager for her, but when they were finally joined as one, he lost his hardness and pulled away. She wondered if it was from her pulling back at the sudden sharp pain.

"Sarah, my love, it has been a long day, and I am so tired. I'm having some pain. We enjoyed so much food … drink, too, I'm afraid. We'll try again after a good sleep." So in spite of their disappointing wedding night, Sarah slept soundly in the belief that it would be better once the newness wore off and Evan's pain lessened.

She spent much of every day planning for his return in the evening, and what to serve for supper. She read the newspaper faithfully so that she could be knowledgeable about the state of the country, and the world, hoping that she and Evan could have meaningful discussions and he would not think her ignorant. She loved simply spending time with him. And their time in bed became more satisfying to both of them, though Sarah wished that Evan was in the mood to make love more often.

After the wedding Samuel announced that he was moving his little family to Greeneville. Although the children had many cousins in Chicago and they liked school there, Samuel felt as if his calling to ministry was better served in eastern Tennessee. The children were very attached to their Aunt Sarah, and now that she was married, they enjoyed the affections of Uncle Evan, too. Bethanne and Eddie occasionally walked to their house, and she always welcomed their visits with open arms and little treats.

The house Evan had rented was near his uncle's and the law office. Most days he would come home for midday dinner, and Sarah anticipated those times with eagerness. At one o'clock in the afternoon, he was often more interested in taking Sarah to bed than in eating food, which pleased her. They both looked forward to parenting their own children.

But after four months she was aware of a gnawing anxiety. Something important was missing, and she was worried about Evan. She'd begun to notice a subtle change in him. In the mornings if he had slept well, he often woke with pain and it took some time for the morphine powder to take effect. Then she noticed he had been drinking before he returned to her in the evenings. At first it was once or twice a week, then most days of work, then every day. They kept a small amount of wine and spirits at home, having received several fine bottles as wedding presents. And Sarah enjoyed the glow of happiness she felt from a glass of wine with supper. But she knew from her experience on the *Rover* that alcohol was a problem for many men.

Equally troubling was his sleep. Occupying a marriage bed with his wife had not seemed to lessen his fitfulness. If he fell asleep quickly, unusual though it was, he always awoke too early from slumber, groaning with pain, sometimes even shouting. Then he would leave their bed, returning only after the morphine took effect. Some nights he didn't return at all, but sat awake at their parlor table, writing feverishly. He could use his left hand well for writing now since he had so much practice at work. But it was still not natural for him, another frustration.

Jane Anne came to call one afternoon, and Sarah was surprised that she was by herself. It was a stifling hot late August day and, although rumblings announced an approaching storm, the clouds were stubbornly holding on to their rain. Sarah was irritable. *I should be used to the humidity by now since I've lived here all my life.*

"Well, Mother," Sarah began, once she had served her the sweet tea with a little ice, just as Jane Anne preferred it. "I am so happy you came to visit this afternoon and glad that James could spare some time to bring you. The weather is much too warm for you to walk all that distance just to see me."

"Oh my dear, I have been looking for a chance to visit, just the two of us, and it is never a trifling matter to spend time with my favorite … confidante—"

The word was out before she could bring it back, and they shared a look. Cara was her mother's first daughter, and before she and Samuel moved to Pittsburg Landing, she had begun to take the role of adult ally. Among the many ways her mother missed Cara, the role of friendship was one that Sarah had not considered. She smiled at her mother sympathetically.

"So it is time, my dear," Jane Anne continued, "to talk just as women, and for me to discover how things are truly going for you, and for Evan, too," she added. "Your home is well kept, and your father and I have enjoyed the Sunday dinners here. You seem to be handling the cooking without much trouble."

Silence. Her mother waited.

Sarah looked at her hands holding the glass of tea in her lap. She set it on the side table next to her chair. "Thank you, Mother. I am fine, and, yes, I am learning the cooking without much effort. I had a good teacher," she said, smiling at her. "It is an adjustment, these early months of marriage. You told me so, and I keep your words of wisdom in my heart."

"What adjustment is the biggest for you, dear? There are so many!" her mother exclaimed. "I remember my early marriage period with your father. Those times when he was preoccupied with things other than me or our marriage. First my mother-in-law's expectations, the endless routine of cooking, and then of course, having children. That," she emphasized, "was the biggest adjustment of all!"

Sarah offered her mother another little smile. "Well, it does not appear that children are on their way yet, but we are hopeful, and, it is early." She wondered how much to tell her mother, how even to put her anxieties into words without inviting her too deeply into the world that belonged privately to Sarah. She decided on simplicity. "Evan is having more pain than I expected. It is the 'phantom' pain that occurs in missing limbs. You know of this tendency?"

Her mother nodded.

"It is requiring more morphine to dull it. Thankfully Dr. Libbert has been able to supply him with what he needs. But I am not sure that the morphine is really helping."

"I have noticed, dear, that Evan seems to be losing weight—his face is so thin. It seems like he regained his health a little after he returned to us, but since the wedding …."

Her mother's words hit hard, and Sarah replied, "I wish I could blame it on my skills as a cook, Mother, but we both know better." She tried to place a smile on her face. "Throughout my time working on the Red Rover, all the surgeons would tell us about the need to be patient with a soldier's injuries. We know the physical ones take their time to heal, and we can see that evidence easily. But the ones inside, those are the most difficult because we can only see what the man tells us. The truth is, Mother, that Evan was affected more than we know by what he witnessed. He holds things inside. The battlefield was very hard on him. He does seem to be sleeping a little more now, and that is a good thing. We—no, I—simply need to give him more time."

"Perhaps it would be wise to set a date when you would expect to see more progress? Maybe Dr. Libbert has some ideas of other approaches to try."

Dark Days, the Call

October 19, 1865
Greeneville, Tennessee

Evan returned home late, much later than usual, well past their time for supper. It was nearly time for bed. Sarah went to greet him at the door. She reached out to hug him and was surprised when he pushed her away. He wore a scowl and was obviously unhappy about something. He had also been drinking, drinking a lot, she guessed, by his demeanor.

Sarah was irritated—no, she was angry. She was tired of being patient with him when it wasn't effective. She was tired of his distance. She was tired of his longer absences from home. Last week when she woke early missing his presence in bed, she found him in the parlor with an empty glass, staring at nothing, tears in his eyes. He had begun to buy whiskey regularly, and she found herself eyeing the level in each bottle and looking for where he kept it. Hardest of all, she began to feel like a jailer or an overseer instead of a loving wife. *Is this what is meant by "for better or for worse"?*

"Why did you push me away, Evan? I was merely greeting you, welcoming you home." She felt her cheeks grow hot.

"I don't need your hovering over me all the time, Sarah. I can close the door by myself."

"Hovering? You call that *hovering*? It is late, nearly ten o'clock, and I was worried about you! This is the third time this week that you have come home late, and it seems like you have been drinking again."

"It is my right to drink whenever I please, Sarah."

"Were you at the tavern with Patrick?"

"No, not tonight."

"Where were you then?"

"I was at the office, working late. Uncle Alfred and Aunt Claire were out for an evening with their friends."

"You were drinking by yourself then, while working?"

"Yes, what of it?"

"Drinking by yourself is not a good thing, Evan. Drinking with others, at a party, at a tavern, that is more normal. How often do you do it?"

"Oh, so now you are the judge of my life, Sarah, for what is normal? Would you be happy if I had been with Patrick at the tavern all this time?"

She had no good answer for this question. They had been standing in the entryway. Sarah took a deep breath and said, "Let's go sit in the parlor, or maybe the dining room. Would you like something to eat? I can warm something for you, or you could have cold chicken if you'd rather."

He shrugged off his coat and let her hang it up. With a pause he continued, "I am sorry for being so late, Sarah. Did I make you miss supper?"

"Oh, no, Evan, I had mine at our usual time." Silently she added, *I am used to it.*

Sarah's Diary: November 2, 1865

Oh, I am struggling so much with Evan, and we are quarreling frequently now. I do not know what to do. I am reluctant to confide in Mother. I do not want her to know the worst in Evan in anticipation of the time he is fully well. Then she will have ugly memories from what I revealed to her, and I fear that would change the affection she and Father feel for him. I made a date for when I think things should be better. It will be my 27th birthday, January 21. Until that time, I will try to be more patient with him. But, in the meantime, I am going to visit Dr. Libbert to see what he recommends. There must be something that I am not doing correctly.

I am not willing to … what? Stand as an observer and watch him throw his life away or destroy the love I have for him? And future children? I am grateful that I have not found myself with child, and yet that is a deep sadness that we both share. I do not know where this will lead, and I feel so unprepared for how to be with him, and to find a balance in myself. One day I am all patience and tolerance, accepting of anything, and another day I am spiteful and ready to argue the moment he comes home. The only bright spot is Bethanne and Eddie.

November 6, 1865

"Come in, Mrs. Rule, and have a seat. I'm sorry that you had to wait so long. I have been unusually busy, and I am the only person here to even greet my patients."

Dr. Libbert's manner was kindly. He was a short man whose vest buttons strained over his round belly. He sported closely-trimmed facial hair, setting him aside from the long beards and bushy mustaches of the day.

"What can I do for you, Mrs. Rule?" His sharp blue eyes peered at her from behind the spectacles on his nose. He waited for her to speak.

"Well, to be candid with you, Dr. Libbert, I am having trouble with helping my husband. I believe you know him, Evan Rule?"

He nodded. "Yes, a nice fellow. What is the problem?"

"Doctor, he continues to have a lot of pain in his right arm, even extending down to the missing part. Perhaps Evan has told you that I had been serving as a nurse? Three years actually. So I have seen a lot of pain. The morphine powder you are giving him doesn't seem to be helping as much, he is needing more. And now he has taken to whiskey mostly every day. I don't know what the whiskey is helping—if it dulls the pain, too, or if it has become such a habit that he cannot do without it."

"And," she added, "he is argumentative all the time. We quarrel about the smallest of things. I cannot remember the last time he sat and smiled at me, or called me by any affectionate term."

She paused, trying desperately to sound professional, then added quietly. "I am so afraid for our marriage."

"What about his sleep?"

"It is disturbed. When he comes home after the drinking, he falls to bed as soon as he can and is asleep in minutes, even sooner. But then he wakes after two or three hours and has trouble getting back to sleep. He gets up in the middle of the night, has more whiskey, and then comes back to bed. It is hard to awaken him in the morning. He is still able to get to work with his uncle—as you know, they are lawyers. But I think he looks unwell."

"What does his uncle say?"

"I haven't talked privately with him yet. And he hasn't come to me."

"Let's see, if I recall, he lost his lower arm about fifteen months ago, is that right?"

"Yes, it was the last day of August. The loss of his arm was traumatic, as for any person, and he had also suffered from dysentery along the way, so that he had lost a lot of his strength. He had also acquired malaria during that summer, though it hasn't recurred since he was treated."

"Well, Mrs. Rule, it seems to me that he needs to get off the whiskey and on to something else that would be distracting so that he can change the habit. I am guessing it will be hard for him to stop all drink suddenly, but by tapering off he shouldn't have any bad effects. I am not sure about stopping the morphine. He may need to continue it for a while longer."

"Fifteen months on morphine? That seems like a long time. And how do I get him to taper the whiskey, Doctor? He is a determined and stubborn man."

"That is the hard one, my dear." Dr. Libbert took off his glasses and rubbed the bridge of his nose. "You are best judge of what will reach him. In many cases, the patient has to have a bigger reason to stop than their own self-interest. Have you told him how much it would mean to you to stop drinking, how much it bothers you?"

"I think I have by my comments? But perhaps not directly enough."

Suddenly the door from the street swung open, and a distraught woman with a bleeding toddler rushed through. "Help, Doctor!" she shouted. "William has fallen out of the tree, and his head is bleeding like a stuck pig. He hit it on a sharp rock on the ground. Oh, help him please! I have never seen so much blood!" William looked to be about three years old and was howling through the mucus that ran down his face. His mother had tried to stop the bleeding with a tea towel, but it was soaked through and dripping down William's shirt.

Sarah and Dr. Libbert both jumped from their seats. Dr. Libbert squatted, with some difficulty, to look at the little boy. William struggled against the doctor's efforts at first, then relaxed. Sarah took the woman's hand without thinking. "Missus," she said, "my name is Sarah. I have seen many bleeding injuries of the scalp. They produce a lot of blood, but," she smiled, "they can be mended. Dr. Libbert will take good care of your William. And you can help your little boy best by calming yourself. Take a deep breath, and look at me." She put her hands on the mother's shoulders. "You must be strong for William and not show your fear. Can you breathe with me?" She looked questioningly at the woman, and they both breathed in unison.

"William," Dr. Libbert said in a quiet soothing voice, "I can help you. You will have to be a brave soldier, but everything will be fine. Would you like me to help?"

William nodded slowly.

"Miss Sarah," Dr. Libbert said, "I have a fine toy soldier in that cabinet over there," nodding to where he kept some supplies, "would you please fetch it for William?" And to William when she brought it, he said, "Look, here is a soldier for you to think on and be brave with. Would you like that?"

The boy nodded. Sarah handed him the toy, asking, "What shall we call him?"

"Willie?" he replied timidly.

"Willie it is. That is a very nice name for this brave soldier."

"Dr. Libbert," Sarah said, "I have some experience with suturing, and I can help if you like."

"That would be wonderful, Miss Sarah. I'll get my suture materials ready. Why don't you help get little William, and Willie, up on my table. You can use some water there," he nodded to two large pitchers of water near a basin, "and clean his wound so we can see what is going on."

When William and his mother had been tended to and left, Dr. Libbert turned to Sarah. "My dear," he said, "you are a natural. Blood doesn't disturb you, and you have a very calming way with children *and* mothers," he emphasized. "And you have experience. I need someone to help me in this office, especially since Dr. Rawley left his practice in town. And Mrs. Libbert is getting more forgetful all the time. Would you consider coming to help me?"

Sarah's Diary: November 30, 1865

I have found it again I think, my calling, and I am so grateful! I have been helping Dr. Libbert in his office. The arrangement we have is that I come to work with him four days a week, Tuesdays through Fridays, for five hours each day. He cannot afford to pay me much at all, since he never paid Mrs. Libbert. What little he does pay me I am saving, not spending it upon myself or household needs.

I have not forgotten what I learned aboard the Rover or at Pittsburg Landing, and my days fly by. I cannot believe it when I look at the clock to discover it is half-past four, much beyond my leaving time! Usually we have two or three patients to tend to who have prior appointments to see the doctor, and then more come to be helped. I have just a little time in the day to sit and talk with him about various questions, and he seems eager to help me learn.

He offered some of his books, and I read through them when I am at his office. It is but a short mile away from our house. I cannot believe my good fortune!

My fortune is not so good when it comes to Evan. He continues the habit of drinking every day, he uses morphine powder, and he is gone long hours. But his sleep is somewhat improved, I think, and it seems we have entered a period of "stable truce." We don't argue, but neither do we talk much. He was not very happy when I told him about helping Dr. Libbert, but I told him that I had many unused hours during the day and that it's best for me to be using my talents. He could sputter and offer weak arguments against that, but in the end what could he say? Forbid me? Ha!

The one day of the week that I do not go to work, I spend making a nice little early supper for Bethanne and Eddie, and we have a lovely time with games and stories, and the toys they bring with them. Then Samuel comes to walk them home, as it is dark by then, and we have all had a good visit. S. has stopped asking me where Evan is. I know the children would love to be with him, but not now, with the way he has become.

My birthday, I will be 27, is in less than two months. My plan is to ask Evan for a special present, his sobriety. Dr. Libbert and I have made a tapering-off plan together, and it will also require him to come home from the office at a normal time. It is possible that E. will ask me what I want for a Christmas present earlier, and if so, I will ask him for it then. But if he does not, I will bring up the subject myself. I am praying that this will work. He is such a fine man, and I know he can be the same as a husband and father. If he becomes sober, perhaps there will be a better chance of him becoming a father, and me a mother.

Resignation

February 16, 1866
Greeneville, Tennessee

Sarah's plan had not gone well. As a matter of fact, it was a total failure. She had several occasions to bring up Evan's drinking, and each time she did, he laughed at her: "I am not a drunkard, Sarah, I can go to my work and perform it just as well as I did before the war. I enjoy relaxing in the evening, and our good Tennessee whiskey helps me do it. You should have a little glass with me now and then."

But Sarah could not bring herself to sit and enjoy whiskey with him anymore. She hated to watch him as the alcohol took its effect on the man she loved. She often wondered if she still loved him. *Can you love someone even when you are so angry and hurt?*

The week of her birthday had been a particularly difficult one. Work at Dr. Libbert's was unusually stressful. The patients who showed up at their door all had a sorrowful story that weighed upon her heart. And not one of them was of circumstances they themselves had manufactured.

One was a little boy's accident on a horse that had been startled by a falling branch. The child's lower legs had been crushed when the horse fell on him. Dr. Libbert doubted he would walk normally again, even beyond the initial healing. Another was a child born with a terrible deformity. He had been the parents' long dreamed-of hope and did not live long. The last was a widow's massive tumor in her abdomen. She had lost her husband three months earlier, and her only wish was to join him as soon as possible. Her adult children were heartsick.

The night of her birthday was magical. Evan had surprised her with a gift of flowers with no hint of alcohol on his breath. They had gone to her parents' home for an elegant birthday supper. Samuel and the children were there as well as James and George, and even Evan's Aunt Claire and Uncle Alfred. She was surrounded by the people who meant the most to her, just as at her wedding. Wilson poured only enough wine for a toast to her health. She was grateful for that.

When they were back at home getting ready for bed, Evan surprised her again. He had found the cherished button from Thomas's uniform, and hired their local jeweler to set it into a pendant. Knowing how much that button meant to her, he decided it needed to be somewhere more fitting than loose in a box. Although it was not elegant and delicate—how could a military button be so?—it was extremely precious to Sarah. The simple silver chain was attached on both sides to a heart-shaped silver setting that held the polished button just below Sarah's birthstone, a garnet. And, he pointed out, it was long enough to wear under her dresses if she wanted.

"Oh, Evan, this is such a thoughtful, wonderful present … I love it! How did you create something so meaningful to me, and clever, and practical?"

"I have long known that I wanted to do something more permanent with that button for you, Sarah, and Uncle Alfred suggested I ask Mr. Thompkins, the jeweler, for ideas. He suggested that we add your birthstone. Do you know that the garnet stands for peace, and prosperity, and health? When you wear it, I want you to remember that I want those very things for you. You are the dearest part of my life, Sarah, and I know that I have not shown you much kindness or love lately. That will change, and I am going to stop the whiskey."

Oh, how her heart soared! Those words, the words that meant so much to her happiness, came from him in a way she could not have imagined. "Let me put the pendant on you, Sarah, to see how it looks. Then," after he slowly kissed her, "let us get to bed. I desire you, right now. It has been so long since I have made true love to you."

Sarah had hoped that night's pleasures would begin new life in her, but it was not to be.

Four days later she could tell he was drinking again. Snow had begun falling in earnest two hours earlier. When she greeted Evan at the door, late again, his speech was obviously slurred and his eyes glazed. She felt the familiar hot flush of anger flood her body. She fought to keep her words and tone civil; she wanted to sound loving.

"Do hurry in, Evan, it is so windy and snowy out there. How did you make it home walking that distance?"

"Uncle Alfred hitched up the team, seeing how bad it was, and brought me home."

"He is such a kind man, your uncle. The soup is still warm on the stove. Would you like some?"

"Soup again, woman? Do you not know how tired I am of soup!? I would rather go hungry than have more bean soup!"

"Go hungry you shall then! If you had come home at supper time, there would still be time for me to prepare what you wanted. But not now. It's late and I am going to bed."

"As you wish then. If you prefer your own solitude to my company—"

"Ha, what is that, company!" she shouted at him in anger. "You call your sitting across the table from me, slurring your words and rambling on about subjects that mean nothing to me *company*? Then, yes, I suppose I do prefer a calm silence."

"*Rambling on,* Sarah, is that what you call my conversing with you? I thought you wanted to understand what happens to me during the day, and all the intricacies of the law, and how I create the best strategies for my clients. I have quite a few, you know, and some very important men, in Greene County even, not just our town."

"Well, good for you, Evan! I am so happy that they are getting the best of Evan Rule. Do they know that your *beloved* Sarah gets the dregs of you at the very end of the day? And with your drinking again, I am surprised that clients still come to you. What does your uncle say about your drinking?"

"Drinking, my drinking? That boring topic again? Sarah, I can handle this and still be a successful lawyer, I have told you that so many times before—"

"You are not the best judge of that, Evan. You cannot see yourself objectively."

"And I suppose you can?"

"Much better than you, I know that. I have half a mind to go to your uncle and ask him—"

"You will do no such thing!" he roared. He took a step toward her and grabbed her shoulders roughly, then shook them twice for emphasis. "I forbid it!"

She would not be deterred. "You may say the words 'forbid you' Evan, but your words or anger will not stop me from doing what I think is right, especially when it concerns our future and how your behavior affects it. I am your wife, not your slave and not your property. You told me last week that you were done with the whiskey," she challenged. "But it is obvious that demon alcohol has wheedled its way back into your life." Tears were beginning to burn her eyes. "But let me tell you this, husband, not *my* life!"

Angry and disgusted, he shoved her hard toward the wall, causing her to stumble against the coat tree and fall with it, landing on her right side across the tree amid a pile of coats, her arms and wrists taking the brunt of the force.

"Sarah! I didn't mean to push you! Are you hurt? Let me help you up. Wait! Let me see if you are hurt."

The shock of it all, then the awareness that he used physical power against her, the wife he supposedly loved, brought the tears to life. She could not stop them from sliding down her face. Once her heart slowed, she raised herself to a sitting position, examining her hands and feeling her arms. They were all right. Her side hurt, and she gingerly felt her ribs, inhaling tentatively. Sarah did not think any bones were broken, but she knew that rib injuries can show themselves late after an accident. Her right hip had been cushioned by the coats, and she thought she might develop a bruise, but that was all.

"I will be fine, Evan, in my body. Nothing broken." She regarded him with a sad expression. Her spirit was numb. She couldn't bring herself to think that he had pushed her. In her mind she wanted to call it a clumsy stumble and fall, but deeper down she knew better. Ignoring his outstretched hand, she carefully made her way to standing and took a slow step, wincing in pain as she bent to pull the coat tree back up.

Evan tried to help her, but he was still drunk as well as stunned at his own actions. "I'm so sorry, Sarah, please forgive me." The words bounced off her back as she left the room.

It would be four more years until Sarah finally mustered the courage to leave Evan. His drinking and morphine use worsened, but at least the shoving and blows had stopped. On several occasions she arrived at work disheveled and tearful. Dr. Libbert, Sarah's parents, Evan's aunt and uncle, and Samuel all urged her, in one way or another, to leave, even divorce him if necessary. But she would not consider divorce. "It will kill his spirit to think that his wife took such a drastic action."

Near the end, Evan was unable to support them.

Heartsick, a Path

Sarah's Diary: May 1, 1870

I can breathe again, though I am so terribly sad of heart for my failure. On the positive side, I am not worried for my physical safety every waking minute of the day, and I am happy enough at Samuel's. Although Mother wanted me to come live with them again, S. offered the extra room in his house. I want to be part of a busy household, especially with Bethanne and Eddie and all that they are learning. S. is happy in his new church work.

But all is not happiness. I am heartsick for myself and Evan and our dreams. I had just been given a glimpse of what a wonderful life as a wife could be like. But our dreams, my dreams, did not take root in the short time we were together. I am ever hopeful that he will stop the whiskey and morphine, thus controlling his anger at me. Perhaps we will be able to live as man and wife again ... oh, I do hope so! But I cannot imagine it in the near term. I have too much memory of his anger and insults toward me. Being away from him helps me to take a broader view of things and remember who we were and who he was when we first met. If only he had never gone to war... that damned war! We would be a happily married couple, with children of our own perhaps.

I can barely bring myself to recall the Sunday that I left him. We had been arguing, but I was keeping my distance to avoid any danger of being hurt. I was in our room straightening things when he came to me, looking for his morphine. I told him I did not know where it was, which was true, and then he launched into a screaming tirade, accusing me of hiding both it and his whiskey! I had learned from Dr. Libbert that hiding a drunkard's alcohol is a worthless pursuit, and so I'd stopped doing that a long time ago.

And then, after he stormed out, a small voice inside my head urged me to leave. "Nothing you have tried, Sarah, has worked. You know that Evan must make changes for himself and not at your urging or inspection or expectation. The sooner you change your situation, the sooner Evan will have to do these things—or not—for himself. Do not waste another minute. It is time. You deserve peace and happiness. You alone are responsible for your life."

And so, just like that, I quickly packed a few items of clothing into a valise, and when he was napping, I walked through our front door and the mile to Samuel's.

E. made no attempt to find me the rest of the day.

On Monday when E. should be at work, S. and G. escorted me back to our house and helped me gather up all the things that are dear to me. I wrote a letter to Evan of my intentions and left it on the parlor table. I hope that my absence will work, and that the farewell is but a temporary one. I deeply wish that the circumstances were different, but they are not. I must gather my courage and hold my head high in town. It is important for me to regard myself as valuable as I do anyone else.

I do so enjoy my time working with Dr. Libbert. He says I am blossoming every day in spite of my life circumstances, and that I should become a doctor, like him. His nephew Jonas has just graduated from the Bellevue Hospital Medical College in New York, and he reports there are plans to establish a nursing school there. Dr. Libbert is a kind and gentle man, and he inspires me to learn more and do better. I have devoured every book that he owns about medicine and surgery and the care of the sick, and all that I have read is most interesting. But I find their instruction to be so far beyond my interests. The questions that consume me are very different from the questions that drive Dr. Libbert.

How will that little boy's mother adjust to the fact that he must now get around on crutches and will never be able to chase a ball like her other sons? And the couple whose baby died? That is a common enough occurrence today when people have large families. But how is it for them to see such large *families, so easily produced, and wonder if they will ever have the joy of holding their own dear child? And for the woman with the tumor in her abdomen … were her children with her at the time she died? Did she have a peaceful death? Was she comfortable, not afraid?*

These are the conditions that I feel called to care for, and from what I saw at Pittsburg Landing and on the Rover, mine is primarily the work of a nurse and not a doctor.

And what of Evan? What demons make the drink so magnetic for him? What lies behind his need to control me? What did he see on the battlefields of Tennessee and Georgia that he cannot erase from his mind? How could I have helped him more? Surely the love I gave him and the knowledge of how to help could save him, could it not? I need to know more.

But I am not ready to help Evan. I must help myself first and gain clarity. I cannot believe that I became a weak and simpering woman, afraid of her husband, reliant upon his good opinion of her to face the day with confidence. I am heartsick for all that I lost with Evan, but I am equally heartsick for having lost myself, and my way. Sometimes weeping comes upon me when I least expect it … an innocent question about the war from Eddie, or while setting the table in the morning.

I see that I am rambling in my writings, and that is surely a reflection of how my life is unfolding at the moment. However, I do know this: My path forward lies in me using my skills and abilities to help people.

Someday I will become a trained nurse.

Nursing School

Sarah barely had the energy to finish the letter to her mother, much less to Bethanne, Samuel, and Eddie, or to Dr. Libbert. It was Sunday afternoon's free time, and she relished the few hours that allowed her to breathe and reflect. She stared out the window at the bleak scene below and adjusted her shawl, grateful for the fingerless gloves, two pairs, that her mother had knit for her. They were so welcome in her cold little room! The cold was not unlike Greeneville's, but the view of the very different city continued to amaze her. All that bustling about! She missed the trees and the rolling hills, and the sense of Tennessee. Most of all she missed her mother and Bethanne.

Wilson Charles Dunlap, Sarah's father, had died suddenly one beautiful October morning in 1870. Her parents had eaten breakfast as usual, and her father excused himself to "attend to his daily constitutional." Her mother had bustled about clearing the dishes and sending George off to open the shop for the day. After a while she missed Wilson's return with the newspaper, so she began searching. She found him on their bed, face down upon the mattress, immobile, breathless, lifeless.

Jane Anne Dunlap adapted easily to life as a widow. Though she had been married to Wilson for forty-six years and had given birth to six children, she had many interests outside the home. Her current focus was on the treatment of Negroes in the South. Although they had been emancipated, they were certainly not treated equally, nor fairly. The cause of women's suffrage was near to her heart as well, and she believed women's suffrage and equal treatment of Negroes were closely linked. She occupied herself by giving more time to those causes, and her house was the site of many meetings with like-minded women, planning actions and writing letters.

Bethanne Beale was almost seventeen years old, and Sarah held a motherly regard for her. The horror of those unspeakable months at Pittsburg Landing had forged a fierce bond, and their recent years together had only strengthened it. Sarah had anticipated her niece's tears when she left for New York City, but she was unprepared for the grey sadness that seeped through her own pores for days afterwards. She was so proud of the woman that Bethanne was becoming.

Sarah remembered her desire to be of use to the Union all those years ago, and chuckled to herself that she was still wanting to be of service. She was certainly used here, she smiled, perhaps even used up. She still could not believe her good fortune at being accepted into this first class of the Bellevue Hospital Training School for Nurses. It was impressed upon them that the success of the well-planned experiment to produce capable nurses and improve the unacceptable conditions of Bellevue Hospital was almost entirely their burden to carry. If the school succeeded, it would be because she and her five cohorts had rewarded the confidence of the people who had allowed them entry.

Sarah was thirty-four years old, the oldest, and the most experienced. She felt the button pendant she always wore, thinking of Cara's letter asking her to come to Pittsburg Landing, and of Thomas, and silently prayed blessings upon both of them. She prayed for Evan as well, but she held very little hope that they would ever be able to live together again. His demons were too powerful.

Her days as a student nurse began two weeks ago, and were fuller than she had anticipated. The women rose before six and reported for duty by seven. They bustled about purposefully, responding to the physicians' directives or the head matron's orders. They were given time off for midday dinner, an afternoon tea break, and a light supper before continuing their work until eight in the evening. Weekly lectures were delivered by the nursing sisters on the topics of cleanliness, order, and patients' comfort. The remaining instruction occurred on the wards while caring for patients. Physicians visited to check progress, and the head matron and employed nurses supervised the students' efforts.

Sarah's Diary: March 21, 1873

What an interesting week it was, as I have experienced the extremes of my emotions in such a short period of time. On Tuesday, just after our midday break when we were returning to the wards for duty, Sister Mary Alice asked me into her office for a little chat. Oh, I was so nervous! I reviewed all that I could recall of my brief time at Bellevue: had I erred? or spoken wrongly?

Before I could spend more time worrying, she began. "Mrs. Rule, I asked to speak with you privately because the other Sisters and I have noted much strength and promise in your work with us. You have a presence about you that conveys a sense of calm to our patients, I have witnessed it myself. And the other students, particularly our youngest, Miss Sterrett, pay deep attention to everything you do and say. If you have any doubts about your abilities, or whether you belong here, you may put those to rest. I'll admit— we took a risk in accepting you here. We had planned for students from New York City only as they would be less homesick. Of course you are here to learn, you are not supposed to know everything that you will know at the end of your two years with us. But we want you to know that the work you have shown us thus far is beyond our expectations. If I may say so, you are going to make us proud, Mrs. Rule."

Oh, how her words filled me with joy!

I wanted to tell everyone, but of course, that is not the type of conversation to confide in others who may be anxious or insecure. I could not muster the right words to thank her and stumbled about in a weak thank you, saying that her words made me so very happy.

She replied more sternly. "I am not saying this to make you happy, Mrs. Rule. I want you to know that you must continue to develop these attributes. They are gifts, indeed, but they must be nourished and polished to continue to shine brightly and inspire others. You have a special kind of burden."

I am a jewel? I wondered—but with pride.

"That is all, Mrs. Rule. You may get back to your ward now. No doubt they are missing you."

Yesterday I had almost the exact opposite experience, which I must say has put me off balance. In the early evening as nourishments were being prepared, I was caring for Mr. Carnes, here for an infected amputation site. He had been improving, but his appetite was not what it had been. He had begun to eat less, saying that he wasn't interested in hospital food. I had heard that many times before, especially when patients are on the mend, and I can understand how they view our food. I am not so keen on it myself.

Then around six o'clock he began to have pain in his abdomen. Dr. Jacobs, who was passing through, in a hurry to get to his own supper, told me not to worry about the pain. It was most likely hunger pains, and the best thing for Mr. Carnes would be a good nourishing meal, soft food of course. Mr. Carnes looked at me questioningly, as if to say "Food? That will help the pain?" The doctor did not examine Mr. Carnes or ask him any questions. That surprised me.

I set out to consult the ward Sister about this, thinking perhaps that the man's appendix was inflamed or had burst, and might need surgery, and so he should not have any food until the problem could be identified. When I could not find the ward Sister in charge, I found a new nurse, Sister Ursula, who knew nothing of the doctor, or the patient, or me. She had just arrived that morning to begin to help with the school. She looked at me sharply. "What did the doctor say, Miss?"

"Mrs. Rule." I corrected her, and then continued, "He said to feed the patient."

"Then feed him you shall." And she scurried off.

And so I reluctantly took a tray of soft food to Mr. Carnes. He refused it, and I was not surprised. He said the pain was getting much worse, and he was sweating profusely. Sister Mary Alice was making end-of-shift rounds then and saw the condition of Mr. Carnes and the tray of food at his bedside. "Mrs. Rule, did you try to feed this man under these conditions?"

"Well, not exactly, Sister. I asked Dr. Jacobs about the pain and he said—"

She interrupted me. "You must use your own judgement, Mrs. Rule, when circumstances like this arise."

"I tried, Sister, and asked Sister Ursula—"

"Sister Ursula has no standing in our school yet, Mrs. Rule. You should have sought me out, or the ward Sister."

"But he is a doctor, Sister, and I thought we were to obey them."

"When you cannot find any one of us to give you guidance, then you must use your own judgement, Mrs. Rule. You were right in your concern for the man's condition, and in the end Mr. Carnes made the correct decision for himself not to take in any food. In the case of a possible surgery, food in a patient's stomach can be dangerous. It can cause one to vomit and perhaps aspirate the stomach contents leading to a very serious lung infection."

"I know that, Sister. But Dr. Jacobs did not examine Mr. Carnes himself. He barely looked at the man. Should he not have given the patient more attention?"

She bristled at my response. "It is not your role as a student, Mrs. Rule, to question the actions of any doctor. If you have concerns about a patient's care by a doctor, or anyone, I instruct you to bring them to my attention. I will handle the situation from that point. Again I tell you to use your judgement, but remember this: you must make your ideas and suggestions to a doctor seem like they are his, so as not to upset the order of things."

The order of things …. That goes the way of hoop skirts on the Red Rover!! Am I to use my judgement or not? I say yes. That is why God gave me an intellect. I will have to work hard on the ways to help doctors think my ideas are theirs, and to avoid the impression that I am overstepping my place.

July 6, 1873

Dear Aunt-Mother Sarah,

I have been thinking about you so much these last weeks as summer comes on, making Greeneville so lush and beautiful. I will not elaborate upon the hot and humid states; you know about them and you need no reminders. I miss you, Eddie misses you, and of course our father misses your adult companionship terribly. We pray for you every day.

My basic schooling completed, I have decided to become a teacher and will attend Tusculum College here in Greeneville in the fall. Since Mama's passing over ten years ago, Papa has not seemed at all interested in marrying again. He devotes himself solely to the church and "my people," as he calls them. Several lonely widows in town seek him out for some unnecessary advice or flutter about him with offerings of cakes or Sunday dinner. I am not worried for him because he seems happy enough.

We visit Grandmother at least every week. I am grateful that she is so kind and loving to us. Since you have gone, she tries to fill in the role of our aunt-mother. But a wise woman to help us, help me, understand womanly things is all that I need at this time.

I have an important young man in my life, Aunt Sarah, whom I have known for nearly a year now. I met him at the ice cream social in the park last year. You were unable to come with us, do you remember? You had one of those headaches that day. His name is Dennis O'Sullivan, the older brother of Eddie's good friend, Timothy. Do you remember him with Eddie when you lived with us? It is unlikely you met Dennis; he was so occupied with reading and schoolwork, and he has a lame leg, unable to get about like his brother. But what a heart he has! Such a very kind man. Although he has not asked Papa yet, we are talking about marriage when I finish my schooling and he is established in his practice. He wants to become a lawyer and work in our legislature.

I am sure the topic of lawyers makes you think of Uncle Evan. Several weeks ago Papa and Uncle James convinced him to seek admission to a farming establishment in Dayton, Ohio, for the care and treatment of Civil War veterans. Perhaps you already know that? Papa learned that many of the men there suffer from dependence on alcohol, and other substances such as morphine and cocaine. Perhaps this little bit of news about Uncle Evan will bring you a smile. We pray for his recovery every day.

Oh, I have so many questions for you! Are the Sisters there still so pleased with your work and skills? What is New York like in the summer? Is it as hot and humid as Greeneville? And the fashions? What are the modest young ladies wearing these days? I have seen the latest hair styles in Godey's Ladies Magazine and am trying to tame my unruly curls by threatening them with execution by scissors if they don't behave. But it is a weak threat. Dennis declares he loves my wild hair. It is easy for him to say—he doesn't have to manage it in this weather!!

But the most important question is this: Aunt Sarah, are you happy? I can only imagine that finally arriving at a school for nurses must be like a dream fulfilled. You spoke about it with longing so many times.

I will close for now. I send you a warm and heartfelt embrace and look forward to a letter from you as soon as possible. I wish the best for you and the patients you tend in the coming weeks.

With much love, your devoted niece-daughter,

Bethanne

Outside the Walls

Sarah wrung the cloth over the basin next to the woman's bed, choosing her next words carefully. "No, I don't think you are wrong to *want* to leave your husband, Mrs. Doyle. Our thoughts and the actions we take are two different matters. Please say more about what you are thinking."

Hannah Doyle was the youngest patient she had cared for during her three months as a private duty nurse, and Sarah felt a sadness at the circumstances. Wed at seventeen to a man nearly twice her age, Hannah was pregnant most of her married life. She had given birth to seven children, five of whom had survived. The youngest was now two years old. Five days ago Hannah visited the midwife who delivered her last three—a midwife who was also known to help women who didn't want any more children.

Hannah had arranged for her neighbor, Mrs. Clarke, to look after the youngest children during the day. Her sister Rachel would take over their care after school. Late that afternoon, while Rachel was reading a book to them, Hannah returned walking slowly, gingerly, pale and in pain. After a few minutes, it was clear to Rachel that Hannah was in no condition to care for herself or her family. And Timothy Doyle was unlikely to be of help. It was impossible to know when he would be home and in what mood. Rachel went next door and asked Mrs. Clarke to watch the children one more day. Then she found a driver and took Hannah to her own little apartment to recover.

Rachel Murray watched over her sister for two more days as she suffered and did not appear to be improving. Hannah resisted every effort of Rachel's to take her to the hospital, but she finally relented enough to permit a visiting nurse.

Sarah was not shocked at what she found. She had heard these stories from the other nurses, but this was the first time she had witnessed such distress herself. When she arrived, Hannah had a high fever and was in terrible pain. Her lower abdomen was hard and distended. She had not eaten for two days even though Rachel had made her favorite soup.

"Miss Murray," Sarah said, handing her a hastily written note, "your sister needs the attention of a physician. If we are to help her, I must consult with Dr. Cornell at the hospital immediately. I'm worried about infection, and she will probably need medication. I can provide some basic care here, but we need the help of a doctor, maybe even a surgeon. We need to send for him right away. Will you get a driver to deliver this message, or take it yourself to Bellevue?"

Sarah stayed with Hannah while Rachel fetched the doctor. She continued applying cool cloths to Hannah's forehead, neck, and arms. She wished Rachel had ice to help with the fever. And she listened.

"He's started to beat me, Nurse," Hannah began in a very soft voice, her eyes closed and facing away from Sarah. "He comes home so angry, and I am the object of his release. I am so afraid he will hurt the little ones, but at least the older ones can fight back some. And we are in danger of eviction because he spends all his wages on gin. I cannot have one more baby to care for; I can barely manage the five that I have now. And my husband is no help at all—he gets in the way, actually."

Tears rolled down her cheeks as she continued to unburden herself. Sarah was tempted to share her own experience with an alcoholic husband but held back. They could not wallow in the mud together if she was going to be a help to her patient.

Dr. Cornell arrived as Hannah's condition worsened. This time the insistence of a man of authority overcame Hannah's stubbornness. She was taken to Bellevue Hospital for treatment and was released after ten days.

Sarah enjoyed private duty nursing, and she was never bored with the routine. In some ways it was much easier than her student days because no instructors looked at her critically, ever-watchful. The more challenging aspect was being on her own and making decisions without the ready advice of another nurse or matron to help her. She had to accept the "making do." She missed the cleanliness, equipment, and supplies of the hospital, but it took her mind back to the days of the hospital tents at Pittsburg Landing when helping the nurses and patients was always a compromise between what should be and what is.

She often had the time to sit at a bedside or kitchen table with a patient or family member and give her undivided attention. Of course on some occasions, anxious supervision of her patient meant she was constantly on her feet, changing a bed, bathing, or cleaning mess after mess. Her sleep was often interrupted or severely shortened.

Sarah would forever remember her frustration and embarrassment when she cried in front of a patient's husband who opposed her treatment of his wife. Mrs. Samuels was a large and pampered woman of sixty-three whose recovery from a fall down the stairs seemed unusually slow. The concussion to her head had healed, and now she had only soft tissue injuries to manage with no broken bones. *Probably all that generous natural padding helped,* she thought wryly.

She had created a schedule with Mrs. Samuels for walking all of the rooms and hallways of the second floor. On this day they were going to walk the circuit together four times. "Mrs. Samuels, it is three o'clock, time for the third one of the day. Let's get you up."

"Oh, Nurse, I don't think so. Tomorrow. I'm too tired for any more walking today."

"But it's what you need to do if you want to get your stamina back."

"I don't feel like it now. Please, just let me rest some more."

"Mrs. Samuels, think of all the progress you've made since I came. None of it was accomplished without some effort. Increasing your walks from three to four will most certainly leave you more tired at the end of the day, which means you will enjoy better sleep at night and get you on to a more normal schedule."

"I don't care what you say, Nurse, I am not getting up now." She pounded the covers emphatically with her fist. "You cannot make me! I am so tired of you telling me what to do all the time and you thinking that you know what is best for me! No, I won't!" she shouted. *Such a temper tantrum for a grown woman!*

A red-faced Mr. Samuels stormed into the room, newspaper and spectacles in hand. "What in heaven's name is going on here, Nurse? Why are you making my wife so upset?"

Sarah tried explaining their plan again, which he helped design, but found herself stumbling to get the right words out. *He gives in to her whims much too easily,* she thought, *and then wonders aloud with her why she is so slow to progress. He is as much of the problem as she is, controlling her in a seemingly benevolent fashion. I thought involving him in the schedule would correct his habit of giving in to her, but that must all be for show.*

"You are pushing my dear wife too much. You need to let her rest."

"Mr. Samuels, getting better is a long process, and some pain and effort are to be expected."

"That may be so, Nurse Rule, but something is wrong with your approach. You just don't understand her, or her needs. Surely you have the training and time to be able to be more patient and understanding. That is what I am paying you for. Isn't that what they teach you at that school you are so proud of?"

Sarah had no control of the red flush to her face, or the tears that came to her eyes, angry tears that trailed down her face and stopped her words. She took one deep breath, then another, and composed herself. She was tempted to begin with "Very well," but she could not use those words. It was *not* very well. She found another beginning. "In that case, I will check back in around five o'clock to see what you need then." She could not help adding "Rest well."

Sarah walked the three steps up to the landing of her tiny first-floor apartment as if she were carrying forty pounds of dead weight. She had spent the last week caring for Sean Davis, a young man of twenty-three, who was recovering from a broken foot, tibia, and femur. Sean had stepped from the delivery cart he was driving when his horse panicked and took off down the street. Holding a heavy milk crate in his hands and unable to steady himself, Sean fell forward, catching his right foot between the step and cart as the wagon suddenly lurched away. Someone finally stopped his horse after he had been dragged over the cobblestones for nearly a block. He was treated for several weeks at Bellevue Hospital.

Now he was on the mend, with only his father to care for him at home. Mr. Davis worked at the newspaper during the day and had hired Sarah to oversee the final stage of his son's recovery. She liked Sean Davis immensely. He was good-natured with a pleasant face, curly sandy-brown hair, and lots of freckles. Sean's manner of talking with his charming Irish accent amused her. She tried to remember and write down his colorful phrases after every visit. They got on well from the first, and his father was grateful to give up the worry over Sean's final improvement. This morning Sean was supposed to learn how to use crutches.

Sarah slowly unlocked her apartment door, removed her hat, and put it with her keys and bag on the little hall table. She took four steps to the kitchen table and sat in her favorite chair with its back to the sunny window. As she slumped forward in the seat, head in her hands, the tears came, really came, the ones she worked so hard to hold back in front of Mr. Davis.

When she had been helping Sean walk, guiding his tentative first steps on crutches … *He had been doing so well,* she thought. *How could I have missed it? I was behind him, holding onto the belt we use for extra support in patients newly walking. Had I been in front of him, and looking, would I have noticed his face slacken and a bluish color to his lips? Something was clearly wrong when he did not take the next step in the pattern.* The right crutch trembled—and tipped out from under him. Sean took one groaning gasp and fell to the left, unresponsive.

No one with her, she tried everything she knew that might bring him around, smelling salts, pounding on his chest, positioning him on his side. He wasn't breathing, and she couldn't find a pulse. Even with her ear on his chest, she could not hear his heart beat. Her own heart sinking, she feared that she knew what it was, a blood clot had been released with his change in activity. The clot traveled to his heart and took his life on the spot. Sean had died suddenly in her care.

She shuddered, remembering her panic as she ran into the street from the Davises' home, searching for anyone who could help her. She found an older woman who agreed to get a message to the nursing registry immediately. When Mr. Davis arrived at home for his midday meal, he was shocked by the presence of Dr. Cornell and Miss Elliott, the head of the registry. They had confirmed with Sarah the likely cause of Sean's demise. Sarah could not recall much of what they had said, other than for her to meet both of them at the registry at ten o'clock the next morning. Her words to Sean's father felt so inadequate.

After nearly an hour at her little table, Sarah moved to make a cup of tea. Then she noticed it, a letter that had been slipped under her door. *Probably for some other tenant, as usual, in this building.* Her spirits lifted as she recognized the name of the sender. It was from Jane! Since departing the *Red Rover*, the two women remained in touch, and Jane had been a faithful friend during Sarah's trials with Evan, working with Dr. Libbert, and throughout her schooling. The last she had heard from Jane was three months ago, when Jane had assumed a new role as the head matron of Pennsylvania Hospital.

July 23, 1875
Philadelphia

My Dear Sarah,

It is always a pleasure to think of you and everything that you must be experiencing in New York City as a private duty nurse. In my role, I must endlessly consider, it seems, the patients as a group as well as their families, in addition to the complex demands and interweaving of the physicians, surgeons, nurses, and attendants. So many to think of! Because of this I can only regard the most superficial pieces of information I am given. And Sarah, imagine this: In a rather short period of time, the first hospital in the United States will become home to its own nursing school! When that happens, concerns for the students and their instruction will be mine, too.

Do you remember our dreaming days on the Red Rover? How both of us sought to expand our knowledge of nursing and deeply desired to help people in better ways than were available to us? Attending nursing school and rising through the ranks of a well-established hospital has helped me achieve that dream. Knowing that I can help more patients, even though I cannot care for each one as I loved to do, gives me a lot of satisfaction.

All of this preamble is to say that I wish that you would come to Philadelphia and work here with me. There are many places you would find yourself useful: in the direct nursing care of patients, in the supervision of that care, or in the newly developing school which we hope to open within the next two years. Would you consider it, my friend? Though I am still quite healthy and spry, I am entering my older years and I could benefit from your more youthful spirit and energy.

I ask you this, dear Sarah, what truly ties you to New York City?

Please write back soon, and let me know what you think of my proposal. Oh, and my dear, I also want to know how you are faring these days. Do you still love your work? Do the days drain you, pleasantly, as they do me most days? What of Bethanne and your dear mother and Samuel? I hope all is well with them. Do you have news of Evan and his treatment at the farm?

How does it look for the possibility that you may live again one day as husband and wife?

No matter what, Sarah, remember that I am your faithful friend who wishes you only the best. New York City is not that far from Philadelphia. Perhaps you could come to visit and see for yourself how Pennsylvania Hospital could become a part of your life as a nurse.

Jane

Sarah didn't know what to think of the letter. Was it a godsend because she was devastated over the death of Sean and she doubted her abilities? *Am I really meant to take care of the most vulnerable people unsupervised? Should I not have anticipated this, and worked harder to prevent it? Did I not owe Sean and his father better than what I gave? Who would tell me?*

Goodbye

November 20, 1875
Greeneville, Tennessee

"Sarah!"

She barely had time to remove her hat and gloves once George opened the door. The family had been expecting her arrival, but even so, no one knew exactly when. Jane Anne Dunlap rushed to grab her daughter's shoulders and hug her as if it were going to be the last time on Earth. *Mother still has a fierce grip! She is even more wily and muscular with age.* "Oh, my dear, oh Sarah, we have missed you so much!"

"Me, too, my sweet little Mother," Sarah replied, kissing her gray-streaked hair. "You have no idea how I have longed to be with you all. Oh!" she sighed, "it is such a blessing to be back in this home with my family all around."

"Aunt Sarah! You're here! Let me go get Bethanne—" Sixteen-year-old Eddie exclaimed. As tall as she remembered Samuel, Eddie must be three or four inches taller. And with his father's large chocolate-colored eyes, Eddie had become a most handsome young man. He had been helping his grandmother unpack some boxes in the pantry. He sprinted out the back door, his coat barely on. In short order Bethanne came hurrying into the house ahead of her father, and immediately grabbed her, too. "Aunt Sarah! It is so good to have you home!"

Within ten minutes the distance between Greeneville and New York City vanished, with the three years that separated them all forgotten. The happy gathering around the table glowed with contentment; stories and laughter filled the room. Samuel and Eddie, Bethanne and her fiancé Dennis, George and James with James's young wife Galena, Jane Anne and

Sarah. They reminisced about Wilson with great fondness, laughing at his favorite stories. No questions about the future needed settling. It was enough for everyone to relax into this joyous evening. They were complete.

Two days later, while Sarah was helping her mother prepare dinner, Samuel's knock at the door interrupted their chatter. A cold front with blustery winds and hints of snow had arrived. Sarah answered the door and turned to fetch Jane Anne. Samuel lightly placed a hand on her arm to restrain her. "It's not her I came to see, Sarah. It's you. Could we have a little time alone?"

"Certainly, Samuel, it will be good to catch up. Let me tell Mother we're going to sit in the parlor for a while. I'll bring you a cup of tea." *It must be about Bethanne and Dennis.* Sarah herself had been charmed by Dennis, and she knew what charm could do to an impressionable young woman. *If not Bethanne, maybe it's his church or maybe Eddie? What on Earth could be the matter with Eddie?*

While Sarah was in New York, she and Samuel had exchanged a few letters, mostly about her schooling and work, what was happening in Tennessee, how he was living out his role as the church's pastor. The letters were newsy and full of adult sentiments and perspectives on the impact of Reconstruction. They were not personal, neither were they heartfelt. They were simply factual.

She sat across from him on the horsehair loveseat, he in Wilson's favorite wingback chair, perfect for reading the newspaper. She smiled. "You have my attention, Samuel. What would you like to discuss?"

His face changed from that of her interested brother-in-law to the kindly countenance of a caring minister. *This must be about me. Have I done something wrong? Is he against my plan to move to Philadelphia?* Samuel leaned forward, his hands clasped together with his forearms resting on his knees. He took a deep breath and then began.

"Sarah, I don't know exactly how to begin. Yesterday I received news from Ohio—"

"Ohio," she said. "The farm where Evan is? Yesterday? Why did you wait until today to tell me?"

He looked at her deeply, as if to deliver the awful news through the force of his gaze.

"He's not … dead, is he, Samuel? He is alive, is he not? What is the news?"

"I'm so sorry to tell you this, Sister, but no, Evan is not alive. He died sometime in the past week." He was silent to let the truth sink into her consciousness.

After a moment he began again. "He was found on Saturday morning, Sarah, more than a mile from the farm, dead. It is believed he lay there for at least two days before someone came upon him. He had left the farm, probably seeking alcohol, I was told. We do not know if it was alcohol poisoning that killed him, or exposure to the freezing temperatures."

Sarah sat like a statue, hands in her lap. She stared, unmoving, tearless, but her gaze was in the past and inward. Years ago, in her heart, she had said her goodbyes to Evan and the life they had hoped to build, the children they would never have. Although Evan had been gone to her, she held onto the slimmest hope that he would win his battles and come back to her as the man she knew before the war. Now that possibility had disappeared. She couldn't quite bring herself to imagine a world without Evan in it, even if they were not together.

"They are sending his body back to us, to be buried in the Greeneville Cemetery. I have already made arrangements with the manager there, and I will be happy to officiate at the burial, Sarah, if you wish. He wanted to be buried next to his parents and uncle in the family plot."

A burial, Sarah thought, *what a fitting way to put this all to rest. My feelings and hopes have been buried a long time … his death seals it. It's time to put this fully behind me.*

Goodbye

"Thank you, Samuel, for sparing me the planning and taking care of the details. When will it be?"

"Four days from now, on Friday. We could have done it on Thanksgiving, but it seems the wrong day for mourning."

She commented wryly, "Any day is the wrong day for mourning, Samuel, but I suppose that is the best choice. And I will only be here a short while myself before heading to Philadelphia. Friday is fine with—no, Friday is not *fine*, no day is fine!" She caught her breath. "Failure defines the situation. Failure to prevent a war in which thousands of lives were lost, families broken. Evan's failure to conquer his demons. My failure to help him. Perhaps we should never have sent him away. Maybe he would be alive today, and we would be living as a married couple, with children even!"

She began to sob. Samuel had never seen Sarah this shaken, even when she struggled with Evan's painful behavior.

"My dear Sarah, we did not send him away. We encouraged him strongly, that is most certain, but before he left, it was of his own free will. At his leaving here, and arriving in Dayton, he truly wanted to get help and return to you and his good life in Greeneville. He was not our prisoner, Sarah, surely you know that."

She slowly nodded her assent and wiped her tears.

He stood and came to her, pulling her to her feet. He wrapped his strong arms around her, placing a hand at the back of her head. Her initial resistance melted at this sign of tenderness, and she let herself be comforted.

Friday was a cold and blustery gray day. The sky was unfriendly, and the ground was dirty with brown patches of frozen snow. The Thanksgiving celebration, if it could be called so, had been quiet and subdued, even with the family's favorite foods before them. Eddie did not know what to say and sat awkwardly, contributing nothing to the attempts at conversation. Bethanne and Dennis were engrossed in each other, although Sarah could tell the end of Evan's story weighed heavily on her niece. She could not help but think of the happy Thanksgiving time eleven years ago when they had been anticipating James and Evan's return. So much had happened in those years!

She had one final task to complete to close the circle—to be present at the burial and pay her respects to the man she had loved and failed.

Sarah's Diary: November 26, 1875

It is nearly midnight, and I am unable to sleep, so I have decided to unburden myself upon this page. What a sad day! I had said my farewells to Evan years ago. If only I had been there when he went to the farm in Ohio. I imagine that both of us would have been hopeful for his cure, perhaps myself more than him. Before he stepped into the carriage, he would tell me that he loved me and hoped to make himself into a worthy husband again. I imagine him gaunt, nearly as thin as when he returned from the war, but not smelling of alcohol. His beautiful green eyes would be sincere and soulful in spite of their redness. We would hold each other for a long time. Then he would put his lovely hands upon my face and kiss my lips and then my eyes, just as he used to do when we were happy. He would pat my curls and manage a smile. "We will write each other, will we not? Let us rebuild our relationship that way first with words on paper." I nod.

Before he turns his back to me and gets into the carriage I would say, "I love you, Evan."

I have often wondered if he needed my assurance of love one last time to give him reason to abstain from alcohol. I will never know, but I must believe that my words on that day would not have carried any more weight than his own desire to get well. I must believe that.

Samuel was my rock today. I will always remember his kindnesses to me and his words. At the graveside his emphasis was as much on the role we are all called to play in helping our brothers and sisters. It is not always possible for that help to make the difference we hope for, he said, because that is God's to decide. But every act of kindness and mercy for those who suffer makes us better for it and strengthens the kingdom of God.

Goodbye

I know that these feelings of sadness and remorse for Evan will dissipate in time, just as Samuel's did for Cara, but at the moment I find myself reliving the few years of our marriage with their hope and their ugliness. I thought I had put all that behind me, and so am surprised to find myself confronting my own little demons and failures again.

After supper had been put away and family headed to bed, the house was still for the first time in days. I stopped Samuel to thank him for everything he has done for me. "You must know, my dear Sarah, that I would do anything for you. You are that precious to me, and to Bethanne and Eddie. My heart breaks for all that you have gone through, but I hold you in the highest esteem. I love you."

I stood there shocked, while he continued to speak of his love for me. My mouth was agape, I am sure, and I was surprised by his flowing expressions of care. A sister-in-law, yes, but it never had dawned on me that his feelings ran deeper.

Then he took my hands in his and pulled me to him. The embrace was welcome, I must admit. Samuel is a most kind and gentle man. But I was most surprised at his kiss … it was warm and tender, and, yes, I felt stirrings for him. His soft mouth lingered on mine for another moment, and then he broke it off.

He stepped back and reached for his coat. "I love you deeply, Sarah, and I have since those awful days after Cara. I watched your love for her and the children blossom even though she was gone. And I felt it, too. But hush. Do not say a word. It is enough for me to tell you of my love. I need nothing from you in return. Now is not really the time. You are too vulnerable, and I would not take advantage of you. Good night, dear Sarah. Rest well."

What turbulence his words have unleashed in me!

A Cure

It was nine o'clock in the morning when Sarah knocked on Jane's office door.

"Well, I am here, friend, just as we wrote. I am ready to be put to work," she smiled, "wherever you need me."

"Sarah, I am thrilled beyond words that you are here. Sit down. Would you join me in a cup of tea? It will be a rare day in the future when we can sit and enjoy tea together, so let us take advantage of this sweet opportunity. I will tell you what I am thinking about where you can best help us now." She smiled warmly at her friend and poured tea into a delicate china cup.

After their days on the *Red Rover*, Jane had moved to Boston, where she worked for several years at the New England Hospital for Women and Children. She graduated from the hospital's, and the nation's, first nursing school in 1872. Then she moved to Philadelphia to be closer to her family.

In response to Jane's offer, Sarah had decided she wanted to work as a nurse on the wards. She did not feel qualified to supervise others, though she felt certain the time would come when she would be ready. She needed to learn the inner workings of Pennsylvania Hospital first. And the possibility of helping launch a new nursing school excited her, for the experience of her own learning had infused her with such confidence and inspiration. She knew she wanted to be party to that same sense of accomplishment in others.

Years later Sarah would look back on this day and define it as the beginning of the third chapter of her life, the time when she came fully into her own as a nurse. Chapter One led her to the major questions of her existence: *Why am I here? How am I to serve?* The second chapter was defined by the upheavals of war, the struggles with Evan, and her preparation as a nurse. *Am I enough? How can I live with a person who is intent on self-harm and an unhealthy life?*

Chapter Three, she would discover, was full of many successes … as a ward nurse, as a supervisor, as an assistant to Jane in administering the nursing service of the hospital, and finally as a teacher in the nursing school. Always, always, she was drawn to the bedside of a patient who needed a nurse. That was the essence of who she was. Though she enjoyed her later roles as supervisor, administrator, and teacher, at every turn she thought of the patient who needed a nurse, a good nurse, a trained nurse. She could still bring the image of Thomas Swain to her mind, grateful that he helped her find passion for her life's work.

For nearly fifteen years, Samuel continued to reach out to her and profess his love. But he never pursued a marriage proposal, nor did Sarah attempt to move their relationship in that direction. It sustained her to know that she was loved by a man, a good and kind man, but that love did not require more of her than to accept it gracefully. Her life was fully occupied by the nursing work that she loved. They exchanged many letters over the years, and she felt that Samuel understood her.

In 1890 she received two letters about her brother-in-law, one from Bethanne, who was now happily married to her Dennis, and one from Samuel himself. They both contained a similar message. Samuel, in his mid-fifties, had become enamored of a widow woman in his congregation, and he had proposed marriage. Samuel told Sarah that the woman, Lucia Epplewhite, carried so many of the fine qualities that he had long admired in her. He added that time was passing and he wanted to have, and to be, a companion in his remaining years.

Bethanne was surprised at this turn of events, but so very pleased to see this spark in her serious and gentle father.

Aunt Sarah, I have never seen him this happy! I was too young to know any different when my mother was alive, and the wartime tensions occupied him while I was a child. But this transformation! Oh, Aunt Sarah, I am so grateful to this woman for her kindness and love for my father! Lucia is three years younger than Father, a very strong and healthy woman, with the confidence of her own opinions. She is every bit as determined as you!

In 1899, two events would continue to shape her life's direction.

One cold February day, as she enjoyed a cup of tea in front of a blazing fire, an article in the newspaper captured her attention. "Kentucky Man Cured of Consumption in Western Clinic." Sarah was very familiar with the deadly disease that attacked and destroyed the lungs of its victims. The warmer and drier climate of the West had recently been promoted as a much healthier alternative than the Northeast's damp and cold.

The article claimed that a young man, Woodrow Swain of Greenville, Kentucky, had left eighteen months earlier to seek a cure in the Arizona Territories, and "by the grace of God and the application of knowledge by his esteemed physicians, he would most certainly be declared rid of the disease." His parents, Benjamin and Suzanne Swain, added that "Woodrow's recovery is most definitely a miracle. Before he went West, he lay at Death's door, which was open to receive him at any moment."

Sarah was intrigued yet skeptical about the article. She had seen her share of medical claims and the often-disastrous results for the unsuspecting public. But she thought there must be a grain of truth in this treatment, harking back to the days when Florence Nightingale's effective ideas were thought to be radical.

And deeper than the story itself, she wondered about a possible connection to "her" Thomas Swain at Pittsburg Landing. Could this young man, Woodrow, be a relative of Thomas's? *And the name Suzanne. That could not be a coincidence, could it?*

Three weeks later she received an answer.

March 1, 1899
Greenville, Kentucky

Dear Mrs. Rule,

What a delight it was to receive your kind inquiry about our son Woodrow. We have received a few letters requesting information after the article in the newspaper, but yours was the most welcome because of your connection with Thomas.

Yes, indeed, Woodrow continues to report that he enjoys the health of which the newspaper boasted. And yes, I can assure you, it was not at all an exaggeration. He is recovering in the Arizona Territory, at St. Mary's Hospital in Tucson. Woodrow writes that the weather is warm compared to our Kentucky winters and much less humid. The time he has spent there, going on two years now, has so improved his health and his state of mind that he has decided to remain there and seek work when he is released. Now that rail transportation is well established and somewhat predictable, we plan to visit him when circumstances permit.

As for our connection to Thomas Swain, that is a much older story. Thomas and I were sweethearts before he went off to war, and we had hoped to marry upon his return. Naturally I was broken-hearted to learn of his death. When his family received your kind letter with the lock of his hair, they suspicioned for the worst. They welcomed me in our collective grief for the wonderful young man we had all lost. As time passed, feelings developed between Benjamin, Thomas's older brother, and me, and we married in the fall of 1866.

Today Benjamin and I are parents to four living children. Stephen is twenty-eight and married with his own family, Woodrow is twenty-seven, Abigail, twenty-four and newly married, and Warren, twenty, who lives with us here at home. Stephen and Warren help their father tend our small family farm. I am occupied, still, as a teacher in Greenville. I cannot imagine a time when I would stop teaching.

Your life sounds most interesting, Mrs. Rule, having progressed so far in nursing. We have never traveled any distance from home here, but Philadelphia is such an important city in our nation's history, and I make sure that my students all know about its part in our Constitutional Convention.

If there should be an occasion for us to correspond again, or even to meet in person, I would relish that opportunity. You would be most welcome here if you were to find yourself in our part of the state of Kentucky. I have always been grateful that Thomas had the attention of such a kind and caring person as yourself, and that he was not alone.

Yours Very Truly,

Mrs. Suzanne K. Carleton Swain

License to Practice

Sarah's Diary: September 3, 1899

It is increasingly curious to me, not to mention frustrating, that some well-meaning physicians regard nurses as their servants, without minds or intellect to bring to the care of "their" patients! For the past few months I have been attending local meetings of nurses here in Philadelphia to discuss our common concerns about our life's calling.

Almost one year ago Jane introduced me to several nurses who have been working to advance the idea that our legislature needs to recognize nursing as a distinct body of practice, and that women who call themselves nurses need to be able to assure to the public that they are indeed trained to safely meet the needs of patients. In other words, these nurses need to have been educated to at least the same level, minimal though it be, and tested to guarantee their fitness to practice. When the test has been passed, the legislature would award that nurse a license, and she would have the right to use the official title of "registered nurse." Other states are pursuing this avenue, following the lead of our courageous sisters in the state of New York.

In order to accomplish this, there must be a basic agreement about what those educational standards are, and how the test of proficiency is best established and graded. Since the legislature's members are not knowledgeable in this area, it is up to nurses themselves to make those determinations. Our little group of interested nurses is in the process of forming an association for this purpose.

It has been enlightening to hear other nurses' stories about why registration is so important. And I have seen with my own eyes examples of patients who received the most disgusting "care" by a person who called herself a nurse. One patient I recall was admitted to our hospital, and the student came to me all in a dither. The young woman had been immobilized from a high spinal fracture and had lain in one position for nearly three weeks at home! She had not been in much discomfort because her senses were dulled from the effect on her spinal cord, and she was also medicated with morphine—too much morphine, I thought. Her hands were starting to look like claws, her knees kept in a position so they would not straighten, and the worst of it was the bedsores! She had rarely been moved or cleaned, and so much of her own waste remained on her body to cause infection. The patient was near delirious much of the time from fever.

The family had hired this incompetent woman who publicly represented herself as a nurse ... why? Because her fees were much less than the nurses who came from the nursing school's registry! It took considerable effort to help this patient, but in the end we prevailed, and her limbs straightened somewhat and the bedsores healed, though she is still unable to move on her own or feel any sensations. The family is reluctant to discuss this incompetence publicly because they feel so ashamed for letting the almighty dollar dictate what care she would receive. They had no idea this woman was not trained. Oh, it is a great sadness, first for the injury, and secondly for the lack of decent and humane care.

I was also surprised to learn that nursing's founder, our dear Florence Nightingale, is against this move. She asserts that no one test can fully ascertain a woman's fitness to practice nursing! I am glad to be among my Pennsylvania colleagues rather than in London. We shall have an easier time of it, I imagine, because the dissenters among nurses are much fewer and without the credentials of the esteemed Nightingale.

I believe that our biggest obstacle is that physicians feel what they consider their sole domain might be threatened. Then, too, the public, as I read about it in the newspapers, thinks this burgeoning move is solely for the benefit of the nurse, to guarantee her status and a higher salary. What rubbish!!

To advance our cause, I have agreed to speak next Saturday at the school's first effort to acquaint the families and friends of our new group of student nurses with what they will encounter. I am positive that most of those who will be attending the afternoon picnic are supportive of their students, but they need to know the broader issues that face their young women. I hope to inoculate them with the passion to speak out and to influence their friends and neighbors. Who knows? There may well be doctors and legislators among the students' friends. Am I anxious about this opportunity? Of course I am. But it is an opportunity I must seize.

September 9, 1899

The picnic lunch had gone very well, Sarah thought. Fried chicken, ham, potato salad, scalloped potatoes, iced tea, yeast rolls and soft butter, and her personal favorite, chocolate cake with an even richer chocolate frosting. *If I could eat that meal every day, I would die a happy woman, though padded with more flesh than I'd like.* The day was beautiful, not too warm, and the weather was fortuitous. Such a blue, blue sky. Sarah loved September, always full of promise and possibility and newness.

A congenial crowd of family and well-wishers had gathered on the grassy south lawn. The head of the nursing school offered her welcome and comments, and then Dr. Blanchard, the physician liaison with the medical school, spoke about the role of nursing within the overall scope of medical care. A few of his comments grated on Sarah's nerves, and she struggled to decide how to gently redirect those thoughts in her address. Overall, though, Sarah liked Dr. Blanchard. He could usually be counted on to kindly interact with her students instead of being a pompous know-it-all like others in the medical school or at the higher ranks in the hospital.

She recalled a time when a physician had arrived at his patient's bedside under the influence of alcohol. Dr. Blanchard had been making rounds on his own patients, and he caught the looks of concern from Sarah and her student. He immediately joined the group. "Good morning, Mrs. Rule. How are things going for this patient and for your student?"

Before Sarah could introduce the student, the offending physician spoke up. "My patient, Dr. Blanchard, this is my patient, and he is doing quite well under my care." The slurring of his words was obvious, and the man's eyes were red, his clothing disheveled.

Immediately, Dr. Blanchard put an arm around the shoulders of the doctor and moved him away from the patient. "I would appreciate the opportunity to understand your fine work with this patient, perhaps in private, as I can see Mrs. Rule has some things she needs to attend to with her student."

Sarah looked over her shoulder as the men moved away. "Thank you," she mouthed as she caught Dr. Blanchard's eye. He nodded to her, grim-faced. *If only they were all so easy to deal with,* she thought to herself.

"And now, ladies and gentlemen, it is my distinct pleasure to introduce one of our esteemed teachers here at the school, Mrs. Sarah Rule. Mrs. Rule has been with us for the past eight years, and the students hold her in the highest regard, as do her colleagues. She graduated in the first class of students at the Bellevue Hospital Training School, and it seems to me, has been on a lifelong quest since to seek ever more knowledge and skill—and thus advance the practice of nursing to the benefit of our patients."

Dr. Blanchard's remarks about her continued for a few minutes that seemed like an eternity. She could sense the audience fidgeting as her heart thudded and her face blazed red.

Stop this, she admonished to herself, *you have spoken to countless groups of students over the years, and at many meetings with persons more influential than yourself. These people care about their students and their education, and Dr. Blanchard has spoken highly of you. What is there to be anxious about? Now calm yourself!*

Sarah checked her lace collar and briefly touched the pendant she was wearing on the outside of her dress. Somehow she maneuvered her way to the podium and gazed out at the audience of well-fed men, women, and a few little ones. She took a deep breath.

"Miss Rutledge," she nodded, acknowledging the woman who headed the school, "Dr. Blanchard, students, and honored guests, it is an indescribable pleasure to stand before you today. Nearly forty years ago at the beginning of our nation's sad and tragic Civil War, I was seeking the answer to my young life's questions: How shall I serve? What gifts do I have to help make life better for my fellow man?

"I found the beginning of the answer at the Battle of Pittsburg Landing, caring for a young soldier named Thomas." Holding out her pendant for all to see, she continued. "It is his uniform button which I wear daily as a pendant, and as a reminder that the answers to life's most important questions are not always clear at the outset.

"My call to nursing was met with many challenges. Highest among them, did I know what I was doing? How could I avoid injuring someone I was trying to help? And even though I might understand what it was I was to do for a patient, did I do it well? Many of these questions were addressed by the opportunity I had to attend nursing school, which brings all of you here today."

Sarah paused. She felt the power of her words overcome her nervousness.

"To the students before me, we cannot promise that you will have success in everything you undertake. There will be struggles and failures, and lessons to learn beyond the ones we put on paper. After all, these are human beings we are caring for, we are human and prone to error, and life is complicated. But I can promise that you will be surrounded by faculty and nurses and physicians who want to help you succeed in every task you undertake. We are so glad that you are starting your journey here with us.

"And, to the family and friends of the students here today, I ask this of you. Support your student. Listen to her, and hear her concerns with compassion, and do not fear when she is distressed at something that has happened in her training. I can assure you that this happens to every student, and it is oftentimes the key to an even greater learning. And in anticipation for how she will be received once her schooling is complete, think on this. An effort is underway to define and regulate the practice of nursing

License to Practice

here in Pennsylvania. We at the school all welcome this, and we hope that you will, too."

Dr. Blanchard looked surprised at Sarah's last words, and sat up straighter.

"When you learn of situations where family or friends are cared for by incompetent people posing as trained nurses, be assured that your student will never have to defend her work. And if you know of someone who is seeking home care, for example, counsel that person to inquire as to what school the nurse attended, how long she has been practicing, and what her references are.

"In order for our legislature to take nursing licensure seriously, we need the support of the public. If you are in positions to advocate for this in your neighborhoods or civic organizations or churches, we hope you will do so. You will be advocating for the public's right, which is your right too as a possible patient, to know that you are receiving care by well-trained nurses. You will be helping to create an environment where your student can flourish. She will know that the nurses practicing beside her have the same standard of education, and the care of patients will be as safe and effective as we can possibly make it."

Sarah reached again for her pendant and held it out.

"And so, in recognition of Thomas and the many opportunities I have had to further my understanding of nursing, and on behalf of the school and the faculty, we welcome your students, and we are grateful that you were able to join us today. Thank you for your kind attention. I believe there may be more cake and iced tea left, so please help yourselves."

Sarah stood still for a moment as the group politely clapped their applause. It was not an overwhelming reception, but she was satisfied with her first attempt at this broader public speaking. She caught the eye of a man in the audience who did not appear to be happy with her comments. *Probably a disgruntled physician,* she thought, *though I do not recognize him. More likely it is a legislator who feels I am stepping on his toes.*

Her thoughts were interrupted by Miss Rutledge at her side. "That was a lovely welcome, Mrs. Rule. Just the right information and in the right amount of time. Some of these people need to be up and moving after such a feast. It is that time of day for napping, is it not?"

I surely wouldn't know about napping, Sarah thought wryly.

Rewarded

February 7, 1900
Philadelphia, Pennsylvania

Sarah rose early and quickly dressed in her most impressive yet serious clothing—no lace collar today. She was headed to Harrisburg to speak to the Pennsylvania General Assembly, and she did not want to give a wrong impression or miss her train. She breakfasted on tea and toast with one scrambled egg. She was too excited to eat more even though she knew the two days ahead would be long ones.

Jane would be accompanying her, along with three other nurses who worked in different Philadelphia hospitals. Two of them would also address the group of legislators. Sarah, Mariah, and Linda had met three days ago to decide who would cover which of the points they wanted to make. They did not want to be redundant, yet the topic was broad with so many ideas to convey. Jane and Eleanor came for support and assistance. Jane had addressed the General Assembly before, but this time, she said, it was important for her younger colleagues to take up the baton. Even so, she insisted on making the 100-mile journey with them. Jane was remarkably spry at the age of eighty-three.

They all arrived at the station on time, boarded, and found seats together. Initially they were overcome with the novelty of the situation, giddy like schoolgirls on holiday, even Jane, remarking at the beauty of the moving wintry landscape. It was gray and bleak and snowy outside their windows, while inside the car they felt festive and snugly safe from the wind and the cold.

All of them felt the air of excitement, hoping that their well-planned remarks would fall like healthy seeds on the fertile hearts and heads of their elected representatives. *Women speaking before lawmakers,* Sarah thought dryly. *Will they really understand our message?* She felt tears rise at the remembrance of her dear mother, gone now a year and a half. She had worked so hard for women's suffrage, and at the end, she hadn't seen her dream accomplished.

Sarah hoped she had enough fight left in her to see her own dream realized. After all, she was sixty-one, just beginning to feel age's effect. Her hands were afflicted with rheumatism, and she was grateful that teaching did not carry the same requirement for physical effort as caring for a patient at the bedside. *My wits and brain are needed most,* she thought, *and lucky I am that both of those are still intact. For the time being.*

It was nearly three o'clock when they reached the Harrisburg station, and although the snow had stopped and the sky was blue, the afternoon air was bitterly cold. They found a carriage to take them to their hotel, where they would have a good rest and supper before the big day tomorrow.

February 11, 1900
Philadelphia

My Dear Bethanne,

I hope this letter finds you and Dennis and your three youngsters all well. It has been unusually cold here the past week, and I have noticed a greater number of friends and neighbors ill with colds of one sort or another. I believe that your little Alana is likely to be more exposed at school than the younger two, and somehow carrying the seeds of a cold home to the rest of you. Be careful, keep warm, drink hot lemon tea with honey, and avoid all who cough if possible. We see evidence, too, that regular washing of one's hands is a very good practice.

It was an interesting two days in Harrisburg. Five of us went there to speak to the General Assembly about the importance of creating a law that would regulate nursing. Who can rightfully call herself a nurse, what is the minimum education she should possess, and what is the test of her competence? Would you not think it common sense? That everyone could see this law should be enacted immediately? No, so many opposing opinions fought each other for dominance. Speeches of resistance and stubbornness, poorly disguised in blowhard questions!

Some said that as long as the nurse is under the direction of a physician, then all should be well, and there would be no need for such a law. Others wondered about the proof of abuses by incompetent women posing as nurses: "Where are the numbers?" they asked us. "It cannot be as bad as you say." I replied that numbers are not so important if it is you or a loved one that has suffered under bad nursing. But, I admit to you, I do wish we had some estimation of the actual numbers.

The most disappointing to me was from a representative who told a recent "story" about his sister who, he claimed, had been wrongfully charged with public endangerment by an upset family member. The sister was providing nursing care to a woman whose time had come to deliver, and sadly neither the mother nor child survived the childbirth experience. The particulars of the difficult delivery were especially distressing. His sister has since suffered humiliation and attacks against her character. And, he emphasized, she had attended a good nursing school and produced acceptable grades on graduation. He was against such a law because it would lead the public to believe that nurses are infallible, which they are not, and that no harm should come to someone if they were cared for by a licensed nurse. The man was on the verge of tears at least twice during his speech, and it was obvious to me that he was speaking from an emotional heart rather than an informed intellect.

We tried as best we could to convey that licensure was intended to create a structure for minimal competence, and that it in no way was intended as a guarantee of perfection, but I confess, Bethanne, our words seemed weak and ineffective against his objections gathering support. I sat down after a few feeble sentences, feeling especially discouraged that I did not have the verbal ammunition to convince him to join our side.

I'm sure you can guess that our efforts failed, and we did not have enough votes to bring a bill before the Assembly. That experience certainly took the wind out of our sails. But today, a new day, we are committed to continue on this journey, just as our suffragette mother and grandmother did. It takes time to make changes, especially important changes. I have often wondered what advice she would have for me, and the loss of her counsel brings me a deep sadness. She was a wonderful woman and I miss her wisdom.

Please let me know how things are there in Greeneville for your Dennis. Is his law practice going well, and is he staying busy? I know that you are likely busy beyond asking, my Dear One, and I think with fondness and love for you often. You made no mention of Eddie in your last letter, and he has not responded to my last one either. I worry about him. Please give my greetings to your father and his Lucia, and assure him that when they can find the time to travel to Philadelphia, I would be most happy to have them visit and stay with me a while.

Your loving Aunt-Mother,

Sarah

April 18, 1907

Seven years passed in a satisfying blur. Sarah taught in the nursing school until 1905, and stayed on longer to help with its running. At the same time, she continued to work toward Pennsylvania's adoption of legislation they titled the Nurse Practice Act. It was signed into law in 1906 shortly after she retired.

In the meantime, she had privately entertained the idea of moving back to Greeneville, just as soon as she was not needed anymore to help get the bill passed. No one knew what she had been thinking. Bethanne's children were adolescents, and she had not witnessed their growing up as she had watched Bethanne and Eddie's. Her brothers James and George lived there with their families, and she wanted to get to know them better. And, Sarah hated to admit, she was sixty-eight, sometimes in need of more help than she liked. Nearer family was the place to be.

She had many friends in Philadelphia that she hated to leave, Jane most of all. Jane at eighty-nine had wits sharp as a razor, but her body was failing. Marsella, Jane's companion and housekeeper, answered the door. "Oh, hello, Mrs. Rule. It is so nice to see you. Miss Jane has been expecting you with lots of anticipation. She is enjoying the sun on the back porch."

"Thank you, Marsella, I do know the way. Has she been well?"

"Oh yes, ma'am, as well as anyone her age. She is slow in her motions, but just as sharp-minded as the best of them. She likes to devour the newspapers from start to finish, and so quickly! I'll bring you out some lemonade and those shortbread cookies that she loves so much. I'll take those flowers, thank you, ma'am, they are surely beautiful. I'll bring them out in a moment."

Sarah handed over the flowers, and slowly made her way through the hall. She took note of the drawing room and kitchen, the dining room and sun porch, trying to capture details she wanted to remember—roses on a soft yellow wallpaper, pewter candlesticks on the dining table, a watercolor of Pennsylvania Hospital. She and Jane had spent many pleasant hours in this house … so much planning, plotting, rehashing, agonizing, discussing, reminiscing about all they had shared.

Sarah had dreaded this day, knowing it might be the last time she sat in Jane's presence in her welcoming home. *We have been friends for well over forty years,* she thought. *I will miss her deeply.* The day's newspaper was spread in Jane's lap, her head bowed and her mouth opened slightly, snoring ever so quietly. Her eyes were closed, and her chest rose and fell rhythmically.

"Jane," Sarah spoke her friend's name softly, "it's me, Sarah, come for our visit."

Jane stirred and smiled up at Sarah. "Oh, yes, my goodness, my dear, the sun just feels so restful and warm. I am like a cat, seeking as much pleasure as it can get from a day. Come here, and have a seat near me. Let us both look at the garden together. Do you see those finches going in and out of their nests? So busy feeding their babies. I just love their color, and the goldfinches, too, such a sweet little sound they make."

Sarah kissed Jane on her soft cheek, and gave her hand a warm squeeze. "How are you feeling today, Jane? It looks as though you are quite relaxed." She settled on the chair next to her friend. *Jane does have a lovely garden,* she thought, *and Nature provides such a healing environment.*

"Relaxed, now that's the word for it," Jane replied, "indeed I am. It is such a pleasant warmth here. And how are you, my dear? All going well for you?"

"I'm fine, Jane, and still so very happy after the legislature's session last winter. I have received a few letters from nurses and some families expressing their gratitude. One came in the negative, but overall, they are quite positive. I am so glad this long effort is behind us. We worked incredibly hard on it, and I feel either like I still need to catch up on my rest, or in the opposite, nothing interests me and I am so bored! Imagine that!"

They both chuckled, and Sarah continued.

"Jane, you must feel so pleased to be at this point, knowing that you were the leader of this amazing effort. When I think of all you have done to help advance nursing, the work, the study, guiding others, and inspiring us all with your perseverance and your ever-calm demeanor. You are a remarkable woman, and I am so proud to know you. And that is before I think of all you have done to help me, to show me opportunities. I am so grateful for our deep friendship."

Jane looked at her friend quizzically, and smiled slowly. "Those sound like words building up to a farewell, Sarah, if I didn't know better. Are you getting ready to leave us here? Maybe go back to Greeneville?"

Sarah swallowed. *Those wits. I should have spent more time on the personal topics to begin with. I surely didn't intend to get right to it even before we'd had a chance to sip lemonade.*

"Well, yes, Jane," Sarah sighed, looking down at her hands. "As a matter of fact, I am finding it increasingly difficult to stay here in Philadelphia with time to spare. I don't wish to start any more nursing work anew while my family in Tennessee blossoms. I hardly know the younger ones, and I think it is time for me to settle back there."

She looked up, surprised to see Jane smiling.

"You must do exactly that, my dear. I am certain that Greeneville is where you belong now. But you do know, I hope, how much I will miss these easy visits with you, living just a few miles from each other, or getting caught up in our important causes. Sarah, you have been like a daughter to me, from that first day I met you at Pittsburg Landing."

Oh, my, she thought, tears coming to her eyes, *Jane has never said this to me so directly.*

"You were so eager to know everything, and you were able to see beyond the horror to understand what it was that you were called to do. I have always admired that about you, you know, your attachment to the question of your calling. I don't think I know anyone else in all the world who is so fixed on knowing and honoring their unique calling in life. And that includes my slow-talking minister, Reverend Bowles, he speaks it regularly, but I do not think he lives it."

She chuckled and rolled her eyes. "If he were committed to his calling, surely he would get on with his sermons faster so as not to lose the attention of even the most loyal of us in the pews!" They laughed, enjoying the easy comfort of each other's presence.

Sarah left her friend's home that afternoon, carefully latching the gate behind her. If someone looked closely, they might have noticed her stopping to find her handkerchief and wipe away tears.

She never returned to Philadelphia.

Rewarded

Michael

June 3, 1907
Greeneville, Tennessee

My Dear Jane,

You asked me to be sure and tell you all the news of Greeneville once I was settled, and so I shall. It has been a most busy period, and I find that I do not have the youthful stamina I once thought would be my companion forever. Moving and resettling require so much of one's energy! Still, I have accomplished quite a lot.

In answer to your question, yes, I am again living in the home where I was raised. After my mother's passing, the rest of the family decided that they wanted to keep the house, and guessing something of my desire to return, did not sell it, for which I am most grateful. Dennis has supervised the transfer of the deed to me, and so I shall always have a roof over my head.

To help with many of the daily chores, Bethanne's youngest son, Sean, is staying with me awhile to make sure wood and coal are stocked, and the house is generally taken care of in all the ways a man might do it. Although Sean is young at 13 years old, he is remarkably responsible, and seems to enjoy helping me out. Dennis has written a plan for what needs to be done, and which routines I should observe as it relates to this property.

Bethanne and Dennis are exceedingly busy as parents of Alana (16), Michael (15), and Sean. It is hard to watch them struggle, Jane, as Alana is often sullen and willful, and Michael prefers to isolate himself in his room, staying up all hours and sleeping late into the afternoon. Dennis works long hours himself, and so the parental discipline must be delivered primarily by Bethanne, which does not suit her personality. Sean is no trouble now, and I hope that he will stay the bright spot in his parents' life.

Michael

Samuel and Lucia seem to be quite content. Their house is not too far from mine, and so we are able to visit regularly. She is a godsend. Even though she speaks her mind freely and has her own will, her expressions are always with kind respect for Samuel and his opinions. I wish I had her example when I was a young wife struggling with Evan. Who knows how things might have turned out then?

I visited the cemetery last week to put flowers on my parents' graves, and stopped to pray at Evan's grave as well. It has been over 30 years since Evan's death, so I was taken by surprise at how those emotions of caring and sadness and regret came over me again. Perhaps it was that I was in the place where it all happened, and reminded of his aunt and uncle, or our favorite picnic spot, or some other pleasant aspect of our life together. It is interesting to me that my reminiscences are more of the happy times and not so much the awful trials anymore.

This causes me to wonder if I took the right actions, but then I talk sternly to myself …. Of course I took the right path! So many were urging me to step away and save myself.

I have also entertained the thought that this longing of mine may have existed for quite a while, but I had so much demanding my attention, so many more pressing matters, that I did not allow myself the time to acknowledge my feelings and grieve for him and what we lost. I did not even take the time to grieve for myself. It doesn't matter what the cause is, because I am still left with a melancholy which I must overcome.

Dear Jane, please let me know what is blooming in your garden now and what little feathered creatures delight you this season. I hope to receive a letter from you soon. Thoughts of you in your lovely home give me great joy. Take good care, dear Friend, to keep your health and vitality.

In deepest friendship,

Sarah

August 14, 1907

Alana rushed breathlessly into the kitchen where Sarah had been kneading dough. "Oh, Aunt Sarah, there's been a terrible argument at home, and Mama sends word to ask you to come right away. She is most distraught, and Michael is gone. Father is away visiting a client's family in Rheatown."

"Gone?" Sarah asked in alarm. "Whatever do you mean by *gone*?" Sarah couldn't help that her first thought was of death.

"He ran away, and Mother doesn't know what to do—she needs you to come as soon as you can," Alana urged. "The neighbor is waiting in his carriage outside, and we can go back together."

Sarah dusted off her hands, covered the dough hoping that it would know what to do without her coaxing, checked her appearance in the mirror, and donned her hat. "Let's be off, then, Alana."

On the short trip to Bethanne's house, she spoke little, but listened as Alana described the chaos that had been visited upon them that morning. She had only to ask two words: "What happened?"

Apparently Bethanne had forbidden Michael to join a friend later in the afternoon, words between them had escalated, Bethanne slapped Michael, and he left. Sarah had heard many similar stories from her friends, patients, and people she worked with, and they usually resolved of their own accord. She knew that Michael's age and the stress for Bethanne of being the primary parent figure could make for a difficult period.

Sarah did not know her great-nephew very well since she had visited rarely while living in Philadelphia. Michael had been a stunningly handsome and somewhat precocious, attention-seeking little boy before the age of five. And then, from what she could deduce from Bethanne's letters, Michael began to develop fears … fears of the dark, of candles, of an encounter with a snake. She thought they were normal enough, but they evolved into more troubling ones as he grew older: the fear of a wolf evolving from a thick limb of a tree and jumping out to devour him, or of a ghost manifesting from a lace curtain. Because he was such an intelligent child,

Sarah guessed that Michael enjoyed a vivid imagination, a tendency that could be very positive as long as it was channeled properly.

Since her return, Sarah was surprised by Michael's appearance when she could see him more regularly. He wore the same trousers and shirt on the last three occasions. They were his favorite, Bethanne claimed. Michael had gained weight at a time when more adolescents were growing out of childhood chubbiness, and his attention to bathing was lacking. His body often carried an odor of old sour sweat, and his greasy hair was longer than that of most boys his age.

Nothing was said of it by Bethanne, and Sarah assumed that the issue was being addressed between father and son, as it should be. Sarah had no wish to meddle although she did recall Bethanne's teenaged years being quite different. Her niece had seemed overly preoccupied with her appearance and cleanliness, in stark contrast to what she was witnessing with Michael. Perhaps that was the difference between growing boys and girls of that age. Eddie had not been nearly as fastidious as his sister. But her recent exposures did not prepare her for what lay ahead as she entered the house.

"Oh, Aunt Sarah, I'm so glad you came!" Bethanne was distraught. "Dennis is gone, and I need another adult to help me."

"What about your father, Bethanne? Surely he would come? I mean, I'm glad to be here, but you have other help around, you know."

"Aunt Sarah, Father his had his own problems with Michael. His advice to us is to turn him more toward the Gospel and insist that he read Scripture every day and go with us regularly to church. Michael will have none of that. I am so worried about him, about—" she stopped, her words hanging in the air.

"What, Bethanne, what are you thinking?"

"He is not like the other boys his age. He spends so much of his time alone, writing and drawing, and when I encourage him to get outside, he claims one excuse or the other—he says it is too hot, he would rather write, or no one likes him.

"He has a new look about his eyes, one that seems so strange. All of a sudden this morning he told me he was going with a friend to a lecture at the library. That's good, I thought to myself, that is progress. When I asked what the lecture was, Aunt Sarah, he said it was being given by the latest spiritual medium, a Madame Lavotsky or something or other like that. He claimed that he wanted to show her his writings and drawings, and maybe she would take him under her wing and guide him. Oh, I was extremely shocked! And I suppose I let anger overtake me.

"I said I would rather he not go, that this spiritual medium business is all tomfoolery, and he had no business subjecting his young mind to such rubbish. Oh, I know that Dennis would have had a much better argument, but he is not here to help me! Our words back and forth got louder and louder, and he finally said I could not stop him because he was so much bigger than me, and all I was trying to do was hold him back from living his own life."

"What did you do then?" Sarah asked.

"I managed to get between him and the door, I could see he was so determined. He came at me, and I grabbed his arms, saying something like, 'You will not leave this house, Michael, I forbid it! You are just fifteen.' He laughed at me then, wickedly, and said 'Watch me leave, Mother.'

"'Oh, no you won't, Michael,' I said, 'You will stay right here until your father gets home, and then we will all discuss this thing together!'" Bethanne stopped, trying to catch her breath and stop crying.

"Then he said, 'That will be too late, Mother, I'm leaving now to meet Charles. Goodbye.'

"So then, and it was surely a mistaken reflex, Aunt Sarah ... I slapped him. I am so ashamed, I have never slapped any of my children in anger—"

"What happened then?"

Michael

"He laughed at me again, and looked at me with that strange look in his eye, and with utmost control he finally said, 'Oh, Mother Dear, you will surely live to regret this day.'"

Sarah felt a chill pass through her … *such a strange and evil-feeling thing for a fifteen-year-old boy to say to his mother.* She put her hands on Bethanne's arms and squeezed them gently.

"Oh, Aunt Sarah, I am so disheartened … at what is happening to him … at my behavior. And what's worse is that Dennis and I seem to be at odds at how best to help, or what to do."

"Bethanne, take comfort. There are many trying times in raising children, and I have never heard one parent say that they did everything perfectly. Young people are subject to many different phases, and it is normal for parents to disagree about the best approach.

"But the most important thing for you at this moment is to calm yourself, and next is to develop a plan, best done with Dennis, on how you will guide Michael in the future. I can surely help the two of you, but Dennis must welcome my involvement, too. You have time, Bethanne. This is one occurrence in a lifetime, and likely there could be others. When did Michael leave?"

"About two hours ago—and if he does go to the lecture as he was wishing, then it should be over by four o'clock, and he would back here by five, I hope … I wonder if I should go to the lecture myself and bring him back?"

"Think about what you are saying, Bethanne. He will be with his friend. He is doing something that he wants, although it is distressing to you. On its surface, attending a public lecture is a normal occurrence. How do you think he would respond to your determination to bring him back home? How could that affect your relationship? What would others in the audience think of you, or him, or how you are managing things at home?"

Bethanne stared at her aunt for a few moments, her eyes glistening. Chastened, she looked at the floor and said nothing. Sarah broke the uncomfortable silence.

"When do you expect Dennis to return?"

"Six or seven? He said he should be home by suppertime."

"Then you need to make your own plan for how to fill your afternoon with something other than fretting, and what you will do if Michael returns home before Dennis. What will you say to him? And then, how will you inform Dennis about what happened? Surely those are not new discussions between the two of you?"

Sarah stayed with Bethanne for another hour and listened and encouraged her thinking. When she was satisfied that all was calm again at her niece's, she returned home, greeted by a pile of dough that had escaped the bowl. She could not help but laugh. *This was the bright spot of my day.*

Late that evening she was awakened by a fierce pounding on her door just as she drifted off to sleep. Sluggishly she found her dressing gown and slippers and made her way downstairs as quickly as her knees would allow. Fearing another urgent message from Bethanne, she was unprepared to discover Michael at the door. Disheveled, wild-eyed and carrying a leather case, he looked at her with relief.

"Oh, I am so glad you are home, Aunt Sarah, I am afraid my mother will not have me, and Father must surely be against me, too. May I live with you? I can do all those things that Sean was doing for you, and more. I am older and stronger and much wiser than him, and I can even provide some income for both of us by my writings. And my drawings, they surely will fetch a good sum. And I won't eat much, in fact it would be good for me to stop eating. And Madame Lavotsky will surely have room for me on tour, so it will be just a short while that I will need to live with you, Aunt Sarah. Will you say yes, please? May I live with you?"

Michael's plea was delivered in one quick breathless ramble as he stood on the porch, Sarah with the door held open, as well as her mouth.

Michael

"Come in, Michael, let us talk about this inside. Will you have something to eat? Let me make us some tea and find the fixings for a sandwich."

"That will be good, Aunt Sarah, I am famished! I am so starved that I could eat a team of horses!"

As Sarah moved about the kitchen, Michael sat, then stood, then paced, then repeated his movements all again. "I am guessing you must be tired and in need of a good night's sleep now, am I right?" she asked as he finally sat to eat what she had prepared.

"Oh no, Aunt, once I have had something to eat, I shall go to my room, you are going to let me stay, aren't you, and write the exciting events of today in my journal, and sketch some scenes of Madame at the library. Oh, she is a wonderful teacher, Aunt Sarah! You would agree, I know, and come to love her just as I have!"

Sarah could find no correct words of response, but even though she tried to interject something into his ramblings, it was not necessary. He was consumed with getting his own thoughts out into the air, and he needed no words from her to continue. She concluded that she would probably not be getting any sleep tonight. When Michael had eaten everything she set before him, she showed him to the room Sean had used when he stayed with her. "This is where you can sleep, Michael, and I hope you will at least lie down and give your body some rest, even though you might want to be writing or drawing. A good night's sleep is so important for our health. And just the simple act of rest will do wonders for your body."

He nodded at her absently even while he opened his case and began taking out pens and ink and his journal. She could see that her words fell on deaf ears and entertained the fleeting wish that she had a lock on the outside of the door. And although it was much too late to go and wake Bethanne and Dennis, she decided that if they were asleep they should not be disturbed. She would deliver the good news of Michael's return first thing in the morning. And since it was still summer, it would be light early.

September 26, 1907

Sarah, Samuel, Bethanne, and Dennis sat wearily in the passenger waiting area of the Knoxville depot. Their train for Greeneville would not depart for another three hours, and they had plenty of time to find a nice meal in one of the restaurants near the station, but they could not. No one was hungry even though it was mid-afternoon and they had not eaten dinner. Each one was lost in their own thoughts about what had happened. They had journeyed together as five to bring Michael for admittance to the East Tennessee Hospital for the Insane, and to a person, even for Sarah who was acquainted with hospitals and healing, it seemed more an acknowledgement of failure than hope of anything resembling a cure.

Bethanne was the first to break the sad silence. "I cannot believe that we are simply leaving him here without family or friends to even visit." Tears ran down her face anew.

"Oh, Bethie," Dennis sighed tiredly, putting his large warm hand over her small one, "you know that we have discussed this all at length. We are not leaving him without care and supervision and meals and attention. They have promised us that, remember? And what could we have provided for him at home any better than we had been already? We could not keep him safe, do you forget that? How many times had we been summoned to fetch him from one place or another, and twice at the train station ready to follow that Madame Charlatan to God-knows-where?"

Bethanne, sitting on the hard wooden bench between her father and her husband, could not find words to argue against those facts or the action they had just taken. Samuel and Sarah had made their own points in different ways that the only thing for her to do was to accept the situation. She understood their words, Dennis's as well, but accept it she could not.

The past seven weeks have been a torture, Sarah thought, *witnessing Michael's decline into madness.* Everyone around him was shocked at what they saw, as Michael seemed to lose connection with the real world and the responses of others. After the lecture at the library, he had been awake for nearly two weeks of continual writing, fevered sketching, and frantic non-stop talking about all manner of spiritual and supernatural occurrences.

Bethanne said that she felt her stomach fall and turn over every time she thought about Michael after the library incident. He claimed to know the will of God through the veins in a maple leaf, the shaft of sunlight as it fell across the dining table, and then the pattern of mud splatters left by a horse on the street in front of their house. "Mother," Michael had shouted excitedly, pounding on the front door, "Mother, come here! You must see this—this is an absolute miracle from the Creator at last! Look at the message He has sent to me—come outside now! You must see this at once!"

Bethanne had just dozed off in the parlor, a victim of a lack of sleep herself as they all tried to keep watch in the house, Alana and Dennis taking turns with her. But this time she had failed to prevent him from leaving through the front door. Fortunately Michael was intrigued by the pattern of what he saw before him and did not get more than a few yards from the house. Try as she would, she could not see any word in it, no image nor pattern, not one shred of meaning. Michael knelt down and with a twig began to pull mud from one splatter into another, insisting that the connections they made were words of God telling him to enlighten more people about how to see Him in the mud. Dennis came out the door just then, and they both were able to maneuver him back into the house.

And then, just as suddenly as he had stayed awake during his phase of what he called "my supreme accomplishments," he fell into a deep despair, sleeping for hours at a time, impossible to rouse or to interest in any of his past pursuits, even spiritualism. He ate but little and lost weight.

Bethanne nodded almost imperceptibly to Dennis, still consumed by her thoughts, "You are right," she admitted, "he could not possibly have continued on the way he was, but Dennis, I do not know how I can continue on the way things are now."

"We will find a way, my dear. We have two children who need us and people around us who will give us support and consolation."

Sarah sadly watched this exchange between husband and wife, but put a smile on her face and stood up to approach Bethanne. "Come along with me, dear niece, and let us take some air for a little while before our train arrives. The colors of the leaves this fall are most beautiful, are they not? They can always take my breath away. Getting some exercise is what I need at the moment, and I want to stop by that little bakery around the corner." They walked out the double doors together into the late afternoon.

Journey to Greenville

April 6, 1912
Greeneville, Tennessee

Who should I write to today?

As was her habit on Sunday afternoons, Sarah sat at her little desk in the parlor, pen in hand and wondered to herself. She mailed at least one letter each week, sometimes more, relying on inspiration from a worship service, or a poem, or something important that had happened recently. As she wrote the date at the top of the page, she was struck by its significance. Fifty years. It was fifty years ago to the day at the Battle of Pittsburg Landing that Thomas Swain was mortally wounded. Two days later she was first urged into service as a nurse.

She decided to write to Suzanne Swain.

Over the years since their first correspondence, she and Suzanne had developed a friendship through mail, although they had never met. Letters passed between them once or twice a year. Sarah learned that Woodrow was thriving in the brand-new state of Arizona. On impulse, she suddenly decided that this year she would travel to Kentucky and meet the Swains face to face. She had lots of time to do this, and at seventy-three, her health and abilities would never be better. Jane had passed away three years ago, and Bethanne's family had entered into a period of stability, but always with a slight air of sadness and longing from missing Michael. She finished the letter by asking Suzanne when would be a good time to visit and inquiring about accommodations in town.

Sarah was delighted to receive word back from Suzanne three weeks later. She suggested that a visit in May would be ideal, but sometime in the month of June the weather for her travel would be favorable, too.

May 3, 1912

Sarah had needed Sean's help to get her valise from the attic, and after it was properly dusted and checked, she assembled what she would take on this journey. It was a long distance, and the train would be the most comfortable and simplest conveyance. At first Samuel insisted that he and Lucia accompany her, but she would not hear of it. The journey of nearly four hundred miles each way would be expensive enough for her alone, and she would not subject them to that kind of expense. Nor could she afford to pay their fares and lodging.

Sarah pulled three dresses from her closet, one more suitable for church and dressier occasions, the other two simpler but with the lace collars she preferred. They were in fine shape for taking to Kentucky, and she finished her planning after shoes, undergarments, and nightclothes were put aside for packing the morning she would board the train. From Suzanne's letters, the Swains appeared to be of very modest means and she had recommended a small guest house within a short walking distance of their property.

What will Suzanne look like? she wondered. *Being a teacher, she will probably be educated in literature and mathematics, but does she have an interest in science? Surely we can talk about the evolution of nursing, especially since Woodrow's treatment for tuberculosis has been so successful. I am hoping to meet a woman that I get along well enough with, but could we become friends?*

May 12, 1912

As the train progressed in the early morning light, Sarah watched the hills of Kentucky unfold outside her window. Trees and grasses and flowering shrubs predominated, similar to those in Tennessee, but they passed through very few towns she would call prosperous. The Greenville station was much smaller than the one she had left yesterday afternoon.

Then she saw them waiting, even before the train hissed to a complete stop. A man whom she presumed to be Benjamin stood there, with a short plumpish woman she recognized as Suzanne from her letter's description—and from her hat, rimmed with bright red fabric flowers.

Suzanne rushed forward. "Oh, Sarah, we finally meet! I am Suzanne, welcome, welcome to Greenville. Are you tired from your long journey? Ben, now you pick up her valise, and let us get going. Are you hungry? Shall we stop and get something to eat? Oh, I nearly forgot. We brought sweet rolls from home in case you need something in your stomach."

Suzanne's greeting burbled out in a rush and in the southern accent that was familiar to Sarah's ear, but with each word more drawn out and sweeter than the speech of her neighbors.

"Oh, it is so good to be here and finally set my eyes upon you! And you must be Mr. Swain?"

She turned to Benjamin, who appeared to be frail but kindly, and he replied, touching the brim of his hat, "Benjamin Swain, ma'am, it is a fine pleasure to make your acquaintance after all these years. Please call me Ben. And my Suzanne, you know her by letters of course, has tole me all about you and read me your letters. You are most welcome here, Miss Sarah. We are so glad you have come."

She looked into Suzanne's brown eyes, still bright and lively despite her age. Sarah could not explain it just then—but a feeling of being home overcame her. *I know this is not my home, I just left it hours ago. I am fully at home with Bethanne and Samuel and Lucia and the people close to me in Tennessee. This is something very different.*

The week they spent together was magical. First was meeting, then learning, the names and connections of all of Suzanne and Ben's children and grandchildren. When everyone was gathered together, the house was stretched to its limits. And just as for Sarah's family, the extended Swains lived close enough to visit easily.

Each morning after a light breakfast at the guest house, Sarah walked the short distance to Suzanne's where she was always greeted with, "Oh, you're here, Sarah, I thought you'd never come! We've been up with the chickens, waiting for you!" That made them all laugh because the Swains kept chickens no longer, the last one having been served up for Sunday dinner several years ago.

Their conversations covered the widest range of topics, and Sarah was relieved to discover they always found something to tickle both their interests. They walked together through the little town, stopping to admire the new house being built. It was so big and grand. They talked of the news, they talked about Suzanne's life as a teacher and the students she regarded as her children. They told stories of great successes and equally tragic outcomes, neither one predictable, as fate would have its own way. Sarah told Suzanne about her time aboard the *Red Rover*, and of Jane, her work in New York and Philadelphia and all she had learned and witnessed.

Both women were sad when their last day came.

They sat on the little porch, enjoying a late afternoon cup of tea and watching a well-fed squirrel scamper up and down the nearest tree chasing what they guessed was a litter mate. Ben opened the screen door and said, "Miss Sarah, our daughter Lily brought over her famous raisin cookies last evening. I know you have a big hankering to try one or two, I just know it."

"You are certainly correct, Ben, I couldn't let this opportunity pass me by. Thank you," she replied, as she took the plate from his hand.

"And if you really like 'em, Miss Sarah, we'll pack you some up to take home to your family tomorra."

"That would be lovely, so kind of you." She gave him a big smile, noting his golden eyes, not for the first time, and Ben left them alone on the porch.

Suzanne began. "You know, Sarah, every day during this visit of yours we have talked the whole day through, but one thing that we haven't covered is this. I would really like to know about Thomas, what you remember about him, how he was, what his last hour was like. Do you even remember? I truly love Ben, and we have made a wonderful life together, but your being here reminds me of Thomas as my first love, and I may never have the chance to hear you speak like this again. We are no spring chickens, you know." With that, her cheeks crinkled up at their unspoken joke.

"Thomas made a very deep impression on me, Suzanne, and being with him changed my life. It was such a short time, and a very long time ago for it to have had such a lasting effect on me." Her hand, without her even being aware of it, reached to absentmindedly touch the pendant's chain. "Thomas was the first person I ever sat with while he died, and I discovered that while I was so afraid of death and what that experience would be like … could I make myself stay and help? Would I witness awful things? Would my presence be a comfort? How would I feel if I could do nothing to help? All those questions were scrambling around helter-skelter in my mind as his life was ebbing away.

"I remember his eyes, those golden eyes, just like Ben's. Thomas had a slow and gentle smile that took over his face, and kindness. Oh, my, he was so grateful to me for any little thing I could do for him. What remains in my mind to this day is the way he told me what to write in his final letter to his family. Thinking more about you all than himself and staying so positive until the end, practically."

Sarah paused, remembering back all those years before going on.

"I remember being sad that he did not have the energy to dictate a second letter just to you, Suzanne. He spoke so warmly about you, and your gift of knowledge, and all the things he would learn and share with you once the war was over and you were married. It was clear to me that he loved you deeply, even for a nineteen-year-old boy. He thought you were beautiful, but he was in love with your spirit and your being, not simply because you were pretty. What an intelligent young man he was."

Sarah was lost in her recall of that battlefield tent, and the image of Thomas dying on his cot, she by his side. She looked over and was surprised to see tears on Suzanne's face as she looked up from the hands folded in her lap. "Those are wonderful words, Sarah, I thank you, but now tell me the truth, how did he die?" Her words asked for the facts of his passing, but her tears belied her need of the truth. She needed to know that Thomas suffered little at the end, and Sarah was grateful that she was able to honestly give that to her.

"He died from the infection, Suzanne, and he became unconscious for nearly half a day. I kept cool cloths on his forehead as much as I could and water on his lips to keep him comfortable. He did not move, or thrash around, or groan. He died quietly, with one long inhalation and a slow release of air. He did not breathe again."

The two women sat in silence for another long minute.

Then Sarah reached up to undo the clasp of the pendant and took it from her neck. "This pendant was made for me by my husband, Evan, as a present for my twenty-seventh birthday. The button it holds belonged to Thomas. I picked it up from under his cot after he died. Something told me that I should keep it to pass on, and through all my years it has served to remind me of the young man who pointed me to the calling of my life. I found what I was looking for because of him. I have no need of it anymore. It is time for it to be with his family."

Tears were in the eyes of both women. Holding the pendant tight in her hand one last time, she gave it a hard squeeze, then held it out it to Suzanne. "Please, give it a new home."

Part Two: Charlotte

Charlotte

August 30, 1875
Indianapolis, Indiana

"My goodliness, you're a tiny thing, aren't you, sweetie?" she marveled, nuzzling her infant niece for the first time. Katy studied the sleeping baby carefully. As she had no children of her own, she was curious about newborns. The baby's fingers were long and delicate with shell-pink nails. Unusually straight eyebrows dominated her face. But her head was misshapen, the result of a long birthing process.

Jacob, her brother-in-law, confided, "The midwife says the dent will fill out in time, and we can help it along by massaging her head with oil after she is two weeks old. I will leave that to Lorena, as my touch is too rough for that kind of work."

Still cradling the infant, Katy sat down next to her sister's bed and watched as mother and child both fell asleep. Not being used to holding such a tender bundle for long, she soon felt her left arm start to quiver. She did not want to move. What if she jostled baby Charlotte awake? For the moment it was enough to stare down at her newest relative. *Such a nice sweet mouth,* she thought. *Will your eyes be green like Lorena's?*

June 20, 1885
Louisville, Kentucky

Katy and Edgar Lane became parents overnight when Lorena finally succumbed to the consumption that had weakened, then destroyed, her body. No effective treatment was known in 1880s Indiana. Jacob Kolb had been killed in a railroad yard accident five years ago.

Ten years after their first meeting, Katy thought, *She's still a tiny thing ... a little breeze could blow her away. But they say her personality and mannerisms are as strong as any ox, except she is so terribly shy. She hardly speaks above a whisper, but when she speaks, she is solidly determined. What a deceivement she is.* Katy always had a ready supply of concocted words.

"Come, Charlotte, this is your room. Uncle Edgar and I hope it will suit you, that you will like it." She gestured to the small room across the hall from theirs. A faded rosebud quilt covered the single bed beneath the window. Daisies stood with some greenery in a simple white vase. Lace curtains draped the open window, and the same lace fabric overlaid a pink gingham skirt around the wash basin. Katy had spent the week working hard to create a space that would make a nine-year-old girl feel special, particularly a girl who'd just lost her mother.

Charlotte stared. *This is so different,* she thought. *I wish Mama could see it. We never had any flowers in the house.* "Thank you, Aunt Katy," she breathed, "it is … nice."

"It was a long trip from Indianapolis, my dear, I know. We'll leave you to yourself for a while. Maybe you'll want to rest? Or get settled? You can put your things away in the chest there. I'll let you know when it's time for supper." Katy wanted to say more, but she didn't know what. Charlotte appeared unreachable.

After the meal, which they had eaten in uncomfortable silence, Katy said, "No need for much of a schedule tomorrow, just get up when you feel like it. But we hope you'll join us early for breakfast." Katy half-winked at her. "You will know when that is. Edgar is a wonderful cook." She leaned over to grab her niece's hands. "We will have lots of time to get to know one another." She tried not to notice as Charlotte pulled back a little from her grasp. "We are heartbroken about the circumstances that brought you here to us, Charlotte. But we wouldn't have it any other way. You're our family, you belong. You will always be welcome."

Charlotte looked at her feet and said nothing.

"Well, then, dear, it's probably time to head on up to bed. Good night, Charlotte. Sleep well."

"G'night, Aunt Katy, Uncle Edgar."

Wonderful odors teased Charlotte awake the next morning—bacon, sausage and scrambled eggs, impossible to resist and so unfamiliar. Before, she was the one who usually prepared breakfast, most often oatmeal and toast. But she remembered the happy sounds of bacon popping and smells of savory sausage, drawing her out of bed and onto her feet when her father was alive. Now her parents were gone, and someone else was cooking.

Charlotte surprised Katy and Edgar. In the month since her arrival, she adapted quickly and made herself useful. She took on garden tasks, and was always moving about, looking at things or trying to tidy up. But she did not initiate conversation with her aunt or her uncle, and she only responded with short replies.

One afternoon as the air signaled rain, changing suddenly from hot and stifling to blustery and cooler, Katy found her standing at the front porch railing, head back, looking up. Thinking that this was a moment for Charlotte to be alone, Katy simply watched. *Is she looking at the clouds and the way the weather is changing? Maybe she is happy with the sudden coolness? Or thinking of Lorena and missing her?*

Katy was startled when Charlotte turned to face her. "Why have you been watching me, Aunt Katy? I am all right, and I do not need you to hover over me like some baby. I can take care of myself. I know how to do things. Goodness knows, I took care of Mama, and everyone says it was better than any doctor or nurse could have done."

A proper response failed Katy. *The girl has not uttered this many words in the time she's been here.* "Well, Charlotte," she said, searching for the right tone, "I was thinking about what it must be like to be almost ten years old with no parents, and a mother gone less than a few weeks. I have no idea what you are thinking, but I suppose that everything must seem a little strange, and sad and hard to believe."

"You are partly right." She looked away but not before Katy thought she saw tears in her big green eyes, *Lorena's eyes.*

"Oh, my dear, you must miss her fiercely, and though I cannot pretend to replace my sister, I want you to come to me anytime you feel the need to talk about her. You know, Charlotte," she said putting hands on her shoulders, "I miss her, too, and I need to talk about her with someone who knew her, like you. Edgar didn't know her much at all."

Charlotte simply nodded, then walked back into the house as raindrops started to spatter.

Katy sighed. *Oh dear, I should have acknowledged the care she took of her mother ....*

Marguerite Parsons was a tall, thin, middle-aged spinster with brown eyes that crossed despite the thick spectacles that only drew attention to her visual problem. Katy was secretly glad she had decided to meet alone with Miss Parsons, who would be Charlotte's teacher next session. She wondered if Charlotte would need some preparation for meeting her and was curious whether students reacted to her appearance. Children, she learned, could be cruel creatures.

"Miss Parsons, I'd like to know what I need to do to enroll my niece in school for the next term. Mr. Lane and I are her guardians now, and I want to make sure that she has no gap in her learning. She has had a most difficult two years helping to care for her mother, who died in June from the consumption."

"And her father, where is he? Could he not be of help?" Miss Parsons asked, her brow wrinkling.

Katy frowned. "Charlotte's father died in a railroad accident when she was barely five, and she had only her mother since then." Katy wondered why she had not just said Charlotte was an orphan, but when she thought of that word, her stomach turned at the coldness of it all. In spite of the love and care that she and Edgar planned to give, Charlotte was still … an orphan.

Surprising Katy at first, Charlotte got along very well with Miss Parsons, and though she made few friends, she was liked well enough. Just as in Indiana, she excelled in her schoolwork. Charlotte enjoyed learning.

Norton Infirmary

August 27, 1892
Louisville, Kentucky

"So, dear birthday girl, now that you are seventeen, what do you see for your future?" Edgar asked, after swallowing the first bite of Katy's perfect sponge cake. Charlotte was not the kind of girl who was interested in getting married or mothering babies, unlike her friend Miriam. She was a delight to be around, and Katy and he would be happy if she lived with them into their old age. But he knew that spinsterhood and caring for elderly family members was not a particularly rewarding life. He had watched his youngest sister, Madeline, care for their parents. She'd turned bitter, a quality sure to drive men away. Charlotte was so quiet, he feared for her future.

Charlotte had plans but had not been ready to share them with her aunt and uncle—until now, until she was asked. She needed advice, but she was afraid to utter the word "nurse" because she had seen Edgar's reaction when nurses were discussed with friends or written about in the newspaper.

Charlotte took a breath, then another, steeling herself for his response. *I am just going to say it without any flowery words.* "Uncle Edgar, I most certainly don't want to be a burden to you and Aunt Katy, so I have decided to become a nurse."

"A burden, Charlotte? You are not a burden to us at all. You could never be! And even if you were such an albatross, that problem can be solved in many ways. But becoming a nurse, good lord, Charlotte, that would be at the very bottom of the list. It's not for you."

Charlotte's face flushed, and her green eyes narrowed as she stared at him, disappointed, verging on angry.

"You could be a teacher if you like. And teachers have an easier life, I am told." Privately, Edgar had also told Katy he was worried that nursing was considered disreputable. "Would it not be simpler for you to become a teacher than a nurse?"

"Perhaps, Uncle, but simpler is not the issue for me. Ever since Mother died, I know more could be done for consumptives, and I intend to be one of those people that could help cure them. Miss Parsons says Louisville has a nurses training school at the Norton Infirmary. It opened just after I moved here. I would be close to you at Third and Oak, and I wouldn't have to travel far at all." She paused to watch his reaction.

"Norton doesn't charge students a fee to attend," she pressed on, "and I would live in the residence during my training. Miss Parsons says I have the mind for it. And I am sure I have the temperament. I saw a lot of the sickness back home, and I was not afraid of it. I was afraid for my mother, but I was not afraid of what I saw. And, I will be able to support myself after a few years, and no longer be a burden to you or Aunt Katy."

Just then, Katy came back into the dining room with their present for Charlotte. "Burden, Edgar, what is she talking about? Charlotte, you would never be a burden to us, nor have you been. You are a blessing, you fill the place of children we never had."

Charlotte nodded, acknowledging her aunt's words, but still determined.

Over the next year, that determination led to her training school application, and, as with almost everything Charlotte put her mind to, she was successful. Charlotte and Katy wore down Edgar's resistance with positive articles, two visits to Norton, and regular conversations about nursing's ability to change its image.

The night before she was to move to Norton, Charlotte sat alone at the dining table, paper before her.

Dear Aunt Katy and Uncle Edgar,

How do I give you my deepest thanks for everything you have done and been for me these past eight years? Mother, father, aunt, uncle, friend, confidante, encourager, challenger ... every role that an orphan girl needed to help her grow into a woman who is not afraid of the world and of being on her own.

I know these things—I know you worried because I'm often shy, and you wondered if I would find a husband or be a spinster the rest of my life. I know you are still not sure that nursing is a good pursuit for a girl like me. But I also know, unmistakably, deep in my being, that I have a natural inclination for healing, and nothing will stand between me and my dream of becoming a trained nurse.

I hope to make you both proud of me and that you will eventually be happy with my choice.

Your loving Niece,

Charlotte

The Norton Memorial Infirmary and Training School for Nursing had operated nearly ten years when Charlotte stood on its doorstep, suitcase in hand, awash in both excitement and sadness. In typical fashion, Edgar had prepared a hearty breakfast with pancakes, her favorite. And in her typical fashion, she couldn't eat when she was so excited.

When she'd arrived in Louisville eight years earlier, she had been so thin that her dresses hung on her bony shoulders. But Katy's baking and Edgar's breakfasts had added enough weight to her petite frame that now she thought irritably of herself as "plump." But she had to admit, she did love her sweets, especially at breakfast.

Charlotte was not fond of the athletics promoted for women of the day or its required restrictive clothing. She would rather read, particularly books about science and faraway lands and the natural world. She felt a deep desire to explore more of the country than central Indiana and northern Kentucky. She longed to see the West. But she knew those were desires for another day. First she would learn to be a nurse, a real nurse.

She turned at the door to face Katy and Edgar. "Maybe it will be easier for us if we all say goodbye here. When you come to visit, I will be better able to show you around once I am settled and have a command of all my surroundings."

Command of her surroundings? Katy thought, *oh yes, she is still our little Charlotte using those words and phrases.*

Charlotte continued, "I will be just fine going in on my own."

Katy held Edgar's hand in one of hers, and a fisted-up handkerchief in the other. Awkwardly she put an arm around Charlotte and said softly in her ear, "Your mother, and your father, too, God rest them, would be so proud of you, dear, I am certain of it. Maybe, at the tender age of eight or nine, you couldn't help her then, but we know you will help many, many others now." She took a step back, smiled, and said, "Let us know when we can visit."

"I will, Aunt Katy, and thank you." She had no more words—"thank you" seemed so inadequate. She hugged Uncle Edgar, then opened the door. On second thought she turned back to them with a grin. "Wish me luck!"

Walking back home Katy found herself feeling jealous of her eighteen-year-old niece.

"I wish I had had her determination when I was her age, and her passion for creating her own life. I hope they will be kind to her."

"C'mon along, Katy-Belle," Edgar drawled, "She'll do just fine. Let's get on home. Work and chores are waiting."

Charlotte woke suddenly from a deep sleep. *Where am I? What are those noises? Why is that woman shouting?* She sat up in the darkness, not wanting to move. Lorena had been talking when the loud sounds stopped her. *Oh, I was so close to having a connection, a real connection again!* Rarely had her mother appeared to Charlotte in the years since she had died.

Sad and frustrated, she tried to will her mother back. She sat a while longer, then lay back down. It was still dark, and she doubted she could fall asleep again. She tried hard to remember exactly what her mother had said. Charlotte was surprised to see her looking so healthy. In her last two years of life Lorena had been painfully thin and pale, with dark circles under her eyes and dull, brittle hair. She almost always carried a pinched frown as if she had pain, somewhere, constantly. Charlotte could never recall her mother having a relaxed and pleasant expression. Maybe in her younger years before a stillborn baby and Jacob's death? Maybe then, Charlotte hoped, her mother's life had been easier. She was too young to remember.

Was her mother telling her how proud she was? Or how much she loved her? *That would be a surprise,* Charlotte thought wryly, *she certainly didn't say those things to me when she was alive.* Deep inside, Charlotte knew she was loved, and her mother had been proud of what a good student she was. But she could not recall hearing praise, or feeling her mother's warmth in an emotional embrace. Never did an arm drape companionably across her shoulders, like Aunt Katy's, or a hand reach out to hold Charlotte's.

She lay back and drifted off to sleep for the briefest of moments before she was awakened again.

"Get up, Ladies," the night nurse hissed at half-past-four. "Your first day as Norton nurses has begun!" The students were housed in two rooms in the infirmary itself. The furnishings were sparse but adequate—a small bed, a nightstand, and a little chest for their limited belongings.

In the dining room Charlotte swallowed the last of her tea, leaving most of her breakfast untouched. She was anxious, and her stomach was uncooperative. She knew she should eat more, something, anything. But she just couldn't.

Mrs. Broome, the matron of the school, abruptly appeared at the head of the table as if conjured by magic. The students were instantly silent. She stood ramrod straight, staring at each one up and down, her sharp eyes looking for all the world like a little rat terrier's.

She pulled a tiny black notebook from the pocket of her crisp white apron, thumbing a few pages. "Roll call, Ladies. I know you may need to return to your rooms for a few minutes after breakfast—you weren't prepared for the schedule details today, I realize. But you are now," she said, emphasizing the last word. "Tomorrow and each day after, at ten minutes to seven, you will present yourselves ready to work on the women's ward. By then you will have eaten breakfast, straightened your rooms, attended to any personal needs, and be wearing a spotless uniform. Is that understood?" Nods and mumblings of assent answered her question.

"Four expectations—breakfast, rooms, personal hygiene, uniforms. When it comes to your being students, timeliness is obviously important, but nothing is as important as your attitude. Studious, attentive, pleasant, ready to do whatever is asked of you without question. You are here to learn and to serve. Period." She continued. "And if you ever have a choice between learning or serving, you are here to serve, first and foremost."

She looked at the wide-eyed students staring back at her. "I am seeing just seven of you. Miss Stardle changed her mind at the last minute. That is unfortunate, because she prevented another eager woman from joining this group. However, I am confident we shall fill her place in no time. When your class is full, the eight of you will be housed in the last two rooms on the second floor of the Infirmary. When Miss Stardle's replacement arrives, she will join the three of you in Room Two. Miss Glenn, Miss Kolb, and Miss Simpson. The other four found your way last night to Room One, I trust?"

Again she looked at each one intently, then continued. "Miss Blue?" A pretty young woman, a little older than Charlotte, nodded at Mrs. Broome. "Miss Blue, and the rest of you, when I or any of the staff or physicians address you, no matter what you're doing except saving a life, you are to stand and reply, 'Yes, ma'am' or 'Yes, sir.' Is that understood?"

They all stood and replied, "Yes, ma'am" in unison.

"Very well, you may sit again." Then one by one, each student stood and responded to her first roll call at Norton.

Sarah Blue, Mariah Crosby, Sophie Glenn, Maybelle Linn, Polly Richter, Eleanore Simpson … Charlotte's cohort and confidantes for the next two years. Charlotte hoped they would all get along. *Some of these women must be fifteen years older than me, but even more, they will have more life experience. What do I know?*

Infatuation

December 16, 1895
Louisville, Kentucky

Charlotte had turned her head just as Dr. Fields entered the ward, which was why she didn't see the heavy china bowl flying at her with surprising force. It caught her full on the right cheekbone, and blood poured instantly from the gash. Her hand moved reflexively to the injury.

She had been patiently trying to feed young Mr. Silas, and for several attempts he kept his mouth shut tight. But as the first real taste of the sweet mixture registered, he opened his mouth like a little bird's, urging Charlotte for more and more. *You like it,* she thought, *good for you. Good for me, too, I was at my wit's end trying to find something you would eat. Maybe there's more in the—.*

Abraham Silas, admitted to Norton a week ago for inflammation of the brain, was improving slowly with fits and starts. Charlotte had spent longer than she liked in the tiny ward kitchen preparing a thickened custard, and she was anxious to see if he would take it. "Horse box nuts," he shouted, "white, white, white!" He pointed at the floor where the pudding lay in a puddle. When he saw blood running through her fingers and down her arm, he began laughing hysterically.

Dr. Fields stopped short at the doorway, then stepped in quickly. "Stop it at once! Stop it, I say!" he shouted, then grabbed a napkin from the tray and pressed it to Charlotte's face to stop the bleeding. With both hands on the sides of her face, he said, "Miss Kolb, look at me, can you move your jaw?"

Her face hurt and she was stunned; her ear was ringing. She stared at her hand. *Is all this blood coming from me?*

"Move it side to side if you can, slowly … slowly. Oh, good. Now open your mouth a little. Good. I'm guessing that all you have is a flesh wound, and we need to see to that first. There'll probably be some temporary bruising to this pretty face of yours."

Pretty? Me? He really said I'm pretty? He must be saying that to soothe me. Hearing the ruckus, Mrs. Broome rushed in. "Go get your injury attended to," she directed Charlotte. Then studying Dr. Fields as he took her elbow and steered her to the door, she finished, "I will make sure the rest of your shift is covered."

Charlotte nodded slowly and accompanied the doctor to the treatment room.

She had helped Dr. Fields, a surgeon, a few times on the ward when she was taking care of his patients. He had also taught two of her evening classes on gastrointestinal surgery and wound healing. He was younger than most of the doctors at Norton, and spoke softly, unlike the typical speech of a physician in command. She noticed at once that he had red hair, like hers, as well as green eyes. *A fellow redhead,* she had mused. *I wonder if he has hated his hair all his life, too, though men rarely think about that.* His manner seemed gentle in tending her wound.

Suturing Charlotte's gash was painful, even though he injected a cocaine anesthetic to numb her jaw and cheek. She noticed that he washed his hands for a longer time than other doctors she had helped. In her classes she had learned that scientists of the day were beginning to understand that antisepsis was absolutely necessary for good wound healing. Once the cocaine had taken effect, he began slowly and carefully, delicately even, to put fourteen stitches along her upper jaw, near the ear. When he finished, he helped her sit up.

"You are quite fortunate, Miss Kolb, that the gash was not at your lower jaw. The scar can easily be hidden by your hair. Normal movement would put undue stress on the sutures if it was lower. Where it is, the wound is not affected much by eating and talking." He smiled at her, and she nodded, carefully.

"You should limit your talking for at least two days to allow for some initial good healing. Liquids and soft food only; two days should be adequate for the food restrictions. I will ask Mrs. Broome to find something else for you to do rather than care for patients."

Charlotte nodded again. Her face wasn't too painful yet, but she dreaded the wearing off of the anesthetic.

"I am so sorry this happened to you," he continued. He looked into her eyes and nodded thoughtfully. "The public has little idea of the personal risk that nurses can face in their work. You are called to be kind and understanding, but not much thought is given to possible danger. I know about this, Miss Kolb. My older sister was a nurse, and she died from cholera, contracted when she cared for patients in the poor Irish section of New York."

Charlotte thought she saw his eyes grow moist as he spoke. "Her name was Jeanne, and she had red hair, too, like us."

He stared off, over her shoulder. Charlotte felt uncomfortable, never having heard such personal details from a physician. Normally she would converse along with him, but since he had just warned her against talking, she moved to get off the table. "Here, let me help you," he said, ignoring the step stool, and putting both hands at her waist, he gently eased her to the floor beside him. Charlotte's face flushed, and she forgot her injured jaw.

"I will want to take a look at my handiwork tomorrow. You can find me here around one in the afternoon. Rest the remainder of today. Ice over the bandaging will help keep the swelling and pain down. I'll see you tomorrow, Miss Kolb." She nodded, avoiding his eyes.

On the way back to her room she stopped to give her blood-soaked apron to the laundress, who gasped when she saw Charlotte's bandaged face and the gauze strips wound around chin to head, immobilizing her jaw. "My goodness, Miss, what a terrible mess! Hope we can get all this blood out for you ...."

Charlotte would graduate in almost a week, and the realization of her appearance caught her off guard. What would Aunt Katy and Uncle Edgar think of her bruised face? Would she still need all these bandages? They were looking forward to this day as much as Charlotte, and she didn't want anything to mar the impression that she was launched onto a wonderful path. Now she had no way to hide the confirmation that bad things could happen to her in the course of her work.

But she could minimize it. She decided to send a note by messenger telling of her excitement about graduation, and of course, seeing them. She added a postscript: *You will see that I am well and healthy except for the bandage on the right side of my face. I sustained a slight injury when a confused patient threw a bowl in my direction, and I needed to have the cut edges sutured together. It looks much worse than it is, so do not be surprised when you see me. I am fine.*

Sunday dawned cold and clear, promising to be bright. Charlotte had packed her things and was ready to leave her home of almost two years. After the ceremony she would move back to Katy and Edgar's. *What will I miss most about Norton? Friendships? Priscilla and Polly first of all.* As Mrs. Broome had predicted on their first day, an eighth student, Priscilla Weaver, quickly joined them. She was young, like Charlotte, and a bit lost at first. Charlotte remembered being alone and unsure. It was the easiest thing in the world to reach out in kindness.

She had been surprised to discover another friend in Polly Richter. Tall and solidly built with unruly black hair streaked with silvery strands, thirty-eight-year-old Polly, a briefly-married widow, spoke her mind without hesitation. Charlotte was always careful with her words, fearful that they could harm as well as help. Where Charlotte was shy and quiet, Polly was quick to laugh and seek out humor. People were drawn to her whether or not they agreed with what she was saying.

I wish I could be more like Polly. It is hard being so guarded and careful all the time.

Priscilla interrupted her thoughts, coming back into their small room, so crowded now with the possessions of four women strewn about in the happy task of preparing for their new lives. "Let me help you finish your hair, Charlotte. If you pull the sides a little forward and add some pomade to make them stay, you can almost fully hide your dressing. And some powder will help with the bruises under your eye. It's good they are not so noticeable; the big bruising has moved down your neck where your collar covers it more. And for our photograph, you can be on the end with everyone else to your right. Shouldn't be noticeable at all," she finished authoritatively.

Charlotte hadn't worried much about the photograph—she was thinking more about Dr. Fields. He had seen her on Thursday and Friday to check the sutures, and when he finished, his final words warmed her. "I will see you on Sunday, Miss Kolb, at your graduation. Mrs. Broome has asked me, Dr. Anthony, too, to address the graduates at the ceremony. I am honored to speak, but I must admit it is with some sadness as well, for I will miss your group of students—well, not students really, now you are nurses. I will miss you *nurses*," he corrected, and after a pause, he continued, "I will miss *you*."

Charlotte treasured those four words. She turned the scene over and over in her head, wondering just what she should take from them. Was he telling her something beyond a physician-nurse friendship? They hadn't really been friends since all their discussions had focused on his patients, but his manner was very kind. *He is kind to everyone, all the students like that about him. It is clear that he appreciates nurses and their work for his patients, but now, he appreciates* me?

Before her injury, she had imagined her new life as a nurse with the registry, taking care of patients in their homes, happy to be away from the hospital and its demanding hours and routines. But now she wondered how she could continue to see him if they were not both in the same environment most days. Before, she was uninterested in women's chatter about men and marriage and romance. *Is that all they can talk about?* Now she found herself thinking, *I wonder what he thinks of me. Although he said he will miss me, what is the distance between missing and affection? What is it that I am feeling? I am so new to this!*

She dared not share her thoughts with anyone. They were her secret, her sweet secret.

Charlotte stared through the mug of tea in her hands, lost in its familiar warmth and the sudden foreign feel of home. Graduation over, she replayed the afternoon and the scenes with Dr. Fields. Aunt Katy and Uncle Edgar had been swept up in the happy occasion and made no comment on her injury. Family and friends and well-wishers of the new nurses filled the reception area, bunching about the tables of tea and punch, and the delicate little cookies and finger sandwiches she loved. Charlotte wished she could stuff her pockets full for later.

But that afternoon she could not eat a single tiny cookie. He had caught her eye, and her heart thudded as she realized he was making his way through the crowd to her. She felt her skin turn hot all over. "Miss Kolb," Dr. Fields smiled, "congratulations. I am very happy for you and your accomplishments. You must be thrilled to have reached this milestone in your life." Charlotte could feel Aunt Katy stir at her side, moving in closer.

"Dr. Fields, thank you, you are so kind. Please allow me to introduce my aunt and uncle, Mr. and Mrs. Lane, of Louisville. They have taken on the role of parents since I was almost ten. Without a moment's hesitation they welcomed me as if I were their own cherished daughter. They have supported my dream of becoming a nurse, this new life. Every break they insisted I tell them all about what I was learning. It was as if they were students, too." She smiled at them.

Katy was surprised at her niece's little speech, and could not miss the blush that flooded her face. Turning to Katy and Edgar, Charlotte continued, "Dr. Fields, whom you heard speak at the ceremony, has been a lecturer at the school, and I have taken care of some of his patients."

"Mrs. Lane," he said, shaking Katy's hand, "your niece has been an inspiration to her fellow students, and I am honored to meet her family. What a lovely young woman you have raised. Mr. Lane," he finished, shaking Edgar's hand as well. Turning back to Charlotte, Dr. Fields pulled a small envelope from his pocket. "Here is an invitation for you and your aunt and uncle. I hope you can come. And congratulations again, Miss Kolb."

Then he disappeared. She felt the cool absence of his presence immediately, but the envelope still held the warmth of his hand.

She left it unopened until that evening when Katy and Edgar said goodnight. She held it a while longer, wondering what they were invited to. Inside she found a folded ivory card with the initials SJF in raised black letters.

Miss Kolb,

My sister, Marissa Fields, and I request the pleasure of your company at an open house, from eight o'clock until eleven o'clock p.m. next Saturday, the twenty-eighth of December. Please know that this invitation includes your family and relatives who may be visiting during the holidays. The address is 2514 North Columbus Street. We hope that you will be able to attend, and I look forward to your presence.

Stephen

Oh, a chance to see him again, she grinned. *Stephen. His sister, I wonder what that means?* She had distanced herself from the usual gossip of nursing students, moving away whenever they clumped together like hens cackling about men. But when she heard others mention Dr. Fields,

Stephen, she thought as her pulse quickened, there was only an aura of respect and kindness. Just a week ago she did not have any special interest in him. *What a short blossoming! Is that how romance and attraction works?*

Lights glowed from the house as the party colors of women's dresses inside moved past the windows. Charlotte and Edgar stood at the entry, admiring the brick facade of the impressive home, holiday wreaths adorning the outside. The afternoon's snow left a light dusting that refreshed the entire scene. "I'm so sorry that Katy is missing this," said Edgar, "I will try to remember every detail for her—you know how she is. She will want to know everything that I have noticed, or not, everything. You'll help me with that?"

"Mmm," Charlotte nodded as Edgar raised the door knocker. "At least she is feeling much better, and her cough is improving. Rest is best for her now, and she—"

She stopped mid-sentence as a tall woman opened the door with two small children behind her skirts. "Oh, do come in, welcome. You must be some of Stephen's friends I haven't met yet. I am Marissa Fields, so happy to welcome you to our home. Come in!"

She closed the door behind them as Edgar made introductions. Charlotte half-listened, taking in every detail that might reveal more about Stephen. "... And here are Esther and Lucas. They are on their way to bed, aren't you, children?" she asked.

"We are twins," said Lucas, and Esther nodded. "We are going to be four in January, and I'm the oldest."

"I was almost first," Esther added. "But I'm the tallest."

"Our mother died," Lucas finished.

"These are Stephen's children, and their father promised they could stay up until the guests started arriving, so it's off to bed with you now. Here's Miss Melanie. Go on with her, children. Good night, dears."

"Good night, Auntie."

Charlotte smiled at them. *So precocious,* she thought. *Stephen was married. Stephen is a widower. Stephen has two children. Are there more? Who is Melanie?*

The entryway opened into a large parlor that flowed into an even larger dining room. Furniture had been moved to allow more space in front of the fireplace, burning brightly and smelling of pine. The large table held fruitcake, candied nuts, little ham rolls, and Charlotte's favorite impossible-to-resist sweet, chocolate. Beverages were arranged at one end; hot mulled cider, hot chocolate, tea, coffee, bourbon, whiskey, rum, and a special wintertime wine.

Stephen appeared as a servant was taking their wraps. "Oh, Miss Kolb, Mr. Lane, I am so glad you could come. I don't see Mrs. Lane, is she not able to join us?"

Edgar shook his head, "No, Dr. Fields, she is improving at home after a rather severe cold this week, and thought it best to stay away and rest. She is most sorry to miss a party, I can assure you."

"Please, please, both of you call me Stephen, 'Doctor' is for another time and place, and we are past that formality. I am so sorry about your aunt," he replied, looking at Charlotte. "Please let her know we missed her. Before you leave, I'll ask the kitchen to send some food home with you. Then she won't have to miss everything."

Piano music drifted from another room, and Edward cocked his head to decide what was being played. "Ah, Chopin, my favorite composer," he declared. "Whoever is playing, is playing the piece very well."

"Let me introduce you to our friend, Mrs. Marshall, who is at the bench," Stephen said to Edgar, leading them to the piano room. "Do you play?" he asked.

"A little," Edgar demurred, "I am very fond of all music, piano in particular. We used to have a piano, and I played for a time, Katy, too. As it began to need more work, we donated it to a program that teaches piano repair."

"I play a little myself, but I don't have much time for it really. Having a piano in the house offers me an excuse to clear my mind, and playing relaxes me. And if one is going to have a piano, it should be played, no?"

Stephen kept glancing in Charlotte's direction even as he was talking with Edgar. They listened to Mrs. Marshall finish the piece, and then he excused himself to attend to some other guests. "Please fill your plates, and enjoy the food and drink," he said, and then, touching Charlotte's elbow lightly, he said softly, "I will find you later. Please don't leave until we speak."

Edgar moved to join others around the piano, who, quietly at first, then with more confidence, sang carols of the season with no regard for loudness or pitch. The mulled wine helped increase the joviality in the room. They had both sampled the food at the buffet table, and Charlotte loved the bite-size pecan and mince pies gracefully displayed on an old silver platter. Edgar was fond of the tiny beef sandwiches with horseradish and cranberry jelly. She tried to keep her focus on the conversation or the people in front of her, but her flushed face and pounding heart made it difficult. Part of her was always on alert for Stephen's nearness.

Charlotte and Edgar met several of Stephen and Marissa's friends, and Charlotte blushed when Marissa introduced her to Mr. and Mrs. Broome. She had wondered if there would be any other guests from Norton but had not recognized anyone until the Broomes. *Why does this make me anxious? I am not a student anymore, and it is perfectly fine for Stephen to befriend me.*

Augusta Broome offered Charlotte a tight smile and a perfunctory "How nice to see you again, Miss Kolb. This is my husband, Mr. Hawthorne Broome. How are you this evening?" She could not tell what Mrs. Broome was thinking, but that was nothing new. None of the Norton students could ever decipher what was behind Mrs. Broome's impassive mask unless it was obvious displeasure.

"I am well, thank you, Mrs. Broome, and," shifting her gaze, "it is very nice to make your acquaintance, Mr. Broome." Where Mrs. Broome was tall and severe-looking with a sharp nose and spectacles over tiny eyes, her husband was short and round-bellied. She stood a full head taller than he. When he smiled, which was often and with a nervous kind of tic, his big brownish teeth were his most remarkable feature. *Large, like horse teeth,* Charlotte thought, and *perfectly straight.* Oh, what a description she would have for Priscilla and Polly when she saw them next. The students had often conjectured about Mr. Broome. Was there a Mr. Broome? Did he command attention and respect like his wife? Did she demur to him? What did he look like? And most important, how did they seem as a couple?

"Miss Kolb, Mrs. Broome, may I interrupt a moment?" Turning away from the Broomes, Charlotte found Stephen at her side.

"Certainly, Dr. Fields," said Mrs. Broome. "I see another couple I would like to introduce to my husband. We will find you later." Then, with a final glance at Charlotte, she steered Mr. Broome toward the buffet table.

"Will you come with me to the kitchen? We won't be interrupted there." Charlotte followed him into a spacious kitchen full of wonderful smells and half-full pots, tended by a cook and serving girl.

Stephen smiled at the women and said, "Thank you for your hard work tonight, ladies. My guests are delighted with the food. I'm very pleased. If you don't mind, I'd like a moment with Miss Kolb. We won't be long." The two women nodded and moved to leave Charlotte and Stephen alone.

He turned to face her, and took both her hands in his. They were large and warm, firm and confident. "Charlotte, you must know that I would like to spend more time getting to know you as a person, not just as a nurse. I am wondering if you can find time to dine with me in the next two weeks. You know my schedule is often hectic and unpredictable, but with enough notice, I should be able to arrange for coverage at Norton. I was able to do that for tonight. Is there a time I might take you to dinner?"

"Dr. Fields, um, Stephen, I would like that, too. Monday my training as a registry nurse begins, and for three days I will have a normal schedule, light actually, as I will not be caring for patients. Perhaps I can avoid taking on a case through the weekend. I am afraid it will have to be sometime in this coming week, as after that my new work schedule is uncertain."

He smiled at her, and squeezing her hands, replied, "Good. I will see what I can arrange. And by the way, I should remove your stitches soon. Perhaps you would like to have Sunday evening supper here with me and my family tomorrow? We can take care of the stitches before." Her heart leapt. *Another time with Stephen! So soon!*

But part of her wondered about the speed of her feelings. And his.

First Home Case

January 6, 1896
Louisville, Kentucky

Charlotte hurried to the registry office faster than usual as a bitter wind whipped around her. Thoughts of Stephen warmed her, though, during the short walk. She was surprised at her quick arrival, disappointed that she needed to shift her attention to the present.

Nancy Trefry, middle-aged, slight, and pale, had a large distracting gap between her two front teeth. But after a few minutes in her presence, one stopped noticing it. She was nothing like Augusta Broome. She moved gracefully, and her manner was quiet and gentle. Mrs. Trefry was in charge of the registry nurses, and Charlotte had enjoyed her orientation sessions. The other trainees were equally taken with her direct answers to questions. She was very kind, and devoted to her work.

Six of Charlotte's fellow graduates were part of the group; the other two had returned to their home cities to take on work there. Charlotte was grateful that she could easily keep up her friendship with Priscilla and Polly.

Mrs. Trefry was at her desk when Charlotte knocked. "Come in. Oh, that's you, Miss Kolb, good, I'm expecting you. I have papers for you to sign, and two cases I want to discuss. I think either one would be good for a first assignment," she said. "Sit down here," pointing to the simple wooden chair across from her desk. On it was a small lumbar pillow, decorated with colorful crewel peacocks. "Would you like a cup of tea to warm you this morning?"

"That would be nice, Mrs. Trefry, thank you."

She poured from a large pot behind her desk and handed the tea to Charlotte. "Now, you remember, Miss Kolb, this requirement that you see me to discuss cases is just in the beginning of your arrangement with us. After I am satisfied with your performance, we can communicate more casually by messenger. But for the first few cases I will want to meet with you before and after an assignment."

Charlotte nodded, comforted by this plan. She hated the thought of floundering on her own without someone to help her evaluate what she had done. She was anxious to get started.

After Charlotte signed the agreement with her general duties and salary, Mrs. Trefry opened the worn green ledger on her desk. "Let's see. The two cases I have in mind for you are both surgical recovery situations. Mr. Johnson, sixty-eight years old, was at Norton for nearly two weeks. He had a ruptured appendix, and surgery was required. Dr. Fields performed skillful surgery, I must say, but not before his appendix burst. Mr. Johnson was very sick with infection afterwards, some days at death's door, but he pulled through."

She frowned and paged through the ledger. "He went home three days ago. One of our nurses is caring for him now, but she needs to be relieved due to her own family crisis. He is very, very weak, and still needs help with all his daily activities. The main focus is on gaining his strength back. Mr. Johnson lives alone and has no one there to help him." She paused.

"The other patient, a new amputee, is a nineteen-year-old girl. She's from a wealthy family, and they are not prepared to do any of her care themselves. Fortunately, hiring a nurse is well within their means. Miss Covington suffered a fall from a horse, with a complicated compound fracture of her ankle and foot. Healing was quite slow, and gangrene set in around the ankle, requiring removal of her leg below the knee." Charlotte grimaced, imaging the effect on a young woman. *How would I handle it myself, if I had such a drastic outcome?*

"She is stable from the surgery and will go home tomorrow. She will need competent and careful wound care, and rehabilitation so that she can get around on crutches, with an artificial leg at some future point." Mrs. Trefry looked up from the ledger. "There may be some conflicts within the family, I gather.

"Well, what do you think, Miss Kolb? Where would you like to start? You will not have the luxury of choosing most of your cases because we are quite busy, and I must get them decided based on who is available. But for a nurse's first home case, I like to allow choice where feasible."

Charlotte weighed both in her mind. *Miss Covington provides more immediate challenge, and it would be good to start with a fresh case. And a wealthy family, that could be nice. Mr. Johnson ... not so much challenge, but maybe a chance to see Stephen? Would he come to the home to check his patient?*

"What would my sleeping arrangements be?"

"All our cases are required to provide you with a place to sleep, if overnight care is necessary. In Mr. Johnson's case, the conditions are basic, and though the care could be thought of as easier, you would be expected to prepare all the meals for you and your patient. A housekeeper comes in every few days, I believe, and brings in food and other items he needs."

Charlotte scribbled quickly to keep up. Mrs. Trefry took a breath, then continued.

"The accommodations at the Covington home are more luxurious, but the challenge with a new patient and possibly tense family relationships might outweigh having to do all the cooking and very basic sleeping arrangements. Well, Miss Kolb, you decide. What is it to be?"

I cannot be sure that I would even see Stephen, that notion is silly. And with Mr. Johnson, I am a little uncomfortable with the idea of sleeping alone in his house. I am not very familiar with families in conflict, but establishing myself at the start with a new situation could be good. Every case will have its challenges, and things that could make me uncomfortable, but also, things I need to learn. That is the purpose, is it not, Miss Charlotte? she admonished herself.

"I will take Miss Covington, then."

"Very well. Here is the address and some patient and family information. You start tomorrow. She should be home after the noon meal, so I suggest you arrive around ten in the morning to acquaint yourself with their routines, her accommodations, and yours, of course. You have the list of what we suggest you bring with you on an overnight case?"

Charlotte nodded, "Yes, from orientation last week."

"Someone from the registry will visit you after two or three days to see how you are getting along." She stood to dismiss Charlotte and reached out her hand. "Good luck, Miss Kolb. I am confident you will do well."

Charlotte took a deep breath and smiled to herself. *I am on my way.* When she left the office she took out the paper to read some of the details. She was pleased to discover that Stephen was Miss Covington's surgeon. *Lucky girl,* she thought to herself.

Angelina Covington met Charlotte's gaze after two more tries. "Miss Covington, please look at me," Charlotte said. Angelina finally looked at her, a dull and vacant expression on her face. *My goodness,* Charlotte thought, *this is a surprise. I hope she won't always be this difficult to engage.* "Miss Covington, I need to ask you some questions." She turned back to Angelina's parents who were hovering behind her.

Mrs. Covington, short and round-faced, had been talking nonstop, to herself, to her husband, to the room, barely stopping for a breath since Charlotte first arrived. "Shush, Isabel, the nurse is talking," said Mr. Covington.

"Perhaps, Mr. and Mrs. Covington, it would be better if you would let me meet with Miss Covington alone for a while." The mother frowned, but Charlotte continued, "I need to make an assessment of her condition, and then when I am done, I would like to ask you both some questions as well."

"If you think that's necessary, Nurse, but I don't see why I as her mother shouldn't be in the room. I know her better than anyone." *Except herself,* thought Charlotte.

"Your views will be very helpful, Mrs. Covington, but we have a process for beginning our work, and when the patient is older than sixteen, it usually begins with him or her."

"Oh, in that case, of course," Mrs. Covington gave in. "I didn't realize you had a way of doing things." Charlotte rolled her eyes as they closed the door.

Turning back, Charlotte noted the faint smile on her patient's face as she spoke softly, for the first time, "Thank you."

"Of course, Miss Covington. First, we should decide how to address each other. What would you like me to call you? Miss Covington, Angelina, a nickname?"

"You can call me Miss Covington, I suppose."

"Very well. Then you may call me Miss Kolb, or Nurse if you prefer." Charlotte smiled and opened her notebook. "So now, how are you feeling at the moment, Miss Covington? Are you in pain?"

"Yes, I am," she nodded, her forehead wrinkling, "although they gave me medicine just before I left the hospital, so it is not too bad. The burning and tingling in my leg is the worst—it never leaves. My absent leg," she corrected.

"Mm-hmm," Charlotte responded, "and how many days is it since they removed it?"

Angelina looked away from Charlotte, her brown eyes filling with tears. "I'm not sure, ten days, I think?"

Charlotte knew that it had been exactly fifteen days and guessed her patient did, too. "And how have they been caring for your stump, Miss Covington? Have you helped them unwrap it yet?"

A look of shock flashed over the girl's face. "Oh, my goodness, no! I can't bear to look at that awful mess! They wanted me to, but I said it was going to make me sick to my stomach to even try! That's their work, anyway."

"I see. Well, everyone has a different sense of the right time. We will work together to find your right time." Angelina looked away.

Charlotte assembled the items she would need, then washed her hands. The stump was fairly dry with only a small amount of ooze. The stitches were in good order, and the surrounding tissue had minimal swelling and redness. *Stephen did a wonderful job, just as he had with my stitches.* The thought warmed her.

She blushed now, thinking of his hands at her face, her "pretty face," he had said. *Stop it!* she commanded herself. *You cannot allow yourself another moment to dwell on him—it is too distracting.* Charlotte rewrapped the stump, reminding herself to refer to it as *leg* in the future. *Stump* was so impersonal.

Angelina dozed off, and Charlotte went to look for the Covingtons. As she came down the steps, she could hear their voices suddenly lower. She stood at the parlor entrance, waiting for an invitation to enter. Red-faced, they were leaning in close to each other from their separate armchairs. Mr. Covington, suddenly aware of her presence, nodded and gestured for her to come in.

"Miss Kolb, ahem, we are so relieved that you are here to take care of our daughter. How do you evaluate her condition? How long will it take before she can walk again—or ride?" He indicated that she was to sit across from them.

Charlotte couldn't believe what she was hearing. *Why don't you worry about now, where so much needs focus right in front of us?* "It is difficult to say, Mr. Covington. I'll need to observe the healing process over time, Miss Covington's ability to get around on crutches, not just a wheelchair, and her overall motivation to do more and more for herself. A patient's mood and mental state are half the battle to a successful outcome. And, I might add, the support and involvement of her family are every bit as important."

Mrs. Covington nodded as Charlotte talked. "What in the world can we do for her, Miss Kolb? She is such a delicate girl, and I am so worried for her, especially since the gangrene. Could it happen again? She hardly talks to us. At the hospital she was as close-mouthed as you saw her just now."

"Now, Isabel," Mr. Covington interrupted, looking at his wife sternly, "She is not a delicate girl at all. She is much stronger than you imagine. If only you wouldn't pamper her so, she would gain her strength back more quickly. We must push her to do more on her own."

"Really, you are both correct," Charlotte mediated, trying to look both of them in the eye, "It is a matter of timing. Sometimes it will be time to do more for her, and sometimes less. But, as a way of starting out, I want to hear more from her about what she is thinking and feeling. I will be what I call 'planting seeds' for her own responsibility in doing more of the care herself."

They both looked at her quizzically, unsure of what Charlotte was saying in this reply. Each of them had been hoping for something more definite. To be told to wait and see was not in either of their natures.

"I'd like to know a few things about your daughter. What is her usual personality, what upsets her, what does she enjoy? And the accident itself, what happened?"

"Well," Mr. Covington began, "she was on a riding party with two young friends. It was a freak accident with our favorite horse, a retired thoroughbred, Barnacle Bill. She was riding at a nice trot through an open meadow in a wooded area, when the horse started as a deer dashed out of the trees right in front of them. She had turned her head to say something to her companions, so she missed the deer and was unprepared for the horse's reaction. He threw her, but her left foot stayed in the stirrup." Mr. Covington shook his head. "We were relieved that Bill wasn't injured." Mrs. Covington gave him a sharp look.

"It was truly awful," Mrs. Covington added, "Angelina was dragged quite a distance before one of her companions could overcome the horse and stop him. It was nothing short of a miracle that she wasn't killed. Or hurt even worse. She had scrapes and bruises, a laceration on her left arm as she was dragged on the rough ground, but the broken foot and ankle were her only serious injuries."

"How did Miss Covington feel about the horse?"

"Bill was her favorite. She loved riding him as often as she could." Mrs. Covington nodded her head. "When Angelina marries, we had planned to give him to her. Now I wonder if that will be the best thing ...."

"Is she planning to marry soon?"

"They have not set a firm date yet, but we were all discussing the spring, after the Derby, as we would have some family and friends already gathered in the area. Her fiancé, Harold Chester, is a breeder of fine horses, and his mind will naturally be more free to concentrate on Angelina after the race," Mrs. Covington added. *A new complication,* Charlotte thought.

"How has Mr. Chester been involved with your daughter since the accident?"

"He wants to be at her side every day, but she won't hear of it. She doesn't want him to see her as an invalid," said Mr. Covington.

"And that awful period when the gangrene developed, the smells were absolutely overwhelming. I couldn't stay in the room more than five minutes, even with a handkerchief at my nose, and then the window had to be opened, even though it was December. Thank goodness we urged Dr.

Mays to consult a surgeon. I think he let it go on too long ...." Her words tapered off.

"And Miss Covington's personality? And her likes and hobbies?"

Mr. Covington stepped in. "Usually she is a smiling and pleasant young woman with enough energy to ride several times a week. She likes riding, and sketching, and reading."

"Oh, and Leonard, don't forget her new interest in birds. She has become awfully fond of watching and sketching them," Mrs. Covington added, "and Harold enjoys watching birds, too. Actually, he is the one who introduced her to the hobby. They sometimes ride out to a pond on some nearby property for a picnic and looking at the variety of birds in the area, so different, they tell me, from those here in the city."

"Except the damned pigeons," Mr. Covington muttered, as he bent to pick up the newspaper beside his chair. "—such a nuisance."

Charlotte stood and nodded at them. "I need a few things from my room first, and then I'll go back to Miss Covington. I am sure we will have many more conversations about your daughter and what she needs, what each of us can do. Ideas are already beginning to percolate in my head."

As Charlotte passed Angelina's room, she heard a light snoring and decided to let her be for another hour. Her room was at the far end of the hall, smaller than she had anticipated but containing well-made and comfortable furniture. Today was unusually sunny for January, and, after pulling some writing paper and a pen from her valise, she sat down at the desk in front of the window.

January 7, 1896

Dear Stephen,

It is less than two days since we said our little farewell, "Just for a while," you said to me, "there will be ways that we can see each other. Let us be patient." And so I am practicing that. I think I will enjoy working with my first home case, Miss Covington. Challenges will appear, I am sure of it. I think half of them will be getting her trust and helping her to see a positive future. You were her surgeon, and your handiwork appears quite skillful. Her parents are what I expected: concerned and anxious, each with a different opinion about her.

Supper at your home last week was special for me, and I enjoyed getting to know your sister better, and your adorable children. How lucky you are to have such an arrangement with Marissa ... a warm and welcoming home for her as she tends to children nearly as close as her own would be. And you, with the knowledge that your children are well cared for, and that you have provided for your sister.

The laceration on my face is healing just as you said, and it is not as bothersome now that the stitches are out. Thank you again, for your excellent care of me.

I look forward to our next time together, eagerly.

Charlotte

She hesitated about including "eagerly." Was it too forward of her? She kept returning to their last parting when he had left her at her door. He had leaned forward to kiss her, and being unprepared for it and unsure, she turned her face so that he kissed her cheek. He laughed at this, kindly, then turned her head with both his hands and kissed her again, on her lips. Gently. She could still feel that kiss and the warm, enveloping feeling that wrapped her in its embrace, promising ... what? Love, affection, a special place in another's heart? Smiling down at her, he whispered, "Good night, Charlotte. I await our next meeting." No, she decided, it was not too forward. But a niggling thought bothered her—this development with Stephen had happened much too quickly.

Over the next two days Angelina slept most of the time, which Charlotte thought was good, up to a point. She needed to heal and recover, and rest was an important part of that. But she also needed good nutrition, and some activity that would increase her appetite so that she would eat more. Mostly she needed a spark to engage her willingness to claim back her life. Charlotte could tell she was depressed. She kept remembering Mrs. Broome's words and her lecture on a patient's mental state.

"From the very first, Ladies, you must keep a patient's mental condition top in your mind. Too many nurses, and, I daresay, doctors, too, focus solely on the body and its healing. For the best and most lasting effect, one must view the mind as a patient, too. It may need healing just as much as, or even more than, the body before you."

Mrs. Broome had gone on to describe a number of mental conditions that could befall a person, and the steps a good nurse should take in caring for these "unfortunate" patients. She had stressed this final piece of instruction: "It is my opinion that one can certainly move too slowly to help a mental patient, but worse is when you move too quickly. It is then that you are liable to lose the patient's trust and confidence in you, and you may not have the time to rebuild those forces. If you fear, Ladies," she admonished, "that you might be pushing a patient too much, you probably are. Slow down. Think, reflect, give it time."

"It is time for a change of scenery, Miss Covington," Charlotte announced the next morning. "We are going on a little excursion, not much, just to the back porch for some fresh air. While you are up it will give the housemaid time to clean your room, open the windows for a while and put fresh linens on the bed."

"But I don't feel well, Nurse, I want to sleep some more. My head aches, and I just want to sleep."

"Miss Covington, your head may ache whether you are sleeping or not, but being up will tire you out more, making your sleep more beneficial. Tell me what day dress you would like to wear."

"Can I not just stay in my nightdress, Nurse, with a robe and a blanket to keep me warm? Who will see me except you?"

"That is an excellent point, Miss Covington," said Charlotte the negotiator, "we can save the dress for another outing."

Getting Angelina downstairs was easier than she thought. Mr. Covington and Charles, the houseman, brought her downstairs in a fireman's carry, following with the wheelchair. Angelina had been cool to the idea, but by the time Charlotte had coaxed her to stay "just a few more minutes; I think I hear a Northern Cardinal," her patient had relented. "Five minutes more, Nurse, then I must have sleep." Fifteen minutes later Angelina reminded Charlotte that it was time to go back inside.

"Oh, right you are," said Charlotte. "It has been such a pleasant winter morning here ... we must look for that bird again." She smiled inwardly to herself. *Well, that was a success!*

Heartstrings

1896
Louisville, Kentucky

A loud thud from Angelina's room jolted Charlotte awake from a deep sleep. She quickly threw on her robe and made her way in the dark. She could barely see a form in the bed, but Angelina was not on the bed, she was on the floor.

"What happened, Miss Covington? Are you hurt? Here, I'm here, let me help you—"

Angelina lay in a heap next to the bed, making no attempt to hold back tears.

"What is the matter? Are you in pain?"

"Yes, it has been nearly constant, and I think the medicine is giving me all sorts of frightful dreams …."

Charlotte maneuvered her to a standing position on her good leg, and pivoted her to sit back on the bed. The bandages were intact, with no blood soaking through. After Angelina was settled, Charlotte pulled the little chair closer to the head of the bed and sat down. "Would you like to tell me about it? Nightmares?" she asked, taking Angelina's hand in hers.

"It was awful, I tell you, Nurse, I can't get it out of my head. I was on the ground, at the accident, and Bill, the horse, you know?" Charlotte nodded. "Bill trotted over to me and nudged my broken ankle, licking it. Then he became enraged and started bucking and pawing at the air, his eyes, oh those eyes, so full of fury. Then he came at me as if he was going to eat me, not trample me, mind you, but *devour* me. I was screaming at him to stop, and then Harold, my fiancé, grabbed hold of his reins, and, before my eyes, Bill began eating Harold's head and shoulders!!!" By now, Angelina was whimpering.

"Oh, Miss Covington, that is truly an awful scene to imagine, let me—"

"—and the worst part, just before I woke up, was when Bill looked at me, blood dripping from his mouth, and smiled, his big horse teeth all bloody. Then he gave me a slow wink as if he and I were conspirators!"

"Remember, Miss Covington, this is a dream, not reality."

"I know, I know. But it was so vivid, and I can't get that last scene out of my head! My Bill and my Harold … at each other."

"Hmm." Charlotte said nothing for a moment. "Miss Covington, some say our dreams may have a basis, even a very tiny one, in the truth. Each person's dreams may reflect some part of their inner world."

Angelina wrinkled her brow, and Charlotte continued. "For myself, I have found it useful to consider the main elements that appear in a dream. Perhaps it would help you to tell me more about Bill and your riding." Charlotte wanted to know more about Harold, but she knew it should not be the first question.

For the next ten minutes Angelina talked about her love for horses and riding from the age of five. She had been thrown many times, but never with an injury. She had begun to feel that she was invincible. Three years ago her father had bought Barnacle Bill, a retired thoroughbred, and from the very start, she and the horse had developed a special bond. She wasn't quite sure how Bill would fit into her new life once she married, but both her father and Harold assured her that she could ride Bill regularly.

"That could be it, Nurse. Maybe my dream is about my fears for the future. Maybe I am afraid I will have to—" she stopped.

"—give up one for the other?" Charlotte finished for her. "—concerned that you can't ride Bill and be married to Harold at the same time?"

Angelina hesitated. "Maybe. Maybe that could be part of it."

"I wonder what makes you think that."

"I received a letter from Harold after the injury. He was so angry with Bill, he called him 'that damned horse of yours'—forgetting how much I love Bill. Suddenly I found it difficult to defend the horse to Harold. It was my fault, Miss Kolb, I am the one who is responsible for controlling myself on the horse, and I was inattentive. I should have paid more attention around the bend, especially around that bend where I couldn't see for a distance. I lost my focus. It was not Bill's fault. That is what a high-spirited thoroughbred does if he is not under the control of his rider. In the end, it was an accident, certainly not a malicious intent of the horse's."

"Did you tell Harold this?"

"No, I didn't. His letter upset me so much."

"Has he come to see you since the accident?"

"Once at the hospital and I said I didn't want him to see me like this."

"Like what?"

"An invalid, with a putrid, stinking stump of a leg. A cripple."

Goodness, Charlotte thought, *those are difficult words.*

"Miss Covington, you had an injury, a severe injury, and you are recovering. You will get better, and be up and around more each day, first on crutches, and then with an artificial limb. You will be able to ride again, but only if you want to. You are *not* an invalid, you are recovering. Mr. Harold can be a very good help to you, *if* you will let him."

"But what if he doesn't love me anymore?"

"Well, Miss Covington, what would that tell you?"

"That I am no longer worthy of his love, of him?"

Charlotte's eyebrows rose. "Hmm … well." She took a deep breath. "This is how it seems to me, Miss Covington. If he is not able to stand by and help you recover, then *he* is not worthy to be a husband, your husband. Imagine all the ups and downs that most surely will happen in your lives going forward. Does one not promise to stay by the other in sickness and in health? It may seem like an unpleasant way to put this, but you might view it as a test of his love for you. And, Miss Covington, you *do* deserve to be married to a man who loves you, and," she added thoughtfully, "who loves you for who you are."

Over the next three weeks Charlotte saw improvements in Angelina. Both women were now addressing each other by their first names. Harold had become a regular visitor at the Covingtons' and had proved to be a willing helper, working with Charlotte to get Angelina safely out of bed and assist her with crutch walking, a slow-going affair. Angelina was helping Charlotte with the now once-daily dressing changes, and although she did not like looking at the end of her leg, she could do it.

The couple had decided to postpone their wedding for at least six more months, when Angelina would be able to comfortably stand at her own wedding. Mr. Covington had arranged for Angelina to consult an excellent prosthetist when the swelling subsided enough to measure for her lower leg. And Barnacle Bill was assured of his pampered existence as most favored horse in the Covington stable.

Charlotte and Stephen continued to exchange letters, but they had not been able to arrange any time to be together. Once Angelina needed only daily visits to check her progress, Charlotte moved back to Katy and Edgar's. She was delighted when Stephen invited her to a piano recital at the home of his friends.

He arrived at the door looking more handsome than she remembered, his green eyes alight with happiness. She could not contain her excitement and stumbled over words as she let him into the entryway. "Oh my, it's you … it's really grand, no, great, no won—"

"Who else were you expecting, my dear Charlotte?" he chuckled, taking the hand that was not at her throat and kissing it. Katy and Edgar were close behind and anxious to greet "Dr. Stephen."

"Will you come in and warm yourself a few minutes? It is awfully cold out tonight," said Katy, hopeful.

"No, I'm sorry, Mrs. Lane, we need to be off now. Our driver must keep the horses moving." Charlotte started to put on her long winter coat, and Stephen turned to help. "You will need a hat, I think, and definitely gloves, maybe a scarf?" *I have lived through cold Kentucky winters, Stephen, and am quite prepared for them. Besides, I've been making daily trips to the Covingtons.*

"Thank you, Stephen," she smiled. "I have all that. Shall we be off?"

The sheltering space inside the closed carriage was the ideal spot to watch street scenes as the horses moved along. Stephen held her right hand, and even gloved, she felt a comforting warmth from him. She took a deep breath and shut her eyes for a few seconds, wanting to seal this moment forever in her memory. When she opened them, Stephen was looking at her. "You too?" he asked. "I'm so happy that we are finally together again," he continued. "And I know you will enjoy the music, and my friends."

She decided to be bolder. "It doesn't matter to me what occupies our time: a recital, talking about books, having supper with your little family, no matter. I simply enjoy being with *you*, Stephen."

He gave her hand a squeeze and moved to put his arm across her shoulders, requiring both of them to adjust their positions. "Better?"

"Much," she nodded and smiled. They talked about the Covingtons and Angelina's progress. "How do you feel about caring for people recovering in their homes rather than working in a hospital?" he asked.

"I like it, I like it a lot. But part of me wonders about those people who cannot afford it, or who live alone, or who have no one who cares for them …." Her voice trailed off. "I wonder if I could be of more benefit to them instead of people like the Covingtons."

"I am sure you will have a good sense of that with time," he assured her, shifting slightly. "Here is our destination. What do you think?"

She was stunned and had no words. Stephen's home was impressive, but this, this palace, made his look like a simple cottage in comparison. "Who lives here? What an absolutely grand home."

"It belongs to my friends, William and Jerusha Bryant. Their family made their living in the distilling business. William inherited this home—"

"This palace—" she corrected him.

"—when his father died three years ago, and Jerusha turned it into a place of culture and art, especially music. They recently bought a very fine Steinway concert grand piano in New York, and the sound produced on it is unbelievably pure in tone. I have heard it played—even played it myself—and I think you will agree. But you will have to be the judge of that, as I am biased in its favor," he finished, helping her out of the carriage. He took her hand again, and they walked the short distance up to the stately entrance.

Stephen introduced her to the Bryants, and they greeted her warmly. "It is wonderful to finally meet you, Miss Kolb. Stephen has told us about you, and we are so pleased to welcome you to our home. We know you will enjoy the recital; the performers are quite accomplished." Charlotte could not see the flush moving up Stephen's neck, but her own face was getting warm as well. *He has told them about me? What does that mean?*

"Oh, there you are, Stephen, I hoped you would be here soon!" A tall and statuesque young woman, more beautiful than Charlotte had ever seen, was at Stephen's side. With a graceful flourish she laid her hand on his arm, leaning in conspiratorially. She looked exactly like the "Gibson girl" of popular ladies' magazines with large blue eyes and thick blonde hair piled artfully, one long curled section resting carelessly near her collarbone. She wore a bodice-hugging dress of dark green velvet with fitted sleeves of green lace that ended just above her wrists. She looked closely at Charlotte. "And who is your young friend here? What a sweet thing!"

Sweet _thing_, Charlotte thought indignantly. *I am not a thing! I do wish I hadn't worn my green holiday dress. I used to think it was pretty.*

"Celeste, allow me to introduce a most special young woman, Miss Charlotte Kolb. Miss Kolb is a nurse, and she and I have worked together with some of my patients. Charlotte, this is an old family friend, Celeste King. For a time Celeste and I were students of the same music teacher when we were young, and we enjoyed playing piano duets together."

"Yes, Stephen, we really need to resume our work at the bench, don't we?" she smiled again knowingly. "We could play for hours together and not even notice the passing of time, isn't that right? And we had such a good sense of musical expression and rhythm. It was so easy with Stephen, Miss Kolb," she added, smiling too broadly at Charlotte. "I am one of the pianists who is playing this evening, and I do hope you will overlook the flaws in my performance. I am going on tour in two more weeks, and this evening is a time for me to play more casually in front of a welcoming audience. Or at least," she said, turning directly to Stephen, "I hope you are welcoming!"

She winked at him, nodded in Charlotte's direction, and strode off to the conservatory.

They were both at a loss for words. After a pause Stephen cleared his throat and ushered her through the crowd to meet more of his friends. The room was filled with people in elegant evening dress, the women's hair fashionably coiffed. *The men are smiling at each other like peacocks,* Charlotte thought, *proud to display their possessions.*

When the host signaled time, Stephen took her elbow and whispered, "Let's find our seats now. They should be starting soon." Two other couples had situated themselves on the conservatory chairs arranged in front of two grand pianos, the new black Steinway paired with its equally handsome cousin, a rich mahogany Chickering.

Charlotte looked at Stephen. "Two?" she whispered.

"Yes, you should hear them in eight hands, two people on each piano. Such a magnificent sound!" he sighed. The room held more than fifty chairs arranged in semicircular fashion, the two pianos facing each other so that the audience could easily observe four pianists at once. Stephen guided her to middle seats in the second row.

When Charlotte allowed herself to be consumed by the music instead of Celeste, she was lost in its tones. She loved the soothing Brahms piece that the first performer, Charles Slocum, played as introduction. Another pianist, Henry Brodkin, played two favorites, one by Mozart and the "Little Sonata" by Beethoven. Both men were very accomplished pianists, and they concluded their portion with a duet on both pianos. Finally it was Celeste's turn. She was the featured performer.

Charlotte was mesmerized by both the power and the tenderness in her playing. When the music was bold, fast and loud, Celeste played so hard her coiffure was in danger of coming apart. Her fingers flew over the keys, and her muscular arms dominated the entire length of the piano. And when it was soft, slow, and tender, it was as if she were caressing the piano, like a baby or a lover, leaning intimately into the keyboard. The expression on her beautiful face was often one of near-ecstasy, her eyes closed, brow lifted, the audience well beyond her awareness. Celeste's connection with the music and the instrument was by far the most captivating part of her performance. The artistic sound she coaxed from the instrument was secondary.

The moment her final piece was complete, the audience was on its feet, the applause held back far too long. In spite of her discomfort with the idea of Celeste and Stephen, Charlotte joined the cheering audience enthusiastically. As the noise died down, Stephen whispered to her, "If you don't mind, my dear, I'd like for us to leave now. We'll say our goodbyes quickly. We can find a little dessert at the hotel near here. It would be nice to be away from the crowd. Don't you agree?"

"What a wonderful idea," she smiled. *Enough of Celeste for one night!*

Two hours later, nearly midnight, Stephen's carriage arrived back at the Lanes'. Charlotte felt as if she could fully breathe again. Modest though her family's home was, it was where she felt truly herself. She could not say she was pretending when she was with Stephen and his surroundings, but it was a world mostly foreign to her. Before he opened the carriage door, he kissed her. This time she was not surprised or flustered or unsure what to do. She welcomed the kiss and wrapped her arms awkwardly around his shoulders. She pulled away slightly, then leaned in to kiss him again on her own initiation.

"It is hard to say goodnight to you, my dear," he whispered, and kissed her ear and the new scar on her cheek. Her heart pounded so loudly she could hear the blood rushing in her head. *What a lovely evening,* she thought, *but the best part, except now in this carriage, was at the restaurant.*

They had discussed everything except Celeste: music, his love of the piano, Charlotte's interest in authors of the day and her dreams of travel. Stephen told her the story of his short marriage and his wife's death in childbirth. She told him about her mother and her sense that she could have done something to prevent her death. "I hope that I will be able to make a difference for tuberculars somehow ...."

"I have seen your way with people, Charlotte, and it amazes me, your patience and kindness. Though if I were your patient, I would not want to improve because I might lose your attention," he smiled again. *Is he making light of me? Of course not,* another voice in her head countered, *he is the sincerest of men.*

Commitment to Love

December 31, 1896
Louisville, Kentucky

The old year, with just a few hours left, had been so many things for Charlotte: a time of learning, nursing challenges, deepening friendships, and struggle. But as she looked back, uppermost in her mind was a time of blossoming love. She and Stephen were now tiptoeing around the subject of marriage, but neither had said the word directly to the other. She hoped a proposal would come soon, perhaps on a special occasion like tonight, the cusp of a new year, a new beginning.

Aunt Katy's knock on the door interrupted her thoughts. "Ready, Charlotte? It's nearly time for our guests to arrive." Katy and Edgar were hosting a late-night dessert and champagne party to welcome the new year with friends. For three days Katy had been preparing special foods for the occasion—little cakes, tiny bite-sized pies, spiced pecans, several kinds of cookies. It had taken over a week for the candied orange and lemon peels to set up and crystallize.

Charlotte wore a fashionable long dress of red silk that she had borrowed from Priscilla. "Those tucks here and there in the bodice helped, don't you agree, dear?" asked Aunt Katy. "The dress now fits you perfectly!" Charlotte nodded and saw that the particular shade of red complemented her red hair and pale skin. She flushed with pleasure at her reflection in the hallway mirror.

Katy and Edgar were delighted to see so many of their friends chatting happily and relishing the food, but Charlotte grew more and more anxious at Stephen's absence. She was used to him arriving late on occasion; he was, after all, a doctor, and could not always arrange for someone to cover for him to fit her schedule. But she was always left with a nagging worry about how they would manage their lives if they were to marry. She hoped that Marissa would continue to live with them and look after the twins, with the frequent absences she anticipated with her work, and Stephen's long hours.

At one-thirty in the morning on the first day of the new year, Katy leaned against the front door, exhaling a "thank goodness" as their last guest departed and Edgar busied himself carrying dishes and glasses into the kitchen. She passed the parlor where Charlotte sat with her eyes closed, her head against the back of the comfortable old chair. "Tired, my dear?" she asked her niece.

Charlotte opened her eyes with a resigned look and nodded her head. "Yes, Aunt Katy," she sighed, "I suppose you could call it tired. I'd best get to bed. Tomorrow, I mean today, is a busy day. Goodness." She put her hands on the chair arms and started to push herself up, but Katy stopped her, covering one of Charlotte's hands with her own and leaning down to look into her eyes. Charlotte fought back tears.

"My dear, I am making a guess here, but I imagine that you are sorely disappointed that Stephen did not show up tonight, especially to see you in your stunning dress," she smiled.

"Oh, well," Charlotte sighed, "I do suppose the dress is a part of my state tonight, yes. I would like to talk, but not now. I am tired and weary, and a little bit sad. I just need to sleep, and I know you must be exhausted, too. While I was working, you were working every bit as hard with all the party preparations. It will keep, Aunt Katy. Good night." Charlotte slowly left the parlor.

Charlotte's home care cases were becoming more frequent and interesting. In the year since graduation she had started accepting work directly from referral rather than the registry's assignment, and she welcomed greater control of the cases and her hours. Most of the time she agreed to work on a shorter-term basis to be available for time with Stephen. She was not surprised when her free time did not coincide with his. Still, they were drawn to each other like magnets every time they were together. Charlotte found Stephen more and more insistent, and she was more and more reluctant to resist him.

At last Stephen proposed on Saturday afternoon, July 3, 1897, as they were seated in a neighborhood park, watching ducks on a lake. Marissa had taken the children to Lexington to visit relatives, and the two of them had more time alone than usual.

Charlotte was beyond relieved to hear the words she had been longing for. "My dear Charlotte, I have been to see your uncle—and your aunt too as she could not be held back." He smiled. "You know your Aunt Katy! They have agreed to give me their blessing to ask for your hand in marriage. And so, dear girl, I humbly beseech you, will you marry me? Will you do me the great honor of becoming my wife?"

Charlotte was pleased that Stephen was not on bended knee as she had always thought the tradition was stuffy. But the idea that her aunt and uncle gave their blessing was both a comfort and a disappointment. Was she not a modern woman? Why did someone else need to give their blessing if she was the one to say "yes?"

He took a small satin pouch from his breast pocket and held it out to her. "Well, what do you say?" Inside was a silver and gemstone ring, with, as he explained later, both their birthstones, set at each end of a scripted "F," holding a simple diamond in the middle. Charlotte's birthstone, a yellowish-green peridot, complemented Stephen's blue topaz. She stared at the ring, amazed at its delicacy and stunning beauty. She couldn't summon the words she wanted.

"Charlotte," he asked again, "what do you say?"

"Oh, Stephen, I was caught by surprise—of course! Of course I'll marry you! I am just so surprised that it was today … I wasn't expecting this. I mean, here we are on a walk in the park, looking at things. In the middle of this ordinary summer day you give me this, this extraordinary ring …" and she tapered off.

"Charlotte, my dear, I have been waiting a long time for the right moment, and other things always seemed to be in the way. Your being tired, my being tired, the demands of being a doctor, and a nurse, the distraction of the twins. But if you need a more romantic setting, I suppose I could arrange something. But it's time to get on with this, don't you agree?"

Charlotte Claire Kolb became an engaged woman to the great happiness of her aunt and uncle. They decided on a September 11 wedding in Stephen's home, which could hold more guests than the Lanes'. They planned a wedding trip to Niagara Falls, New York, and Canada, where Stephen's mother was born. Stephen had visited there once before he started medical school. "You should see it Charlotte, you *will* see. The water is impossible to describe, and the power of it, the sheer power of it, thundering, pounding over the edge down into the river, it demands the senses pay attention to only it. The water is all one can imagine. One's body is consumed by it!"

Charlotte was thrilled: one of her very first trips, a real trip of travel, and to visit a place that had become so popular. She had read about the New England area in the fall, too, and knew about the captivating change of colors and the lobster and blueberries, so different from Kentucky's pork and bourbon. *What a wonderful time to become Stephen's wife!*

Priscilla was delighted to learn of the engagement. She thought that Stephen was a wonderful doctor, most kind and considerate. "Think, now, Charlotte, how easy your life will become, with your beautiful home and servants to help. Marissa is going to stay, isn't she?" The question of Marissa's permanence was still undecided. According to Stephen she was torn between returning to her old life in New York and the two little children she had become so attached to. Charlotte hoped she would stay. Stephen was unsure.

Polly was less enthusiastic. "Oh, Dr. Fields is a wonderful man, he is—but the age difference between you is something you need to think about. I know it is considered correct to marry a man who is older and wiser and with more experience. But his experience also includes a marriage and raising two children to this point. Is he not looking for a nurse-maid for them? What do his children think of you? And, besides, you don't know much about the social life and the trappings of wealth that he lives with." Charlotte was almost twenty-two, and Stephen would turn thirty-three in November.

"I know I'm young, Polly, but that is one of the things he loves about me." When she heard herself say those words aloud, she stopped. *Really? Everybody has an age. Why was that such an important aspect of love?* She took a deep breath and continued. "I am prepared to learn all that I need to know to manage this new life. Look at how I learned and adapted to nursing. I can be flexible. And the wealth that Stephen has should allow me the freedom to continue with the work that I love. If Marissa decides to move back to New York, we can easily afford to hire a woman, a governess, to watch over Esther and Lucas. And they seem to love me, Polly, really they do."

Polly's expression said she needed to be convinced. "They run to hug me, and they call me 'Mama Charlotte.' They asked me if it was all right to call me that, and I was thrilled. They did not know their real mother, but Marissa has filled that role very well. They have always called her 'Aunt Marissa' and seem to understand she's not their mother. Stephen thought their request was very sweet and he approved of it. I imagine some day they will just call me 'Mama' and drop the 'Charlotte.'"

Polly sighed and hugged her. "I am happy for you, Charlotte, if you are happy. Your happiness is the most important thing to me in all this, not Stephen's, not his children's. And if you say you are happy, then I choose to believe you."

Charlotte bristled. *'If you say you are happy' and 'I choose to believe you' sounds as if she doesn't really believe it.*

Polly continued. "And, of course I want what is best for you. We are friends."

Two months flew by in a flash some days and dragged most of them. Charlotte couldn't wait to begin her new life but took on three short-term nursing cases to keep her mind occupied. One was a young man, living alone, with a mysterious ailment that caused him to go blind. Debilitating headaches required the regular use and monitoring of powerful narcotics. Another was a case of pneumonia that had left her patient alive, but extremely weak. The third was a pregnant woman in her last trimester who needed strict bed rest. Her husband was working on an engineering project in Ohio for two weeks.

Each time Charlotte took a case or simply went to work, she was reminded just how alive and full of purpose she felt. This was *her* life, no one else's, and she alone could make a positive difference for someone. Waiting by a sleeping patient's bedside or making some nourishment, her thoughts often wandered back to her mother. Those memories were dimming now. At first it panicked her, as if in losing a memory she was actually losing her mother, but she understood it now as normal.

On the evening of Charlotte's birthday, she and Stephen were alone in his house. He presented her with two books, one of poetry and one about travel to the West, along with a beautiful leather-bound journal and an exquisite ink pen, suited for her small hand. She kissed him in delight at these thoughtful gifts. The delight turned to tenderness, the tenderness to intensity.

"Just two weeks and a little more until I can carry you upstairs to my bed, our bed," he said, breathing hard, correcting himself. She nodded, smiling, imagining what it would be like. They had many occasions of kissing until they couldn't breathe, of his hands exploring her slight frame, her breasts, her buttocks, her thighs, although they'd both remained clothed.

She had enjoyed the feel of him, too, his sweet neck, a shelter where she could bury her cares in the moment, his strong arms, his powerful back, his growing hardness. Although Polly had described what to expect on her wedding night, and assured her that it was something that many women looked forward to, Charlotte still couldn't imagine being naked with him.

"I just don't know how I'm going to be so, I don't know, so … free? So free with you? I know that I want to be closer and to have these feelings continue, but I can't imagine—"

"Oh, dear girl, please don't give another moment's worry about our being husband and wife, about our being intimate. I will teach you, and I promise, I will be gentle. You will discover that every step is most natural. I love you, Charlotte. You mean the world to me, and I would never want to cause you a minute of harm or worry, or pain. You will look back on these times of fretting about a man and a woman's relations, and laugh that you were so anxious. I know something about these things …." He kissed her again, moving from her mouth to her ear, then with his tongue he traced a line lightly from her ear lobe to her collarbone, and then around her neck.

"Oh, Stephen," she shuddered, "that makes me want more, you know that, don't you? You are a devil," she insisted, smiling, eyes closed, "*my* devil."

He stood up suddenly and walked to the window. "What happened, Stephen, why did you stop? I thought you were enjoying this."

"Oh, Charlotte, I am, most definitely, but a man can only take so much of this business before he wants to, mmmm, finish things. I think we should slow the pace. We still have weeks until our wedding, and you said you want to remain a virgin."

"Sometimes. I don't really know if that is all that important to me, Stephen, but I suppose it's best if I have time to think on it … again," she smiled at him. "I think on this a lot."

He grinned back at her. "Oh, not nearly as much as I do, my love, as you will see."

Commitment to Love

To hear Aunt Katy tell it, their wedding was beautiful, although Charlotte had been too nervous to recall the carefully planned details. The September afternoon had brought a front of gloomy and blustery weather, but inside Stephen's home, their home, all was bright. Esther and Lucas were excited, Esther more, and being nearly six years old, they could maintain their childish decorum longer than two years ago.

Charlotte and Stephen passed their wedding night in Stephen's grand bed and, as he had promised, he was gentle and patient. Charlotte enjoyed their lovemaking, and the short-lived pain was minimized by her happiness and excitement. She trusted Stephen and Polly's wise counsel, and she believed it would get better. She slept well and deeply.

Their wedding trip was a blur of sightseeing, eating wonderful food, and spending more time in each other's arms in unfamiliar beds. Charlotte enjoyed making love with her new husband, initiating and responding with increasing passion to his knowledge of how to arouse and satisfy her. *Oh, if every day could be like this,* she thought, *not one care in the world. No worries about Marissa's leaving, or how the children will adjust, or directing the house staff.* Marissa had offered to stay with them through the holidays, but they had all agreed that it made most sense for her to return to New York in early November, before the weather turned. Thoughts of Stephen's work, and her work, fell into the background. Work would always be there, and she could enter into it whenever she wanted.

Charlotte stayed busy in October. Marissa helped her learn the running of the household; she planned meals with Mrs. Rachel, the cook, and directed the cleaning and upkeep never obvious in a well-run home. Charlotte did not like Mrs. Rachel very much, and she sometimes wondered if she was reliable. But Stephen thought her meals and her dependability were first-rate.

One morning Charlotte found Stephen sitting beside Lucas, talking quietly with his son. Lucas lay curled on his side under the covers, with his back to his father. "I don't want to get up, Papa, I am sick in my stomach." Stephen smiled up at Charlotte standing outside the door. "Let me feel your head, son, to see if you have a fever. No, no fever. Tell me about your sick stomach."

"It doesn't want any food, it doesn't want me to get up."

"Are you having pain, Lucas?"

Lucas shook his head, "No, not really, I just don't feel good."

"Hmm, maybe some weak tea and toast would be good for it. Turn around a bit so I can feel your stomach. I certainly hope we won't have to operate." With his skillful surgeon's hands he assured himself that his son was in no immediate danger.

"When did it start, Lucas? Just this morning?"

"I don't know, Papa, maybe in the night, no, it was after supper when you were all talking."

"Hmm … I see, was that when we were talking about Aunt Marissa and New York?"

A tear slid down his cheek as he nodded. He did not look up at his father. "You are feeling sad about her leaving, is that it, Lucas?"

Lucas nodded again. "I don't want her to go—why does she have to go? Doesn't she love us anymore?"

"Look at me, son. Let me tell you that I am sad about her leaving, too, did you know that?"

He shook his head, and looked up at his father. "Really, you too?"

"Oh my, yes, Lucas, Marissa has been a most important part of our family since you were born. But since Charlotte came into our lives, Marissa has been longing to go back to her home in New York. A person can love someone and still want to leave to have her own life. Of course she still loves us, Lucas. We all just feel it is the right time for her to go back to her life and friends there."

Lucas sniffed and sighed.

"She wants to go, Lucas, and we should not keep her here if that is truly her heart's desire, now, should we?"

The boy shook his head again.

"The most important thing, son, is that we let Marissa know how much we love her, and will miss her. It is normal to be sad about this. And, maybe in a little while your stomach might feel like eating some breakfast. You let Charlotte know if it doesn't feel better by midday, all right?"

Charlotte and Stephen consulted the twins about Thanksgiving, their first one without Marissa. Should they celebrate the holiday as they had in the past, or would they like to start a new tradition? Thinking it might involve presents or even tastier food than they were used to, the children brightened at the idea of something new. Charlotte had been thinking about this for a while and unveiled her idea. "You know in my work, and your father's, too, we see so many people who are less fortunate than we are. I was thinking that we could share our Thanksgiving with another family. They might not be able to come here and join us at our table, but we could take Thanksgiving to them. We could have Mrs. Rachel make extra, and then all of us could go as a family to their home. What do you think about that?"

The twins were silent. "What if they don't like us?" Esther asked. "Or what if they are dirty, or smelly, or don't have manners?"

Stephen frowned. "It could be strange or awkward at first, but many people live their lives very differently from us. I like Charlotte's idea, and I think it is high time that we do something like this, something different."

"But Aunt Marissa wouldn't make us do this, she would want to keep things nice and happy," added Lucas.

"Perhaps," Stephen said, "but you might be surprised. Your aunt has a big and generous heart, as does Charlotte, and it is time for us as a family to share our good fortune with others. It is one little step. Maybe we can save a special treat for ourselves until after?" Stephen's words settled it.

Polly told Charlotte about a family she worked with in a poor part of town. The mother, Mrs. Walters, was newly afflicted with swollen and painful joints and could barely get around. Preparing even a simple meal was beyond her this year. Mr. Walters, a fireman, was recovering from serious burns to his arms and chest. He had tried to save a little boy from a fire and bravely went back into the burning house to find him, but he could not.

The Walterses had three children under the age of nine. The youngest was thin and pale for his age and lacked energy. Polly assured Charlotte that the family would welcome their Thanksgiving offering, and it should not be "too frightening" for Lucas and Esther. She cautioned Charlotte about expecting to be invited in. This year a pall of pain and sadness had overcome the family, and they might not be very hospitable.

Charlotte thought Mrs. Rachel seemed irritated when she heard the plan to take extra food to a needy family. "There's them that's needy here, ma'am, nearly right under your nose. And the food won't stay hot as you're carrying it across town."

"Taking it to them piping hot is not what's important," Charlotte countered. "We have no knowledge of when they will want to eat. We shall carry the food wrapped and secure for their meal, or meals, whenever they would like. I want them to be able to warm it as they need."

Mrs. Rachel pursed her lips and stared at her new employer. "Very well, Missus, what do you want me to make?"

"Well, exactly what we are having, so two of everything. I know this will mean extra work for you, and I can help if you will instruct me, and our young neighbor, Miss Clark, has said she will come and help, too. We can make a party of it. Just think of the joy this will give the family."

Charlotte was quite sure she heard Mrs. Rachel huff, "Party indeed," as she left the dining room.

At midmorning on Thanksgiving the food for the Walters family sat on the dining table, wrapped and ready to carry in the baskets Mrs. Rachel put out. Stephen was expected back any minute. He had operated on two patients yesterday, and he needed to check on them this morning. "Esther, Lucas!" Charlotte called upstairs, "Are you ready to go? It is nearly time." Both children made their way down slowly, their arms full of toys.

"What is this?" asked Charlotte. Over the past two days, she had watched their anxiety melt into an attitude of anticipation. Perhaps it was the laughing that came from the kitchen when Miss Clark talked of her grandmother staring down a turkey and turning tail as the turkey chased her into the barn. Maybe it was the smell of pies baking yesterday, or of today's turkey and ham.

"Well, we know it's not Christmas and time for presents yet, but we thought we could give the children some of our old toys. We don't use them anymore. Maybe they don't have very many?"

Or any, thought Charlotte. "That is so thoughtful and generous of you both. I am so proud of you! They will love these toys, I am sure, and they are hardly used. Your father will be so pleased to see your generosity." Lucas beamed.

And then it was Christmas. Nearly four months had disappeared in a happy daze. The four Fieldses grew more comfortable with each other, and Esther and Lucas fretted less about their aunt. Charlotte eased into her duties managing the home even though her exchanges with Mrs. Rachel still felt prickly. She learned to expect it and ignore it at the same time.

Stephen radiated a quiet delight at the end of a tiring day, observing his peaceful little kingdom with a glow Charlotte had never seen in him. She loved the intimacy they shared in the privacy of their bedroom, and the way he desired her body sparked her longing for him just as much as he wanted her.

But a growing sense of unease at her life began to gnaw at her. She had spent two arduous years learning to be a nurse, and she questioned whether she was turning her back on a desire to help others. *What is happening to that yearning I had to care for people like my mother? Am I exchanging it for an easy life?*

Whatever the longing was, it was calling her to do more, to be more than a wife and mother to Stephen's children. And in spite of their frequent lovemaking, she was not yet pregnant. *We need to settle things. It's time to hire a woman to help with the twins. I will broach the subject with him, soon.*

April, 1898

"Stephen, I want to talk with you about something." He looked up from his newspaper.

He patted a seat next to him on the loveseat and smiling, took her hand. "What shall we discuss this morning? Do you have some special news for me?" Stephen had begun talking about another child in the family, a sibling for Esther and Lucas, and his hope that he and Charlotte would have several children of their own.

Blushing and smiling down at him, she admitted, "No, Stephen, that is not it today, but I hope very soon. What I need to tell you is this. I am eager to return to nursing and take on cases that I can help, really help. I want to work with some of the longer-term cases, like Miss Covington— remember her?—or patients with serious, perhaps even terminal illnesses. I feel so strongly pulled, Stephen, I do. And to make that work, we need to hire someone to help with the children and the house while I am away. How should we go about that?"

She watched as his expression changed unexpectedly from pleasant hopefulness to disappointment. "Oh, my, Charlotte, this is a surprise. Aren't you happy with our life?"

"I *am* happy with our life. But that's just it, Stephen, it is 'our' life, and just a part of mine, a wonderful part. But another part of me yearns for *my* life, the life I was preparing for when we met."

He sighed, looking thoughtful. "What about the children, Charlotte, they love being with you. What will this do to them?"

"I don't think it will do anything to them. They will see their step-mother enjoying her life and loving them when she is here. And Stephen, I will be in control of when I take cases, so it is not as if I will be gone all the time. You and I can agree on the amount of time I should work. Maybe I could take a case that we would expect to last one to two weeks—and then be home for a month or so before I take another case. What about something like that?"

"Entirely unworkable, Charlotte. In the first place, how do we find someone that we trust to come in on such a sporadic basis? It is one thing for the children and me to be flexible with your notions, but not necessarily someone I would hire."

"Notions, Stephen? You think this is a *notion*, my desire to help others?" Her face flushed, and she felt pressure start to build in her chest.

"Maybe that was the wrong word, Charlotte, but it seems to me that you are being selfish, my dear, putting your own needs before the children's, and even mine. Needs that would take you away from us, and when the children are so young. I don't know. Could you not seek a regular nursing role, like at the Infirmary, where you would have a predictable schedule and be home every night? It might be easier to hire a day woman than someone who would live with us for short periods of time."

"Hmm," she said, swallowing back her desire for more words and a resolution to this. "I will have to think about that."

"Good," was all he said, and he returned to reading the paper.

She felt the bright edges of her thought, her plan, her hope, curl in and darken just a little. It was not what she had imagined. She had been so happy to leave Norton as a freshly graduated nurse and the years since had shown her the gifts she possessed. To go back to the Infirmary seemed like a big step back. She wasn't even sure she had the skills to supervise people. As very few positions for bedside nurses existed, students provided most of the care.

And she was disappointed in Stephen. His concern seemed to be for the impact on him and the children, not her feelings or her needs. Before they married, had he not implied that they could hire help to replace Marissa; was this not the exact circumstance they had discussed? She decided to think on it some more. Although redheads had a reputation for quick tempers and fiery arguments, neither she nor Stephen had that tendency. She had learned that words thrown about in anger rarely solved anything.

Mrs. Broome looked at her quizzically across the desk in her little office. "Really, Mrs. Fields, you want to come work here?"

"Well, I am just trying to decide what to do with myself these days. I long to be of use and use my training to help others. I love the work of a private-duty nurse, and the challenge, I might add, but it does not lend itself easily to caring for a husband and young children. Stephen, Dr. Fields, I mean, thought you might have a position here that would accommodate my needs and our family's schedule."

Mrs. Broome lowered her chin and frowned sharply over her glasses at Charlotte. "Mrs. Fields, you are sadly mistaken if you think I can create work, willy-nilly, for the individual needs of nurses. My sole concern here, aside from the nursing school, is the care of our patients. The schedule convenience for nurses is not something I worry about. And I have all the ward supervisors that I need. We have no vacancy. I think your best avenue is private duty."

Charlotte looked down at the hands in her lap and set her jaw. She was not surprised, but she was embarrassed at how her words had come out, selfish and immature. She was sure Mrs. Broome's opinion of her, if she had one, had lowered because of her request.

Mrs. Broome spoke again. "Why don't you go see Mrs. Trefry and explain your circumstances to her? She may have some ideas that could fit your, ahem, 'schedule needs' better than I do." Charlotte studied Mrs. Broome, and thought she saw a softening in her face that was not apparent initially. "Perhaps the two of you can create an arrangement," she added, before consulting her watch and standing. "I am sorry, Mrs. Fields, but I must get back to the wards. The new students are only a few months into their training, and they need lots of supervision. I'm sure you remember. Good day."

She was gone, but Charlotte had another little hope to cling to.

Mrs. Trefry was more welcoming than Mrs. Broome. However Charlotte was shocked at her appearance. Now dark circles underlined her eyes, her hair was dry and thin, and her frame, once delicate, had filled out to the point of overweight. She was almost unrecognizable. But the radiance of her smile was the same as Charlotte remembered from two years ago, and she still offered "a cup of tea to warm you," although the May morning was sunny and pleasant.

Charlotte explained her situation, carefully choosing her words this time, so that she emphasized her need to be actively involved in nursing even though she had a family to tend to. Did Mrs. Trefry have any ideas for how she could take on cases and still have a family life with a more predictable schedule?

"Well, my dear, those are difficult needs to reconcile at the same time, but I have two ideas that you might consider. The first would be to pair up with another nurse who would be willing to work as your partner for the nighttime. The two of you would receive half the pay that one would get, and the family or patient would have to be willing to take on two of you, but

I think that could be a benefit, actually. Another perspective, another nurse to work things out with would be an advantage for the patient, I imagine.

"The other thought I have is to work with me, and learn what I do."

Charlotte looked at her in surprise. "Are you that busy that you need an assistant?"

She shook her head. "No, my dear, but the time is coming for me to lighten my load. I have not been feeling well lately, and my doctor suggests that I work less." Changing the subject, she continued. "I know that you understand the work and the need to make sure we are offering the best match for the patients, and a solid base for new nurses to launch themselves. They don't stay with us for very long, just as in your case, my dear, before word gets out and they begin to be hired directly. But it is a challenge of a different sort to make sure that patients get the best care by providing the best nurse possible. What do you think?"

Charlotte's mood lifted immediately. Neither of those ideas had occurred to her, but she was concerned about Mrs. Trefry. "I do not mean to pry into your personal affairs, Mrs. Trefry, but how is your health? And how do you think we could work together? Would this be on a part-time basis?"

Her blue eyes filled with tears. "It is kind of you to inquire, Mrs. Fields. Some days are better than others. I am tired mostly, though I'll admit I have pain, especially at the end of the day. Midday is best for me. Dr. Strang, the German doctor in town, is going to try me on a special tonic. He is highly respected by other doctors here. For the time being, I am to rest as much as I can to gain my strength back. He is not very happy about my working, but I need to do this work while I am able. My husband is not very well …."

Charlotte nodded thoughtfully. Mrs. Trefry continued. "I think you could learn the work by coming in with me daily for a week, perhaps two, at my best times, say from ten in the morning until one or two o'clock. I would have the most energy for explaining things to you then. Once you are comfortable with the work and assigning, you could work in the afternoons. So, for the time being, it would be part time. What do you think?"

Stephen was pleased with Charlotte's choice. The children seemed to take the change in their routine in stride. She was with them in the mornings, overseeing their breakfast and getting them ready for school. She had time to read the newspaper or write letters and consult with Mrs. Rachel about dinner. Mrs. Rachel reluctantly agreed, with a small pay adjustment, to give more attention to the children when they returned from school until Charlotte arrived home from the registry office.

All the pieces seemed to fit nicely.

July 1898

It's so hot for this time of year, Charlotte thought, sweat running down her back and the sides of her face, though both windows of the little room were fully open. She was checking over an agreement with a new nurse when dizziness and a sudden wave of nausea overcame her. Heat rose up her chest and neck, and she located the wastepaper receptacle just in time as she lost her midday meal, which hadn't been much in this weather. She grabbed a handkerchief from her pocket to wipe her perspiring face before she leaned over to vomit again.

She was still slightly dizzy, and as she sat at the desk, her eyes closed and her head in her hands, it hit her with a most definite realization—*I am pregnant, I am sure of it now.* For a week she hadn't felt like herself, nothing she could put her finger on, it was just, well, different. Her head in the clouds, her attention often elsewhere. As they lay in tangled sheets after making love, Stephen had commented on the increased fullness and sensitivity of her breasts, but he had not guessed the reason. She had thought he was happy about her ever-increasing interest in making love with him, but maybe he knew something else?

She grinned and spoke aloud in amazement, "We are going to have a baby." *Oh my stars, we are going to have a baby!*

New Beginnings

December, 1898
Louisville, Kentucky

The house was most festive as they looked forward to Christmas and the promises of 1899. In her sixth month of pregnancy Charlotte answered the twins' question about why she was getting so fat. At Sunday dinner Lucas announced, "I'm glad we're getting a baby. I'm tired of Esther now, and I want a baby brother to pal around with. It will be more fun to do things with him."

Esther retorted in disgust, "Brother, you don't know anything! When he comes here, he will be a baby for a long time and you will be getting older. Pal around, that is ridiculous. I want a baby sister that I can take care of and dress and teach things to." She lifted her little nose as she speared another carrot, her favorite vegetable.

"My, my," Stephen said, smiling across the table at Charlotte, "We certainly have some interesting expectations about this new little one. What are you wishing for, my dear?"

"I am hoping for a healthy baby, that is all. Boy or girl, either is fine with me. I do hope he or she has the Fields's green eyes and red hair— although if it is a girl, I would hope her hair is curly and thick. If he's a boy? I pray he has the good sense to look up to his big brother." The smile on Lucas's face was a gift.

Charlotte worked at the registry for another month. She felt positive and energetic, and Mrs. Rachel took care with the sweets that were served. Mrs. Trefry was able to resume her past schedule, and she welcomed the income. Her condition had been diagnosed as a disorder of the thyroid gland, and the tonic that Dr. Strang prescribed was proving to be effective.

She had more energy and sparkle. Her face was thinning a bit, and the bodice of her jacket was not so strained.

February and March were typically cold and blustery months in Louisville, and Charlotte was grateful to be able to stay inside and warm. Before Christmas, she occasionally visited Katy and Edgar, and lately Katy had taken to visiting her, enjoying tea before the fire, chatting and knitting baby garments. She was as excited as any grandmother-to-be and secretly wished for a little grandniece. She imagined the sweet baby days she and Edgar had missed before Charlotte came to them.

"So I assume that you will now stay at home to care for the baby, and not return to nursing? Is that how things will play out after he or she arrives?"

"Yes, Aunt Katy, now I'll put my knowledge to work caring for my own little family. I am lucky that Esther and Lucas are excited about the baby, not to mention Stephen. He is absolutely over the moon about this— you would think he invented children, the way he goes on about it!"

"Hmm," Katy replied, "Drat, I have dropped a stitch. These tiny needles and the fine yarn are hard to see clearly, and my fingers are not as nimble as they used to be." Charlotte smiled at her wistfully. *My dear aunt is getting older.*

April 2, 1899

Charlotte finally wakened Stephen at 4:30 a.m., the pains growing harder and more frequent. Stephen wanted to contact the midwife when they began last evening, but Charlotte resisted. "No. Let's wait a little longer. First babies usually take a long time getting here, and I would rather not have the midwife here, underfoot, until she is needed. Not yet."

Stephen agreed, although he thought she was uncharacteristically irritable. "I'll let her know when you say, dear. I just hope it's not the middle of the night."

She held off until nearly dawn before shaking him awake. "It's time, Stephen. Get her here as soon as you can—"

The baby arrived at 2:30 in the afternoon, a fierce loud cry announcing his entrance, ten fingers and ten toes, with a fine light fuzz covering his head. Charlotte was exhausted from her uncomplicated but long labor. The midwife had arrived early in the morning, and she and Stephen had worked together to comfort and encourage Charlotte.

Stephen had decided months earlier that he would stay with her for the duration. For six years he had carried a deep regret for not being present during his first wife's labor. He could have been some small comfort to her during some of the process, but he did not think of that at the time. If something bad were to happen, he did not want Charlotte to be alone, or know that he hadn't been there for her.

Uncle Edgar had come early in the morning to take Lucas and Esther for the day. Being Sunday, they went to church, and he promised them a visit afterward to see his friend's thoroughbred horses. The twins loved horses and were distracted enough they did not think about what was happening at home. The same was not true for Katy. After a hasty Sunday dinner, she shooed Edgar and the twins off to the horses and walked briskly to Charlotte's.

Mrs. Rachel opened the door. "He's here, Missus, a boy. Our baby is finally here, what a long day we have had!"

Nothing could stop Katy and she headed for the stairs. "Oh, my stars, this is marvabulous! A boy!"

She tapped lightly on the frame of the open bedroom door. "May I come in? Are you all right?"

"Come in, Aunt Katy," Stephen smiled, "Come in and meet our newest Fields, Charles Edgar."

Through tearing-up eyes, Katy regarded her exhausted niece and the tiny bundle in her arms. She moved quickly to Charlotte's side and kissed her cheek. "Charles ... Edgar?"

"Yes," said Stephen behind her, "we named him for our fathers, the men who have loved and influenced us."

Katy remembered that August day twenty-four years ago when she first met Charlotte, and offered a silent prayer of thanks to God, and one to her sister. *I will stand in your stead, dear Lorena, and do everything I can for your sweet Charlotte, and your grandson.* She held the new bundle in her arms, and kissed his head. *What a blessing,* she thought, *he is here and they are safe.*

Charlotte was not prepared for the way she instantly fell in love with this baby. She couldn't stop looking at his sweet perfection, silently willing him to wake when she wanted to see his eyes. Initially they were a grayish-blue, but she believed they would turn green like everyone else's in the family. His little nose, his fingers curled around hers, the funny way he would yawn and shudder, then fall back asleep, eyelids fluttering. Once past the initial period of sore nipples, they both adapted easily to breastfeeding. Charlie had a good appetite and gained weight.

Stephen had thought he understood being a father, but he was newly transformed. Watching Charlotte and Charlie, he knew he could not penetrate that powerful connection that stood like an invisible wall. Sometimes he felt a twinge of jealousy at their bond. He had missed watching his first wife care for her babies when the twins were born. Six years ago his world required that he meet the demands of two helpless infants, grieve the loss of his Emma, and adjust to Marissa's assistance, for she had immediately come to help. The awareness of what he had missed with Esther and Lucas saddened him.

But his involvement in this special period of bonding with Charlie affected him deeply—it felt like another honeymoon. He was caught up in the experience and loved holding the baby on his chest when Charlotte needed to rest. The twins were excited about Charlie as well, and although Esther had wished for a baby sister, she was happy simply to have a baby to care for. And Lucas quickly changed his expectations about being pals so soon with his little brother.

Charlotte was surprised that her intention of returning to nursing easily receded into the background. She was so taken with Charlie that she could not imagine leaving him for an entirely different world, even for an hour. Her friends had visited and exclaimed about the perfection of this new little one. Although Polly had no children of her own, she did have seven nieces and nephews and lots of experience with the early life of a young family.

"So, you're not ready to think about going back to work, is that right? Well, let me tell you, Charlotte, I have seen it before. Sometimes mothers want to stay at home and dedicate themselves fully to their husbands and families. I know of others who have a different calling. Family is one part of their life, but their profession is another. It is not wrong to want a part of your life that is totally your own. Both approaches are right, depending on what the mother wants."

Charlotte nodded her head thoughtfully, but Polly could tell that she was not convinced. It was too soon after Charlie's arrival for Charlotte to know what she wanted.

Blame

November 3, 1899
Louisville, Kentucky

Edgar's unexplained two-day fever had spiked, and Katy was frantic. Charlotte expected to be gone only an hour, but her evening visit to check on him stretched into the early morning hours. She and Katy sat by his bed worrying, changing cool cloths repeatedly, their hands chapped from constant immersion in water. Katy had never seen Edgar this ill. Charlotte was anxious too and relieved when his fever broke around three in the morning. Her breasts were aching, and she knew Charlie would be more than hungry. He was a ravenous little monster at seven months of age. She wished she had brought him with her.

She had just kissed Katy's cheek in farewell when a sudden banging at the front door interrupted them. A sweaty red-faced policeman stood before them. "Ma'am, are you Mrs. Fields?"

Katy pointed to Charlotte, just behind her. "That's her. I'm her aunt. What's wrong, officer?"

"Come with me, Mrs. Fields, there's been a fire." The heavy cold fingers of dread clutched at Charlotte's chest.

"A fire, oh my God!" Katy said, "Go, Charlotte, go!" prodding her niece who was standing like stone.

When Charlotte and the policeman arrived at the house, their wonderful happy home, it was nearly gone. All that remained was the back porch and part of the kitchen. *My Charlie, Stephen, the children, where are they?* A black unthinking terror took over. She saw neighbors standing outside and a man about Stephen's height in the group. He had a blanket draped over his shoulders, and someone was trying to make him sit down, but he wouldn't.

Where is Stephen, where are the children? Maybe someone has taken them into their home for safety and warmth? Maybe they are some-where else? As she ran to the cluster, her heart fell again, the man was indeed Stephen. *Oh, thank God, he is safe. The children must be safe, too.* "Where are they, Stephen? Where are the children?"

Stephen turned, staring through her with a questioning daze. He was covered with soot, and tears had dried leaving a horrible mask she could never have imagined on his beautiful face. He recognized her. "Oh, Charlotte, finally, there you are!" he cried, overcome by deep engulfing sobs, grabbing her so tightly she thought her ribs would break.

Her own tears came instantly to see him so crushed. She pulled back to look into his eyes and watch the words come out of his mouth. "Where are they?" she demanded. "Where are the children, our babies?"

He could only shake his head, sobbing.

"No," she cried, gulping air, "no, no, no, no, NO!! Answer me, Stephen, tell me this minute!"

The neighbor who had been standing next to Stephen tried to put out a comforting arm, but Charlotte pushed it away. "Mrs. Fields, the fire went so fast, and everyone was asleep, and Dr. Fields came running to us for help—"

"Where were you, Stephen? You weren't with the children? You weren't in the house?"

The neighbor interjected again, "He was called to the hospital, Mrs. Fields, he said he had to go for a patient who needed an operation, and that your Mrs. Rachel was looking after the children."

"Where is she? Does Mrs. Rachel have the children with her?"

The neighbor shook her head sadly, "No, Missus, they're all gone, Mrs. Rachel, too. She must have fallen back asleep."

"What!? Where did they go? Someone has them, right? I want to see them, NOW!" Now she was shouting, but at no one in particular.

Stephen turned to her again and put his arms around her, tightly, until she stopped fighting against him. "Charlotte, we will do that—later. They are gone. They are gone, I tell you. Our children have perished."

What can one say about a despair and depression with a magnitude so massive? Charlotte and Stephen moved in with Katy and Edgar who cared for the grieving couple. Silence shrouded the somber household without much to do. Cooking was minimal that winter; no one had an appetite. Marissa came immediately from New York and found a modest house for the three of them to rent. Stephen went back to work after one week, declaring that "work will be my savior," but he used up all his energy at the hospital and had none to give in the evening when he sat brooding in front of the fire.

Each was inconsolable in their own way. The fire took almost everything, including the rooms once filled with noise or the hope of finding the shred of a childhood reminder. No toys, no clothes, no tangible sources of anguish or comfort from the little person who had touched those things. All was lost. Marissa and Katy and Edgar surrounded the couple with as much care and love as they could muster, but nothing could reach them. Neither Priscilla nor Polly could engage Charlotte for more than a minute or two. The minister made visits, and kind neighbors left food and condolences. Daily life went on but time stopped for Charlotte and Stephen.

Stephen was still capable enough at the hospital, but he was slow and less able to communicate warmth and empathy to his patients. He was brusque with the staff and students, and curt with his fellow doctors. Mrs. Broome and Dr. Hotchkiss urged him to take more time away. When he did not accept their urging, they insisted. "You have had an unspeakable blow, Dr. Fields," Dr. Hotchkiss said, "and you need time to recover from this tragedy. There will always be patients here who need you, always. But you will not always have this time to grieve and to be with Mrs. Fields in your shared grief. You must make your recovery the focus of your attention. Do not come back until at least the middle of January."

Marissa tended Charlotte. She selected her clothes and told her when to bathe and wash her hair. She sat with her at the little dining nook and made her take toast and tea and oatmeal. It was harder for Marissa to direct her brother, but she tried. She could see that both of them were pulling away from each other.

Thanksgiving and Christmas passed without ceremony. Marissa and Katy and Edgar, grieving themselves for the children, made half-hearted attempts to recognize the holidays. They put up some fresh greens inside. Katy bought a few presents, clothing mostly, for Charlotte and Stephen. The couple refused to go to church. Religion was sore comfort to their grief, and the notion of God was a profanity. Stephen was more and more irritable, and his anger often fell on Charlotte or Marissa. Charlotte, usually sensitive to Stephen's critical remarks, barely heard his words, and if she did, their ability to affect her was gone. She didn't care.

Marissa was finally able to persuade them to get outside for a walk. The sunny January afternoon was still and cold. The sidewalk was clear of ice and snow, and the three of them walked to a nearby park. No one spoke until Charlotte took a deep breath, eyes closed, as she stopped and raised her face to the sun. "Damn you, God," she cried. "This hurts so much—take it away, take … it … AWAY!! How *dare you* shine your sun when my world is so black?"

Stephen put his arms around her, and for the first time since the day of the fire, she let him. Marissa watched for a minute, then turned and walked back home.

"My world is black, too, Charlotte. I cannot …," his words fell off. "I don't know what to do to make you or myself feel any better, or do what I need to do as a physician. I cannot see …." Again his words trailed off.

"This blackness is awful, Stephen, but at least it keeps me from remembering what happened. I prefer the heavy blanket of darkness to this, this pain of reality!"

"Charlotte, we must both face this pain. It is like the pain after surgery, if one lies abed without moving to avoid it, the recovery is longer, and many times more complicated."

"Don't give me your stupid medical platitudes, Stephen Fields! Recovery be damned! How does one recover from the love of children, and the pain of losing that love? Use those words with your patients but not here with me! I know that, and that knowledge is useless to me, especially now. Especially knowing that this situation, this tragedy, was absolutely avoidable. Why did you let Mrs. Rachel be in charge? You know that she was—"

"What, Charlotte, you're blaming me? I did everything I could think of to make sure the children were watched over for the few hours I would be gone. Mrs. Rachel was awake and perfectly lucid. She had knitting that she said would keep her up until I returned. I expected you home at any time, certainly by nine o'clock. Edgar's fever was not a matter of life or death!"

She stared at him, unbelieving, as he continued. "And the least, the very least, you could have done was to take our little Charlie with you. We would have one child left at least. He was the fussiest I have ever seen him after you left, and even the bottle that Mrs. Rachel tried to get him to take did not satisfy him. He finally cried himself to sleep. I know, *I* was there."

Charlotte's heart stopped. Stephen had just shot an arrow at her; did he mean it to hurt as much as it did? A truth so shattering, its sharpness left her cold. Her baby Charlie's last hours were without the comfort of his mother—a mother's worst imagining. She had no reply to this; it was something she blamed herself for already. But to hear Stephen express it ripped the scab off her wound. Charlie's death was her fault. She should not have left without him.

Stephen returned to the hospital, and the time away from his demands had helped his attitude at work. But each night when he went home, he was disgusted by Charlotte. He could not shake Charlie's death, nor Lucas's and Esther's, and his anger at his wife grew. He had lost three children; she, just the one. Charlotte could feel the cold weight of Stephen's feelings. She had no words to change anything.

One evening in April, Marissa had had enough of the tension between the unhappy couple. "Stephen, don't you think it's time to forgive Charlotte? Can you not see it for the accident it was?" Stephen turned from his book and frowned at her, as she continued. "Of course she never intended that helping her uncle would result in this tragedy! I know the anger you hold toward her, and it is only getting worse. I can see hers, too, and the loss and sadness both of you feel. I feel it, too. Not only have I lost a niece and nephews, I have lost the happy relationship I used to have with each of you. What will it take for you to forgive Charlotte?"

He was red-faced by now. "Marissa, she did the unforgivable. She abandoned her role as mother in favor of her uncle, and that priority I cannot live with. Every time I look at her, I see our Charlie, and the memories of Lucas and Esther tear my heart out. I don't want her to suffer more than she already is, really I don't. But I cannot envision myself trusting her as a wife, nor as a mother, anymore."

"Stephen, she is young. Don't you think she would do things differently if she could?"

"It is too painful for me, Marissa. Every day is worse, not better. I am going to move out. You should leave as well."

Stephen's plan did not surprise Charlotte. "I will save you the trouble, Stephen, I am sure my aunt and uncle will welcome me. I need to be somewhere away from you and the awful memories as well. Being with you is no comfort at all. I agree. It is best for us to be apart."

"Not just apart, it's best to end this marriage, Charlotte. But for now, it will be enough for me to not have to look at you every day."

Katy and Edgar rescued Charlotte. In July she began taking as many home cases as she could. Polly invited Charlotte to live with her, but she declined. For the time being she needed a familiar place of comfort and welcome. To put herself into one more new situation was too much. Maybe later.

Heroine

August 30, 1901
Louisville, Kentucky

Charlotte's heart galloped as the man's dirty hand clamped down hard over her nose and mouth. She had sensed his presence a split second before she saw his shadow in the room. His rough hand was calloused, and he reeked of alcohol. The grimy sour smell of him in his unholy embrace, coupled with her panic, made her want to vomit. For a crazy moment Charlotte thought that might make him loosen his grip on her. But she did not vomit, and he pulled her away from the window so she could not be seen from the street below. The moon was full, and the view from the window was stunning. *What a contrast,* her thoughts spinning, *between the peace on the street below and my terror in this room! How did he get upstairs?*

"Don't you dare make a sound, missy," he hissed, "or I'll use my knife to shut you up for good." She could feel the tip of his knife now at the left side of her neck just above the collarbone. *Oh, please, not my artery,* she begged silently. She took several slow breaths to help calm herself.

Her fear turned to determination as she began to gather her thoughts, remembering why she had come into this room. Mr. Ellerton, her patient— she had awakened to check on him. He often had sleepless nights, and they would talk quietly until he fell back asleep. The tightness in his legs eased if she massaged them.

The intruder backed her toward the door so that he could shut it, and she was able to see Mr. Ellerton from the corner of her eye. He was awake, eyes wide as hers. He slowly moved a finger to his lips in warning. She had always liked him, but she had not appreciated his cleverness before.

The man's grip on her loosened, and as the door quietly shut behind them, the intruder continued hissing in her ear. "The old man is rich, and I know he keeps his money in the mattress. Git over there, and blindfold 'im so he don't see me. Then help me git under the mattress to the money. Don't try anything funny. I'm right behind you, and I'm much bigger than you, missy. I'll kill you, I swear. Here." He thrust a dirty bandana into her hand and shoved her toward the bed.

Charlotte bent over Mr. Ellerton, clearly awake now, and tied the bandana as loosely as she could, whispering "I'm sorry" as she did it. She could feel him nod his head twice as she tied the knot. "The gun?" she whispered.

He nodded again. Mr. Ellerton insisted on sleeping with a gun beneath his pillow, a habit she could not get him to break. She was grateful a second time, this time for his stubbornness. Although the man was paralyzed below the waist, he still had strength and mobility in his arms and hands.

The intruder grabbed her and pulled her back from the head of the bed. "I'll pull the old man over on his side, I know he cain't move, but I ain't never counted on you t' help me," he half-chortled to himself. "Git under the edge of the mattress, and gimme the money." Charlotte knew where he kept the money; she had seen him fumbling to put it away one night as she came to ready him for bed.

Slowly she felt around for the packages of bills Mr. Ellerton had wrapped and marked so carefully. Seven in all and quite bulky when piled together, but he could easily sleep on them when spread out. She handed the intruder one package. Her heart's pounding increased. *What will he do now? Will he simply leave now that he has what he wanted? Will he hurt us?* He was masked so she could not identify him, although she imagined he could recognize her on the street if they ever met.

Where is the gun?

As she put her hands on the mattress at the head of the bed, she felt hardness under one of the pillows. She sneaked a look over her shoulder to see the intruder counting the bills, the knife on the bed all but forgotten. *How stupid, he must not have any experience at robbing people.* Emboldened by this awareness and Mr. Ellerton's gun now at her hand, she quickly turned and knocked the knife to the floor away from the intruder. Hoping that she might wake someone, she decided to shout, her voice the only weapon she knew how to use. "Get out, you filthy robber! I am not afraid to use this gun," she lied, "and you had best leave that money where you found it and go!"

"Oh, yeah, who's going to make me?" he replied, nearly as loud. "You're no match for me, missy, and the old man cain't move. I ain't afraid of a scrawny girl like you. You're lying, you don't know how to use that damn thing. Gimme that gun." Unarmed and unafraid of Charlotte, he lunged at her.

The door of the bedroom burst open, and a tall muscular man strode in and grabbed the intruder around the neck. "Miss Charlotte, give me the gun. I'll take over guarding this criminal. Bring me one of Father's belts, and we'll tie his hands behind his back."

She found a belt in a dresser drawer and handed it to him, trying to keep her hand steady. "Help me walk him down to the kitchen. We'll tie him to a chair until I can get the police to come take him away." Mr. Ellerton's son, Joshua, and his young wife had arrived from Denver yesterday to check on him and tend to some business after his spinal cord injury. If the robber had been watching the house, or knew the comings and goings of the family, he might not have known about the latest visitors.

Later, after the night's flurry had died down and the occupants resumed a somewhat normal morning, Charlotte sat upstairs with a snoring Mr. Ellerton, thinking about her actions. She smiled to herself. *My family and friends would be proud of me,* she thought, *I am proud of me. Using one's physical strength is but one way to meet a challenge. I wish I*

242

were bigger and stronger, but my wits came through for me last night. And for Mr. Ellerton.

September 20, 1901

The day had been warm, but autumn was well on its way. The early evening had a new smell of cooler earth and leaves crisping on their edges. Katy checked the dining table, and, feather duster in hand, bustled to the parlor where Edgar was reading the newspaper. "She'll be here any minute, Edgar—aren't you excited?"

"Of course, Katy-Belle," he chuckled, "I'm ever' bit as anxious to see our niece as you are. She's worked with the Ellertons quite a while now. I'm just as curious as you about how she's doing after that robber. But—" he shook the paper at her and peered over the top with a knowing look, "there are other things happening in the world that we need to know about, too. The globe doesn't spin around Charlotte," he winked.

"Of course you're right, Edgar, but her note sounded so different from the others we've had. Sounded to me like she's got a more important reason than just wanting to visit. Maybe a reconciliation? Though I could hardly imagine that she would have time for that, not with her taking care of that old man." Katy's speculations ended as Charlotte knocked twice, their signal, then opened the front door.

"Aunt Katy! Oh, it is *so* good to see you," Charlotte exclaimed, smiling widely. She relaxed into Katy's warm hug, holding it a bit longer than usual. She wanted to remember this sensation.

"Well, dear, what about me? Did you forget you have a doting uncle as well?"

"I was just giving you time to fold the paper, Uncle," Charlotte smiled, stepping into his embrace. "It is so good to be here with you both. I have missed you and this house, and of course your cooking, Aunt Katy. Cook at the Ellertons does an adequate job," she said, rolling her eyes, "but it is nothing compared to your meals. Is it beef stew for supper?"

"Most surely, Charlotte, your favorite," replied Edgar. "How could she fix any different?"

"Come sit down, you two," Katy said. "I'll bring in the stew, and, Edgar, you can ladle it out. Cornbread's done, too, I'll bring it next, then we can eat."

They chatted about Edgar's work at the newspaper and the assassination of President McKinley. Katy wasn't sure about Roosevelt, but Edgar thought he would make a fine president. They waited for Charlotte to reveal her news. She would start when she was ready.

"Well, I know you must be wondering why I wanted to visit tonight." They both nodded. "Overall," she continued, "Mr. Ellerton is doing quite well. He is much stronger now, the skin on his back is almost fully healed, and he has a wheelchair for getting around. We've been working with him on transferring from the bed to the chair, and he is more comfortable moving about now. His son from Denver hired a handyman to make a ramp so that he can easily be outside."

"That's good to hear, Charlotte, I'm sure you've helped them quite a lot. So you'll be taking a new case, then?" Katy tried to jump ahead. "How much longer will you be at the Ellertons'?"

"Just one more week, until the twenty-eighth."

"Then you'll be coming back here to stay with us between cases, is that it?" she questioned. "You know your room is always ready for you, any time."

"I know, Aunt Katy, and I'm so grateful to you both." Charlotte hesitated. "I have a new patient already, two of them at least. Maybe three."

"Whatever does that mean, Charlotte? How can you not know how many people you'll be taking care of?" Edgar asked.

"Well, Uncle, Clara Ellerton, the younger Mrs. Ellerton, is my new patient. You remember both the Ellertons came to help out his father? She is expecting a baby in February and has had some problems with her condition. The doctor thinks she is fine to travel by train back to Denver as long as she goes soon and is looked after on the journey. They want me to be their nurse until after the baby comes. There might be two babies—the doctor wasn't—"

Katy interrupted. "Train to Denver? You're leaving us then?"

"I'll be back, Aunt Katy, as soon as I'm done taking care of Mrs. Ellerton. Who knows, it could be sooner if she has any more trouble. But yes, I'm going to Denver. We leave in a week."

The week flew by. She resigned from the nursing registry and shared her exciting news with Polly and Priscilla. She busied herself with packing and shopping, making sure she had the proper clothing for the Colorado winter. She visited the Ellertons, checking on Clara as well as old Mr. Ellerton, who no longer needed much of her attention.

Two nights before their departure, the elder Mrs. Ellerton invited Katy and Edgar to join the family for dinner as a chance to meet Charlotte's family and say their thanks and farewell properly. The Ellertons had spared no expense to entertain them. The finest linens and crystal, the best wine, and a menu Charlotte had not seen in all the time she'd been in their house. It was a beautiful late September evening, the windows open to a light breeze. Candles flickered everywhere for a softened effect of graciousness and elegance.

In spite of the imminent departure of Joshua, Clara, and Charlotte, Mr. Ellerton had regained his former good spirits, telling the visitors haltingly but clearly about the night of the attempted robbery, amplifying the account of Charlotte's bravery and the intruder's fearsomeness. *The robber grows bigger, taller, and more menacing with every retelling,* Charlotte thought with a tinge of embarrassment, but a tiny bit of pleasure at her elevated status. *Have I ever been so important?*

It was clear to Katy and Edgar that the family thought highly of Charlotte, and she seemed quite fond of them. Joshua Ellerton was a banker every bit as established and well-off as his father. On their walk home,

Katy said, "It's too bad he is married. The young Mr. Ellerton would be perfect for our Charlotte if Stephen is never going to be her husband again. She's a lucky one to have found a wealthy family to work for."

"Who knows," Edgar added, "maybe she will have an easy life while she is out West. Our girl surely deserves it."

Denver

Thursday, October 10, 1901

Dearest Aunt and Uncle,

Finally I have time and energy to write you! I trust my telegram answered any immediate concerns you had for my safety and well-being on this journey. Mr. Ellerton is a most generous employer, and he insisted we wire you as soon as we arrived.

Oh, dear family, I am well and pleased with everything I am seeing and learning. Who could have imagined that I would be able to live in a very different part of our country, a wild place, partially at least? Not I—I never dreamt it! I feel a bit of my old self returning as I am immersed in such new surroundings.

When we arrived at the Ellerton home, we arranged a visit by their physician, Dr. Thudbury, to check over Mrs. Ellerton. She has insisted that I call her Clara, and so I do. She is just two years older than myself, and we could possibly be friends if I were not her nurse. Dr. T. is very pleased with Clara's state and praised my watchful vigilance of her during our journey back to Colorado. His biggest concern is that she may be having twins, for she has gained so much weight and girth for this stage of her pregnancy. She still has nearly half her confinement ahead of her.

Clara and Mr. E. have been wishing for a family for most of their ten-year marriage, but their hopes have been dashed on several occasions. So the arrival of this baby or babies is of the utmost importance to them. I can sense anxiety in every look her gives her. Privately he has confided that he wishes she had never come to Kentucky with him. But she was so insistent to be with him, in the event that his father would take a turn for the worse. And the older Mrs. E. would say almost anything to see her son ... she may have led him to believe that his father was more ill than he was.

Colorado is such a beautiful place, especially this fall. The very bluest of skies and in the distance are the snow-capped Rocky Mountains— yes, snow already! While we have the beautiful maples turning color in Kentucky, here I can look at the hills and mountains covered by aspen trees, shimmering gold against the dark green of the pines. Fall is so short here, the trees seem to change by the minute.

I have had to make some adjustments to the climate, it being very dry here compared with Louisville. We must drink more water, and for a nurse, especially, one must keep the skin moisturized. Clara has introduced me to Vaseline, a petroleum jelly that is good for all sorts of skin-healing issues. Aunt Katy, you should get some, too. I use it on my hands and feet at night, and sometimes my face. The dryness of winter is very hard on skin.

Clara has been well, and frankly, I feel a bit useless. There's not much for me to do to help her. Tomorrow I plan to visit the library to see if I can find a book about pregnancy with twins. Clara has arranged for a local midwife to attend her when the time comes, but the Mr. seems to want Dr. T. In the end I believe Mr. E. will win out, as Clara seems to defer to him on most of the important decisions around here. He does insist, and she complies, that she is now to remain on absolute rest with her feet up.

At this point I am more a companion than a nurse. I look forward to the time when my skills can really be put to use. But while I am here, I am committed to try and learn everything I can about the unique nursing challenges that Colorado presents.

The Ellerton home in Denver is grand, and the "little" room I am given to stay in is twice the size of my room in Louisville, most comfortably appointed. They employ a cook and a maid, and now, a nurse. The home was completed in 1890, the year before their marriage, and they both took an active interest in the design and construction oversight. It is obvious that—

The noises of loud arguing interrupted her writing. Mr. E. and Clara were having words again, and although her bedroom was on the opposite end of the upstairs hall, she could make out the topic clearly. "You are being ridiculous," he shouted, "my full attention is given to you and these babies, our children, that you are carrying!"

"That is simply not true," Clara retorted. "You spend more time talking with her than me, and especially after I have gone to bed. I can hear you. I see the way you look at her, Joshua, and more recently, she has a similar look. She pretends to be my friend, but I know that is because she wants to get next to you. A woman in my condition is no competition for a younger and prettier one."

"Prettier," he sputtered, "Clara, no one is more beautiful or desirable to me than you are. Charlotte cannot hold a candle to you. Your condition is just temporary, my dear, and you must keep the end of your confinement in mind, the family we have always dreamed of—"

Her sobbing stopped his words. "Joshua, this is the family you've always wanted, but now I am not so sure. I am so alone, and I have no idea how I will be as a mother, and a mother of two babies at once? I will never be able to keep after them the way I should."

"We will get you help, my dear, I have already begun to make inquiries."

"Really, Joshua, help? Help like Charlotte? Other women to come into our home and tempt you away from me? I had no idea that you would fall for her charms."

Me!? Charlotte was shocked. *Their argument is about me!* She had heard some arguing before, normal for all married couples, but this was the first time that she could decipher the topic. She was heartsick that Clara thought she was merely pretending. *Mr. E. is very handsome, and most kind, but I would* never *intrude on their relationship or the feelings they have for each other. I know my place.*

The next morning Charlotte left for a brisk walk after breakfast. The day was crisp and cool, with the sky sporting a soft turquoise color. She was invigorated by the mountaintop snow to the west.

What should I do? Confront the issue head on, or wait and see how or if Clara or Mr. E. approaches the topic with me? Having Clara get so upset can't be good for her pregnancy, especially if she is carrying twins.

Charlotte decided that from now on she would have conversations about Clara with both Clara and Mr. E. present, and avoid any time alone with him. She should be more observant of Clara, concerned that she could be falling ill to a more serious mental disorder than the simple ups and downs of pregnancy.

When she returned to the house, all was quiet. She made a cup of tea and picked up the *Rocky Mountain News. Clara can have another half-hour to herself,* Charlotte thought. Inside was an article about the National Jewish Hospital for Consumptives, which had opened its doors in December of 1899. *I wonder if such a place exists in Kentucky?*

The days moved by, too slowly, an opinion shared by both Charlotte and Clara. October's weather had been beautiful, and November was warmer than usual with only a trace of snow. The relationship between the two women continued to be strained, and although Charlotte had kept to her plan, it did nothing to melt Clara's icy attitude. The doctor confirmed that she was indeed carrying twins, and stable. Decorating the house for Christmas was left mainly to Mrs. Flores, the housekeeper, and Charlotte, who looked for anything to occupy her time when she wasn't checking on Clara.

Wednesday, December 18, was Clara's birthday, and in spite of the tensions between them, Mr. E. had decided to stay at home with his wife. Charlotte was pleased to have most of the day to herself and had arranged to visit the consumptives' hospital. She exited the streetcar near Jackson and Colfax and enjoyed the brisk walk, imagining a future with a real purpose. As she approached the hospital, the motto over the entrance captured her attention. "None may enter who can pay—none can pay who enter." *What a legacy,* she thought, *how can they afford to provide this free care?*

Mrs. Berg, a board member, made time to give her a tour. Everywhere Charlotte looked was a sense of kindness, quiet, occasional laughter, and order. It had been years since she had seen her mother up close; now she was surrounded by consumptives. She remembered her mother's last few months, wasting away. She saw her pained expressions again, heard the short breathy words, recalled her paper-thin skin stretched over nothing but bones. Compared to the streets, where the poor lived in crowded, often unsafe and nearly always unclean conditions, this hospital was a refuge of hope and healing.

Charlotte didn't stay long in the presence of so many ill patients, in case she might possibly bring the sickness back to Clara. But the tour of the hospital made her wonder. *What if I stayed in Denver and worked with consumptives, maybe even at this hospital?* Mrs. Berg had acted very kindly towards her and was interested that she was a nurse. She had a relative in Kentucky that spoke highly of Norton Infirmary and nodded approvingly when Charlotte described her training. *Maybe she could help me?*

Since the fire Charlotte had only been able to view life through gray lenses, but since coming to Denver, she'd begun to glimpse occasional spots of color. *I needed this change,* she thought. *I need to make a new life, and now I have a sense of what it might be.* For the first time in nearly two years, she felt a little lightness she had not imagined could be hers again. The pain and sadness she carried about Charlie and the twins and Stephen's change of heart were always just a thought away. She could conjure those bad feelings with no effort. But she had built a walled-off place inside her heart for them and was more able to lock her private griefs away during the day.

A thick letter from Aunt Katy was waiting when she returned. She took it upstairs to her room with a cup of tea, closed the door, and made herself comfortable in the little rocking chair. Holding the letter over her heart, she smiled to herself, though with a little sense of dread. *How will they take my idea to stay in Colorado after Clara's confinement? One thing at a time,* she admonished. *Don't go looking for problems where none exist.*

Inside the letter was another envelope addressed to her, from Stephen. Her heart tripped at the single page from Katy. No real news, just a note that Stephen had sent this to her in Louisville, and she knew that Charlotte would want to read it as soon as possible. Katy signed the note, "… ever hopeful, your loving Aunt Katy." *Hopeful for what?* She knew how much Katy and Edgar both wished for a reconciliation.

Charlotte, his letter began, not "Dear Charlotte" or "My Dear," just her name.

"I hope that you are well. I trust that your Aunt and Uncle are in good health, too, and that they have forwarded this letter to you if you are no longer living with them. I am living in New York now with Marissa, and have set up a surgeon's practice here as part of Bellevue Hospital. We are comfortable in a house near the hospital, and Marissa has rejoined her friends and her life in the arts and literary world. It is an adequate existence and has served my need for a fresh start, absent the ever-present reminders of my prior life.

I release you from all attachment to me or my life, and I wish you no ill will. I do not intend to marry again, as the prospect of trusting another woman and of having more children is most distasteful. Life's circum-stances have taught me that I should only rely on myself and my calling for any sort of happiness.

If you wish to remarry, I will cooperate with whatever is needed, but at the moment, the requirements for divorce are most complicated, and I do not wish those complications for either of us. Infidelity must be proved, therefore perhaps abandonment could be the basis if you want a divorce.

If things change for you, you may contact me at this address, and I will
cooperate in any way I can. I ask that you refrain from using my name.

Stephen

PS. I wish things could have been different.

Although Charlotte had harbored no illusions of a reconciliation, the
complete absence of any affection or fondness struck her again like a cold
and leaden weight, just as she was beginning to see some hope for her life.
She did not rise from her seat. She simply let the tears flow.

National Jewish

March 31, 1902
Denver, Colorado

Clara's baby boys arrived three weeks early, healthy though small. She had been attended during her long labor by Dr. Thudbury and the midwife. Mr. Ellerton was overjoyed with his two infant sons. Clara seemed relieved but unsure about motherhood. Charlotte's presence the last two months had been merely tolerated, and she did her best to keep out of the way, checking on Clara only when necessary.

She was grateful that Clara did not insist on her dismissal before the delivery; it gave her time to set a plan in motion. Mr. Ellerton hired an older woman to help with the babies, and Charlotte said farewell to the Ellertons when the twins were two weeks old. Dr. Thudbury was sure that Clara did not need the constant presence of a nurse any longer. Charlotte was paid well for her time with the Ellertons, and thinking that times ahead might be lean, she had carefully saved her earnings.

Aunt Katy and Uncle Edgar had taken the news well enough, as her letters to them since Christmas gradually revealed her idea to find work in Denver. They knew a separation might come someday but had always hoped she would be closer to Kentucky. But they also respected Charlotte's longing to care for consumptives. Colorado was an ideal location for their niece's dream. Charlotte hoped that Katy and Edgar would visit soon to see her new life for themselves.

Mrs. Berg had helped arrange Charlotte's employment at National Jewish as soon as she was sure she could leave the Ellertons. Fortuitously, one staff vacancy opened, and on Sunday she had moved into the nurses' quarters at the hospital. Although her room was small, she felt cocooned and relieved to be free of any household decisions. She prayed it would give her time and space to heal and get on with her life.

Charlotte had never spent time around Jewish people, and she had wondered if everyone connected with the hospital was Jewish. Mrs. Berg assured her that being Jewish was not required as staff and patients of any faith were welcome. The founding of this hospital was a major initiative of the local Jewish congregation, supported by congregations across the country, thus giving it the designation of "National." Charlotte assumed she would notice some difference in dress or speaking style and was surprised that she didn't see anything unusual other than men wearing the traditional skullcap, called a *yarmulke*. Some men wore one all the time, others only on special occasions.

Monday was a beautiful day, and Charlotte could smell the coming of spring. Despite the morning chill, the sun warmed the damp earth, and crocuses and tulips dotted the hospital grounds. *What will my new life be like, I wonder? Anything is possible!*

Mrs. Charles, the head nurse, was waiting for her. She noted Charlotte's arrival a few minutes early with pleasure. "I am assigning you to the women's ward for now, Mrs. Kolb; it is the easiest place to start." *Mrs. Kolb? That was certainly a surprise, but one I'll have to get used to. I am not going to use Stephen's name.*

"The women have many needs, and they will tell you about them. You can also learn much about their lives and their circumstances." She noticed Charlotte's wrinkled brow. "The men? Well, they are easy enough to care for, don't let yourself be mistaken. But they are less likely to let you know when something is amiss, and they do not easily tell their stories. With the women, you will learn what is important, and you can then apply it to anyone with tuberculosis that you care for."

Mrs. Charles gave her a thorough tour of the hospital, beginning with the men's and women's wards, which were mainly large outdoor sleeping porches. Each bed was on wheels and could be moved indoors when the weather was bad. Patients who were extremely ill or recovering from surgery were housed in a special area. She introduced Charlotte to the cooks in the large kitchen and to the male attendants, who had the strength to carry and move people and beds. Charlotte also saw the operating rooms and noted approvingly that medications were kept in a separate area. A well-supplied laboratory provided space to examine specimens and determine treatments.

After the tour Mrs. Charles left her with Myrna Trimble, the nurse who would orient her. "You may call me Miss Myrna," she said to Charlotte. "And I will call you Miss Charlotte. We call everyone here Miss or Mister with their first name, except for the doctors of course." She rolled her eyes. "They are always Doctor So-and-So. Our patients stay here a long time, some for months, and it helps to create an atmosphere of family for them." Charlotte nodded. "Let's begin with the patients that you and I will be caring for."

They stepped to the porch where every woman was in a bed in the sunshine. Miss Myrna made introductions at each bedside. Most of the patients were pleasant to Charlotte, even though almost all struggled to breathe. Sometimes it was the difficulty of getting in enough good air, so the struggle was on the inhale, and for others it was the effort to expel the bad. The lung tissue itself had lost most of its elasticity.

The last patient she met, Miss Tema Milyavsky, stopped Charlotte cold at the bedside. *Oh! My mother! I have just met my mother all over again!* Miss Tema looked to be the same age as Lorena when she died, with the same hair and eye color. She even carried the same look on her face and fluttery hand movements as she whispered a few words.

Tears filled Charlotte's eyes immediately, and she too had trouble breathing. Her face and neck flushed red. How many times had she tried to conjure up her mother, get one more good look at her, talk with her, hold her hand, give her a hug, say "I love you"? She told herself firmly, *This is NOT my mother, this is my patient,* but the sadness and pleasure she felt at seeing Miss Tema overwhelmed her. "What is wrong, Miss Charlotte?" Myrna asked, noting the change, "Are you all right?"

Charlotte beckoned her away from Miss Tema's hearing and said, "I will be fine, please don't worry. Caring for consumptives is a goal I have long been wanting to meet, and, well—" she blinked back tears, "my mother died from consumption when I was nine, and Miss Tema looks exactly like her. The sight of her caught me unawares."

Myrna nodded at her and squeezed Charlotte's hand. "You have the heart for this work, Miss Charlotte, I can tell. But," she took a breath and looked deeply at Charlotte, "you will need to take care that you keep your perspective. Miss Tema *reminds you* of your mother; she is *not* your mother. Repeat this to yourself often."

Charlotte swallowed. "I know, I know. And thank you."

Myrna continued, "Why don't you spend some time with Miss Tema to discover more about her interesting life, if she is able to talk comfortably. Sit down with her. Take your time. Their words are slow."

After lunch Charlotte returned to the porch to find Miss Tema awake and eager to talk. She was thirty-one years old when she traveled with her brother from New York in the hopes that she could be cured in Denver. She had developed tuberculosis after arriving in New York. She and her family had emigrated from Kiev, Russia, in 1896 to escape the official pogroms of Alexander III against the Jews. She dreamed of being a teacher one day, she loved literature and reading, and had mastered the English language. But the required effort and stamina were beyond her abilities, at least while she was sick.

Miss Tema's parents and two sisters still lived in New York, and she spent much of her time writing voluminous letters. Receiving mail from her family was a highlight, and it was a special occasion when more than one letter appeared in her box. She had a nine-year-old niece who was learning to write and express herself, and Tema took great pleasure in helping her young one.

Myrna is certainly a clever woman, Charlotte thought at the end of the day. *Making me spend more time with Miss Tema so that I could understand the differences between her and my mother helped a great deal. I have come a good way today.*

Woody

Charlotte welcomed her long days. At night she could not help but think of Charlie and Stephen and the twins. When she allowed herself to dwell on them, especially Charlie, whose absence left her still with an inconsolable aching, she could hardly sleep or eat. Peace came only in facing the demands of her new work with something to attend to every minute. She could be busy twenty-four hours straight and still not accomplish everything that needed to be done. Her work provided the solace and absolution she didn't know she longed for.

Charlotte had begun to attend the local Presbyterian church, and she looked forward to her new Sunday ritual. She enjoyed having the afternoon to herself to plan for the week ahead. One summer day she sat down at her desk and tried to begin a letter to Aunt Katy, but after a minute she recognized a sadness and longing that she could easily name after two and a half years. Grief, still grief. The sharpness of it had dulled, but grief was, in its simplest form, still a knife. No words of cheer or interesting news could be coaxed from her pen. She got up from the chair and decided she needed to walk. She craved fresh air and a bigger view than the empty page.

She carried a basket to give her the look of a woman with purpose. She pulled air into her lungs, deeply, and closed her eyes to the sun. The day was warm, not as hot as it could be for June, but she was glad she had on a light cotton dress. For a while, her thoughts kept her company and she had no plan or destination for this time outdoors, just a time to clear her head and ground herself. After a few blocks she decided to turn down a street she had not yet explored and found herself in a modest neighborhood with simple homes and children playing in a few yards.

She noticed a little boy running after his dog. The dog, full of energy and fun, turned suddenly and began chasing the boy, who was giggling with delight. She stood for a moment enjoying the scene. Suddenly the dog chased the boy toward a tree stump, and as the boy looked over his shoulder at the dog, he stumbled on an old root and fell to the stump, hitting his head—hard. He began to wail. Lifting her dress above her ankles, Charlotte rushed over to the boy and knelt at his side. "Are you hurt? Oh my, yes, you are, there's some bleeding here." She found a handkerchief in her basket and pressed it to his head. "Does that hurt you?" she asked.

At that moment a man came out of the house, calling, "Daniel, time to come in—" Seeing the boy on the ground next to a strange woman, he hurried to his side. "What happened?"

Tears running down his face, Daniel exclaimed, "Brownie chased me into this stump, and—and—" Frightened by the quick turn of events and the concerned attention of two towering adults, he began to cry harder.

"There, now, Daniel, it looks like you will be right as rain in no time. And you got this nice young lady to come to your aid. You work fast, young man!" the man said, smiling at Charlotte. "Woodrow Swain, ma'am, I am this boy's uncle."

"Nice to meet you, Mr. Swain," she nodded. "I am Charlotte Kolb. I was out enjoying a nice walk on my day off, and I noticed this young man in need of some help. It looks like a simple small wound, and I agree, he should be fine." She got up to go, brushing off her skirt.

"Miss Kolb, perhaps you'd let us rinse out your handkerchief? And then I am sure Daniel's parents would want you to stay for some cake. We were just getting ready to break into dessert after our big Sunday dinner. Won't you please join us?" By this time Daniel's parents and an older boy had come onto the porch to see what was taking so long. *A family,* Charlotte thought, *a nice healthy family. I think I will join them.*

Over coffee and a tangy lemon cake that Charlotte found most delicious, she learned that Woodrow's family was from Tennessee and that his sister Abigail had married a man who worked with the railroad. His work brought him to Denver, where they had built a home for their three children; James, the older boy, Daniel, and a baby sister, Lucy. Uncle Woody, they called him, had come from Arizona for a long visit to learn more about the railroad business. Woody was a short thin man, not much taller than Charlotte, with dark curly hair and large brown eyes. *Kind eyes,* she thought, *nice manners.*

"And what about you, Miss Kolb, have you always lived in Denver?" asked Abigail.

"Oh my, no, I lived most of my life in Louisville, Kentucky, but I was born in Indiana, near Indianapolis. I have only been in Denver since October—such a fine time to enjoy the beauties of nature here, isn't it? The area has made quite a pull on me. I have always longed to see the West, and last year presented the opportunity to come. Once here, I learned of National Jewish, and it seems I have now found my place working as a nurse with consumptives."

Abigail nodded. "Well, we have a few things in common, Miss Kolb. We are from other parts, too. Our parents, Woody's and mine, raised us near Greenville, Kentucky, and both of us made our way here to the West at different times. David brought me, and the consumption brought Woody." Woody flushed a little as his sister started to tell his story.

He decided to take over. "I came to the Arizona Territory a few years back to take the cure in Tucson at St. Mary's, and I was one of the lucky ones. I have regained my health. I left Tucson for the nearby mountains of Cochise County and have been happy there since. And healthy. I am grateful to have my health back, although I think it is the mountains that have inspired me to work hard and get stronger." He flexed both of his muscular hands absentmindedly.

"The mountains here in Colorado? Well, sure, they are something … there's so many all pushed up together. But those in Cochise County, well, they stand like one huge ring around several valleys, and it is possible to know each of them by name. Here? There's too many to know." He smiled. "I am a simple man with simple tastes. But I surely love my sister's lemon cake. Could I trouble you for more, Abigail?"

She glanced at her brother affectionately. "Anything to put more weight on you, Woody, even a *third* piece, if it hasn't yet disappeared." She rose to get him some more.

Conversation continued amiably around the table, and Charlotte noticed that the two boys were well-behaved, their baby sister less so. When she began fussing, the mood shifted, and Charlotte pushed back from the table and stood. "I think it is time for me to be heading back to the hospital—I live in the nurses' quarters. After church I usually spend Sunday afternoons writing my family and getting things in order for the busy week ahead. And you, Daniel," she said, "It looks as if you have recovered from your encounter with the tree stump. It is likely you will have a bruise on your forehead to show for it, probably some swelling, too, but I imagine you will be fine. Mrs. Johnson, Mr. Johnson, Mr. Swain, thank you all for your hospitality. It has been a delightful visit, and I am pleased to have met you all."

Woody pushed back his chair and stood, too. "Miss Kolb, one moment—don't forget this," he said, handing the handkerchief back to her, damp from a washing. "I would like to walk a bit after my sister's wonderful dessert. May I accompany you to the hospital?" Charlotte flushed. *Oh dear, is this man interested in me? I will have to clear the air so that he knows I am not really a 'Miss' Kolb.*

"Well, um, of course," she replied, at a loss to say more. As they stepped off the front porch, she asked, "What is it like where you live, Mr. Swain? Is your West full of the renegade Indians that we hear so much about?"

He laughed at that. "Full, oh no, Miss Kolb, not full, 'though I have seen my share of Indians in Cochise County. But most of them come into town in pairs, looking to trade. What we have more of, in our part of Arizona, is Mexicans, and of course, some mixed-blood people, too. Hard to tell which is more in someone sometimes, the Mexican or the Indian. Or the Negro blood."

"Are they troublesome? Are you ever afraid?"

"Mostly no, Miss Kolb. Though I am a small man, or maybe because of it, they don't bother me much. And I stay away from skirmishes if I can. Truth is, I feel sorry for their plight. Yes, one reads reports of occasional conflicts, but newspapers are known to blow things out of proportion, jumping high over mouse droppings." She could not suppress a laugh at his expression, and he smiled, happy to get a reaction from this serious woman. For Charlotte, it felt good to laugh.

She learned that he lived in a small place called Ramsey's Canyon, and until recently he had been the postmaster of the little town. Woody worked with some men who were hoping to get into the mining business, but after a few months of "studyin' the numbers and dangers," he decided it was much too risky, for him at least. It was then that his brother-in-law David suggested that he go to work with the railroad. Since Woody had not visited his sister or her family since he left Kentucky, he decided to travel to Denver to see a different part of the country.

"Oh, Colorado is a most beautiful place, it is, but Arizona and the mountains where I live have captured my heart. I must be crazy, but I love the high desert, the warmth ... some call it heat, not me, and of course, the dry climate. And when the monsoons come! You have never seen such big, bold, powerful loud thunderstorms nearly every afternoon in the late summer. And then the torrents stop, and the desert is all fresh-smelling again, just in time for the most beautiful sunsets—orange and purple streaks against delicate shades of blue. A fella' can set his clock by 'em. Mother Nature is a massive power. And the winters, oh, my. Yes, ma'am, we got snow, but not too much in the valleys. The mountains, some. Most years you can still see a little of it left at the tops even in summer before the rains."

Woody painted such a vivid image of southeast Arizona Territory that Charlotte was intrigued. She listened to him talk on about how much he loved it. *I wonder what it would be like to live there? Although I like what I am seeing in Colorado, Arizona could be wonderful too ….*

Suddenly they were at the hospital.

Woody touched her wrist, lightly, and those kind brown eyes looked directly at her. "Miss Kolb, I have really enjoyed our chance meeting this afternoon, and it would be nice to see you again. You said you have Sundays off work. How would it be if we met next week? I would be happy to accompany you to church, and then we could have Sunday dinner at my sister's. You only had a taste of her kitchen skills with that cake, but she's a very good all-around cook, I can attest. I surely have put on weight in the three weeks I have been staying with them."

Charlotte hesitated. *I need to tell him now, it's the best time. Not later. If he has ideas ….* "Mr. Swain, I want to tell you something—" He looked at her quizzically, kindly, and nodded in encouragement. "I don't really want to go into the long story, but the truth is, I am a married woman. My husband and I have chosen to live apart, and so I am not really free to pursue a relationship with a suitor—" She stumbled, not knowing what she should call this, this thing, and thinking, *a piece of lemon cake—well, two pieces— and a brief walk is hardly a courtship. Why did I even start this conversation?*

Woody nodded again. "I see. Well, is there anything in your, um, arrangement with your husband that prevents you from having a man as a friend, not a suitor? Could we spend time as friends, you getting to know me and my family? I'll be returning to Arizona in another month, but they are living here permanently, at least as long as the railroad keeps my brother-in-law in Colorado. What would you think about that?"

"I'm not sure," she said. "Truthfully, I don't know how I feel about that."

"You can always use another friend, can't you? A person can't have too many, they say. And as much as I love Abigail and her family, having another adult to talk to who doesn't know me or my background, it's good for me. I am a quiet man, but I have started to realize how much I like the company of others, women especially."

Charlotte looked at him, eyebrows raised. "I don't really have any friends who are men, so I suppose it would be good for me, too. I don't see the harm in going to church together next week. Your sister won't mind me being a guest again at her table?"

Woody smiled. "I'm sure it will be fine. She's been after me to broaden my circle of … friends. I will send a note to you at the hospital about next Sunday."

She nodded. "Very well, then, I will hope to see you next Sunday. Goodbye, Mr. Swain."

Relapse

October 23, 1902
Denver, Colorado

Denver's summer was a welcome contrast to Louisville's oppressive humidity. The afternoon rains and the "freshing-up of things," as Woody said, left the air clean and surprisingly dry. When storms came up, staff scurried about to get patients' beds under a roof, and those that could appreciate it delighted in the drama unfolding before their eyes—the drama among harried hospital staff as well as the ominous clouds menacing the mountains.

Caring for her patients demanded much from Charlotte, but she grew accustomed to the pace of work. As in her days at Norton she learned when to take a break and rest. The hours were still long ones, rising before dawn, falling into bed after a little supper and sleeping soundly. But she woke more rested, able to put the sadness of her life aside for twelve hours.

She enjoyed the routine and structure of work, and spending weeks with each patient allowed her to get to know them, almost as family, and gave her a deeper sense of purpose. She knew she was important in these people's lives, and they became equally important to her.

Woody had returned to his beloved Arizona in July and, since then, had written four letters to Charlotte. His words were clothed in a surprisingly elegant penmanship. During their time together he seemed a genuinely quiet and homespun sort of person, shy, but always sharp-witted. She had not expected that his letters would be as long, eloquent, or as entertaining as they were. She had reluctantly written back at first, feeling that she didn't have much to say other than the hospital routines and stories about her patients. He was especially curious about Miss Tema and wanted to know more about her life in Russia. They had taken to addressing each other as Miss Charlotte and Mr. Woody.

While she was writing to Woody one September Sunday afternoon, the thought struck her … she had been in Colorado nearly a year now. And it was almost a full year since Stephen had completely removed her from his life. She realized that she hoped he was happy, which seemed like a healing, of sorts. She couldn't say that she was happy, yet, but her routines gave her meaning, and her friendship with Woody gave her a place to understand herself through relating to another.

A month passed before his next letter showed up in her little mail cubby, but she was so tired that evening she didn't have the energy to read it. *It can wait 'til later,* she thought. Two days later she remembered the unopened envelope and set aside some time, with a cup of tea, to enjoy it.

October 15, 1902

> *Dear Miss Charlotte,*
>
> *It has been a beautiful few weeks here with the weather beginning to bring out the shivers and sweaters. It is a time of high and final energy for many of the animals as they seek to locate winter food, or fatten themselves for the long and welcome sleep known as hibernation. Did you know that bears sleep much of the winter, and give birth to their cubs then?*
>
> *Winter is, for me, a time of curious and watchful waiting. Although the weather may be harsh, one can still witness many changes. The fallen and snow-soaked sycamore leaves gradually decompose to nourish the soil from which the trees grow. The brilliant orange hues make their way to the color of earth. The fall here in Ramsey's Canyon is a most delightful time. I believe you would like it too—the aspen trees changing their colors in Colorado is a most wonderful sight, too, according to Abigail.*
>
> *I have some news about my health, Miss Charlotte. I began coughing again and have had a lot of tiredness. The doctor says it is the consumption coming back, that one may never fully rid oneself of it. He thinks it likely that*

the stresses of my railroad work may have brought it back to life. He tells me that I should return to St. Mary's in Tucson and have another try at a cure. This is sorely disappointing to me, I can't deny it. I thought I had found the magic formula. It has been hard for me to tell you this, but I know you, of all people, would understand my mental state.

I will write to you with my new address when I am back at St. Mary's. It may take a while if they do not have room. In the meantime, Miss Charlotte, please keep a kind thought for me.

Woody

She was stunned. He thought he had conquered the disease, and she wanted to believe that more cures were possible. But watching her patients every day she knew that "cure" was not part of the language with consumption. It was more often described as "improved and stable." She decided to pay a visit to Abigail.

"Come in, come in, Charlotte," she said. "We were just wondering how you were getting along. Woody writes us that you two have been corresponding—" She let the sentence drop to see what Charlotte would do, but she simply nodded. Abigail pointed in the direction of the parlor. "Won't you have a seat there by the window? I'll get us some tea—would you like that?"

Again, Charlotte nodded. "Thank you, that would be lovely."

Abigail brought the tray with two appealing slices of spice cake to the cozy parlor, and served them both cups of tea. "It is so nice to see you again. I was hoping that we would be able to continue seeing you even after Woody left for Arizona. Is everything going well with you?"

"I am fine, and, yes, I'm very busy with my work, and feeling more comfortable in my role. I usually know what is expected of me now. We spend a lot of time with our patients, and their progress seems as important to us as if they are family." Abigail nodded. "And you, Abigail, how goes it with you and your family? Are the children well? And your husband?"

272

Abigail launched into tales of the usual domestic occurrences: children with a fall cold, returning to school, a toddler's demands. Just then her blue-eyed, dark-haired little daughter came looking for Mama, a sad and threadbare doll in one hand and the other thumb in her mouth. "Come here, my Lucy, do you remember Miss Kolb? She came to visit us a few times when Uncle Woody was here."

Lucy stepped in close to her mother looking quizzically at Charlotte. Charlotte leaned forward, her eyes meeting the little girl's. "Hello there, Lucy, it's so good to see you again. Does your dolly have a name?"

Lucy looked seriously at Charlotte, thumb still in her mouth, then with her mother's coaxing, reluctantly took it out and whispered, "Betsy. She's asweep."

"Oh, I see," Charlotte said, lowering her voice. "We don't want to wake her, then, do we?"

Lucy shook her head.

"Well, I'll be quiet then. Your mother and I will talk softly. I am so glad I could see you again, and it's very nice to meet Betsy."

As if on cue, Lucy turned around and left the room.

Abigail looked at Charlotte and said, "You have a way with children, Charlotte, you will be a wonderful mother someday."

Before she could even blink, her eyes filled with tears. She shifted her gaze downward and swallowed, trying to stop them.

"Oh my, Charlotte, I can see something I said has upset you—please forgive me! Would you care to talk about it?"

Charlotte shook her head, unable to meet Abigail's inquiring look. "No, not now. Maybe another day …."

Lucy came rushing back in to the room, "Betsy's awake so you can talk loud now. She said it's all right with her."

Charlotte managed a smile and sat up straight. "That's good," she said to Lucy. "And I do want to talk with your mother some more, is that fine with you?" Lucy nodded and left the room again.

"I'm glad you came to see me today, Charlotte. We received a distressing letter from Woody this week."

Charlotte nodded. "Yes. I heard from him, too. He mentioned that his consumption has returned and he needs treatment again. Is that what you are referring to?"

Abigail nodded. "Yes. We were wondering what you thought of him coming here, to Denver, for treatment at your hospital. That way he would have family close, and a friend. Although I know he has many friends in Arizona, we could visit him here as he improved—is that not right? We would feel so much more comfortable, knowing what we do, if he was close to us." She sipped her tea. "But do you think it would be wise for him to travel on the train to get here? It's a several days' journey."

Charlotte thought a moment. "It would be the easier on him, I think, since he would not have to change from one type of conveyance to another. Although several days by train can be tiring, he is already tired, and having the time to do nothing on the train should not be too stressful. Getting him here, with his railroad connections and your husband's, should be fairly easy to arrange. But he might need a private car, and that might not be possible. I'm not sure if trains have rules preventing consumptives from traveling. The real challenge will be finding available space at National Jewish."

Charlotte hoped that she had some influence at the hospital and decided to put her reputation as a dedicated and excellent nurse to the test for Woody. Rather than start with Miss Myrna or Mrs. Charles, she sent a note to Mrs. Berg asking to meet with her.

Charlotte had mulled over the question of her approach and concluded that being direct was best. She decided to argue that Woody's being a patient at National Jewish would be beneficial to them. Woody and his family were railroad people, an important business for Colorado. Woody had already been treated in Arizona and being cared for in Colorado could provide a useful test for relapsed consumptives. Woody's family would take him back the instant he was ready for release … finding discharge placement would not be a problem. And he had already shown the will and discipline to maintain his health after treatment at St. Mary's.

It was not to be.

The hospital was near full and committed to taking in Jewish people and refugees first, Mrs. Berg explained, kindness evident in her large brown eyes. "I have a great respect for what you are trying to accomplish, Mrs. Kolb, and I appreciate the stress Mr. Swain's family must be under. But he has care available very near him in the Tucson area, and the climate, well, it is not as high as our Colorado mountains, but the dry air and warm temperatures are good for consumptives there, too."

Charlotte knew it had been a gamble, glad that she and Abigail had not pinned their hopes on bringing Woody to Denver. Still, it did not prevent them from being downhearted at the news. Charlotte was grateful that she had not written Woody about the possibility of coming to Denver. He was disappointed enough with the return of his sickness.

And then a telegram arrived from Uncle Edgar, rarely good news by that method.

Katy had stroke Wednesday. Very serious. Recovery doubtful. Come home?

Mrs. Berg and the nurses were very understanding, but Charlotte knew that her position at the hospital would soon be filled. It would be hard to find work there again. She wanted to stay in Colorado; she had made an independent life there. Yet, how could she not go? Katy and Edgar were all the family she had. But Louisville, with all its memories?

Home by November 1. Charlotte.

Edgar and Charlotte sat in the little parlor, too tired to do more than stare into the fireplace. Katy's funeral was over, and all the guests had gone. The day was a sad one for both in different ways. Edgar bade farewell to his wife, friend, and partner of more than fifty years. Charlotte's grief was different ... her second mother, the mother of her longings and fulfilled dreams, the one who knew her tragedies and happiness, the one who stood beside her and behind her, always encouraging.

Another grief shadowed her heart. Like her mother Lorena, Charlotte could not save Katy. Charlotte reminded herself that Katy's death was not her failure. She did not know how to prevent the disastrous stroke. Who could know it was coming?

Over the week that Katy had lingered, Edgar and Charlotte talked a lot, much more than in the past. Edgar told Charlotte of his and Katy's early years and their courtship. Charlotte slowly unveiled the intensity of her grief over Charlie and the twins, and of Stephen. Now they were both quiet, waiting for a flame or a spark, anything, to nudge the next topic, the big topic that lay unspoken between them. Edgar plunged in.

"What is next for you, my dear? I assume you'll not be heading back to Denver since you're expecting your position to be filled." Silence. "You know that you are more than welcome to come back here and take up your life where you left it, sort of ...." He drifted off, realizing he was now on eggshells. "I mean, you should be able—"

"I know, Uncle," she smiled at him, "I know. Yes," she sighed, "opportunities exist, but with Aunt Katy gone and all the painful memories here, I cannot stay. I simply cannot." She took a deep breath, not only to steer away from the past, but to consider a new future. "I have been thinking that I might like to explore more of the West. From Woody's letters I have a yearning to see the desert and some of the places that he's described, but, well, I'm not sure. It's an awfully big change, but I don't know what else to do. I do know that I do *not* want to stay in Louisville."

"What would it take for you to be sure, my dear? You know that I would support your decision, no matter what, and you would always have me to come back to if it didn't work out."

"I don't know, Uncle, I suppose I'm just afraid that I couldn't tackle all the decisions about travel and work and life. I don't feel like my usual self—without Aunt Katy. Somehow I think I would feel more alone than ever." She smiled at him sheepishly. "I know, I know I'm not alone with you here, but—"

"—I know, too, Charlotte, I won't always be here either. I'm getting on in years myself. I'm seventy-three next birthday. But—" he winked at her, looking for an instant like the Uncle Edgar she remembered. "I don't feel a day over seventy-two."

He continued. "Along those lines I've been doing some deep thinking myself. Hear me out on this idea, Charlotte. What if I were to come with you, accompany you until you got settled at least? Then I would come back here to Louisville, and … to where Katy is. But to see you properly settled would make me so happy, and if it didn't work out there, well, you might change your mind about Louisville. You could always come back here with me. That is what Katy would have wanted me to do for you."

She looked at him wide-eyed. *The thought had not occurred to me!*

Edgar had more to say. "And, Charlotte my dear, on the other hand, I need a change. With Katy gone, there's nothing to hold me here either except her burial place. And you know, I want to be a part of your life, and not just in letters and maybe, occasional visits. If you must go further, might I come along too?"

The Sun of Tucson

November 1902
Tucson, Arizona Territory

They had settled it in the space of five minutes. Edgar would accompany Charlotte to Tucson. Many details needed to be addressed; arranging for the house to be looked after while Edgar was gone, communicating with Woody, finding a place to stay in Tucson, purchasing train tickets. And, Charlotte knew, she needed to find work.

She had set some money aside, as was always her habit each time she was paid. Edgar and Katy had also saved money for her future. So although she didn't have to work to survive, the deepest part of her needed to work, which was more clear to Charlotte than ever. She was driven to use her skills and knowledge to help sick people. Just where she would find those sick people was the question of the moment.

In his latest letter, Woody urged her to write to Sister Cecelia at St. Mary's Hospital, inquiring about work there. "It seems to me they could always use more help … I see it all around me. They are always talking about expanding the hospital and its services. I will mention you, so your letter won't come as a surprise. Be sure to tell them about your time at the Jewish hospital in Denver."

It was a sunny day, the temperature fifty-five degrees as the Southern Pacific train pulled into the Tucson rail depot, so very different from the Louisville conditions they left in November. Their travel of nearly a week had been tiring, but as the landscape changed from snow-covered and cold to brownish-green, with a little snow still visible on the far-off mountain tops, Charlotte began to feel tinges of excitement. The saguaro cactus, ocotillo, and succulents were plant and tree forms neither she nor Edgar had ever seen except in books. *This is all so new to me!*

Even though he was a patient at St. Mary's, Woody had been doing well enough to write letters and use his prior contacts. Sister Cecelia had a cousin in town, Mrs. Charleston, who ran a reputable boarding house and was willing to rent rooms to Edgar and Charlotte. They were relieved to find Mr. Charleston waiting for them at the depot. The rooms were sparsely furnished with thin quilts and tired bedding, but they were clean. Both their windows faced the Tucson Mountains, a view that delighted Edgar.

The following morning, as they finished breakfast with three other boarders, Charlotte pushed back her chair and started to excuse herself. She was anxious to get to the hospital and see for herself how Woody was faring. Just then Mrs. Charleston came into the room and handed her a small white envelope. "This came for you, Mrs. Kolb. I've held it three or four days until your arrival. I almost forgot to give it to you."

Charlotte was not expecting mail, but she could see that it had not been posted; it must have been carried by hand.

Mrs. Kolb,

Allow me to introduce myself. I am Sister Cecelia, the head matron at St. Mary's. Your friend Woodrow Swain speaks highly of you, anticipating your arrival with much eagerness. He tells me that you are a trained nurse, with excellent experience at the Jewish Hospital in Denver, and that you are looking for work here. I wish that we could use your skills at the hospital, but we have no vacancies, and any one that might become available needs to be filled by one of our own sisters. I imagine this is disappointing. However, I would like to meet you when you come to visit Mr. Swain, and discuss some ideas about where you might be able to find work. Please let someone at the hospital know that I would like to see you, and I will do my best to be available.

Such a kind woman, Charlotte thought as she left their meeting. Sister Cecelia had given her the names and addresses of two doctors who were caring for consumptives. Dr. Craig MacBriar saw people with no means to pay, and he treated mostly Indians and Mexicans with consumption. His financial support, according to Sister Cecelia, came from local donors and church people, gained from occasional talks he gave to interested groups concerned for the welfare of the poor.

Dr. Abraham Nesbitt also had a small practice visiting homebound people, many of them consumptives. His financial footing was much more unstable than Dr. MacBriar's, although neither man's could be described as solid. Charlotte thought both of them were probably doing admirable work, but seeing as she needed to be paid, she decided that she would first contact Dr. MacBriar. Before that, however, she had to see Woody.

She made her way to his bedside. He looked thinner than she remembered from six months ago. But he had color in his cheeks, and those kind brown eyes, seeming bigger than ever in his thin face, sparkled when he saw her coming toward him. She held out her hands in greeting, and his grasp of hers was immediate. "Oh my, Miss Charlotte, so much has happened since we parted. I am so very—" he took a quick breath, "de— glad you're here. Sit down." He was almost panting for breath. "Sit." He pointed to the simple wooden chair between his bed and the next man's. "Sit and tell me how you are. No first, first, Charlotte, just let me gaze on you."

Their smiles spoke loudly in spite of the silence between them. "I have friends who visit, but there's no one like you." And as she sat there, looking at him with warmth and fondness, their hands still grasping each other's, she recognized a comfort and a kinship that she had sorely missed. It felt like coming home. *Being with Woody feels like home.*

She did the talking, and for an hour she told him of Denver and the beginnings of winter there. It had snowed heavily for the two days before leaving to go to Katy. She told him about his sister and family, and of the antics of little Lucy. She talked about Katy and Edgar, unable to hold back tears as she described Katy's last hours and Edgar's heartbroken sobs. She told him of her gratitude that Edgar was with her now, and how much she valued his presence, because his presence was the only thing she had left of Katy.

"There have been so many things to do, you know, Woody, and they have all kept my mind a-jumble just like little children daring me to chase them. But on the travel out here, with things set in motion as much as possible, at last I had the time to ponder the question of *What next?*"

He nodded, smiling at her charm, her pull on him.

She then became serious. "Three nights ago I dreamt that my mother and Katy were sitting on a porch swing together, shelling peas and talking about me. Aunt Katy said to my mother, 'What do you think she'll do now, Lorena? Who will take care of her?' And my mother got up from the swing, peas falling all over the porch, and screamed at her, 'That was YOUR job, Katy!! That's why I let you have her. You failed me, you failed my baby!!'" Charlotte fought back sudden unexpected tears and tried to smile. "I woke up then with this strong, strong sadness that I just couldn't shake. I couldn't take care of either one of them, Woody, but by the grace of God, I *will* certainly take care of myself. I just wish they knew that."

Woody smiled at her again, nodding. "They know that, Charlotte, they know you're a strong one."

Doctor Mac

When she first met Dr. MacBriar, his appearance and thick Scottish accent surprised her; Charlotte had assumed he was born in America. He was a large man in his late fifties, at least six feet tall, she guessed. Thinning, silver-streaked, sandy hair tried to cover his head. He had a ruddy complexion and carried more weight around his middle than he should. His most distinctive feature was white mutton-chop sideburns and beard, the area directly beneath his wide and full lips clean-shaven. Bushy eyebrows perched above kind, yet piercing, blue eyes.

"Aye, it's bonny fine to meet ye. Miss Kolb, is it?"

"Mrs. Kolb," replied Charlotte, "Mrs."

He nodded. "Well, Sister Cecelia told me she was passin' along my name t'ya, and I'm happy to make your acquaintance. Sit down, Miss Kolb, let me move my papers first. It's a wee mess, I know, but I know where ever'thing is, if ye gimme the time t' recall it." She did not correct him.

Charlotte's second surprise was the state of the man's office. It certainly didn't seem to bother or embarrass him to invite a guest in for a chat. She could not see one square inch of his desktop. On the floor at the side of his chair were books stacked at least three feet high, two of them held open by other books laid across their spines. *I couldn't breathe if I had a work space like this!*

He offered her a cup of tea, and she sat, spellbound by both his speech and his story. He told her of his decision to come to America after his infant son died from cholera at one year. Then, before they could move, his wife and a second child, a daughter, died soon afterwards, cholera again. He had always had a fascination with the American West, and he knew it was a place where consumptives sought treatment because of the good air and sunshine. He had heard about St. Mary's from a priest friend of his, and after some time in New York, determined that Tucson would be the place he was meant to be, to heal others and be healed himself.

He saw many patients who needed to be in the hospital, but sometimes a bed was not available. The expansion of St. Mary's, while a laudable goal, took time and money that no one had. It was not at all unusual that some of his patients died from a lack of care. He asked her a few questions about her training. He was looking for an assistant, someone to help his hospitalized patients be released sooner if they could be cared for at home. The assistant would also check on the sickest ones at home who were waiting for a hospital bed.

"I learned about you from Sister Cecelia, and she told me of your experience with consumptives in Denver. I never heard of the hospital, that Jewish one, but from what I have learned, the care there must be very good. What do you think, Miss, er, Mrs. Kolb? Are you interested in this sort of position? I really need some help—my patients are needin' more than I can give. I need you, they need you, and I think that St. Mary's needs you, too. Will ye consider my offer?"

"Dr. MacBriar, what an interesting role! I do think that it would suit me, but as with all big decisions in my life, I want to think it over first. You know that I just arrived in Tucson three days ago? My uncle and I need to find a more permanent place to stay, and I should find out if a nurses' registry or some form of organization exists. That could take a little time. Would it suit you if I gave you my answer within the week?"

Charlotte liked Dr. MacBriar right away and was almost sure she'd agree to work for him. He seemed to be very compassionate—and tactful. She suspected he wanted to ask about her husband when she mentioned her uncle, but he did not. She was impressed by his thoughts about his patients at either end of hospitalization. She wondered, though, about the state of his office and whether she should infer that he was disorganized in his care as well. She hoped not.

Several days later Charlotte and Edgar rented a small, two-bedroom, territorial-style house not far from the hospital or Dr. MacBriar's. She claimed the tiny bedroom at the rear of the house, leaving Edgar the larger. She thought it only fair as he was providing the rent at first, and she needed less space to get around than he with his diminishing eyesight.

The house had been built ten years ago, and the walls were of thick insulating adobe, cool in the summer and heat-retaining in the winter. Their next concern was the availability and preparation of local food. They both knew plenty about soups and stews and beans, and fortunately, enjoyed such simple fare. Mrs. Charleston had recommended a Mexican woman, Consuelo López, who agreed to cook for them and teach them how to cook with unfamiliar ingredients. Along the way she and Edgar would learn some Spanish, and Consuelo some English.

Charlotte did indeed agree to work with Dr. Mac, as he requested she call him. "'Doctor MacBriar' takes up too much time to speak it and is hard for the tongue to get around. You call me Dr. Mac, and I will call you—?"

"Nurse Kolb," she finished for him. If he was going to rely on titles, she wanted a reciprocal one. And addressing her as "Nurse" avoided the uncomfortable issue of her marital status.

At Charlotte's suggestion, they established a daily routine. They would check in with each other at his office to report on yesterday's work. They discussed which patients he wanted her to visit that day, whether to see how they were doing with their home treatment or to get an idea of which hospitalized patients could be discharged soon. In between, she assisted him with patients in the office if he needed.

It took her several days to get used to the outdoor privies and the earthen floors in some of the poorer patients' homes. Often those homes were one room only. She discovered that morning home visits were generally best, feeling that it gave her the most accurate view of a person's circumstances and their ease or difficulty in getting around. After a quick lunch at home with Edgar, she would go to St. Mary's to see Woody, then the hospital patients. When she knew a patient was soon to be discharged, she visited the family, if any, at home, and taught them what they needed to do to continue the patient's recovery.

Most of the time her focus was on cleanliness and hygiene, getting patients out of doors as much as possible. But she quickly learned that good nourishment was a more pressing matter. Bringing Consuelo along on her visits proved indispensable. The first time Consuelo accompanied her, at Sister Cecelia's foresighted suggestion, Charlotte also brought an interpreter. Alberto was one of the local handymen who worked at St. Mary's.

She described her day at supper that evening to Edgar. "First off, Uncle, imagine three people visiting the wife of Mr. Martínez, with the family dog, three puppies, and two goats wandering in and out of their one-room house. Remember, Consuelo is not a small woman in the least. And Alberto? He's twice as tall as her, and he is no small man in the middle either. So we quickly moved out of the tiny room and sat under the shaded ramada in the yard, with chickens scurrying about our feet. I tried to make some notes of unfamiliar words for Alberto to help me translate—but they speak so fast!"

She took a breath. "So now the four of us, in the middle of dogs, goats, and chickens, were sitting on two hard wooden benches in the shade of the ramada. I started by asking Mrs. Martínez if she would be doing the cooking, and if so, did she know about cooking for a person recovering from consumption. I would look at her, but Alberto would be translating, so she would be looking at him. He told me she didn't know a thing. And then he asked me, 'What is consumption, anyway?'"

Edgar put down his spoon and shook his head.

"So then I had to explain it for him so he could tell her. And then? Consuelo got in the middle of the conversation with Alberto, and then Mrs. Martínez, asking questions about consumption and her own dry cough. At the end of all that, I asked Alberto to summarize the conversation about consumption. Amazingly, they all seemed to grasp the important points.

"Finally I got the conversation back again, and then I asked Consuelo, through Alberto, if she knew what was required of a good diet for consumptives. She didn't. So then I told her about high-calorie foods and frequent feedings. Fortunately, with their goats, milk is no problem, but I don't know much about the fat content of goat's milk versus cow's. I have a LOT to learn, Uncle Edgar! Not the least of which is Spanish for health reasons. That visit took us longer than two hours. And that was with lots of fast talking!"

"Hmm," he nodded, and still chuckling, "think of everything you will be learning. And your Aunt Katy would be so proud of you and thrilled with everything you're experiencing."

Charlotte finished, "I'm going to make a list of questions and sentences that will apply to my patients and ask Alberto to translate. Maybe Sister Cecelia has a book of Spanish I can borrow."

The day came in late March when Woody was deemed well enough to be discharged, but not to his cabin in Cochise County. It had not been checked for months, Charlotte argued, and Ramsey's Canyon was too far away. She wanted him in their little Tucson house.

Woody put up weak arguments for returning to his Huachuca Mountains, but Charlotte had planted the seeds of her campaign almost from the moment she and Edgar had arrived in Tucson. If Woody wanted to get out of the hospital sooner, what better arrangement than to be under her care, and with Consuelo's cooking? And with Uncle Edgar as chaperone, what sort of impropriety could there be? And who gave a fig about propriety anyway? She had important work to do among people who only cared about her healing skills. As Edgar knew and Woody was discovering, Charlotte's arguments and persistence were powerful forces.

Meanwhile Edgar had been looking for a larger house that the three could rent, one with at least three bedrooms. Surprisingly, Dr. Mac held the solution. An elderly patient of his had just died, leaving her heirs with an empty house to manage. The wealthy old woman had lived alone in a large four-bedroom home. It was one of the first homes in Tucson to have running water, and a bathroom inside. It was close by, had a central great room, a big covered porch, and an indoor and outdoor kitchen. The distance to Consuelo's house was even shorter. Sitting around the cluttered great room at the end of moving day, Charlotte, Edgar, Woody and helper Doctor Mac pronounced the new location 'perfecto.'

Edgar was thriving in Arizona. The change of pace, a new sense of purpose, and the weather all agreed with him. One evening in late July, as he and Charlotte were sitting on the front porch after a monsoon storm had refreshed the air, he turned to her and declared, "My dear, I am at home here. I am at peace, and I know my place. Oh, yes, I miss my friends in Louisville, and being able to tend Katy's grave. But I can send and receive letters, and Katy would be the first to urge me to claim the West. Louisville is a place of old memories, but this, this Arizona Territory of yours, is life and a future for me. I don't think I will ever go back to Kentucky. I will always have my memories. This place feels like my home now."

"Oh, Uncle," Charlotte exclaimed, jumping up from her rocking chair to hug his shoulders, "I could not be happier! I feared that you would be thinking just the opposite, looking for the first opportunity to leave. But I could see that you were liking it here, and you have been invaluable help to me. Just know that wherever you are is home to me. I am so pleased with the way all the circumstances have aligned themselves."

But it would not be long before those forces would un-align to upset the happy arrangement the three took for granted.

Melancholy

Fall 1903
Tucson, Arizona Territory

At first Charlotte didn't think anything was wrong when she arrived at Dr. Mac's office. He was not at his desk where she usually found him, even when she arrived early. The skies were gray and blustery, and she recalled that November night four years ago and the fire that destroyed her life. To keep the desperate feelings tucked away, she began to busy herself tidying his ever-messy desk. He had recently allowed her to do that for him when he couldn't locate the notes they had just discussed the day before. Charlotte's first thought was to sort them by date, and she scanned the pages for hints of which were more current.

She held old papers in one hand and a pile of newer notes in the other when he stumbled through the door. Normally a well-dressed man, Dr. Mac appeared in rumpled clothing. He was wearing striped pajama tops half-tucked into baggy trousers, suspenders partially holding them up. "Whas goin' on in here?" he bellowed. "Oh," somewhat taken aback, "oh, iss just you." He stopped, tilting his chin down as if to understand what he was seeing. "And what are ye doin' in me office, and wi' me papers, yet?"

Charlotte stood there, mouth open, with no idea what to say. She had been coming to his office for months now, their usual arrangement, and she had never seen him like this. She put the papers down and moved around the desk toward him. Was he having trouble seeing her? She took another step and smelled what she thought was alcohol on his breath. "Dr. Mac, it's me, Nurse Kolb. I'm here for our daily meeting about your patients, remember? And helping to tidy your notes. You asked me to do this for you some weeks ago."

"Damnation, woman, I should be able to remember what I asked of ye, and fussin' wi me papers is never something I would permit! Now get out of here, 'fore I throw you out myself—you're just a wee thing, don't think an old man like me can't still handle that. Get out! Leave now, dammit!!"

She was stunned and remained rooted to the spot, wondering if she should protest. But she knew enough not to aggravate him more, and the business they had with patients could wait another day since nothing was urgent. He might still be drunk. She quietly closed the door and left.

Who can I talk to?

She hesitated to confide in Sister Cecelia if it was a problem with alcohol, but then again, if it was a problem with alcohol, should she not be told about it? Charlotte had never encountered Dr. Mac like this, but maybe he had had similar "spells" before, or then again, maybe it was the very first time something like this had occurred. She decided to focus on what she had observed, his behavior, and not speculate about the cause of it. After all, she wasn't sure about alcohol on his breath, and perhaps it had not been the reason for his behavior. Charlotte did not know much about alcohol.

Sister Cecelia was in her office when Charlotte reached the hospital. After an awkward start, the words tumbled out, and Sister admitted her surprise: she had never known Dr. Mac to be impaired. They developed a plan to observe him over the next few days. Charlotte would check back into the office in the evening, and she would do her usual visits in between. If anything was amiss in the afternoon, Charlotte would then involve Sister Cecelia, who might be able to get Alberto to help.

In the meantime Sister Cecelia would attempt to contact Dr. Nesbitt, and without divulging any details, ask if he could help with some of the more urgent patient care, if required. Charlotte was relieved that she had informed Sister Cecelia, but she felt burdened at the same time. She had taken on a broader role than she wanted. They parted, agreeing to each think about what else might be necessary.

The next morning Dr. Mac was his usual talkative self with no hint that anything was amiss. She didn't know how to open up the conversation, and she found herself sneaking glances to look more closely at his hands or to check on his buttons and fastenings. Everything looked normal.

Two weeks later more of Dr. Mac's problem became apparent. The office entrance from the street offered no protection on this blustery winter morning, rain pelting sideways. She fumbled with her key and discovered that she had no need of it. The door was open. *Did he forget to lock it last night?* she worried. *He has some valuables in the office and medications that some folks would want.* Dr. Mac was always careful about discussing medications in public, and he took pains to make sure the little locked box and record book were also kept beneath the padlocked floorboard.

Although it was dark in the office, she could make out his form slumped across the desk. He was moaning. "Oh, my head, my head! I canna' stand this pain anymore! Is that you, Nurse? Finally! Help me, *please* …. Get my medicine box, I need laudanum drops. They will be faster."

"Dr. Mac, whatever is the matter? Let me look at you. Laudanum? What is wrong?"

"It's my head, my head is splitting, maybe I'm going to have a stroke, or a tumor. The pressure is so great—" He fumbled in his pocket for the keys and gave her the bunch. Immediately he pressed his hands back at the sides of his head, squeezing his eyes shut. "The first key is the black padlock one, you know, the floorboard under the rug. The key to the box is the little one with the dab a red on it. Hurry! This pain may kill me—"

Charlotte quickly brought the little box to the desk, unlocking it with deft precision. She was surprised to see the laudanum was almost two-thirds gone. The last time she had seen the medicine box, the bottle was full. Was it a month ago? She couldn't remember.

"Count the drops for me, Nurse? I'm not seeing things well … the light's unbearable. So glad you came along! Water's back there," he said, pointing to the sideboard that stood against the wall behind his desk. "Pour it half water, and count me out twenty drops."

"Twenty, that's too much, is it not? Dr. Mac, are you sure?"

"Twenty!" he shouted. "I know how much I need!—now!"

In less than ten minutes he began to relax, still draped across the desk top. Charlotte found some blankets in the closet at the back of the office. She made a pallet of sorts on the floor. Before he fell into full slumber from the drug's effect, she helped him get down on the floor, with a rolled blanket under his knees and another folded for a pillow. Then she covered him and got busy making a fire in the wood stove, the office's only heat. For her? A nice cup of tea was exactly what she needed.

But hot tea could not help Charlotte, nor Dr. Mac either, over the next fifteen months. The episodes became more frequent, and his behavior more erratic. In January of 1905, when he was clearheaded, he asked her to stay at the office a while longer after discussing the next day's patients.

"Nurse Kolb, I am feelin' that it's time for us to talk about your future."

"My future, *my* future? What about yours? You are still needing help, I can see that with my own two eyes, and it is undeniable. Some days you are unable to have even the most basic of conversations. Whatever is going on with you? Let us get you some help, another doctor, treatment for you, maybe fewer patients. The amount of laudanum you are taking is too much, and taking it with alcohol is likely to kill you."

"Who said anything about alcohol!? Somethin' will kill me soon, that's for sure, but I know one thing. I miss my Mollie and the wee ones more and more ever' day, and I feel them calling me from the other side. I'm so tired of this pain, and you are more than capable of takin' over the work with these people, with or without a doctor. I dinna' want t' get help. Actually, no treatment can help me now, probably never was one. I'm sure I have a growth in the brain, and since last week I have had more and more trouble with vision. The damned thing must be pressing on my optic nerve."

"Dr. Mac, I find it impossible to believe that you can't get better. We can send you to a doctor who specializes in these things in New York or Pennsylvania. There *must* be someone—"

"—Oh, you think that, do you Missy?" he interrupted. "You think I havna' tried to seek out help for myself? You think I want to go like this? This life here in the Arizona Territory has been a godsend for me, just as my personal life was falling apart. St. Mary's, and the Sisters, and the people here, and—and you, have all been indispensable. You saved me from livin' a life of despair." He stopped for a moment.

"But now I can see the end, with no hope of a cure. I am resigned to go with dignity and be with sweet Mollie and our babes again. Being with them will be a blessing, no, it will give the last days of my life purpose, and something t' look forward to as I depart. I welcome this change, Nurse, and only worry that I may harm someone by my wrong action before I die. *That* would kill me."

They looked at each other knowingly, the truth of his words undeniable.

"What can I do, then, until it is time? If I cannot help you be saved, at least I can help you while you're still here."

"You can help me leave in dignity, Nurse. You can make sure I do no harm. You can ease me way, and be the friend at my side. When I leave," he added.

Charlotte looked at him, unsure of what he was saying or asking, and a coldness crept over her as her suspicions grew. But she could not bring herself to ask more. He spoke more quietly. "And one more thing, Nurse? May I call you by your given name?"

She nodded, swallowing the growing lump in her throat. "Yes, yes, of course," she replied, "please, please call me Charlotte. And I will call you Craig."

When she confided in Woody about Dr. Mac's requests, he had the same questions she did. "Can you take care of his patients by yourself,

Charlotte? You are not a doctor. And what does he want you to do for him? Making sure that he doesn't cause harm to patients … isn't that a doctor's judgement to make? How can you, as a nurse, determine that?"

She explained that over the time she had worked with him, they had developed plans for how certain types of patients should be treated. They called those plans "protocols." Most of the care they were providing did not involve medications or surgery. In fact, most of what they were doing was monitoring the effect of the climate, and the rest, nutrition and exercise. He had taught her the signs to look for that should cause concern, as well as what to do about them. And the truth was, their patients were more than grateful for the attention that Dr. Mac and Nurse Kolb gave them. They would dare not complain, and to whom could they complain?

Charlotte, too, worried about these things. Patients might not complain, but what about a disgruntled doctor who felt that his reputation was being challenged? She had heard stories of physicians getting up in arms because someone's care of a patient went against accepted medical practice. She was confident in her own skills, but she had no real allies to stand beside her. Dr. Mac's support would not be there much longer. But an official medical board did not exist in 1900s Arizona Territory.

Uncle Edgar had already gone to bed, and it was late. Charlotte and Woody held mugs of chamomile tea, his favorite at the end of the day. Charlotte knew that a cup could help bring on relaxation and reduce the day's stresses. She sipped thoughtfully. "The things you bring up, Woody, are all good questions, but the one thing he said that bothers me most was what did he mean by 'helping him leave in dignity?'"

"You didn't ask him?"

She shook her head.

"Why not, Charlotte? You are usually so keen on clarifying things that could be vague or misinterpreted. It is not like you to leave that to question."

"I don't know why, Woody. I suppose it took me by surprise and caught me off guard. I didn't know how to answer, and so I guess I just let it pass. I wasn't ready to hear him say something like that."

"Like what, Charlotte? What do you think he was saying?"

"I think he was telling me he wanted me to help him take his own life, help him die. Isn't that what you think of when someone uses those words? They don't want to suffer the indignities of not being able to control how death takes them?"

Woody studied her face and then nodded his head slowly, looking at Charlotte with understanding. "What are you going to do?"

"I don't know. I mean, if a person is intent on taking their own life, and I can see the reasoning behind it, even then I could not give the drug, or shoot the gun, or suffocate them with a pillow. As a nurse, my training directs that my first duty is one of compassion for what my patient is experiencing. But if I cannot agree with why they want to take their life, should I not argue against it and present hope and help? Would that not be more compassionate than helping them suffer an unnecessary death? Arguing against it would be the very opposite of giving in to death. Nurses encourage people to live, Woody, doctors, too."

"But Charlotte, you would have to be sure a treatment or a cure was available. From what you have told me Dr. Mac said, none is assured."

"It is impossible to know that, Woody, under the circumstances." They sat there in silence for several more minutes.

"Charlotte," Woody said finally, "I see that you are confused about the right thing to do. You can argue both sides strongly in your head. But that is not helping you right now. It is late, and I am weary. Let me leave you with this to ponder on. Is uncertainty not the way of life? Even if you knew a treatment was available for Dr. Mac, who is to say that it would work? Or that he would take it. Not much in healing is fully certain. Some people respond, some don't."

She looked at him with tears in her eyes as he continued. "You try to do the best that you can for a patient, but in the end what you do for another is based on what you know at the moment, the person's condition, your skill, the ability of the body to fight the disease, the will of the patient. So many factors—and they can all easily change. Who knows, could it not also depend on the alignment of the stars? Or how you hold your mouth while thinking? The point is, Charlotte, life does not give up its secrets easily. You do your best. That is all that can be done. You do your best."

She looked at him and nodded almost imperceptibly.

"And Charlotte, you should go to bed now. I can see how this situation is draining you." Woody stood and reached for her empty mug, and made sure the fireplace was secure for the night. He picked up one kerosene lamp, then turned to look at her once more.

"Thank you, Woody. Your counsel is wise and you are such a good friend to me. I am so grateful."

"That's good to know, Charlotte, but I think that I am the grateful one. Good night, my dear."

Charlotte pretended not to hear the "my dear." She continued to stare at her hands in her lap and gave him a simple nod. "I'll see you in the morning."

March 27, 1905

She opened the office door and was somewhat surprised to find that Craig wasn't there, ready to begin their work. He had seemed chipper and in better health on Friday. Instead of Craig, she found an envelope with her name on the outside. *He must have left it over the weekend.* Ten short words, "Please come to my house. Find me in the bedroom." Charlotte felt a coldness grip her from throat to stomach, and she fought the urge to vomit. *Is today the day? Will I find him dead?*

She looked around and noticed a general sense of tidiness, most unusual for this office and his desk. And then she saw the rug moved away from the hiding place under the floor. Her heart pounded so loudly she could hear the blood swooshing in her ears. Her face burned. *Oh, God, no, not now. I am not ready*—She needed to get to him as quickly as she could.

She found Craig fully dressed except his shoes, lying on top of the bed. She watched his chest rise and fall, shallowly, and his eyes were closed. He opened them when she stepped into the room, and gave her a slight smile. She noticed the bottle of laudanum on the bedside table. He held a glass of water weakly in his hand. With his free hand he patted the bed, and she sat down next to him. He took two deep breaths making an effort to gather his strength.

"Charlotte, I know what I asked of ye was too harsh for such a gentle nurse, and so I made the final glass myself. I finally realized that I just dinna want t' be alone, and I knew ye would understand, and be willing to stay wi' me. You are strong. I dinna' have much breath left for talking, I just want t' sleep and wake up wi' Mollie. Here is a letter for ye. And Charlotte, they will be coming for my body in the early afternoon. Be gone then." He indicated a thick envelope the glass of water had been resting on, and began to raise the glass to his mouth.

"Oh, Craig, please, please, just a minute, just one more minute, and then I'll let you … go. I need to tell you how much I have valued our relationship and the kindness you showed me. You took me in over two years ago, trusting that I could do the work. And your encouragement and teaching helped build my confidence. I don't know how it will be without you and your vision for these poor people. I am sure that I will be fine, well, I hope I will be fine, but you need to know that I will also be grieving you, mourning and remembering. And yes, smiling, too." She fished in her pocket for a handkerchief to blot the tears that filled her eyes.

"I will think of you and your Mollie fondly, and I will be grateful that you will have no more pain, no pain in your head, your body, or your heart. Thank you, Craig, for what you have been for me … teacher, colleague, and friend. I promise I will stay here with you. Sleep now."

Tears tracked slowly down his face as she spoke. When he could tell that she was finished, he shakily drank from the glass and handed it back to her.

She took both his hands and held them firmly for a long time, then switched to just one gentle handhold as his breathing slowed. Before his final breath, she leaned forward to kiss his cheek, tears clouding her vision.

"I love you, Craig," she whispered, *"Vaya con Dios."*

A Gift

How Charlotte made her way home she couldn't say, but she knew she could not see patients that afternoon. Craig had already arranged for the removal of his body and burial in the town cemetery. Nothing was left for her to do for him now. When she opened the door to their house, the house Craig had made possible for them, Uncle Edgar and Woody looked up from the kitchen table, surprised.

"Charlotte, it's early for—" said Woody, who then stopped, her face and posture saying everything. He scooted the chair back from the table and rose to meet her, wrapping her in his arms. "Dr. Mac?" he asked softly into her hair. "His time?"

She nodded, unable to speak. "I'm so sorry, Charlotte. You lost a good friend."

They stood like this for a time before she pulled away, looking at Uncle Edgar. "I need to be by myself now, I hope you both understand."

An hour later she came back into the sitting area holding Craig's letter. "You must read this," she declared to Woody, Edgar having gone out to tend the garden. "I can't believe it. Tell me what you think it says."

Woody read the letter once, then a second time more slowly. He looked at Charlotte with a smile at the corner of his mouth. "It means that you have no worries about money, Charlotte. Your friend Dr. Mac had some wealth that was not apparent, and he left much of it to you in the tending of patients with consumption. Do you know this lawyer he writes of?" She shook her head.

John Barillo, Esquire, a solidly built gruff man nearing fifty, sat behind his massive desk and looked squarely at Charlotte, seated across from him. "Well, Mrs. Kolb, you have obviously made a big impression on Dr. Mac since you've been here. None of us in the area, including Sister Cecelia, knew that he had such family money. Some of us wondered how he could afford to treat so many poor people for nothing, but nobody ever asked. I suppose we were just glad those people were not our problem. We assumed he was using his prior earnings, and that the lack of funds would catch up with him sooner or later. I saw how he lived. Modest, simple, no extras to speak of." He shook his head. "Not a clue, we didn't have a clue."

He continued. "News of his death was not a surprise to me. At the end of February, he asked me to make his will and said he reckoned he had a month or so to live. I always wondered how doctors could be so specific about how long people had. Seemed at peace with it. You were a big part of him being so calm about it all."

Charlotte sat very still, her pulse quickening. *Does he know the plan of Craig's end? And that I knew about it?* She wondered. *Is this illegal? Could I be arrested?*

Mr. Barillo leaned across the desk and looked at her conspiratorially. "I can't help but wonder if the good doctor hastened his own demise, or if someone helped him. Someone who might benefit from his grand gesture?" She could feel her face redden, but she did not offer any response. "If he had a life insurance policy that was providing the money, and if suicide was suspected, that could be a real problem for a beneficiary." Seeing no reaction from Charlotte, he leaned back. "But," he sighed, "since this is a case of family money passing through, no one has grounds to investigate."

Spring made its way into summer, then into the season of monsoon rains. The mornings started out blue-skied and cloudless, but more humid than May and June. The humidity had a dampening effect on the temperature, which Charlotte liked after the higher heat of the desert summer. Then clouds would begin to gather, building powerful white thunderheads across the sky, graying into the afternoon. A flash of lightning or clap of thunder would announce the change. One could smell the rain coming, and the wind that might have been negligible in the morning picked up and cooled the air.

And then the rain would begin in earnest, big solo splats at first, then a torrent, as if many-galloned buckets of water were released all at once. The downpour might last half an hour, filling arroyos and creek beds, flooding the streets. And then, just as quickly as it had begun, clouds moved and rain stopped, leaving the area renewed. Charlotte had lived in Tucson for three monsoon seasons now, and she fully understood Woody's passion for this season in this part of the country.

Craig had also left money to St. Mary's Hospital. The board began fleshing out dreams for an addition that had been put on hold. Charlotte was busy, too, with her plans for a clinic that would be tied to the hospital, but independently managed by her. She needed to recruit a physician just for the clinic, and in early September she received a response from an advertisement she had put in several large newspapers. Doctor Lyda White, from Chicago, was interested in the position and wanted to travel west. Dr. White was quite familiar with tuberculosis, especially rampant in the crowded poorer parts of the city, and she hoped to be part of the sanitarium movement so she could add her own efforts to the search for a cure. She had family in Silver City, New Mexico, that she could more easily visit.

Charlotte sought the advice of Sister Cecelia and Dr. Nesbitt about hiring Dr. White. There had not been a woman doctor in the area before, nor a clinic managed by a nurse for that matter. Would that be too much change for Tucson and St. Mary's?

Some of the more established doctors, especially Dr. Lance and Dr. Simplot, thought she should search for a "real" doctor, one who was a man and wouldn't be swayed by "the high emotionality of the female mind." *Hogwash,* Charlotte thought to herself as she listened to them offer their opinions. She was glad that the structure of Craig's gift made it clear that the administration of the clinic was hers to fully operate. In the end she decided that Dr. White would be a good fit, and two women working together side by side would be a wonderful example. Later she wondered why she had worried so much about the hospital and the city. It was the patients she really cared about.

October 17, 1905

On a warmer than average Tuesday, Uncle Edgar was fretting about planting his winter garden, afraid it could be too late. "This is the perfect day for it," he declared. "The weather should be cooling soon, and the conditions are just right for my stiff knees." He wanted to try two new varieties of lettuce and put in broccoli again.

Charlotte smiled as he headed to the back door. "I'll be home in a few hours," she said. "Dr. White and I are reviewing the clinic setup, and going over plans for how we are going to bring patients in. I may go see Sister Cecelia, too, depending on the time. But definitely before supper. What are we having, Uncle?"

"It depends on what Woody brings in from the market, but I thought we would have the posole I made two days ago, with some fresh cornbread and greens dressed the way you like them."

"Wonderful as always, Uncle. I'll be hungry for that, I'm sure. You have become a superb cook, and Woody and I are lucky to have you!" Edgar raised one eyebrow, and smiled back at his niece.

Charlotte could not have guessed that words spoken about a menu would be the last ones she would ever hear from Edgar. When he returned from his errands, Woody found Edgar outside, flat on his back, dead. Edgar's face was frozen in a macabre mask of pain, his hand clutched at his sternum, as if he had grabbed at his throat. At first Woody thought it was a heart attack, or maybe a stroke, that felled Edgar. But as he looked at the rest of the body, he noticed Edgar's left lower leg swollen to at least twice its size, stretching the fabric of his trousers like a sausage.

Woody cut the pants to above the knee and saw unmistakable fang marks and bruising. Snake bite. He looked around for the culprit but could not find one. He knew of at least one rattlesnake species, the Western Diamondback, that was still common in town and could have been responsible. Edgar was familiar with rattlers as they all knew to keep an eye out for them. How cruel it was that one simple act of diverted attention could make the difference between living and dying.

Woody's heart ached for Charlotte.

Blooms

Late fall into winter was a bleak season, and Woody's efforts failed to draw Charlotte out of her sadness. She kept telling him to "give it time, Woody, I will get better, I know myself." Work occupied her during the day and she enjoyed the time with Dr. White. But she dreaded coming home now, finding only Woody. She was grateful he was there, such a good friend. But she missed Edgar deeply, his supportive kind words and twinkling eyes, his obvious love for her. The history they shared.

When she thought about her new status without any family, she chided herself. *You are nearly thirty-one,* she thought, *and much too old to be feeling like an orphan. Look how many years you had with Katy and Edgar. Stop your moping around.* But the effect of her self-talk was short-lived, and in minutes the vacuum of sadness could pull her down again. When she felt like this, the losses of her life piled higher, weighing her down with memories of her parents, Stephen, Charlie and the twins, Katy, Dr. Mac, and now Edgar. Woody was all that remained of her family.

It was a Sunday morning, and Woody had scrambled eggs and cooked bacon. Since Edgar's death, Woody had taken over most of the cooking. Occasionally Charlotte made a meal, but she had much less experience and interest than Woody. They sat at the little table, and when she reached for another piece of toast to shuttle the berry jam, Woody put his hand on her wrist.

"Charlotte, we need to talk … I mean, I need to talk—to tell you what's been on my mind. I can't keep this inside any longer." She opened her mouth to speak, to say something, but he continued. "Go ahead, sweeten your bread, I didn't mean to stop you from that. Edgar's jam is too good to postpone." He smiled.

She broke off a piece of toast and spread the jam, looking at him quizzically. She nodded at him to go on. "I'm listening, Woody."

"Charlotte, there's no easy way to build up to this." He looked down at his hands, and back at her, at her green eyes, earnestly. "We have known each other over three years now, and you must know that I grow fonder of you every day. I have mentioned you in letters to my family, and they know how much I admire you. I care about your welfare, and I cannot imagine my life without you in it, us under the same roof. I have seen you under difficult circumstances, as well as times when things were going well. You have taken good watch over me, and I know that you have my welfare in your heart."

He paused. Swallowed hard.

"I suppose what I am saying, Charlotte, is that I love you, and I think we should marry. Now the two of us are alone here in this house, with Edgar gone. Well, it seems rather like we are already a married couple … in most respects, that is, one without a chaperone now. I know I don't have much to offer you. I would like to go back to work, and I feel strong enough to do that, but here in Tucson, not back at Ramsey's Canyon. We would have a few things to take care of, but first, Charlotte, the most important answer I need is this. Do you, or rather, could you, love me?"

She sat there in silence, trying hard to collect her thoughts. She looked back into his pleading brown eyes, *beautiful eyes,* she thought. "Woody, you have taken me entirely by surprise. Yes, I have feelings for you, and the truth is, I would like to be married again. I would like to have more—" she stopped herself. Woody only knew about "a husband." He did not know the story of Stephen and the twins, the fire, and, Charlie. It was time to tell him.

She stared off over his shoulder, eggs untouched. "I have something I must tell you, Woody, I can't keep it back any longer either. You know that

I am still married. My husband, Stephen Fields, is a doctor, and he lives in New York with his sister Marissa, last I knew. We parted painfully, each of us blaming the other for …." She swallowed as tears filled her eyes. "… for—" she exhaled, "—for the tragic house fire that took the lives of his six-year-old twins, and our sweet baby Charlie."

Woody inhaled a breath of surprise, and Charlotte kept talking, afraid to stop, afraid to continue.

"He was just seven months old when the fire—" She stopped, unable to finish the sentence. They sat in silence. Charlotte shifted and sat up straighter. "Any feelings I had for Stephen are long gone, all except sadness for what could have been, and terrible regret." Tears began to trail down her cheeks and she made no effort to dry them.

She talked of her life before the fire. She told him the details of the fire and its aftermath, and of Stephen's last letter releasing her from any ties to him. Although they were still legally married, she had no inclination to pursue a divorce. It would be too difficult, and costly. "The sadness I feel now about Edgar is simply heaped upon my already deadened spirit and the accumulation of all the painful goodbyes in my life."

Woody let her words hang in the air before he spoke. "Come sit here, Charlotte, and let me hold you. I cannot imagine—" She moved to his welcome embrace as he stroked her hair and gently massaged her back. "You were saying that you would like to marry again, and to have more … children? Is that it? You would like to have a family?"

She nodded, tears falling freely again. "Yes, Woody, I would. I really would. My life with little Charlie was just beginning, and it was a glorious time for me." She stopped to wipe more tears away. "But now, with my work, work that I love, I don't know if I have it in me to be nurse and mother at the same time. And wife." She pulled back to look at him.

"Charlotte, since Dr. Mac's gift has taken away any worries about money, plus the small inheritance from your uncle, let's think about this. What if we marry and have children, and what if I can be the parent taking care of our little ones while you work? I know that is not the way it is normally done, but we don't have to do things the normal way, do we?"

Stephen hinted to me that we could have someone look after the children while I worked, but he didn't mean it. Could life be different with Woody? Can I trust that he means what he says? That I can really have a family and a career?

She looked at him in surprise. "I had no idea that you wanted a family, too, Woody. I thought you were quite content to live on as a single man. I know you dote on your sister's children, but it didn't occur to me that—" Those kind brown eyes twinkled.

"There's a lot that you have yet to learn about me, Charlotte."

Weeks passed, and Charlotte began to see another side of Woody. He could be gentle as well as intense when she let herself be kissed, which happened more and more frequently. She had never wondered what kind of lover he might be, but as she began to look at him through new eyes, she noticed the way he took care of his hands, and the effort he made to keep his thick hair combed. She began to wonder more about his hands and what they might feel like under her clothes. After their conversation about marriage, they had both begun to take liberties with each other.

Though they slept separately, they embraced on seeing each other in the morning and before bed. They spent more time kissing. At the end of the day when Charlotte returned home, they developed the ritual of a cup of tea after supper, holding hands and talking about their days. Each said "I love you" regularly to the other.

In February, Charlotte announced that she was ready to write Stephen about a divorce, as well as talk to Mr. Barillo about the process. Woody was thrilled. More than ever now he wanted to be married to Charlotte, and both of them struggled to resist the intimacies each longed for. He worried that the neighbors and Charlotte's colleagues would gossip and he didn't want that stain on their relationship.

Charlotte had just finished writing the letter to Stephen when Woody brought in the day's mail. "Letter for you from New York, my dear," he said flourishing a thick white envelope. "I wonder what this could be," he asked, one eyebrow raised, a feature of his that she found particularly attractive. Noting that the return address said "Fields," Woody assumed it was from Charlotte's husband. And as he handed it to her, he said, "I hope he doesn't want to reconcile with you."

That thought had not occurred to Charlotte, and her heart thudded. Just when she felt strong enough to overcome the hurdle of asking Stephen for a divorce, she could not possibly imagine having any kind of a life with him again. "It's probably news," she said, "about a move, or even about Marissa." She held the fat envelope in her hand for a moment, then tore it open.

Inside she found two letters, one addressed just "to Charlotte" in Stephen's handwriting, the other to "Mrs. Stephen Fields." She opened Stephen's letter first. She quickly scanned the two pages to get the gist of the message.

Charlotte was stunned and had to read it a second time.

Stephen wanted a divorce, a divorce he said, in order to marry Celeste, the pianist. *That woman obviously continued to seek after him and finally got what she wanted!*

She felt her face flush, and her heart began to thud again in her chest. On the surface this was welcome news, but she couldn't believe that Celeste had been in the background all those years. She began to wonder about Stephen's true affections for her after all. *Maybe I was really just a convenient young woman to look after his children. What was it Celeste had called me? A 'sweet thing'?*

Woody had been sitting quietly by, watching Charlotte read the first letter. He could hold back no longer. "What is it, Charlotte?" he asked, "Is it good news? Is everything all right?"

She took a deep breath and then worked to steady her face. "Yes, Woody, everything is just fine. One of our big obstacles has just been solved without our having to do anything about it. That letter I just wrote to him? I can tear it up." His face relaxed and she continued. "Stephen wants a divorce, and he has included the papers for me to sign. This must be them," she said, opening up the bulky letter.

The first page was from his attorney, and the second and third pages had the terms of the divorce with places for her signature. She read the attorney's letter thoughtfully, and tears began to well in her eyes. "Abandonment, Woody," she muttered, "he is accusing me of abandonment." She had expected something like irreconcilable differences, the popular term of the day, or even loss of marital consort. But abandonment, and on top of the news about Celeste? He was accusing *her* of abandoning the children, abandoning *him*? How could she live with that? Stephen had wanted no part of her, could not imagine living with her, especially after "what she had done." *He was the one who abandoned me! Not the other way around!*

Then, as clearly as if she had been standing behind her, Charlotte heard Aunt Katy's voice. "Go forward, Charlotte. Go forward. What's past is done. You cannot change Stephen's mind, only how you react to the situation. This is still, underneath it all, a gift for you. You are free to marry Woody. You are free to have your family."

May 6, 1906

As she pulled the dress over her head, Charlotte noticed an unmistakable tingling in her breasts. She felt it first, and seconds later her thoughts caught up with the familiar sensation from years ago. *Could I be pregnant?* She and Woody had first made love in March, when they knew the divorce was imminent. They had tried to avoid pregnancy, but the methods of the time were not foolproof. They were waiting for a time when Charlotte was less busy with work to plan a wedding. But that day had not come; she and Dr. White were busier than ever. Charlotte decided to keep her suspicions to herself a little longer. She might not be pregnant, and that news could disappoint Woody.

But as the days wore on, other signs became obvious: the morning sickness, and unusual tiredness, even for Charlotte who was used to having hectic days. She gave Woody the news one morning after a bout of vomiting.

"Really?" he asked, incredulous. "Are you sure?" She nodded, grinning at him in spite of the lingering nausea. He picked her up even though they were both the same size and swung her around, crowing, "I'm going to be a father, Charlotte, I'm so happy! A father! Me! We are going to be a family!"

They guessed that the baby would come near the end of December and decided to marry as soon as possible before her condition was obvious. They felt it was important, after all, to consider the Sisters, and others who might gossip. Woody sent a letter to his family announcing their impending marriage. He did not mention the baby as that message would come later. They were thrilled to learn the news, though his mother was concerned about the effect on his health and his stamina.

Their baby girl arrived on December 27, the exact date Woody had predicted, a little over seven months since their wedding. "Let people count," he told Charlotte. "You and I are the only ones who matter. And our little one, of course." But Charlotte had already learned a very important lesson—that she was valued for her work and her knowledge and compassion. They were worth much more than others' opinions of her and whether or not she and Woody conformed to the norms of the day.

The baby was small at five and a half pounds, but perfectly healthy. After some experimentation they created the name Katarena Sue for their three mothers; Lorena, Katy and Suzanne. "What a mouthful of syllables for such a tiny babe," their friends declared.

Woody and Charlotte couldn't care less. Their tiny daughter brought them immeasurable joy, and as he had promised, Woody was more attentive and helpful as a parent than Charlotte had imagined or wished for. All her hopes were justified.

Partnership

1907
Tucson, Arizona Territory

Charlotte fell into a satisfying and respectful working relationship with Lyda White. Friendship followed. During the last weeks of her pregnancy, Charlotte needed more flexibility in her schedule and frequently asked for modifications. Lyda agreed to them without question. Being practical women dismissive of formality, they used first names. Lyda valued Charlotte's understanding of the way that people lived their lives, and what needed to be adjusted to achieve the best health possible. Charlotte appreciated Lyda's deep gift for understanding and applying the science of medicine and illness.

In 1906 it had just been announced that an Austrian, Dr. Robert Koch, the man who identified the tubercle bacillus as the cause of consumption in 1882, was awarded a Nobel Prize. The resulting infection, tuberculosis, could be spread by contact and frequent exposure to an infected person's cough or spit. Scientists conducted many experiments in search of a cure. Tuberculosis was a leading cause of death in America, as well as much of the known world. International conferences were organized to report on scientific findings. Lyda shared the journals she subscribed to with Charlotte, and answered her questions about some of the more complicated research processes and results. Although she knew that Charlotte was intelligent, she was surprised at her easy grasp of many of the finer details.

June, 1907

Charlotte approached Lyda with an idea one morning. "I know we have been keeping records on our tubercular patients, and I have been wondering something. What if we wrote down the same information on every patient at the same interval, then compared the results? Your journal said that scientists hope the development of a medication won't be far off. But since we don't have that luxury yet, maybe we should study the effect of all the things we do know about, such as exposure to fresh air, diet, sleep patterns, rest and exercise. Maybe we would discover other helpful actions. What do you think?"

"Wonderful idea, Charlotte! Then when we have new treatments, we can compare those new results to the best that we know now. Will a new medicine really make any difference? We have already heard about people using iodine and mustard plasters, and all kinds of mechanical experiments on the lungs. Who is to say that a new approach or medicine would be any better? All that is reported now is deaths from tuberculosis, and so many things can influence that."

"Exactly," nodded Charlotte. "That's exactly what I was thinking. And we could add some sort of note about their overall health status at the beginning of the time when we see them, and then compare it at certain intervals. Certainly not every visit, but how would every six months be? That should be enough time to see progress."

Lyda smiled. "Charlotte, you're as sharp as a pin; you would make a wonderful physician!"

Charlotte set to work looking through the notes on their patients and created a form to record each person's results at the same intervals. How many hours of rest they got on average each night; did they nap during the day; how would they rate their energy level on a scale; whether they ate lightly, moderately, or heavily; did their diet contain milk, cheese, eggs, fish, or meat, and how much? How much exercise did they get each day and what type? How much time did they spend out of doors in fresh air?

She began to notice that the very process of talking with their patients about keeping track of their progress resulted in subtle changes in many. Some became more interested in improving their diets and exercise just to please Charlotte and Lyda. She had never thought about collecting information as a form of treatment.

"Woody," she said late one night over their tea, "I have gained a new level of interest and excitement about my work that I haven't had for quite a while." He smiled and took her hand, squeezing it gently. "That's wonderful, Charlotte. I can see a new spark about you too since little Kat arrived, but I thought it was all about me," he winked. "Or perhaps the baby. She surely does take a lot of care, doesn't she?"

"Yes, Woody, she does. All babies require that, I think. You know that I am beyond grateful that you are willing to look after her so much, more than most fathers would today."

"It is no sacrifice, Charlotte, at all. Willing, you ask? I *want* to do this. I would not want to miss the changes I see in her every day." She smiled wanly, remembering all the little milestones that had thrilled her so about Charlie. He continued. "I am just sorry that you don't have the same chances as I do."

Again she nodded. "I know, Woody, and sometimes I feel the same. But the delight that you show in telling me all about her development every day makes me so happy. And I get to see those changes on the days I am not working. It is all for the good, and I am the luckiest woman in Tucson."

"Don't you mean the world?" he chuckled.

"Maybe," she smiled, "that might be the right word. Let's see if you can convince me of that tonight—" as she rose to turn down the lamp and lead him to bed.

Hitting Stride

1907 to 1912
Tucson, Arizona Territory
November 15, 1907

Lyda burst through the door as Charlotte was readying the items they would need for the day's clinic; clean thermometers, alcohol, Lyda's favorite stethoscope, pitchers of water, and of course the inevitable patient notes and pens. "Charlotte, you'll never guess! Our little project has been accepted for publication! Here," she smiled proudly, thrusting the official-looking letter at her.

Charlotte was stunned. She knew that Lyda was working on an article about their year-long study but had no idea that it had been submitted anywhere. The return address read St. Louis, Missouri.

Dear Dr. White and Nurse Swain,

I am pleased to inform you that your article entitled "Results of Monitoring Tuberculosis Patients' Health Maintenance Indices in a Southwestern Medical Clinic" is accepted for publication in our journal 'Advances in Rural Medicine'. You can expect it to appear in the May-June, 1908, issue.

As you may know, our fledgling publication is working hard to expand its readership, and as we operate on a limited budget, we are unable to offer an honorarium to authors at this time. But it is articles like yours that will help us increase subscriptions, and we sincerely thank you for thinking of us for submission. You do understand that this is an exclusive arrangement, and you are prevented from publishing this anywhere else. Your future speaking engagements, of course, are not limited.

Enclosed you will find a letter of acknowledgement that you will need to sign and return to us at your earliest convenience.

Several months earlier they had summarized what they had collected over twelve months. They had complete records on seventeen patients. Of those, three were significantly improved, ten were stable, two suffered a decline in their health, and two had died. The fact that three-quarters were stable or improved was impressive. Besides the measures they collected and the health status at the beginning and at twelve months, Lyda believed passionately that seeing each person regularly was a critical part of their work. She stated that in the study as well as their opinion that helping patients understand why they were interested in such information had a subtle, but powerful, therapeutic effect.

"This is notable, Charlotte, for two reasons," Lyda continued. "First, we are women. People regard us as lower than men in our 'wild west' culture. And a woman doctor, and a nurse? Two women? Well, that is unheard of."

Charlotte nodded in agreement, and kept scanning the letter in disbelief.

Lyda continued. "The fact that we are not connected to a prestigious university is against us, too. I suppose we could have tried to enlist one for support, but I didn't want to wait and wade through all the political procedures and hobnobbing that would be necessary. I thought that submitting to this new little publication would get us a start at least."

"Lyda, I am surprised that you did this and, well, without my help, not that you needed it."

"Be realistic, Charlotte. I know how busy you are at home, and I value your time. I have no such entanglements, and I was anxious to get this off. And help? You gave me such invaluable help along the way, and your records are first rate. I could not have written the results so easily without the clear implications they pointed to. And the fact that you keep such wonderful notes of our discussions made writing the final report so effortless. You could not have done anything else to help before I sent it off."

Somewhat mollified, Charlotte dropped the topic. But she noted with pleasure that Lyda had included both their names as authors, even if hers was listed as the second author. She was published! What a milestone, and one she had never dreamed of.

Lyda and Charlotte received their ten copies of the journal in April, sent by the publishers as a token of gratitude. *Gratitude,* thought Charlotte, *I'll warrant that they want us to spread these around to help them 'increase their readership' instead of paying us.* Nevertheless, when she brought her copies home to Woody, she couldn't hide her sense of pride.

Charlotte wished that she could show similar academic letters behind her name as Lyda. She had been listed on the registry in Louisville, where she received her training at Norton, but that was an entirely different state. Since then she had also provided nursing care in Colorado. She wondered about nurses like her who moved from one state to another. Should there not be a symbol, a universal one, to show that they had received a legitimate education?

It was a hot day in late May when the post arrived with a letter for Charlotte, and what appeared to be an identical one for Lyda. She had been ready to walk out the door to go home early. She was pregnant again, and at this early stage of pregnancy, she was unusually tired. Lyda had urged her to leave; they were not very busy. Charlotte looked forward to joining Kat for an afternoon nap in their darkened bedroom, with cool cloths draped over her if she was still uncomfortable in the heat.

She called Lyda into the front room of their three-room office. "These letters just arrived, Lyda. One for each of us. What do you imagine?" They both eagerly opened the envelopes, and Charlotte, who had been standing, sat down suddenly, her mouth open in surprise. She had been sent an exact copy of the letter that Lyda received, from a Dr. Somerall, of the Pima County Medical Society.

"This is ridiculous," exclaimed Lyda, "they are questioning our findings?"

"And," added Charlotte, "they want to examine our records, and our patients as well?"

They sat in silence, Lyda looking at the paper and muttering. "I have a nerve to go to Dr. Somerall this minute and ask him what on God's green earth he thinks he is doing, asking questions about our findings? This is hogwash!"

"Lyda, think on this with me. We need to take some time," said Charlotte. "He is writing on behalf of the entire medical society; it is probably more than him. He is simply the secretary. Maybe he is not behind this at all … he could just be doing his duty. I am upset, too, but at this point, we don't have much to be angry about, just curious. Why are they contacting us now?"

"Hmm," replied Lyda. "You have a point there. And Charlotte, you and I both know that I can be hot-headed at times. Maybe I should calm myself before we decide on a course of action."

Charlotte smiled at her. "I know, Lyda, it is just a little miracle that my temper does not match my hair. But just imagine what they would think if they saw us marching, uninvited, into their meeting, both of us red-faced, fiery-eyed and fuming. They should have a healthy fear of us!" Charlotte shook her head. "I wonder what they really want. What is behind this letter?"

Three weeks later they sat at one side of a long polished table, across from the four officers of the medical society. June's sweltering temperature stayed stifling until just after sundown. The special meeting had been called for 6:30 p.m. to give the doctors time to finish their office practices for the day, and to have something light to eat. It was so hot, no one was really interested in food.

"Ladies, thank you for coming to our meeting so that we can get some answers about the, ahem, research that you have been conducting," said Dr. Melvin, the group's president. He was a youngish man, in his mid-forties, with thinning brown hair curled over his shirt collar. The men had removed their jackets in the airless room.

Charlotte felt her ears get warm under his words. She was already aware of her heart pounding in her chest, and she told herself to *breathe, take deep breaths, calm down.* They had agreed that Lyda, as the physician, would do the talking unless questions were addressed specifically to Charlotte. They had both been upset at this turn of events, having expected that the local doctors would welcome the results and encourage the two women further in their pursuits. *Why in the world had we thought that?* She positioned her hands on her belly to cradle the baby. She needed to remain calm for this one.

They had tried to guess at the motivation for the meeting, but all they could come up with was resistance to their findings, which was laughable. They felt it best to gather information rather than assume they knew what this was all about. To that end they had not brought any study notes nor patient records. Those were private and belonged between the clinic and the patients. Lyda insisted that they be kept locked. It was almost impossible not to feel defensive.

Three hours later, she returned home.

"Well, Woody," she said, closing the door behind her. "I'm here. So glad this is over. Time to get into my night things and put my feet up. Well, hello, you," turning to Kat who excitedly threw her arms around her mother's knees. "You will never guess how this all turned out," she said, reaching down to hug her little daughter.

"I'm all ears! Tell me, Charlotte."

"Well, four of them squared off against us two women. They looked like they were expecting to brawl, shirt sleeves rolled up. Yes, I know it was a very hot day, but just the same, the sight of them matched up against the two of us 'little women.' Too bad I'm not eight months pregnant! We would have taken up all the rest of the space. You would have enjoyed it, Woody."

He nodded for her to continue.

"Their first questions were about our education. Where did I receive my training, what kind of marks did I get, where did Lyda go to medical college. Although neither of us planned to take our patient notes, we had decided to bring along our school certificates, just in case. And my goodness, Woody, you could not believe how impressed they were with Lyda's credentials. They were astonished to think that a woman could weather the rigors of medical school at such a young age. They were not nearly as impressed with mine, I tell you.

"But then one of them wanted to know where I had studied research and writing for publication. 'Studied it?' I replied, 'it just comes naturally to me. I like to keep track of things, and the ideas that Dr. White and I had made sense.' I told them that we were determined to do the best that we could before a cure for tuberculosis could be found, and surely we could do things to help patients maintain the sense of health that they already had.

"You would have thought that we offered some lunatic prize. That seemed like a foreign idea to them. And even more surprising was when we talked about the value of educating our patients so they could take care of themselves on their own. We emphasized that their health was their own to manage and take care of, not a doctor's, not a nurse's, nor a hospital's. It was their responsibility. Seeing a doctor or a nurse was a kind of consultation, but always, always, the decisions are in the patient's hands."

He smiled at her. "And how did they react to that idea, Charlotte?"

"They were dumbfounded to hear us talk like that, and yet, we saw two heads nodding slightly in agreement. They know full well that a person's health is his own, not someone else's."

"So, did that discussion loosen things up a bit, were they more willing to accept your work in Tucson?"

"I think so, but it was hard to tell. We met for another half-hour, talking more easily about our findings. They kept calling it research, but we had not done any experiments at all; we were simply summarizing our patients' information and their health status. Nowhere in our article did we use the word 'research.' Just before they dismissed us, one of them wanted to know why Lyda was not a member of the medical society. She was shocked at that question, I tell you. She looked the questioner boldly in the eye and said, 'Because you never approved my application. I sent one in to you more than two years ago when I came to Tucson, and did not hear back. So I sent an additional inquiry, and still no reply. I concluded that if you were too busy to consider my application, I had better things to do than beg for standing. I have had this experience before, doctors, I can assure you, and my time is every bit as valuable as yours.'"

Woody applauded, startling little Kat.

"I wish you could have been there, Woody, you would have been so proud of Lyda, standing up for herself and all. She is so impressive."

"So are you, my dear, so are you."

In the months that followed, several events occurred worthy of celebration. First, Lyda was made a member in good standing of the Pima County Medical Society, retroactive to the time she had first applied. Her application was discovered buried in a stack of papers on the desk of the recently-retired secretary. Although she was not as warmly received at meetings as she would like, she had a seat at the table and she was judicious in the use of her voice. Dr. Somerall, the current secretary, invited her to consult on a difficult case of his, a man with long-standing tuberculosis. And after a few months' acquaintance, he invited Lyda to dinner, and they began to see each other socially.

The clinic that Lyda and Charlotte maintained was being sought as a model in other parts of the Arizona Territory as well as New Mexico and Nevada. Their days were so busy that they had added another nurse,

Melissa Phillips, a trained nurse from Wichita, Kansas, whose husband worked for the Southern Pacific Railroad.

In January of 1909, Charlotte and Woody welcomed their second child, a son, Arthur Charles, and they began to appreciate the complexities of frontier life with two children under three years of age. Woody was overjoyed, and Charlotte was delighted to see her husband so fulfilled by his role as father—and holding his health stable. From time to time she had concerns, fleeting though they were, that maybe the demands of a growing and active family were getting to be too much for his energy. But he assured Charlotte that all was well. As tired as he could be, he told her that his enjoyment of his children made up for it. Charlotte thought him a most remarkable man.

His claim that his energy was fine was tested when Charlotte announced in the fall of 1910 that she was pregnant again. Woody looked at his growing wife in resignation. "Well, maybe, love, this should be our last child. Now that we have both a girl and a boy, this new one can be whatever it chooses. I may have reached my limit."

Charlotte smiled at him in full understanding and appreciation. She had her career and her family. And she had a strong partner for a husband. She knew she was fortunate, unlike most of the women she knew. The welcomed their last child, another boy, on July 1, 1911. They named him Richard Alan and called him Dickie.

Its Rightful Place

September 10, 1912
Greenville, Kentucky

Dear Woodrow,

I am sorry that I cannot deliver this package in person, but travel is impossible for me now with your father being so ill. I keep hoping in my heart that you and Charlotte and the children could make the trip to Kentucky instead, but I know from your letters how very busy you are; Charlotte with her work, and you with the household duties. When I think about those arrangements, I am surprised that they work for you, but on the other hand, I am so glad they do work, for you have been given a way to maintain your health, help your wife with her dream, and learn what it means to take care of children on a daily basis. Those are three very important things, my dear. We are so proud of you, son, for your determination and your ability not to be influenced by the nags and gossips of the day!

Do you remember my telling you about my friend Sarah who was called to be a nurse at the Battle of Shiloh? It used to be called the Battle of Pittsburg Landing. That was the battle at which your Uncle Thomas was killed. I had promised to marry him after the war ended, do you remember that? When the war was over, I fell in love with your father, and we married. The rest of that history is known to you.

I had a most pleasant visit with Sarah a few months ago, and she gave me a pendant, this odd little pendant which I am sending on to you. When the box, addressed to Charlotte, is opened she will see in the center of it is a brass button, a button that came from your uncle's uniform, which Sarah found when he died. The garnet is Sarah's birthstone. Sarah's husband had the button made into a pendant and gave it to her as a birthday *present, I believe. Sarah had never taken care of anyone before she was pressed into service at Shiloh. And she had never cared for someone who was dying before she took care of Thomas.*

Something in Sarah was awakened then, and she decided that she had a calling to become a real nurse and pursue the education that she needed to achieve her goal. Every day she wore the pendant as a reminder, and at our visit a few months ago, she gave it to me, saying that it rightfully belongs with Thomas's family. Well, Woodrow, Charlotte is our family now, as are Kat and Arthur and Dickie. So, on behalf of your father, we would be most pleased for you to present this gift to your dear wife, our daughter-in-law, as a much-belated 'welcome to the family' from the Swains with the message that we honor her calling, too. I have enclosed a little note inside, just for her.

With all our love,

Your Mother and Father

Farewell

October 15, 1940
Tucson, Arizona

Charlotte sat at the bedside, her warm hand over his bony one. His skin was dry and paper-thin. His face was gray, and his closed eyes were sunken. He was exhausted from the effort of coughing and trying to get his breath. The morphine she gave in the past hour had blessedly calmed his breathing. His shallower breaths were coming less often now, which helped avoid the coughing trigger. Her notes about his care were on the bedside table, and she picked them up again, searching. *Did I do everything?* She wondered. She flipped to the page that preceded it with the doctor's orders. No. Everything was on time. Everything that she could do for a dying patient had been done.

With her other hand she felt for the pendant at her neck and enfolded it in her palm. So many things had happened since Woody's mother sent it. The Arizona State Nurses Association was founded in 1919, and two years later, the Arizona Nurse Practice Act came to life. Those had been long and cumbersome processes, but now she could claim the title of Registered Nurse, knowing that she represented the best that nursing had to offer.

The Spanish Flu pandemic of 1918 had devastated the country and much of the world for three years at the same time the "Great War" was being waged. Arizona lost more than 6,000 lives in the pandemic alone. Lyda and her husband, Dr. Somerall, both died in 1919 while caring for patients on a military installation. Charlotte's clinic continued its operation until 1933 when it was assumed by St. Mary's Hospital as an outpatient clinic.

Their three children were grown now. Kat and her husband Gregory had two girls, Emma and Rosemary. Arthur and his wife Mary Alice had one daughter, Suzanne; their son, Jacob, had died from a malignancy. Dick, having outgrown 'Dickie', was serving in the Army in Hawaii. Charlotte and Woody were the happy grandparents of three girls.

Still, although life was busy around her, Charlotte made time to work as a nurse, and she often sought out private duty care, a role she had relished in the beginning of her career and still loved. It would be another five years until a treatment for tuberculosis was discovered with the advance of the powerful antibiotic, streptomycin. That led the way to more research and even more effective treatments. In the 1950s most of the TB sanitaria would close, no longer needed.

Although many things had advanced, she was gratified that the heart of nursing seemed the same as in Miss Nightingale's day. To touch, to care, to be present ... such holy gifts to offer.

"Charlotte?" he asked, moving his head a little so that he could whisper easier. "Are you still there?"

"Of course, my love, I'm here. For as long as you need."

Part Three: Will and Ella

I'm Going to Be a Nurse!

1956-1968
Indianapolis, Indiana

"C'mon over!" six-year-old Ella Swensen would shout at the top of her little lungs. "It's office hours! We're open!!" Holding clinics for the neighbor kids in her parents' carport, she treated most of her "patients" with "shots." The lucky ones might get one or two of the tiny sugar pills she kept in a safe place.

From the first time someone asked, "What do you want to be when you grow up?" her answer was immediate. She was born to be a nurse, and her certainty never wavered.

Ginny and Ginger, the two women who worked in Dr. Topmiller's office, sparked her imagination the first time she saw them. Ginger was the gravel-voiced, red-headed receptionist who always wore a white uniform, confusing Ella at first. *Don't all nurses wear white?* She wondered. *Isn't Ginger a nurse?* And their names were so similar. But Ginny was the one who wore *all* the nurse things: white dress, white stockings, white shoes, and, the giveaway, a white cap.

Ginny was the real nurse, businesslike and unfussy. Ella could not recall one smile from her, except for the time that she had to see Dr. Topmiller when she was eight. Someone at school pulled a chair out from under her, and she fell, fell really hard, on the linoleum-covered concrete floor. She didn't mention the incident at first, forgetting all about it in the middle of supper. But when she got out of bed the next morning, she was stiff and achy.

The pain continued for a week. Ella was convinced that she had cancer, and she hated for her mother to know it, afraid it would break her heart. But even more than her childish fear of the cancer taking her life, she didn't want Dr. Topmiller to look at her, there, on her bare bottom. When Ella finally admitted her fears to her mother, she gently wrapped her arms around her daughter and said, "We will face this together, you and I. I'm sure that prank with the chair had a lot to do with it. Hard falls can hurt a long time, I know. Don't you worry, sweetie."

While she and her mother waited in the exam room with Ginny, Ella gathered her courage. "Will Dr. Topmiller have to look at my tailbone?" Ginny looked up from her notes and caught her mother's eye, a smile ready at the corner of her mouth.

"I'm not sure about that, Ella," she said, putting down her pen, "but I do know that he likes his patients to keep their clothes on as much as possible." She smiled. "I'm pretty sure he'll begin with having you move and bend for him, and just pointing to where it hurts. He might touch your lower back. I will be right here with you, and your mother, too, if you want."

Ella nodded, her fears starting to melt.

Ginny continued, "And Dr. Topmiller has daughters of his own, Ella. He knows what can bother young girls." Being with Ginny relaxed her when she was scared.

Ella loved learning. Almost everything interested her, and she rarely had to work hard to master a subject. Sometimes she got lazy, but she could always overcome that with a little serious study. Her parents supported her dream of becoming a nurse, but her father insisted on one concession. He had investigated the nursing schools she was considering, surprised that her list contained only diploma programs based in hospitals. Although he guessed that her choices were reputable, he pressed her to study nursing at a college or university. "You like school, and it would only be one year longer than it would take you to earn a diploma. You, my dear Ella, need to go to college. And with your excellent grades, you should be able to get a scholarship."

She applied to several colleges with strong nursing programs, but the University of Evansville was her favorite. When the envelope arrived, "U of E: Class of '72" printed in bold purple ink, she took the stairs two at a time to share the news with her siblings. "I'm in, I'm in!! I'm gonna be a nurse!" she shouted to Lynneah, the five-year-old baby of the family.

"Right now?" Lynneah asked.

"No, silly, in a few years. I have to go to school first."

"Don't you go to school now?"

"Yes, sweetie," Ella replied, patting her sister's curly head. "But this is a special school where I'll learn more and more how to take care of people when they're sick. Oh, I can hardly wait to go! And, it's not too far away."

Instantly Lynneah's face darkened. "You're going away? Leaving me?"

Ella wanted to swallow her words. *I should have thought this through a little more. Of course Lynneah doesn't want me to go. I'll be the first to leave, and she's been like my baby since Mom went back to work. Bernie and Chuck weren't much help in caring for their little sister.*

Will, University of Evansville

October 1968
Evansville, Indiana

Mary inhaled, one eyebrow arched in question. She held it in, then slowly let the smoke escape. "Could you tell us again how you felt about that, Will? I don't quite get the picture."

"Well, as I already said, it wasn't like I imagined. It was much easier than the instructor made it out to be. It was just talking." He shrugged his shoulders, his mouth turned down at the corners.

"So, I'm looking for more of a *feeling* word here …. For example, were you surprised or pleased, or relieved—something like that?"

"I suppose you could say I was pleased. No big deal, really."

She waited.

Will studied his pen thoughtfully. "I'd wondered if this nursing thing would be for me … like, was I cut out for it? Could I handle it? But after my first session today, I realized I could. All the hurrying about and noise on the hospital unit distracted me at first, but, after a minute or two, I found I could talk to my patient without getting all nervous about it. It came to me then that I do it all the time. Talk, I mean." He looked up.

Mary Westhoven nodded and smiled to herself. Will was describing a student's first clinical experience of sitting with a patient for a solid hour. No procedures, no care, nothing to do but "get to know your patient," they were instructed. This first clinical assignment often stressed them. Students would take many steps on the journey to becoming good nurses: from talking to someone, to really listening, to using that information in light-ning-quick assessments. Mary's DIR group, Dynamics of Interpersonal Relationships, was meeting for the third time. *Someone should find a better name for this class,* she thought. *Sounds like it belongs in an engineering curriculum.*

Mary had agreed to lead a weekly meeting of ten students to help them make sense of their nursing school experiences. They would be together for four years. By graduation, most cohorts had dropped to six, sometimes seven. Her officemate, Sue, created the course three years ago. Convinced that students would benefit from guided support, enough faculty volunteered to facilitate. Mary was proud to play her part. This was her third group.

At the beginning of each session, Will fished out an expensive-looking green pen from his book bag and laid it on top of his notebook. She hadn't seen him write with it, but he touched it a lot. When he spoke, he often held it up vertically, moving it with emphasis or sometimes like a pointer. She wondered if the pen was a gift. *His question about being cut out for "this nursing thing" is a good sign. He's showing some reflection. Maybe humility? C'mon Mary, don't go there. Humble is saying a lot.*

Mary found Will attractive, if not model-handsome. He looked to be about 5'10" and fit. The first class met on an unusually warm September day, and that afternoon his short-sleeved shirt exposed muscled forearms hinting at sculpted biceps. *He must work out or lift weights—good for him.* His brown eyes seemed knowing, partially hidden behind dark-rimmed glasses. Though he favored fashionable turtleneck sweaters tucked into slim-fit corduroy jeans, his curly brown hair was short, defying the long-hair convention of the day. His large nose sat above the full lips that he often chewed.

Besides Will, her group included Dale Ann, Sandra, Beth, Ella, Elaine, Nancy Joe, Sarah, Patti, and Clara. Sandra and Elaine offered Will more eye contact and head-nodding than the others. Sandra often tried to fish a response from his solid, quiet presence. Nancy Joe, who was engaged; Clara, who was overweight and self-assured; and Patti all seemed unaffected by his presence. It was hard to know how the others reacted to his masculinity. At the moment she didn't dwell it on it. Time would tell. The class of 1972 included three men in a sea of sixty-three women. Male nurses were still a novelty even though the first of them had graduated nearly thirty years ago.

Dale Ann had married three months ago, a week after her beloved grandmother died without warning. First a Candy Striper and then a nursing assistant, she felt at home in a hospital. Science fascinated Clara, who was drawn to potential cures for cancer. Ella arrived at each meeting cheerful and upbeat. She seemed to connect with what the others were saying and established eye contact with each of them. *She might be an anchor for this group.*

The turbulent Sixties was a decade of shocked witness to the assassinations of President Kennedy, Robert Kennedy, and Martin Luther King, Jr. Racial strife intensified. Increasing tensions accompanied the signing of two Civil Rights bills. Feminism claimed its power and influence. Last year's "summer of love" drew the nation's attention to the changing mores of the hip generation, as drugs and music provided a raucous backdrop to news of the war in Viet Nam.

Ripples of unrest on campuses across the country were percolating. Protests would come, but when four students were shot dead in Ohio, the escalation in voice and passion ignited campuses everywhere. The University of Evansville was no exception. However, the mission of the nursing school, to produce fully competent and capable nurses, served to insulate the program somewhat from outside pressures.

Will Swain still wasn't sure that nursing was right for him, but his mother was a nurse, as well as his great-aunt and others further back in his family tree. When he first enrolled in college he had planned to become a psychologist. Human behavior and the unpredictable ways that the mind worked had intrigued him for years. Now in his third year, he had just switched his major, not sure that psychology was really where he belonged. Hearing about the experiences of his roommate, Ron, the previous spring,

Will, University of Evansville

made him think about nursing as a path he should consider. Their conversation after Ron's maternity evaluation nudged the decision.

"Was I ever surprised at that final conference!" Ron had said as he flopped down on the old couch in the dorm's lounge. "I'm glad that's over!" He gave a big sigh and kicked off his comfy Earth Shoes.

Will glanced up from his sociology text. "What kind of surprise? Good? Bad?"

"Good, I guess. Y'know, I went into this rotation with all kinds of concerns about what it would be like in the delivery room and how patients would feel about me. I didn't even think about how others would see me, the nurses on the unit mostly. So, you know, it's been the anxiety about my being a man on top of all the other stuff. I know some of them think I'm a homosexual, and that makes it harder for them to see me as a real person. They get to imagining all the sex stuff. And I'm not. At least I don't think I am—" He laughed. He had made that joking comment to Will for two years.

"Yeah," Will said, closing his book. "I get it." He shifted his position in the overstuffed chair to get a better look at Ron. "So what was the surprise?"

"The nurses on the unit, especially the head nurse, really like me—" Ron flushed, a little embarrassed. "They were so complimentary. Like saying I seemed sure of myself, but not pushy. The one thing Mrs. Brills said that really stuck with me was that I was approachable, but not overly friendly. I carry myself confidently, and, here, let me read her words. I wrote them down, I was so surprised. And I quote: 'He does not appear to get caught up in the emotional speculations and chit-chat of the staff,'— unquote—but she said the staff still see me as someone they can easily talk to. What do you make of that?"

"That's pretty good, don't you think? I'd be pleased if it was me," Will replied thoughtfully. "So what about the patients? And how they accepted you?"

"Well, except for breastfeeding teaching, patients were generally fine with me in places like the delivery room and on postpartum. They had the option of me observing or caring for them, so the ones I got to work with were fine with me. Hell, they have male doctors all around, so what's so strange about one more man in the room? Really, I thought the biggest challenge for me was going to be the fathers. But I could tell a couple of them, first-timers, were really pleased with the way I paid attention to them as well as the mothers and babies. I think it caught them off guard, and helped them see me as a nurse, not simply a man."

After that, Will began to wonder what it would be like for him to be a nurse. *Can I do it? Is it too messy? What if they think I'm a sissy, or gay?* Another part of him countered. *What does it matter what they think? Who's in charge here, anyway? Guess there's no way to know except get in there and try. I should talk with Mom.*

Will's mother, Estelle Swain, was a nurse, but she had not worked since he and his sister Sherry were born. During the summer break at home in Lafayette, he found her after supper one evening in the fragrant garden. Flowers were her passion. Estelle was not very interested in growing vegetables; she didn't care much for cooking. But she loved her summer peonies and roses, their sweet and pleasant smells so strong "and compelling," she always said.

Estelle was tall and thin, *too thin,* Will thought. *I wish she'd put on some weight.* His father, Dick, called her "lanky." She had salt-and-pepper graying hair that she kept short, and large brown eyes, her best feature. She kept them hidden, though, behind thick glasses. He wondered why she didn't wear contact lenses. She wore no makeup other than lipstick occasionally when they went out. Her favorite summer attire was an old pair of blue denim pedal pushers and a white sleeveless blouse. *I have to admit, Mom does have nice arms, kinda sinewy. Must be from her work out in the garden.* He was glad she could show them off.

"What do you think about me becoming a nurse, Mom? Do I have what it takes?"

She shifted from kneeling and sat back on her heels to look at him. Taking off her muddy gloves, she gave him her full attention. "What brought this on, Will? I thought you wanted to become a psychologist?"

"I've been reconsidering things. Ron's helped me see nursing in a new light. The notion that the mind and body work together, not separately, could give me more options for a career. Nursing may have it all. Plus, the four years it would take to earn my degree is short compared to the time and money I'd have to invest in getting a PhD in psychology, or becoming a psychiatrist."

"A psychiatrist, Will? You haven't mentioned that before. *That* would take you a long time."

He nodded his head. "Yeah, I'm not really serious about it. But do you think I could be a nurse? What about the work?"

"Oh, you could, Will, yes, you could, I'm certain of it. You're a great student, and your determination will take you far. But here's my one bit of personal wisdom. Caring, it's a delicate thing, a fine line. You must care enough, enough so that your patients feel it and its power. Not everyone has it, Will, it's a special thing. On the other hand, if you care too much, you can become unbalanced and lose your way, even yourself. Especially yourself."

Thanksgiving break, 1970
Lafayette, Indiana

Will's sister Sherry, younger by two years, shot him the look that signaled "Let's get out of here." Grabbing her purse and keys, she urged, "Let's go for a drive—I want you to check out my new wheels." She yelled back at the house that they would be gone for a while and headed out the door. Will, feeling ever more out of place at home since college, followed quickly.

After admiring Sherry's shiny new red Toyota, a trendy Japanese car that her friends envied, Will leaned back in the passenger seat, took in a deep breath, and sighed. Watching him from the corner of her eye, she asked, "That bad, huh?"

"What, your driving?"

She smiled and continued. "You know what I mean, Buster. Home. Mom and Dad. Mom especially. But before you say anything, I want you to know, since you've been home, she's better. Putting on a good face and all that."

"That's good," he replied.

"Yeah, I guess," she admitted, "a bit of a break, you being here. But you should try living with it day in and day out."

"So, how bad is it then?"

"Well, except for her time planning next year's garden, she spends most of her days in bed. She gets up before Dad comes home from work and rushes around to throw something, anything, together for dinner. But the drinking is the worst part. He drinks a lot, too, and then they both get bleary-eyed and don't make sense. Their fights are doozies. I usually leave the house and stop by Chuck's place before I go to work. I'm working at Bell now, you know, mainly because they pay well and have a night shift. I'm basically waiting till I can save enough to move out and manage the upfront costs myself."

"Oh, Sher, I don't know what to say. I hate it that you're stuck here, with them, and in a job that doesn't advance much. Tell me again why you're not going to school?"

"You know very well that I'm not college material. I've said it a million times! I never did like school, and with my grades? Besides, there *is* a lot of advancement potential at Bell, and with the union, I can have a good life *and* a great retirement. You don't know everything, y'know."

"What about the military? There's lots of roles for women."

"You gotta be kidding, Will!" She took one hand off the wheel to gesture vigorously. "These days? With Viet Nam? I hate that we're there, and I want nothing to do with our killing machine. I'm definitely not gonna be a soldier, or a support person. And I wouldn't be a nurse—*ever*. Who knows what Mom really went through?"

Will sighed again, shaking his head. *Mom and Sherry. Hopeless, why won't either of them listen to me?* Yesterday he had tried talking with his mother about getting help for her depressed mood because he knew it was useless trying to address her drinking head on. He was learning about the effects of alcohol on all parts of the body as well as the brain, so he tried approaching the topic through the impact on heart disease and digestive problems, which she often complained about. *If she didn't have alcohol in her system, I know her overall health would be so much better. She probably doesn't take her blood pressure pills either.*

Although his mother hadn't worked since he and Sherry were born, she had served in the Army Nurse Corps during World War II. Whenever he broached the subject of her career and her jobs, the answer was always the same. "You know about war, Will, and I'm sure you can imagine how difficult caring for men with war injuries and illnesses was. It's best left in the past. I don't want to talk about it."

When he had asked his father about her experience, sure that he would fill in the details, he was disappointed. "Your mother went through a lot during the war. She told me some things, sketchy details, so I know a little bit. But she insisted that I not press her, nor ever discuss it with you kids. I made her a promise, Will, I did. And I intend to keep it. It is her story to tell, if she ever wants to. I will be as eager to know it as you and Sherry, but until she's ready, I'm not pushing her."

"Thank you, Will," Estelle had responded firmly, when he tried to talk about her alcohol use. "I know you're trying to help. But the truth is, son, you don't know everything, and some days are just too hard without my vodka. I need it to sleep, and I need it to get up and keep me going during the day—"

"Alcohol messes up your sleep, Mom, and all that—"

"Don't interrupt me, Will, don't. I have *tried* stopping, I really have. And your father, too. We just take it day by day, one day at a time. And we are really glad to have our favorite son home for Thanksgiving. So there. Case closed. No more."

"Mom, what if you talked to—"

"Will, I said no more, and I mean it. I am *not* going to talk about it!"

The longer he was away from his parents' control, the more awkward it was to visit. And nursing school wasn't giving him all the answers he wanted either. During his cohort's most recent DIR session, Ella summarized one frustrating morning. "I'm getting to the point where I hate my books. They tell me everything I need to know for the best scenario, the textbook case. But in the real world, trying to help real people with all their crazy problems? Nothing fits that best scenario, and I can't figure out how to modify the real-life version in a way that will help." She shook her head and looked down at her shoe. The other students regarded her wordlessly.

Mary nodded. "It's hard, Ella, I know. It can get really complicated." Will understood exactly what she meant. *Nothing in my books tells me what to do about Mom's drinking.*

May 12, 1971
Evansville

Will was headed to the dining hall after his last class when Cliff, a friend from the dorm, caught up with him, breathless, and handed him a note. "Will, man, you've got to get to a phone. Dick Swain, your dad, right? He called, says it's urgent." Will looked at the pink slip with nothing on it that Cliff hadn't already said. He stared at the paper in dread.

He phoned the house from the dorm's phone in the hall. "Dad, Dad, what's the matter? Are you OK? Is it Grandma?" he asked, afraid to ask about his mother, or worse, Sherry.

"Will, son, are you by yourself? Is there someone with you?"

Was that ice he heard, clinking in a glass? "Dad, I'm fine. I'm at the dorm, on the hall phone. What's going on?"

A long sigh. "I'm afraid it's your mother, Will. She's gone."

"Gone, Dad, gone? Where did she go?" But he knew.

"No, Will, gone … *gone*. Will, she's dead. She died this afternoon."

Will sat down abruptly on the floor, oblivious to others walking around him. At some level he had been afraid of this call for years, worried that her drinking would defeat her. But when he was home at spring break, he thought her skin tone was pinker, not so gray, definitely not jaundiced … yet. *It couldn't be her liver? Could it?*

"What happened, Dad? Was it her heart? A stroke? Did she have an accident?"

"At this point, Will, they think it was a massive stroke. We won't know for sure until after the autopsy, but that was their best guess."

"Didn't Sherry hear any noises or anything?"

"Sherry moved out to an apartment the first of the month. She's been gone a couple of weeks now."

"I don't know what to say, Dad, I really don't. Or feel. I'm just numb."

"I know, son, I know. I can't believe it. I'm in shock, too."

Estelle

May 17, 1971
Lafayette, Indiana

Will lay on the bed, studying for next week's psych nursing exam. Although he was excused from the last week of clinicals, he needed to get back to campus in a few days. His father stood at the partially opened door. "Hey, Will, OK to interrupt?"

May in Indiana brought unpredictable weather, and Will had propped open the window in his old room. He pulled the curtains away to allow as much air flow as possible, but it didn't make a dent upstairs. His father carried a cardboard banker's box into the room. "Your mother left us this, Will, and I know you will want see everything that's in here."

Will eyed the box warily. "What's in it, Dad?"

"Memorabilia mostly, several smaller boxes, some things from the war, even a couple of books. Some pictures. Most important though, she wrote letters for the three of us." Will shut the heavy text and sat up, swinging his legs over the edge of the bed.

"I'm going to take mine and leave you alone with all this stuff. I'll have more time later to go through it myself, so you can have first stab. Come find me after."

Will nodded and took his letter from the top. The envelope was taped shut, and across it in his mother's flowery handwriting, was written TO WILL, MY SON, and the second line OPEN ONLY UPON MY DEATH. The thick envelope contained eight pages of ivory vellum, with burgundy script letters 'EBS' at the top of on each page.

February 3, 1971

My Dear Son,

I am writing this letter, Will, to fill in the details of my life when I was in the Army Nurse Corps, a subject which is the most difficult for me to talk about. I can write about it easier. You deserve to know these things, you really do. You especially need to know this if you are ever called to be a nurse in wartime.

I am writing a similar letter to Sherry, to Dick, too, though he already knows much of this. I made a promise to myself and to him, after your visit last Thanksgiving, that I would write this letter. Dr. Connelly tells me that my health is deteriorating rapidly, and that if I do not stop drinking, my life will soon be over (as if I didn't know that!).

I do not intend to stop drinking. It is the only thing I have found to help me manage the nightmares. I wish this wasn't the case, but more than anything now, I need to be honest with you—and with myself. My life was a living nightmare, Will, and somehow I managed to survive, God only knows how. I refuse to relive them at night. Why do I go on, one could ask? I am a coward to intentionally take my life. I drink to help the nightmares, not to commit suicide. I know it is a fine line, I know.

Today is the 26ᵗʰ anniversary of the liberation of Santo Tomas in Manila, in the Philippines. It is, for me, a day of tears and loss and surprising great joy—and every year, I am more disappointed in our government. Many celebrate that date to honor the sacrifices of heroic fighters, but to me it is a date that marks a turning point in my life. In spite of the horrors being over, I have not been able to rid myself of them.

But I should start closer to the beginning.

I was a prisoner of war, along with 65 other Army nurses, from 1942 until 1945. And although those years took a terrible toll on countless American (and Japanese) soldiers, not to mention the innocent civilians who were in the wrong place at the wrong time, it also took a dreadful toll on Army and Navy nurses, doctors, too. We may not have faced combat with rifles and big guns and bayonets, but we faced the after-combat hell. I can't tell you how many times I prayed for a bullet or a bomb to take me quickly, instead of ounce by ounce of my flesh, and hope by hope of my spirit.

After I finished high school in 1934, I went to nursing school in Great Falls, Montana. It was a grand time for me even though it was the Depression. Though I had to work hard, I enjoyed what I was learning and looked forward to a different life. I graduated in 1937 and worked for a while at the hospital. But wanderlust and a sense of adventure called me, and in 1940 my friend Melissa and I joined the Army Nurse Corps.

We had heard that Manila was the premier duty station—easy work, exotic tropics, eligible men, everything that a twenty-one-year-old girl could want. But Melissa went to Hawaii, and I was stationed at Sternberg Hospital in the southern part of Manila on the island of Luzon. We tried hard to be assigned together, but the ANC wouldn't budge.

At first things were fine, and I enjoyed the work, the friends, and the wonderful life after work. I learned to play golf and became quite good at it. I had a lot of dates but was never serious about any of them. Nobody was in a hurry to get serious or marry. Being an Army nurse was the best thing in the world: I was good at medical and surgical recovery nursing and could pick up new skills whenever I wanted. I had confidence in my ability to heal, learn, and even teach, so it wasn't long before I was helping to orient new nurses.

Then came December 7, 1941. We could not believe what happened at Pearl, and I immediately feared for Melissa. Who could guess the Philippines would be next? Fort Stotsenberg, 80 miles to the north of Manila, was so heavily bombed that at the briefing that evening, they put out an immediate call for five more nurses from Sternberg. Four in our group raised their hands, and to this day I have no idea why mine went up, but in an instant, I became the fifth. We were given just minutes to collect our things. What does one take to a war? I wondered.

We arrived just as night was falling. No one was prepared for the total and complete devastation before us. We did the best we could to help, but where to start? Another nurse and I began to sort the injured into who would

Estelle

likely survive and who would not. The first impressions that hit me, those sounds and smells and sights of human slaughter, are still with me today. What does one do with parts of bodies? And all that blood and debris? Sort them? Into what? Boxes, garbage cans?

The day we called 'Black Christmas' came, and we were so thankful when it was over. Mess hall cooks had planned an elaborate meal, which we all looked forward to. But the relentless shelling and bombing changed everyone's plans. Patients hid under their beds. At the end of an exhausting day we 'celebrated' with cold turkey sandwiches.

Equipment and all the other things we needed were extremely limited. We nurses had to improvise almost everything. Yes, we were still working—we had more and more sick and injured to take care of.

When the Allies surrendered in March of '42, the Japanese made us prisoners of war, trucking us across town to the grounds of Santo Tomas University, which had been converted to Santo Tomas Internment Center, the 'STIC' we called it. We captured Army and Navy nurses became the first large group of American women in combat. What a disgusting accolade!

The Japanese moved us several times in the next few months to stay ahead of the active bombing and fighting, but the sounds ... we could always hear and feel those shuddering bone-vibrating sounds! For a while we worked in Malinta Tunnel, a fairly well-secured underground 'city,' the closest thing to a real hospital. Generators powered the lights and fans though we still had many blackouts.

On July 2, 1942, they moved us back to STIC.

For several months things were tolerable there ... barely, but tolerable. At first they kept us nurses in the convent on the grounds, and we shared tiny rooms where we could pretend that we had some privacy. I kept what little was left of my sanity by burying myself in work, and like the others, welcomed the blessed exhaustion at the end of a shift. Yes, we had a schedule, and we kept to it, rigorously. The schedule was our savior.

At the end of August we were moved back to the main STIC dormitory where our quarters were even more cramped. We had to sleep packed in next to each other on the floor, head to toe. We could not get away from anyone—perhaps that is why I need so much privacy today.

The next months passed in a blur. There was a kind of openness to STIC at first, and outsiders could come in and sell us things. The warden set up an organization of internees but in truth we were prisoners. We created all kinds of groups who provided services for each other, like a library, gardens, schools. STIC had an elementary and high school for almost 600 youngsters, can you believe it? The medical people were a tiny part of the camp; the rest were Filipinos and wounded enemy soldiers. At its peak, about 3,800 of us were housed there.

Things changed again, and the government turned the prison over to the Japanese Imperial Army. It was then that our lives really got bleak. Many things upset me, Will, but most frightening then was the sense that I had no hope, none.

Everyone, and I mean everyone, *was malnourished, and our food was reduced from 960 calories a day to 700 in the last months. Every day we became weaker, but still we worked, though our shifts were short. I weighed 125 pounds when I joined ANC—when we were liberated, I was down to 83. We suffered the same illnesses as our patients: malaria, dysentery, beriberi (which, as you know, is a serious vitamin deficiency).*

We watched more and more men die, usually with nothing at all available to ease their suffering, except someone at their side if they were lucky. The morgue was overflowing, and transport of bodies out of the prison became impossible. Sewage piled up. The morphine was gone, the quinine was gone, the aspirin was gone. Christmas of 1944 was the dismalest. We were all relieved to see December 26, so we didn't have to think of home and wonder if we would spend another Christmas as POWs.

It was hell, Will. I have no other way to describe it.

Estelle

Then on the night of December 29, a date I'll always remember, I left myself.

I cannot explain how, but the forces that worked on me for so long had weakened and changed me beyond recognition. I came upon a Japanese soldier ready to use his bayonet on an unconscious Filipino woman, a teacher, who had miraculously hung on to life for a week. I screamed at him, I rushed him to beat him with whatever energy I had left. He turned to me, his bayonet held high, just as another soldier came to see what the noise was. They shouted at each other, and then the second soldier nodded his permission, and the first one stabbed the woman three times in the chest. The other soldier held me back by the arms but twisted my face trying to force me to watch. Then he threw me to the ground. I waited for the bayonet's stabs; I prayed for them, really, did they know that? I made gestures for them to kill me, too, but they laughed at me and strutted off.

I left myself. I disappeared. I dream of bayonetting them almost every night, yet still the woman dies. I carry the memory to this day and am so filled with hatred toward the soldiers, and of course, at my inability to change the circumstances.

In early January of '45 the Allies landed at Luzon, and the push to our freedom began. STIC was liberated on February 3. Though we were malnourished and many of us sick, all of us nurses survived. I don't know how, really, except for our work, and the sense that our group had a purpose. That kept us going—the cohesiveness was everything.

The next month was transition. Everything changed in an instant. We were replaced by fresh nurses. They gave us medical tests and hospitalized some. They gave us new uniforms that actually fit—well, after pinning and tucking, and automatically promoted us one grade. We were awarded the Bronze Star and some got other medals as well. Gradually we could hold down real food again. Then they flew us to San Francisco to begin the process of getting back to our hometowns, me to Great Falls. And on to our lives.

What a weird time that was. This may not make any sense to you, Will, but I had such a connection to those nurses, and our patients and mission, and it had been so intense for YEARS! Finally we were FREE! But in spite of the surface happiness, deep down I felt as if my soul had been ripped away from me, and I didn't belong anywhere anymore. Suddenly I was freed from my purpose and my fellow compatriots. What is freedom if it takes away your own sense of self?

I began the hard time of grieving, which I never finished. I was a fragile shell outside and hollow inside. But I went through the motions because I couldn't think what else to do.

Gradually some of the old Estelle returned. I continued my nursing work with the Army Nurse Corps at Fort Leavenworth, where I worked until I met Dick there, on the golf course. He was also returning from the Pacific command. For a while I was distracted and happy with a new sense of purpose, being a wife to him and a mother to you and Sherry. But then the baby blues blossomed into full-blown depression. I kept thinking I would get better and finally, about a year after Sherry was born I did, somewhat. But still I grieved. I ached for so many things that didn't really make sense. I still grieve today.

When I close my eyes, I see the many soldiers I abandoned during their greatest need, their eyes sunken into the ghostlike cavities of their faces. I hear the screams of captives: men, women and children—Will, children!—calling for the torture to stop. I see parents torn apart watching babies beaten by the Japanese. And that poor woman on December 29—and my failure to save her. I cannot see a Japanese person on the street today that my heart doesn't pound and bile floods my throat. Thankfully, not many of them live around here.

I hope this letter has filled in the most important blanks about my life. I am sorry, Will, that I wasn't a better mother. You must know that I am so proud of you and your dreams of helping people by becoming a nurse. You

Estelle

will succeed. I hope you will be able to care where I failed. I hope you have a happy life.

I pray that you will forgive me.

With love,

Your Mother

Will sat frozen on the edge of the bed, staring through her blurry words, tears sliding down his face. His throat was tight and his chest hurt. He ached, but he didn't know what for. To hug her, to cry with her, to comfort her? … be comforted himself? *I will never have that chance again. What absolute … horrors, horrors that she lived through! My poor, poor mother. She's gone. She's really gone.*

Ella, University of Evansville

1968
Evansville, Indiana

The picturesque campus of the University of Evansville did not overwhelm Ella like the scale of Indiana University in Bloomington, and it was far enough from Indianapolis that she wouldn't be expected to come home every weekend. Besides learning to be a nurse, Ella craved wings. She hungered to be fully in charge of her own life without her parents' expectations dictating her choices.

Years later she would tell her father how valuable his advice had been, to study nursing at a college or university, and how it had simplified her educational journey. She often wondered whether he truly understood its impact on her career. In 1965, the American Nurses Association officially promoted the bachelor's degree as the "entry level" for the title of Registered Nurse. Many of Ella's diploma-educated friends chose to attend classes and study after long hours taking care of patients in order to obtain the bachelor's degree. Completing her basic education at one time over four years was so much simpler.

Ella liked her classes, and for the most part, the faculty. Mrs. Jean Kellogg, their nursing arts instructor, required them to write a philosophy of life as one of their first assignments. Ella thought this was ridiculous because most of the students were all of eighteen or nineteen. *How can we possibly have a 'real' philosophy of life? I hardly know what life is all about, much less a framework from which to make sense of it.*

She lived on the first floor of Moore Hall's south wing, one of ten girls who bonded quickly over canasta and a shared flair for mischief. Susan Michaels, her roommate, was a serious med tech student with a wicked sense of humor. Susan studied more than Ella and kept her side of their room tidy and organized. She could find anything in a few seconds, while it took Ella time to dig through the pile of clothes on the floor of her tiny closet. It was Susan who nicknamed her Bella, and Susan became Mikey.

Although Ella was one of the shortest girls in the dorm, she never saw it as a problem. She liked being petite. "I can have my pick of men," she boasted, "including the gems you all ignore. And if I need to reach something, I have a reason to talk to a handsome stranger." Girls were often jealous of her thick and naturally curly shoulder-length hair. Secretly, Ella liked that her hair got so much attention. It helped to counter her insecurities about being ten or fifteen pounds heavier than she wanted. She hated the way short skirts exposed her thighs and was relieved miniskirts seemed to be going out of style.

December, 1969

Ten days before Christmas, in the wee hours of morning, bleary-eyed Ella could hardly stay awake. She had been prepping for finals with two other sophomores in a basement study room. It was windy and snowy outside, and the library was closed. Ella knew that if she stayed in her room to study, she would be too tempted to crawl under the covers and fall asleep.

Ella quietly opened the door to her room, keeping the light off so she wouldn't disturb Mikey. She was so weary, she expected to fall asleep immediately. But after a minute she sensed that something wasn't right. Mikey was a deep sleeper and almost always snored. *No sound coming from her side of our room. Odd. And something else too … a smell. It smells like someone's had an accident in their pants.* She could feel her heart start pounding.

She spoke softly, then louder. "Mikey? Mikey, can you hear me? Mikey, wake up!" No reply. *Oh God, oh God!*

She switched on her bedside lamp, took one big step over to Mikey's side, and saw dried spittle around the girl's open mouth. Her lips were blue, and if she was breathing, Ella couldn't see it. She shook her, no response.

She threw open their door and yelled, "Help, I need help!" Hall doors opened and lights came on. Bonnie, a senior nursing student, rushed into the room, and Ella shouted, "Mikey, it's Mikey, she's not breathing!" Barb, the resident assistant, ran for the emergency phone to call the housemother.

Bonnie started to perform CPR. "Help me get her on the floor, Ella, this bed is too soft, and we need room on both sides." It took all of three seconds. Another senior came in, and began helping Bonnie, pushing Ella aside. Shortly the housemother arrived, then campus security, finally the paramedics. Ella was pressed out of her room into a crowd of curious students.

Even from outside she could tell no one was having any success. The lead paramedic barked, "Hospital," and in an instant they packed up and disappeared. Barb put her arm around Ella's shoulders as the housemother shepherded the other girls into the lounge. "Let's go to my room," Barb said, and Ella let herself be led.

In one way or another, Mikey's death affected every student in the dorm. She was one of them—young, healthy, a full life ahead. How could this happen? Was she sick? Did anyone know that she was sick? Rumors began to surface that she had been drinking, taking drugs, maybe it was suicide. The truth was none of those. Autopsy revealed that Mikey had undiagnosed epilepsy and most likely had a massive grand mal seizure in her sleep. No one could have predicted this. Not even her roommate who knew her the best.

Her DIR group was uncharacteristically silent the next session. "Please, tell us about that night, would you, Ella?" Mary had asked. "Give us a feel for what it was like for you."

Ella had never witnessed the death of someone so close, nor in front of her. In her own words and voice and away from the dorm, she began to relive the shock. Tears slipped from her blue eyes. "I liked Mikey. A lot," she sniffed, fingers under her nose. "Everybody liked her. Really, I loved her, like we were sisters the same age. And she thought of me as a sister. She didn't have any siblings.

"She wasn't an attention-grabber. She didn't stand out to others, not at all, but she was the type of person the world needs—kind and thoughtful, gentle. She loved understanding how our bodies work and how problems reveal themselves in lab tests." Ella paused. "She would have been wonderful at her job."

She wiped her eyes with her palms and took a breath. "You know," she sighed, "her parents were beyond devastated. I have never seen anyone treat their loved ones' things with such reverence. She was a saint to them, their only child. They sat for more than an hour in our room, not speaking, just taking it all in. I tried to leave them alone but they insisted I stay. I guess they thought they could keep her somehow, one minute more, through me." Her tears started fresh again. "They gave me her favorite scarf and hat." She held out the items, then gently put them back on her lap. "This is all I have left of her."

The next semester Ella took an increased interest in diseases of the brain, part of her personal mission to make sure Mikey's death had some kind of meaning. On the outside she presented a good front and stayed focused on her studies. She found a part-time job serving catered events on campus. Keeping busy was the therapy she needed. The rest of the year she remained roommate-less, and even though Barb and the housemother pushed her to change rooms, she pushed back. It was just for a few more months, she insisted, she could handle it.

At the beginning of their third year, nursing students began to consider whether or not to specialize. Pediatrics, maternity, emergency? Those courses and clinical rotations appeared later, so the discussions were hypothetical. Listening to the older students made Ella anxious to figure out just where she fit in the nursing world.

Medical and surgical courses created the foundation of hospital nursing, offering the first views of the realities of nursing's work. As juniors and with faculty recommendations, students had the opportunity to work for pay as nursing assistants. Gaining more clinical experience was crucial, and of course, the extra money always helped.

Ella's question about specializing was answered in her psychiatric nursing course by Mrs. Abernathy. She was tall and elegant, her posture and movements worthy of a model. Sue Abernathy made a striking first impression, slim in her white uniform, brown hair in the short bouffant style of the early seventies—teased, sprayed, unmoving. She wore little makeup except mascara and a light lipstick. Her smile was kind, her voice gentle, *rather like Mikey's,* Ella thought. *Funny they were both named Sue.*

Ella found it impossible to compare Mrs. Abernathy with her other instructors; she was heads above them all. But was it the instructor that drew her to psychiatric nursing? Or was it the field itself? In prior clinicals, she found herself assembling and carrying things to patients' bedsides, giving medications, performing treatments, worrying about doing it right or hurting someone. In this rotation, Ella witnessed firsthand what "therapeutic use of self" was all about.

Theorist Hildegard Peplau coined the phrase in the 1950s to suggest that the intentional use of the self in interaction with another could produce positive "therapeutic" results. Is the patient agitated? The nurse should approach him calmly, unhurriedly, with soft speech and a kind expression. Is the mother crying? The nurse might choose to make eye contact and lean in, demonstrating that tears are welcome. To Ella, the concept made perfect sense, and Sue Abernathy embodied it.

Mrs. Abernathy never carried a procedure tray or gave a medication when she asked a patient if she could sit with them. She kept a little notebook tucked away in a pocket in case she needed it. And most of the time the patient, perhaps agitated or staring off in a dream state, came around to connect with her, becoming more relaxed or more engaged as a result. Ella watched Mrs. Abernathy carefully, and thought that whatever she was doing must be magic. Ella wanted it. She wanted to be that magician.

She knew what her specialty would be.

Ella, University of Evansville

Graduation

June 10, 1972
Evansville, Indiana

Ella secured the cap with another bobby pin through her thick strawber-ry-blonde hair, the light breeze lazily moving the tassel back and forth. *So neat that we're together at this milestone. Funny how our friendship all started because of the alphabet,* she mused, *Swain and Swensen.* She reached for Will's hand. "Well, this is the last one, buddy. We're almost launched now." He nodded at her over his shoulder and smiled broadly.

Farewell parties and packing up had highlighted the past week, and most students had stayed for graduation. The pinning ceremony, a sol-emn event second only to the sophomore capping ceremony, was held last Sunday. Sadness, and an unfamiliar tenderness, overcame Will as Beverly, one of their classmates, sang "Bridge Over Troubled Waters" with a poi-gnancy that cramped his throat. "We've known her for four years, Ella," he whispered, "with no idea she could even sing, and so beautifully."

Beverly had introduced the music by saying she thought being a nurse was like a bridge, providing support and a path from the side of illness to the other side of healing. When Will heard the solemn piano chords fill the small chapel, thoughts of Estelle Swain tugged at his heart. Over the past year he had revealed some of his mother's story to people he knew would understand his drive to honor her. That it brought tears to his eyes or down his face was no longer a big deal—DIR had helped him over *that* hump.

Will and Ella were lost in their own thoughts as speaker after speaker droned on through the anticlimactic proceedings of the graduation cere-mony. Finally they were able to snake their way in a long line to the stairs and claim their diplomas. How could that single piece of paper represent what had taken Will six years, Ella four?

Afterwards, Ella introduced Will's father and sister to her proud family: her parents, three siblings, and Melody, her lively Florida grandmother. Her father had reserved a private dining room at an elegant restaurant on the outskirts of town, where waiters hovered with crumb scrapers to clear linen tablecloths. *Do people look at Will and me and figure we're a couple? Well, we are in a way, but a couple of friends only. Will and I will always be friends. But romantically involved? No way.*

In his first two years of college Will had dated occasionally, but his attraction to the opposite sex waned as his interest in academics increased. Ella dated a lot, but she didn't consider anyone a serious partner until her junior year, when she met Jim Cullen, a local. Ella could never put her finger on why she fell so hard for Jim, or so quickly, but fall she did and their relationship evolved at lighting speed. Years later she would look back on this attraction and realize it was her insecurity in managing her own life. Jim seemed like a man of the world. He owned a little sports car; he had his own apartment. Ella had always been surrounded by capable others.

Jim met the partygoers just in time for dessert. Ella was disappointed that he couldn't make it to graduation, or to the restaurant earlier, but he claimed he couldn't get away from the car lot because Saturdays in June were big days for sales. Jim was twenty-seven, and although he was six years older than Ella, he had only been at the dealership for a few months, making him junior on the sales floor.

After everyone else said good night, Will, Sherry, Ella, and Jim decided to continue their celebration with more drinks, maybe some dancing. Jim suggested the Northside. "It has a decent band and the owner is a friend of mine. I'll bet he can get us a good table." Will wasn't sure, but Sherry and Ella wanted to go, so they took Sherry's car as well as Jim's and drove to the popular hangout. After one round of drinks they all decided, Jim included, that the band should be downgraded to "passable."

Jim's manager friend came to the table before they could leave and, learning that Ella and Will had just graduated, ordered another round of drinks, on the house. The band's playing seemed to improve, and they decided to dance a while longer. After another drink they conceded the band was definitely better. Before they knew it, the bartender's rude lights flashed the 2 a.m. closing.

The summer's night air had cooled slightly but the humidity of the river city stayed steady. A thick haze reflected downward from the lights. Anything that could be called a breeze was absent. Crickets, cicadas and insects gave the darkness its own special music. As they walked to the parking lot, slightly tipsy, Ella noticed two piles of laundry lying close together in the crosswalk. She opened her eyes wider, trying to bring more detail into focus. "Wait," she shouted, "that's not laundry, it's *bodies*!! Will, c'mon, help me!" She ran to one body, Will the other. Two elderly men lay crumpled in the street. "Sherry, run back inside and call for an ambulance!" she commanded. "Jim, stay here and watch for traffic."

Will and Ella had completed their fourth-year clinical rotations in the Emergency Room, and were well-versed in CPR. Will's victim was pulseless and unresponsive after five minutes of hard compressions and rescue breaths, and he had probably suffered severe head trauma. Will thought he saw gray matter on the pavement just under the crushed part of skull, but he couldn't be sure in the poor light.

Sherry ran out with the manager, each with a flashlight and adrenaline-fueled urgency. "Oh no, I know these guys!" groaned the manager. Sherry looked at Will's victim and immediately turned away to vomit.

"The light, Sherry—give it to me if you can't stand this." Sherry wiped her mouth with the back of her hand, then held the light for Will, looking away from the scene. "I'm pretty sure he's gone, but I should keep trying anyway." He continued the pattern of fifteen compressions and two rescue breaths. Will wondered if his efforts were effective with the man's head so unstable. *Am I even circulating anything useful? Is his airway really open?*

"I know CPR," said the manager, "I can help."

"Come help me with my victim," Ella said. "Get in position, ready to take over compressions on my 'now.' I'll do the breathing for a couple cycles and give my arms a break. Then I'll help Will." They could hear sirens getting louder, and soon paramedics were taking over. A police car arrived, and two officers began asking questions, thinking it was most likely a hit-and-run. When they learned that Will and Ella were nurses, they complimented their command of the scene. After a short period of questioning and thanks, the four were free to go.

Jim and Ella left, and Sherry drove Will back to the restaurant. She idled the Toyota and turned to her brother. "What a wild day for you with graduation and then all this tonight. Maybe you could be cut out for ER work? You and Ella looked pretty good working that horrible scene."

He shook his head. "No way, that stuff's too much. I want to work with people who can talk about their lives. I doubt Ella would do it either. She's really into psych."

Sherry smiled. She couldn't tell if there was any kind of spark between the two. She liked Ella a lot, and her brother needed someone good like her. But then she remembered Jim. *Oh well.*

"Before I go, Dad wanted to make sure you had this, since we're leaving for home early in the morning. I don't want to forget it in our packing up and all that." She handed Will a small brown paper package taped to within an inch of its life.

"Do you know this return address? In Phoenix?" Will asked. "I don't know anyone in Arizona except Aunt Kat, and we haven't heard from her in years. Didn't she remarry after her husband died? A George, or Greg, or something like that? I think that's what Dad said. I can't remember her name now."

"Too bad we didn't have a stronger connection with them," Sherry said. She kissed his stubbly cheek with a half-sideways hug. "What a night! Really, what a day, actually. Congratulations again! See you at home in a few days." Will nodded and got out of the car with the package. *This is going to have to wait until tomorrow,* he thought. *I'm dead on my feet.*

Dream Job and Marriage

June 11, 1972
Evansville, Indiana

Ella pulled back, hot and sweaty, from Jim's lazy embrace as the sun crossed into her eyes, blazing through the thin drapes at 9:30. Shielding her face with her arm, she announced, "Dear God! I've got to get up—it's so hot in this little apartment! Time for a shower. Where's the aspirin? My head is killing me—too much …." She sat up, gingerly, squinting. "I had too much to drink," holding her face in her hands, then running fingers through her thick hair to massage her scalp. She got up and padded off to the bachelor bathroom. "That was a night," she muttered to herself.

Two days earlier when they were both sober and clear-headed, Jim and Ella had finally set a wedding date for October 14. Why wait any longer? Fall was her favorite time of year. She had always imagined her wedding in picturesque Nashville, Indiana, Jim's hometown, where the rolling hills exploded in orange, red, and yellow, Nature's last hurrah before winter claimed the barren landscape. Brown County Inn outside Nashville was the perfect venue for the small reception they wanted. Her future mother-in-law Merlie was soft-spoken and pleasant, with kindness in her heart, but a deep red scar slashed her lower face, twisting her smile into a grimace. Ella had to concentrate hard to pay attention to what she was saying, but soon discovered Merlie was expert at making big plans meet tight budgets, and she was happy to help the couple with any details she could.

Yikes! Not even eighteen weeks to plan a wedding, Ella thought, *but I guess that's good because it will give me something else to think about during the grind of review for the state board exams in July. And Mom will be happy to plan most of it.* Though it was unlike her to be so methodical, Patti, her friend from nursing school, suggested she devote three times as many hours to study as to wedding planning. Passing the state board exams was critical. She and Jim would need two incomes to buy a house and start a family in the next few years. They had settled on four children as the perfect number. And of course she wanted to work as a registered nurse—the ideal profession with the flexibility to work around a family's needs.

The stress of July's state board exams dissipated as soon as the two days of testing in Indianapolis was over. A few weeks later, the envelope addressed to Miss Ella Swensen, RN, arrived in the mail.

"Yes, yes, yes!" she screamed, jumping up and down at the mailbox in spite of the hot August afternoon. She raced upstairs to phone Jim at the dealership. When he called back two hours later, he was thrilled for her but not at all surprised. She immediately resigned from the hospital where she had worked as a glorified nursing assistant.

Then she phoned Mrs. Caraway, the nursing director at the Evansville Psychiatric Children's Center, and told her the good news. When Ella had first learned of an RN vacancy at the new specialty hospital, she set up an interview. She was impressed with the facility and grounds, and, as they finished their meeting, Mrs. Caraway agreed to hold the position open, assuming positive reference checks of course, until Ella learned the state board results.

Ella began her nursing career in August as a day shift nurse for the twenty-eight-bed hospital, thrilled to have landed her dream job. The patients, emotionally disturbed children five through twelve years old, were referred from across the state. The hospital was divided into two dorms, one for younger children and girls, and the other for older boys. Weekdays the kids were occupied with classes, therapy sessions, and structured recreation time. Back at the dorms they slept, ate meals, and spent their free time with the attendant staff, called counselors.

Ella was a human sponge. Every day she learned something new and deeper about emotional needs and disturbances. But one issue irritated her. Being the only nurse on a dorm, she was expected to watch over all the activity in the common area, but from the glass-walled nurses' station so she could answer the phone. Her job was to interact with the kids and supervise the counselors. But the counselors could only take their smoke breaks in the nurses' station, and sometimes the smoke cloud was too much. Ella hated smoking.

The older counselors, grandmothers mostly, were friendly enough to Ella and gently teased her about the upcoming wedding, especially about sex. But they did not take kindly to any guidance from her, even though she was their supervisor. Ella tried hard to create consistent plans for them to follow, and one or two of the younger staff understood where she was headed. But most gave her ideas a wink and a nod—and then ignored them.

They resisted her instructions about a behavior modification plan for nine-year-old Matt, who insisted that the counselors dress him each day although he was fully capable of dressing himself. She suspected that Matt's manipulative charm met unfulfilled grandmotherly needs. Nor were they able to ignore tiny five-year-old Patrice's shrill and expletive-filled outbursts that occurred any time she did not get her way, especially in public. "Ella's so young," she heard them say to each other one day. "She has no real experience with children. What can she possibly know? All these kids need is love."

Willa Caraway stopped by daily to check the status of the dorms; her office was in another building. Ella liked her a lot even though she was all business and much older than other nursing directors. She enjoyed talking with the kids on her visits and studied the best, most modern therapies, frustrated with the outdated mode of medication management only. "What do all those drugs do to their developing brains?" she worried. "We need to use less invasive approaches." She kept putting fliers in Ella's mailbox, suggesting a class or a book the hospital would pay for. After the wedding flurry had passed and a year at the children's hospital, she told Ella that she should think about going to graduate school.

Jim was interested in her work, up to a point—the point where his enthusiasm and excitement about what she was learning gradually stopped matching hers. Before they married he had asked questions about the kids, wanting to know how this one got along with her parents' visit, and whether that one was having a better time at school since his meds were adjusted. Then, the questions stopped, though just when, Ella couldn't say.

She would always remember the time she told Jim about Mrs. Caraway's suggestion. They were having their first anniversary dinner at the little college bar and restaurant she had liked so much, Midway on the One-Way. The food arrived, and Jim had just finished his first beer. Ella sipped her wine, then dipped a famous micro-fry into ketchup. "You'll never guess what happened today," she opened, popping the savory crunch into her mouth.

"I'm sure I can't. So many strange things go on there," he replied.

She frowned, surprised at his word choice and tone of voice. "Ummm, I don't think this is one of those things you'd call strange."

He nodded in her direction as he signaled for another beer. "OK, then, Ella, shoot. What is it?" He leaned in across the table and looked at her intensely.

"Well, Mrs. Caraway says I should go to graduate school."

"What? Graduate school? What for?"

"Well, she thinks I have potential, and that I could do so much more with a master's degree. In time I could become a manager, a director of nursing, maybe a clinic director. Or I could learn therapy and open a practice. Teach at a university. All those could earn us more money."

He frowned. "Really, grad school? You're barely out of school as it is."

She looked at him, surprised and yet not surprised at his reaction.

"Are you serious about this?"

She nodded. "Well, uh, yes, I was thinking about it."

The waitress returned with Jim's beer. Ella kept still while he took several swallows. "Ella, where does that leave me? Where does that leave our dream of a family? We would have to move, wouldn't we? And how would we pay for it? You wouldn't be bringing in any money. I can't leave my job here. It's taken me too long to get to assistant manager, and I can't just go jumping to another car dealership. I'd have to start at the bottom again."

She sat in silence. She knew the practicalities had to be confronted. But he hadn't even acknowledged the encouragement in Mrs. Caraway's comments, nor congratulated her on making such a positive impression.

"Jim, it doesn't have to be either-or, or right now, does it? Can't we just play it by ear, and see how things fit in time?"

"By ear, yeah, that's not much of a plan. You know, I've been working long hours to make sure we stay on track to buy a house and get started with a family. And remember, I'm six years older than you." She studied the coaster on the sticky varnished table. She exhaled. *Let it go, Ella, and try to put on the happy face Jim loves.*

On a weekend visit to Jim's parents, Ella and Merlie were browsing Brown County Inn's little gift shop. Merlie turned to her. "Jimmy tells me that you've been thinking about going back to school. Is that true?" Ella was taken aback, surprised that he had actually told his mother. She had assumed he considered the issue dead, and she had certainly not planned to raise it.

She tried to smile at her mother-in-law. "Well, yes, we have talked about it a little, but, well ... I'm not sure, and Jim doesn't think it's a good idea right now."

Merlie nodded encouragingly. "He's right, Ella. Sometimes in a marriage it's important to sacrifice one's dreams for the new dreams of the couple together. And besides," leaning in conspiratorially, "think about the effect on Jimmy's ego. He only went one year to college. All that college work wasn't for him, he said. It's hard for a man to see his wife do better than him. If you want my opinion, I think you should leave your education where it is and not go for any more. You already have more than him."

Ella couldn't believe her ears, and no, she didn't want Merlie's opinion. She was sure a telltale flush was creeping up her neck by now. She didn't know what to say against the growing wall that was beginning to reveal itself. *First Jim, and now his mother. Am I not cut out for marriage if this is what it means? And to have his ego at stake. Is that fair? Do I love Jim enough to limit my own dreams?*

1975

After a couple of years, the staff were beginning to listen to her, and Ella started to appreciate the wisdom in some of their suggestions. The smokers continued to smoke, but they agreed on scheduled times rather than a constant flow of staff taking breaks. When Ella was out in the dorm's day room during their breaks, a counselor would signal her for a phone call. She began to feel as if she belonged.

But at home the situation was different. Most of the time Ella had to approach Jim for sex, and often as not, he wasn't interested, or able. How would she ever get pregnant if they weren't having sex? He was drinking more and more. Late one afternoon she was driving home from the laundromat in Jim's car; hers was in the shop. She was lost in thought and not paying attention when she rear-ended the car ahead. It was just a minor bump, but the driver insisted that the police be called for the insurance report. When she returned to the car, she was shocked to see a pint bottle of Gilbey's gin that had slid out from under the seat at her sudden braking. She quickly slipped it into her purse. *Thank God it fits in there! How much is he drinking during the day?*

Prior to their marriage Jim had opened up about an incident that he claimed had changed his life. He had been at a friend's house "just sitting around having a good time with a few beers." Jim left abruptly when Merlie called, needing a ride to the local emergency room to wait with a friend whose husband had been in a serious accident. After picking his mother up, he drove too fast, misjudged the location of a culvert, and lost control, flipping the vehicle. Merlie suffered two broken ribs and a significantly disfiguring facial laceration. Jim had a concussion. Although he was not cited for being under the influence of alcohol, he admitted to Ella that he should have been. The responding officer knew his father and took pity, writing Jim a ticket for reckless driving.

"Consequently," Jim told Ella, "I promised myself that never again will alcohol affect me or my judgment. Every time I look at my mother's sad crooked smile, I remember that night, and how I maybe caused it."

"Do you feel guilty about it?"

"Wouldn't anyone?" he asked.

She nodded. She was glad he told her, but he "maybe caused" the accident? She wondered what effect the accident had on his life, and guilt, and happiness. Now, three years into their marriage, he seemed to be pulling away from her, not getting closer.

September, 1976

Patti invited her to a women's discussion group. Ella had no idea what format the meeting would take; Patti had said it was just getting started. Women's liberation protests, marches, and rallies were in full swing, and Ella was curious. Her time at school had been so focused on getting through, she never took the time to become an activist. Some of her friends protested the war in Viet Nam, and while she was against it, she didn't join them. Women's liberation? Not for her. *I don't think I have been held back by male domination before, have I?*

"Patti, I know I've benefitted from the attention gained by women's lib, but I have never felt pulled to be angry about things or join groups or march. But lately, I'm beginning to wonder if I've been an ostrich about this."

Patti raised an eyebrow. "Really? Well, that's good then. Maybe this meeting will help clarify things for you. I know and respect some of the women who'll be there. Mike is anxious to hear all about it." Ella frowned.

She hadn't told Jim the real purpose of the get-together. He thought it was a Tupperware party.

Patti's friend, the hostess, ushered them into her living room and pointed to name tags and marking pens. The event had an organizer, but no moderator, and as it turned out, one was definitely needed. The evening was dominated by Melanie, who was big, bold, loud, and articulate. And angry. After a few quick introductory comments, she launched a passionate appeal for each woman to join in her personal struggle for women's equality. Get organized, she challenged them. Write letters, make phone calls. Invite your friends. "This is a war we must win!" she shouted. "Why haven't you taken up the mantle for your sisters long before this?"

No one could share an idea or defend a position without being shouted down. One woman, Sheila, tried to offer a contrary point of view, explaining unequal pay by comparing women's dependability when it came to responding to the needs of their children. "And just why do you think that is?" Melanie demanded angrily. "Men don't share the damn domestic duties, including child rearing! And we let them get away with it! They have us coming and going and that's the way they want to keep it! Under. Their. Thumbs!"

Two older women who appeared to be in their forties left abruptly, one in tears.

Afterwards at the coffee shop, "I'm not sure what that was really all about," Patti began, after ordering pie and coffee. "I was hoping for a sense of sisterly support and encouragement, but we were all blasted out of joining Melanie in anything. I won't be associated with her, but you know, Ella, so many of the points she made were right on. Equal pay, control over our bodies, shared parenting, no more domination … I'm for all those things. Maybe we should continue to meet, just three or four of us, without Melanie."

Ella agreed. A spark had been kindled in spite of the confusion and chaos that evening. *I would like to have some women friends, besides*

Patti, who think like I do. And maybe some who challenge me, though not like Melanie.

January, 1977

Ella started to meet with a smaller group and after a few months, decided it was time to tell Jim what it was really all about. She didn't feel comfortable continuing to make up excuses, even though he seemed disinterested. He often got home long after she did. Inventory, late customer calls, meetings of the sales team over dinner, he said.

One evening Jim actually made it home for dinner, and Ella described the women's common interests, questions they were uncovering, and the support they offered each other.

The look on Jim's face grew colder and harder. "I have only one thing to say to you, Ella. If you need them, then you sure as hell don't need me. You decide." She felt as if he had just swung a sledge hammer at her chest.

And then three long black hairs pushed her over the edge.

Headed to Kansas

June 14, 1972
Lafayette, Indiana

Home is sure different now without Mom and Sherry. Just a bachelor pad, thought Will, *what a joke. Some swinging bachelors we are, a man over sixty still in mourning, and a newly graduated nurse ready to fly the coop. I'm definitely not interested in meeting girls here. Wonder what they're like in Topeka?*

He couldn't wait to start his new life. His application to Menninger Hospital was on its way to Kansas. Menninger Hospital's reputation as the premier location for advanced and innovative psychiatric care in the United States impressed Will the first time he heard about it during his psych nursing rotation. *I want to begin my career at the best place possible.*

His dad was in the kitchen, fixing dinner. Will brought the unopened package Sherry had given him at graduation to the breakfast nook, thinking he would share the surprise. He needed scissors to cut through the miles of tape that secured the box. *Must be little Fort Knox in here. A gold coin maybe? More?* An envelope was taped to the box, and on it, in distinctly feminine handwriting, were the words, "*Will: Your Graduation Present, Read This First.*"

OK, I will. The envelope contained a letter and a copy of another letter, as well as a newspaper clipping.

Dear Will,

I expect that by now you will have graduated from the nursing program, as your mother kept me updated on your progress before she passed away. My brother Dick was never very good at corresponding—me neither,

I'm afraid!—but after she died your father tried hard to make sure I kept tabs on you and Sherry.

I am so pleased to be able to pass this little item on to you. The necklace belonged to my mother, your grandmother, Charlotte Swain. It was given to her by her mother-in-law Suzanne Swain. Suzanne received it from a friend, Mrs. Sarah Rule. Since it has passed through the hands of nurses it seems only fitting that you should have it now. I am not a nurse—heavens no, I could never have the patience for that kind of work! I am a naturalist in Arizona, and that suits my interests perfectly. Plants and trees, birds and animals, they are what capture my attention.

I have included a copy of the letter Suzanne sent to Mother, as well as Sarah Rule's obituary. I thought you would like to know these things. The little gift was originally made in the late 1890s, and I have no earthly idea what you will do with it, being a man. That is your question to answer. I hope your search for the answer and the practice of your profession will lead to a most fulfilling life. Please drop me a line from time to time. I would love to know how my nephew is getting along.

Congratulations, Will!

Your Aunt Kat

He read Suzanne's letter and Sarah Rule's obituary notice. "Hey, Dad, look at this. It's from Aunt Kat." Will held the necklace up, its heart-shaped silver setting holding a brass button, above it a small garnet. A simple silver chain connected both sides of the heart.

"Oh, really?" Dick said, turning from the stove. "A necklace? that's an interesting graduation present to give a guy."

"I guess she gave it to me because of the connection with nurses. The button must be a hundred years old. It's from the Civil War. Interesting … maybe it'd be worth something? It was nice of her to send me this, I need to thank her."

The timer dinged, and Dick put four small pieces of sweet corn in a bowl. Hamburger steaks were softly sizzling on the back burner. "I just need to slice some tomatoes and we can eat."

Will smiled. "You're getting pretty good at this cooking thing, Dad."

"Well, I had a great example, did you know that? My dad loved spending time in the kitchen. Mom used to say he was a much better cook than she would ever be; she never spent much time at it. And he loved tending his garden."

"I wish I had met him."

"Woodrow Swain was a fine man and a great father. He died when I was only twenty-nine. And your Grandmother Charlotte—you didn't really get a chance to know what a wonderful woman she was either."

"Yeah, I was what, twelve? Thirteen? Something like that, when she died?" Will put the pendant back in the box. "Well, Aunt Kat's right that I won't be wearing this, but it's symbolic. That's cool. An heirloom? Maybe I'll have it on a desk, someday, or display it on a wall."

1972 to 1976
Topeka, Kansas

Will had happily accepted an RN position at Menninger Hospital in the summer of 1972, and he traveled west in late August. After two years he moved from his first apartment to a rented two-bedroom house in a much nicer neighborhood. The screened-in back porch and easy-to-manage yard convinced him. The landlady was weird, but she took care of the occasional issues that arose. He paid on time, by check, in the mail, so he didn't see her much. Sherry visited a few times, and once she strongly considered moving to Kansas. But after weighing the pros and cons, she didn't think it was much different from Indiana, windier perhaps, definitely a negative. Besides, she knew her new husband Chuck wouldn't like it.

Will began his career as a nurse working on the evening shift, 3 to 11 p.m. At first he wasn't sure he'd like the odd hours when so much of the world was oriented to a nine-to-five schedule. But to his surprise, he found he really enjoyed it. After living in Topeka for a year, he splurged on a Motobecane road bike that Sherry talked him into—Chuck was a bike enthusiast. He enjoyed quiet mornings by himself, exploring Topeka and sampling the bike trails that were being constructed. He made a few friends, joined the bike club, and regularly began riding in small groups to interesting places.

Will dated several women in Topeka, two of them from the biking club, but the timing for a potential mate never seemed quite right. Sometimes he questioned what was wrong with him. *Why is it that when I'm ready to really get serious, the only women I find to date just want to be friends? And when I'm not feeling the chemistry with someone, she wants to get married? Is it the male nurse thing?* He wondered if he was destined to be single the rest of his life. And besides, working rotating evening shifts didn't allow for much of a social life. *Maybe I need to get a day job?*

In the fall of 1974, Will was approached by the head nurse, Mary Springer, a woman he liked a lot. She suggested that he apply for the new position as her assistant. He would still be working the evening shift with the occasional expectation that he be available for some overlaps into the night shift. *Well, it's certainly worth a try, and I've shown them what I can do. Besides, it's an increase in pay, and that's always good.*

Will thrived in the role and while he enjoyed the direct care of patients, he discovered that he was also good at coaching staff, even occasionally participating in performance evaluations. It was obvious that Mary trusted him and he began to wonder if he would be happy as a nurse manager.

Margie

October 1976
Topeka, Kansas

"Hey Will, do you have a minute?" she asked. "I need to run this specimen down to the lab. The damn tube system is all screwed up again. Can you sit with our new admit in 109? She's depressed, suicide attempt, and Dr. Frase wants her bloodwork STAT. Here's her paperwork," she said, thrusting a clipboard at him.

And before he could answer, or offer to run to the lab himself, Mickey was gone.

"Just like her," he muttered, "I bet she wants some time with Jerry."

Will tapped on the doorframe, Mickey's paperwork in hand. "Mrs. Luce? May I come in?" The new patient was lying on her side with her back to him. *A tiny thing,* he thought to himself. He checked the admit sheet: *48 years old, married.*

She offered a soft "Mm-hm," but did not turn to look back at him or sit up.

He walked over to the guest chair at the foot of her bed and asked, "Mind if I sit a minute? Your nurse, Mickey, had to get to the lab, and she asked me to introduce myself and get acquainted. I'm Will Swain. I'm the assistant head nurse on this unit, part of the evening shift. You'll see me most evenings here … this is my home base."

Her eyes were closed. *Terribly thin, her skin looks yellowish. Jaundice, maybe?* Her long, mousy-brown hair was greasy and pulled back in a low pony tail. She wore bell-bottom jeans and a dingy shirt, several sizes too large, that once might have been white. She didn't answer, but he sat down anyway. "How are you doing?"

No response.

After a minute he tried again. "Being here on this unit can be pretty strange at first, but after a few days, it feels a lot more like home." *Oops, wrong word.*

"I doubt that'll happen," she commented, finally opening her eyes. "A hospital is not a home. Well, this locked loony bin is not a home," she corrected herself, "but at least they're safe."

"They?"

No reply.

"Mrs. Luce, is there someone at home that you're worried about?"

She shifted her gaze to his face. "Not any more, well, except for who's taking care of them. But I'm not there now, and that's the best thing for them."

"I want to understand more, Mrs. Luce—can you tell me about it?"

She was quiet. Will had lots of practice giving patients time, time to process their thoughts, time to protect their inner worlds with carefully chosen words. *Time. I have plenty of it, you'll see. I can out-wait you. That's what they pay me for.*

She looked at him this time. "My kids." Tears seeped, then rolled down her face. Silence again.

"Your kids?" he asked. "Tell me about them."

She heaved a heavy sigh. "They're great. They're really great, better than I deserve for the mother I've been." *Hmm. Another depressed woman feeling guilty about her mothering.* Her words stopped again. More silence.

He decided to go with facts first. "How many do you have?"

"Four." Will nodded at her, encouraging more. "Three boys and a girl, twenty-three, twenty-one, ten and nine. Two families really. The girl is the ten-year-old."

"Mm-hm."

"We wanted a boy of our own, so I said we were done after Toby. At forty with two little ones, a year apart, well, that would send anyone to the loony bin, wouldn't it?" She tried to smile before continuing. "They are going to be so freaked out when they find out everything, but maybe they know now? And George, he won't be much help there. Shit, he's had it in for me for a long time."

A goldmine, thought Will. A tap on the doorframe. Mickey was back. She gestured to Will, did he want her to switch places and get back to what he was doing before? He shook his head, she signaled "OK," and left.

"Can I ask their names, Mrs. Luce? We like to know about people's families."

She sat up on the edge of the bed. "You can call me Margie. Adam, he's the oldest, he's not at home anymore. And Jonah. Those two live together in Lawrence. Then there's Gail and Toby. Adam and Jonah had a different father."

Will nodded again, making notes. "George is—?"

"My husband, though I doubt that will be the case much longer. He's put up with so much crap in my life, I know he's so damn tired of it all. He thinks *he's* tired!"

Will mulled over several ways to get at the next question, but he knew simplest was best. He leaned forward. "Margie, can you tell me what happened?"

"I got fired." He nodded again, waiting for more. "I was stealing narcotics, and they found out." Will kept a blank expression on his face. *Narcotics?*

"I knew I couldn't keep it up much longer. I could feel their eyes on me, watching me every minute. And then, well, my patients started to complain."

"Your patients? Are you a nurse?"

She nodded and shifted her position. "God, I need a cigarette. Can you get 'em for me? They took 'em when I first got here, my belt, too … my favorite macrame belt, made it myself."

Will didn't smoke, but he knew that he'd likely get more information if she could. "Tell you what, there's no smoking in the rooms or on the unit here. Why don't we take a little walk, and you can smoke outside?" He retrieved her cigarettes from the patients' locked storage area and escorted her outside. The day was comfortably warm for October. Each patient room looked out onto a large grassy courtyard with white rocking chairs, little side tables, and two round patio tables with umbrellas. A stream bubbled through a rock garden.

Will often found that walking with patients while they told their stories helped them open up. And being outside, in the fresh air of nature, had a calming effect. *But Margie is so thin, I wonder how long she'll be able to walk with me. Ha*—his arguing-other said, *she's a nurse and used to being on her feet.*

"Let's go over to that corner." They stopped in front of the stream. "A lot of people come out here to smoke, or just to enjoy the weather when it's nice. The only thing we ask is that folks pick up their butts." He pointed to the trash can.

Margie nodded. He took a deep breath and started again. "Tell me about being a nurse."

"Well, you know what that's all about. You've been through the training, you know what it's like. They teach you all the right ways to do things, and then they throw you into the lion's den with little support. Constant battle between what you know you should do, and what it really comes down to. I mean, it was OK in the beginning, I liked being a student. But once I graduated, wow, that was a trip! Reality trip." She shook her head.

"How long have you been a nurse?"

"I started late. Graduated in '62 after my first husband, the bastard, up and left one day. 'It just dawned on me that I'm not cut out for fatherhood,' he told me. His exact words, I'll never forget 'em. Left me with two young boys to raise alone. He disappeared from our lives, along with the money. You think that didn't have an effect on their emotions, not to mention mine? I had to do something, and I figured nursing would always pay the bills. So, let's see, fourteen years now, though I took some time off with my younger kids." She paused to draw on her cigarette, hungrily. "How long have you been a nurse?"

"Just a few years," Will answered, "going on five actually." They talked a while longer, and then he checked his watch. "We should get back in, I guess. Your orders should be all entered by now, and you may have some meds to take. To be continued?"

Margie looked at him. "Let me stay out here to finish my cigarette first, OK?"

She thought about the circumstances that brought her here. After she graduated from nursing school, Margie had found work in her little town's nursing home. The work didn't demand much of her, and the patients were stable. That was a good thing. Adam and Jonah were nine and seven and required constant planning to keep them out of trouble. Night shift suited her situation best, although it was against her nature as an early riser. She was at home just as they left for school and awake when they got home. Her sister came over around ten to spend the night with the boys, and get them up and fed the next morning. The arrangement worked for three years until she met George Luce.

It wasn't long before George stepped into her sister's overnight role, then the bedroom. They were both lonely for adult company and marriage followed quickly. At first the boys didn't like George, but they warmed to him when he began to take them fishing and camping. Within a year they had a baby sister, and a little brother a year later.

Margie stopped working seven months into her pregnancy with Gail, and stayed home until Toby was almost three. Life with four children strained their finances, and she went back to work in 1970, this time at the hospital on rotating days and evenings. Two pregnancies in quick succession at nearly forty had left her with chronic back pain, sometimes so bad that she couldn't get out of bed. But the muscle relaxers and pain pills the doctor ordered helped—a lot.

When she started having trouble getting her prescriptions refilled, she found she could turn to the steady supply at work, if she was careful. If her patient had an order for pain medication that he didn't need, she would slip the pills into her pocket, then make a note in his chart that she "gave pt. meds for headache; headache relieved." What relief—she felt *so much* better after an hour. It didn't take long to accumulate a small supply of her own, but she needed more and more pills to relieve the pain.

For a while the deceit was sporadic and only when she had flare-ups. Then she noticed that taking pain pills at home helped her cope with the demands of her growing family. Adam was away at school, but the other three were a challenge with the diverse needs of their ages and personalities. She found that she could conceal her habit by working rotating shifts, and she often volunteered to work an extra so she could continue to build her supply. She told George it was to bring in more money.

Then she tried injecting herself. Such quick relief, no longer having to wait a half-hour or more. Stealing injectables was harder than pills because she had to change needles to give herself the rest of the drug. After a while she stopped trying to get a different one. She just wiped off the used needle with an alcohol swab, pocketed the syringe, and took a quick bathroom break. When the hospital instituted a policy of having another nurse witness a partially used, "wasted," dose of a narcotic, she began forging nurses' signatures. She was good at duplicating their hurried and sometimes sloppy writing.

She was caught shortly after the evening shift began, when she'd just found a patient for her first dose. As she headed into the staff bathroom for her "break," a hand grabbed her shoulder. "Stop right there, Margie." Her heart started pounding hard in her chest, and she could feel the pressure rise in her neck. Peggy Sprute, the usually friendly head nurse, wasn't friendly this time. Margie's heart sank as she saw **Drug Diversion Investigation** at the top of her clipboard. Behind Peggy, stern-faced as well, was the director of security, a young man she had often joked with in the cafeteria.

"We have some questions for you, Margie," Peggy said, "and we also need you to give us a urine sample." Peggy handed her a plastic cup. "Witnessed."

Margie looked around, grateful no staff members were nearby.

Peggy continued, "But before you and I go into a bathroom, we need to see what's in your pockets, and then your locker. JoAnna will take over your patient load. Let's go."

Margie wanted to melt into the floor, wake up from this bad dream, disappear. She was just trying to do her best and show up, able to work without pain, was that so wrong? And she had legitimate pain, at least it was legitimate a few years ago. She handed Peggy the sample, sure there would be narcotics in it. The most damning thing was the syringe in her pocket. At least she had given the patient a partial dose. She cared enough to make sure they had some pain relief. Didn't that count for something?

She sat in Peggy's office with the security director and answered their questions honestly; no point in lying now. At the end of the meeting, Peggy fired her. Tomorrow she would be reported to the nursing board and the Topeka Police Department. Peggy offered to call George to drive her home. "It's either your husband or a taxi. I cannot in good conscience let you go by yourself."

George came to the front door, wondering why Margie was home mid-shift without her car. She pulled him into the bedroom, away from the kids, and told him she'd been fired. "I can't talk about this now. Right now all I want to do is sleep. Will you bring me a glass of wine? I need to clear my head. I don't want the kids to see me all upset at dinner. Tell 'em I'm sick or something."

George left the room. He was disgusted, angry, and ready to say more, but he could smell the lasagna burning. They'd be having "the talk" tomorrow for sure. Margie went to the bathroom and found the bottles she kept hidden behind the carefully folded towels.

Reunion

October 1977
Evansville, Indiana

Will and Ella reconnected at the University of Evansville Alumni fifth reunion. Ella had written to their DIR group to urge them to return for their first milestone, and she needed a pleasant distraction. Within the weekend's homecoming activities, she had invited their group to a picnic at nearby Wesselman Park. Four came with spouses, and Clara and Will were both single. She did not invite Jim.

Will had always loved autumn in southern Indiana, and he felt renewed on this first trip back to campus. The jovial shouts, hugs, and introductions reminded Will of his student days, the "buzzing around" he called it, "before the flies landed." He knew it was necessary, but he never felt at ease with small talk. The spouses were a lot less interested in the lively chatter, even though two of them were alumni.

Patti and Sandra were both married, without kids, and working as RNs on medical-surgical units. Clara was thinking of going back to school, maybe teaching nursing. Nancy Joe enjoyed the flexibility and challenge of public health nursing. She and her husband Walter brought their two-year-old, Kurt, to the picnic, and, when he got fussy after a few hours, they went back to their hotel.

Elaine was pregnant and planned to quit her job in two more months, just before Christmas. She winked, "What timing for the holidays off!" She loved her job on the pediatric unit and had big dreams to learn ICU nursing when she returned from maternity leave. Ella and Will were content as psychiatric nurses, which did not surprise anyone.

Will, Ella, and Clara stayed on, enjoying the late afternoon and picking at leftovers, after the others said goodbye. "So, what about your back-to-school thoughts, Clara?" asked Ella. "Where are you thinking of going?"

"Well, I've looked at IU Bloomington, and then Indianapolis at the Med Center. Kentucky has a strong master's program, and Wayne State in Ohio does, too. I'm not sure. It means a lot of upheaval, moving for sure, and putting myself back in the student thing again. But I liked school, and it would be less disturbing to my life and my parents now than if I waited. They depend on me more and more."

She looked at her watch. "Oh, gosh, I've got to get back. They were expecting me half an hour ago. Seems like I never have time for myself anymore. I have no idea how I could really manage at school, but," as she rose from the blanket, "one day at a time. I bought a poster the other day that I love. It's some sort of prairie dog, standing up in a field of dandelions, eating one, and it says 'Learn to Eat Problems for Breakfast.' That's my motto now. Probably will be for a long time."

They said their goodbyes, and Will and Ella were silent as they watched her walk away.

Ella spoke first. "I'm going to make a big change, Will, and soon. I can't take much more of this pretend life."

He raised his eyebrows. "Pretend?"

She nodded. "The marriage … what a mess, and I'm just grateful we don't have kids. Being around the group again, remembering how I felt when my life was all ahead of me. And seeing the other husbands? They all seem so normal. Nobody drank much, and they're supportive of their wives. When Clara mentioned school, did you see Mike nudge Patti and say 'You should too?' I don't have that. Even Jim's mother is threatened by my education. They are both freaked out about my wanting more. What does that tell you?"

He nodded and said gently, "Maybe you made a mistake?"

The sadness and resignation on her face was answer enough.

"I get it, Ella. And … are you thinking of divorce?"

She looked down at the ground. "Mm-hm. Here's another thing. I'm sure he's having an affair. He came home late a few weeks ago, a Friday night. He went right to the bathroom and then started to fill the tub. Weird, I thought. A bath at eleven at night? He showers in the morning. I went in to talk with him, you know, sit on the toilet lid and try to connect. Ha! I looked down at his discarded underwear and saw his T-shirt, inside out, the way he always takes them off. Long black hairs, two or three, clinging to the fabric. I lost it, Will, I really did."

Tears began to track down her cheeks. "I picked it up and practically shoved it in his face. He was sitting in the water, defenseless. I definitely had the upper hand there. 'What is this? Who is she?' I was screaming at him. He shook his head and said lamely, 'It must have gotten picked up in the laundromat. You never like going there with all those other people you don't know anything about.' I couldn't believe it! What an insult on top of the cheating! 'That is utter bullshit, Jim, and you know it.' Then I slammed the door, actually I turned out the bathroom light and left him to sit in the dark. I took my car keys and got outta there."

Will frowned and took one of her hands. "Go on."

"I don't remember much about the drive, other than at some point I could hear myself screaming. I was so full of rage and anger. I drove, and drove, and finally got back home around three. I slept on the couch that night. Jim was gone when I woke up."

She sighed and took her hand back. "I'm really glad I didn't hurt anyone." She took another deep breath and wiped her face with her hands. "I've been staying with a friend since, and next week I'm moving to a tiny apartment close to work. There's nothing I want from the house, I can tell you that. Planning this reunion has been the bright spot of my life, and today gave me a glimpse of the life I want. So that helps. In a way."

They sat together longer, talking about work and the possibility of Ella going back to school. She wasn't sure how she could afford it, but she was thinking of moving to Indianapolis to be closer to the Med Center and figure things out as she went along. She'd get a job first. Nancy Joe had mentioned an opening at the public health station where she worked, and Ella thought the job might be interesting.

"Let's stay in touch," he'd said to her. She nodded. They hugged for a long time before heading out, each in their different direction.

Later, turning their conversation over in her mind, Ella realized that she had done all the talking. She hadn't given Will much of a chance.

Ella, Public Health Nurse

1978
Indianapolis, Indiana

Ella hated to leave the children's hospital, especially Mrs. Caraway. But she knew she needed to get away from small-town Evansville and memories of Jim. She had seen him twice recently with the black-haired woman: once at the movies and once when she was at a park outing with the hospital kids. Both times distressed her, but she took perverse pleasure that he was with the same person. Her name was Monica, he later told her. *Could I have been the affair that interrupted their relationship?* She wondered. *Maybe Jim was originally with Monica?* Even so, the question didn't take the sting out of his betrayal.

The divorce process was quick, and he had even offered to help her move. She politely refused. *The less he knows about my new life, the better.* Besides, she needed to manage all the details of adulthood now. As soon as Ella decided to move to Indianapolis, Nancy Joe recommended her to fill a vacancy at the public health station, and she was tentatively offered a job.

Everyone knew of her psych interest before she reported for her first day of work. Not one other nurse felt comfortable with mental health referrals, so they often traded cases with her. TB medication monitoring, hospital-to-home follow-ups, and new-baby checks dominated their work on the west side of the city. A nurse could quickly become expert handling chronic conditions like congestive heart failure and diabetic complications. She didn't find much of a challenge there; she knew where her gifts lay. Ella welcomed the trades.

With her geographic assignment she automatically became the school nurse for Washington Elementary. Mrs. Shelby, the public health station's director, required that each nurse oversee one public school, no trading out. They conducted eye and TB testing, followed up on lice outbreaks and lost vaccination cards, and maintained limited office hours.

It wasn't long before Ella noticed that Dave Charles, a fifth-grade teacher, frequently hovered to offer any help with "whatsomever" she needed. He was flirting with her, she knew. She wasn't attracted to him, but he was likable, and it was nice to have an admirer who reminded her that she was still desirable.

Other than school coverage, nurses could specialize as much as they wanted within the available cases, Mrs. Shelby had informed her during orientation. "All our patients must be cared for, but how you nurses arrange to do that is completely up to you, as long as we maintain the quality for which this station is known."

One day a referral came in that she held just for Ella. "The nurses at the hospital are concerned about this little girl and her home environment, especially the father. Social Services visited the home a year ago and could not establish anything to act on. The referral was from a neighbor, it says here, and those are always hard to pin down."

She held out the form to Ella and continued. "This child needs follow-up this afternoon from her hospital stay. I want you to use all your skills to observe conditions in the home, especially her relationship with the parents and between them. There are other children there. You'll bring a fresh set of eyes, and the timing is perfect for another view. Depending on what you find, we may be calling in the police. I would make this visit myself, but I have a meeting downtown." *Right, I haven't seen you make a visit in the six months I've been here,* Ella thought. *Sure hope I am up to this* ....

Dramatic thunderheads started building before noon. Ella got out of the car and reached into the backseat for her black nurse's bag. *Both temperature and humidity must be hovering around eighty-five,* she thought. *How oppressive.* She checked the case card. Her five-year-old patient,

Tuesday Anderson, was discharged after five days in the hospital. She had been treated for injuries from a fall at home: a broken arm that had to be surgically reset, lacerations, and bruising to the back. Prior X-rays revealed one older healed break for which they could find no documentation or follow-up.

Ella took a breath and knocked on the door.

The visit was inconclusive, she later reported to Mrs. Shelby. Except for the fact that the two other girls, Monday and March, and the newborn, July, were given such unusual names, she had seen other families behave like the Andersons. Both parents were present. Mr. Anderson had just awakened to get ready for his afternoon shift at the airport. Mrs. Anderson looked more than tired, but the newborn seemed to be gaining weight on schedule. Ella took the time to evaluate her skin and check for diaper rash. Everything appeared normal. The diaper was freshly changed.

Mrs. Anderson complained of being tired, *but who wouldn't be with four young children?* Her hair was limp, and she had dark circles under her eyes, but what stood out to Ella was how unusually thin she was. Without being asked, she mentioned several times how hard it had been for her not to see Tuesday in the hospital. She had no one to care for the others, nor any way to bring them all with her. Her husband had made all the visits to the hospital.

Mr. Anderson sat in the recliner, dressed in wrinkled trousers, an undershirt barely covering his bulging belly, trying to yawn himself awake. He held coffee in one hand while March fidgeted in resistance on his lap. "Let your Mama be a minute, Marchie, she needs to tend the baby," he cautioned. Mrs. Anderson gave him a glance and picked up the fussing infant from the corner of the threadbare couch.

Tuesday was a friendly little girl who seemed happy with all the attention. Her cast was intact, and she complained about itching, a normal condition. The bruising on her back was turning green now, and the sutures looked clean and ready to be removed in two or three days. Ella

Ella, Public Health Nurse

said she would see about an order from the doctor to allow her to remove them at home. Mr. Anderson said he was glad that they wouldn't have to arrange a trip to the doctor's office. *A return visit would give me another chance to reassess the situation,* she thought, *but for the moment, I don't think I need to worry.*

She was wrong. Two days later she called in to work to say she'd just discovered a flat tire and would be in late. The station was unusually quiet when she walked in the door. The note on her desk read "See me the minute you get in—R. Shelby."

"What is this?" she asked out loud. No one met her eyes.

"Sit down, Ella," said Mrs. Shelby as soon as Ella entered her office. "You need to hear this." Mrs. Shelby then told her the police had been called to the Andersons' the night before. Mrs. Anderson had been severely beaten, and her survival was doubtful. The oldest sister had run to the neighbor's for help, and, when the police arrived, they found Mrs. Anderson unconscious. The two other girls were hiding in a bedroom closet, and the baby was dead. Mr. Anderson and the car were gone.

Was she a coward, or lazy, not wanting to look deeper? Did she know enough? Could she have prevented this?

School, Again

September 1979
Indianapolis, Indiana

Over several long phone conversations, Ella and Will decided to go back to school, same university, same program. Will moved to Indianapolis from Topeka, and in January both were admitted to the incoming class of the Psychiatric-Mental Health Clinical Nurse Specialist program at Indiana University-Purdue University at Indianapolis, IUPUI. "What a crazy mouthful of words," Ella laughed. "Do they make up these titles on purpose, just to test our recall or pronunciation?"

Will had become comfortable and skilled as an inpatient psychiatric nurse in the years since graduation. He was pleased that he had chosen Menninger's and grateful for the solid foundation he had gained there. Sherry and his dad were thrilled that he was returning to Indiana: Lafayette was close to Indianapolis, and they would get to see him a lot more often. Will was OK with that, too. Sherry and Chuck were anxious to have kids. Will's dad was romantically involved with Marian, a family friend, and he had blossomed in a way Will had never seen.

Will and Ella learned it was possible to finish the program in a short eighteen months, although completing thesis requirements often extended the time to two or even three years. Their cohort of psych nursing students was small, nine in total. Other students joined them in the basic courses; Research Methods, Statistics, and Thesis Seminar. Ella rented an apartment with another student, Marcia Corley. Will had an apartment by himself in a nearby complex.

Of the cohort, Will felt most comfortable with Ella and rarely chose to study or socialize much with the others. "I had no idea you were such a loner," Ella chided.

"I just can't see the point in getting distracted by all their dreams and chatter. Focus is the name of the game for me, and I have to make the most of my time here." Funding from federal grants for nursing education had recently dried up, so both of them were paying the costs on their own. Ella's parents were helping her, but Will was using money his mother had left to him.

"I hear you, Will, but their 'dreams and chatter,' as you call it, really help spark my imagination and curiosity. I need others' examples … I'm not at all creative on my own. You know me, I'm interested in *everything*."

At the master's level, pursuit of one's specific passion was encouraged, and thesis seminar was the place where ideas and possibilities blossomed. One student was fascinated by the emerging field of sex therapy, another with psychological interventions for children newly diagnosed with cancer. Ella wanted to be back in school to give her life a new springboard. She wondered about working in the field of child abuse, but didn't have a strong notion of where this degree would lead her. She trusted that Mrs. Caraway had encouraged her for a good reason.

Will was haunted by Margie. After two weeks on Menninger's locked unit, Dr. Frase had discharged her as "much improved." Will had been on vacation when it happened and was horrified by her release. How could she be "much improved" in such a short time, especially with all the legal challenges she faced? Sure, the recommendation for outpatient therapy was there, but Will knew compliance without additional support was slim. Shortly after she left the hospital, Margie had ended her life, combining vodka with a full bottle of antidepressants.

Her death continued to gnaw at him, especially because she was a nurse. He could only imagine the effect on her children. *What a waste of nursing talent,* he thought. *Wasn't there something that could be done to save her?* Obsessive thoughts kept circling with nowhere to go.

He was relieved to finally meet with Sharon Markles, the professor he had asked be his thesis advisor. "So, what have you been thinking about, Will?" she began. "Do you have some thoughts about what you'd like to do?"

Will watched her cradle an IUPUI coffee mug in her hands as she leaned back in the chair. He told her Margie's story, and stopped. Then something else urged him on. *Tell her Mom's story, too.* When he finished with Estelle's, he said "So, you can see I have this desire to do something that will help nurses."

"Where you ultimately decide to go with this, Will, is the big question. What can you reasonably accomplish within the program and its time limits? Are you framing this problem in substance abuse terms, as in, for the individual? Are there special interventions just for nurse clients? Are you more interested in prevention or intervention? Why would either one be worthy of your time?" She seemed truly interested, which pleased him.

She took a thoughtful sip from her mug, staring off somewhere. "Or, try this on for size. You could take the perspective of the regulatory agency. What about protecting the public? What are the current disciplinary approaches across the states? Compared to here in Indiana? And have you thought about the nurse who does not have a substance use disorder, maybe has not broken the law? Say for example, a nurse who has problems that affect her safe practice, like depression, or a brain condition? How about post-traumatic stress disorder?"

He scribbled furiously as she threw out questions, amazed at her flow of ideas. What began as wishing he could have saved Margie and his mother was turning into a Pandora's Box of possibilities.

She recognized his expression as it shifted from engaged to overwhelmed. "Will," she smiled, "this is the normal process. Don't look so stunned. I am here for you, and this inquiry is exactly what you should be doing at this point in the program. You cannot have all the answers. That is what the rest of the coursework is for. Let's discuss some resources, and," she said, pulling out her appointment book, "let's schedule regular meetings right now. You are on to something, Will, and I don't want us to lose it."

When he got up to leave, she added, "Oh, and one more thing. You should bring this up in seminar. I notice you haven't shared too much there, compared to what you've discussed with me."

Really? Will thought to himself. *Seems to me they're just chatting away most of the time, caught up in their own worlds. I'm not sure they could offer me anything useful.* "Oh, uh, well, I'll think about it. You could have a point."

They stood side by side at the single mirror in the compact apartment's only bathroom. "Bathroom therapy" they called it. Ella was struggling with direction for her thesis. "What did your thesis advisor tell you?" Marcia asked.

"She said that I needed to do more reading about therapies, and stick with the course work assignments for now. 'Ideas don't come easily for everyone' was her phrase."

Marcia nodded, taking care with the eyelash curler. "We have another few weeks before the thesis plan is due."

"Yeah, but that's such a short time really. I wish I was as clear as Will on an area of interest at least."

"What's his topic?"

"He's not certain, but I think he's narrowed it down to nurses and PTSD."

Marcia nodded again and continued. "How do you feel about your Brief Therapy clinical work? Is that going OK?"

"I enjoy it. I like that it's brief, six or eight sessions. I'm discovering that I have a talent for listening broadly for themes, and for what's not said. Normally I don't get caught up in details. When I reflect something back to my client, they're often surprised, and it takes us to a deeper, richer place. Who knew? Maybe I have a gift for therapy."

"Let me ask you this, Ella. What pushed you to go back to school? Was there an event that triggered you?"

"Um, well, remember my time with that family of four daughters? I told you about that, right?"

Marcia nodded. "Yeah, those mental health needs of patients in the community."

Ella smiled at her friend. "Bingo, Marcia, that could be it!! I wish I had seen it earlier. That could be my topic!" Ella shook her head. "Back to the library—again."

Road to the Program

1982 to 1984
Indianapolis, Indiana

After graduating with his master's degree in 1982, Will took two part-time jobs. He was invited to fill a lecturer/clinical supervisor position at the nursing school, guiding undergrads in their psych and community health rotations. But he was "just satisfied" with his second job as research assistant at Larue Carter Memorial Hospital. He made rounds on patients and completed the prescribed paperwork to document outcomes and possible side effects. He enjoyed the patients and staff but found himself frustrated with the pace of clinical research.

At a Christmas party that year for just-graduated students, he and Ella found themselves alone for a moment in the host's kitchen. "How's your work going at Carter now, Will?" Ella asked. "Do you like it?"

"It's a job," he sighed, "and it keeps me close to the University and other options. The Board of Nursing, too. But I'm not really that excited about it."

"That surprises me, Will. I see you as someone who always has the bigger picture in mind, and you're so steady and, hmm, well, I guess … determined. I thought research would attract you when no one else would find it interesting."

Ella was energized by her work. After she graduated in 1982 and took a little time off, she was hired as the Mental Health Clinical Specialist at St. Alphonsus Hospital on the south side. Her role was to help the nurses with the mental health needs of patients who were admitted anywhere in the hospital. She liked the challenge of working with the staff on the twenty-bed locked unit. She typically spent half her time there, talking with patients, stepping in when a nurse was called away or needed help. She held case conferences to review or adjust care plans.

Other units in the hospital referred cases to her; a complicated pregnancy of a sixteen-year-old, a new cancer diagnosis in a pediatric patient, a college athlete with a life-changing broken back. With her communication skills and ability to comfort distressed patients she was welcome everywhere. Ella often said she had the best job in the world.

One year later Ella rekindled a relationship with Dave Charles, the persistent grade school teacher she had once dismissed. Now she saw him in a different light. He was more attractive than she had remembered, and he made her laugh. He enjoyed hobbies that encouraged her to seek different ones herself. She started running, which she enjoyed, especially after seeing the effect on her weight, her shape, and most important, her attitude. A flier at the grocery store advertised yoga classes, and she decided to give that a try, too.

In January, 1984, Will asked Ella to help him create an alternative-to-discipline program for nurses with substance abuse disorder. He wanted to turn part of his master's thesis into reality. He couldn't do much for PTSD, but he could help a nurse keep a license to practice. If a nurse was reported to the Board of Nursing because of drug or alcohol abuse, she or he could be "diverted" onto a different path from discipline; a path of intensive monitoring, counseling, and rehabilitation. If the nurse completed the program successfully, the license could be reinstated.

Ella agreed, but her availability was limited. Meetings would have to be on her time off. Will was fine with that. *She has walked with me nearly every step of the way, and I could not have a better partner in this project, even if she can't devote as much time as I would like.*

May, 1984
Indianapolis, Indiana

The director of the Indiana State Board of Nursing, Mrs. Janes, emerged from her office to greet Will and Ella and asked if they wanted coffee. At 10:30 a.m., it was bound to be acidic and stale, served in little plastic cups in brown plastic holders. They declined.

As they walked back to her office, Ella smiled. She recognized Clara's "Learn to Eat Problems for Breakfast" poster over the director's desk. Noticing Ella's reaction, Mrs. Janes said, "My staff gave me that last year when I complained about all the fires we were putting out. Have a seat. Now, what can I do for you?"

Will told her about their interest in helping nurses struggling with substance abuse, and he summarized what they had been learning about alternative-to-discipline programs. "We're wondering where the Board of Nursing stands on the issue. We'd like to get some background on the Indiana experience to date, and if you have been thinking about a program."

She frowned. "Well, as you know, our mission is to protect the public, not nurses, and we see that our primary purpose is to make sure we respond to complaints in as timely a manner as possible." She raised her eyebrows at Will, inviting him to comment. He did not. He and Ella had planned how this first meeting should go and agreed to gather as much information as possible without stating a position.

Mrs. Janes took a breath and continued. "A couple of our members have expressed some interest in 'diversion programs,' that's what we call them, easier to say than 'alternative to discipline.' But our caseload of complaints has been increasing, and, unfortunately, we don't have the staff to dedicate any time to this."

Ella raised another rehearsed question. "What do you think a diversion program could do that is not already happening with your current approach?"

Mrs. Janes smiled and nodded. "That is the $64,000 question. It's a terrible waste of nursing talent when we have to rescind a license. Some of these nurses had quite stellar histories and were good at what they did. Then alcohol or drugs got in the way. It's so unfortunate when they get caught." She reached down to pull out a folder from her desk drawer. Putting on her reading glasses, she consulted the page in front of her.

"If we had a successful approach to handling these nurses, maybe they wouldn't job-hop from hospital, to nursing home, to outpatient clinic, to nursing home. And maybe the message about a program would encourage nurses to self-report first instead of getting caught. As you know, according to the law, if they get caught, they lose their license. If they self-report, things could possibly be easier for them—and they wouldn't have to automatically surrender their license. It would all come down to compliance. Maybe our complaints would go down, and patient care would improve? We would have to look at the enabling legislative language to make sure a program fits the framework."

Will smiled to himself as he made notes. *'Enabling language.' 'We would have to look.'* He wrote her exact words. *Is she interested?*

Will and Ella planned to brainstorm while attending the Cincinnati Music Festival over a free weekend. Will was a jazz buff, and Ella loved all music. She was ready for a break from work. Dave initially planned to join them, but a last-minute fishing trip with his brother was more appealing. Dave was friendly toward Will and not threatened by his relationship with Ella. She'd reassured him they'd been just buddies for more than fifteen years— nothing was going to change.

Riverfront Park and the hotel were over an hour's drive with plenty of time to drift back into conversation about a diversion program. "The Board of Nursing might be where the program properly belongs," Will said, "because licensing is the main issue, and they collect license fees for every RN. But as a backup, maybe we should check out the support of other groups, like the nurses association, maybe even the hospital association." Will was driving, and Ella scribbled notes as they talked.

"Hmm. Will, do you ever get tired of thinking about nursing all the time? I know we're hoping to map out our next steps, but, really, do you ever get tired of it?"

He looked at her. "What? All the time? You think I think about it all the time?"

"Well, yeah, I do. If we're not talking about an approach with the Board, you're consumed with students or your Carter patients."

His face reddened. "Well, Ella, I've spent eight years of my life studying to help make a difference, and I want it to pay off. I like what I do, Ella—no, actually, the truth is I *love* what I do, even the challenges. Thinking about the 'what ifs' really makes me come alive. I'm not like you, Ella. I don't really have the friendships like yours or groups to do things with. Really, I hardly have friends. I am perfectly content to be by myself."

It was Ella's turn to flush. "What about me, Will? We've spent a lot of time together over the years. You'd call me a friend, right?"

"Of course you're my friend! You're my best friend, don't you know that? Really, Ella, I don't know what I'd do if you weren't in my life."

Ella nodded. "Same for me, Will, same for me."

The only sound for a few minutes was highway noise and Stevie Wonder's "I Just Called to Say I Love You" on the radio. Ella spoke again. "Y'know, Will, Dave sometimes doesn't get it. He acts like he's OK with our relationship, and other times he gets kinda … twitchy, like he's not really sure. Like he doesn't quite believe me when I say he doesn't need to feel threatened."

"Wonder why, Ella?"

"Don't know … maybe I should ask him about it." Silence. "But you know, Will, I'm really glad he's not here this weekend. It's so nice to be with just you on a little holiday of sorts. But no more nurse talk this afternoon, OK?" She winked at him and continued. "Unless *I* bring it up of course."

"Of course," Will chuckled. He signaled the turn, and they exited the freeway.

The Focus Group

December 1984
Indianapolis, Indiana

Will and Ella scanned their questions once more and decided to leave them just as they were. Why a focus group instead of individual interviews? Mrs. Janes had asked.

Will said they were going to do both eventually, but if they could first gather a small group of nurses whose licenses were revoked, it might be healing for them to hear others' stories. Besides, they could see what kind of consensus, if any, might evolve from new ideas—and, more important, to see what kind of ideas might be sparked by group discussion that might not come out in a one-on-one interview.

Ella was going to be the facilitator, Will the recorder. Since most nurses are women and the subject so personal, they thought the nurses would connect more easily with Ella.

Carter Hospital provided easy parking and an available meeting space. Finding nurses to participate was harder, and there were no funds to pay them. They had hoped for twenty positive responses to their request, and they were relieved to receive fourteen. With date and time conflicts, last-minute problems and no-shows, seven nurses sat in front of them, six women and one man.

Ella took a deep breath and then smiled at them.

"Thank you all for joining us this afternoon. I'm Ella Swensen, and Will Swain, my colleague, back there behind you, will be taking notes. As you probably remember, we are both nurses. Your thoughts will be incredibly helpful to us as we work to develop an alternative-to-discipline program for nurses here in Indiana. We thank you for your courage in coming forward." Will raised his eyebrows and nodded encouragingly at Ella.

"As we told you in our letter and on the phone, we will not be asking for specific details of your experiences—no names, no employers, no details of your stipulations with the Board. First names only. If you share something specific, we will not record it. And we ask that all of you respect the confidentiality of the others. What you say here, remains here. Agreed?"

She looked around. All seven heads nodded. "OK then, let's begin with the first question: When you were first licensed as an RN, what did you know about the reasons for losing a license?"

A nurse named Petra, a bouncy blonde with triple-pierced ears and heavily made-up brown eyes, was first to break the ice. "To be honest, I didn't think a thing about it. One of my last classes was about our responsibility to the profession, belonging to organizations, and all that. I don't remember learning much about how I might lose my license. Documentation was a big deal—they talked about the acceptable way to correct errors so we wouldn't be in trouble if we ever had to testify in court. No changing notes, definitely no White-Out. That's what I remember most." Several others nodded.

"I was taught that administering narcotics was really risky," replied Francine, a thin Asian woman with dark circles under her eyes. "There were so many safeguards at my hospital, and it seemed like they were watching you all the time. I knew that if I stole narcotics I could lose my license. So, for a long time I was glad that I was only an alcoholic—I could stop any time, you know?" She said it with a wry smile, and a few chuckles sounded in the room.

Wally, a stern-looking African-American woman with close-cropped hair and big sad eyes, spoke up. "My sergeant went over everything in such detail, and so often, that it was easy after a while to ignore the information about infractions and punishments. In actual practice they overlooked all kinds of violations, and so you got the idea that all those reasons to lose a license would be ignored, too. I served in 'Nam at the end of the war, but even then, what I saw, what I heard, the smells ...." her voice trailed off, and she looked at the floor. Ella waited.

"Go on," she prompted.

"Even then, at the end," Wally replied, "I couldn't get those things out of my head. Nobody wanted to believe that the experiences of war could cause a nurse to have alcohol problems. Nurses are used to blood and screams and stress and pressure and long hours, right? People think nurses should be able to handle it—after all, they say, it's not like we were shooting or in hand-to-hand combat." Wally took in a deep breath. Behind her, quietly, so did Will.

She continued. "Well, I did handle it, for a while that is. Hardly anyone noticed when I stopped handling it, they were all too tied up in their own worlds. It took them years to catch me."

Ella looked around for more responses. Silence.

"Thank you. OK, let's go on to our second question, but as we go along if anyone wants to come back to a previous one, feel free. Where would a nurse go for help today if he or she had a problem with their ability to practice?"

Michael shook his head and spoke up. "That's tough. I found my way to Narcotics Anonymous after hitting bottom, after my wife left, taking my kids. Even then, it still took me a while to reach out for help. The staff at the Board gave me a list of numbers to call, but, shit, half of them were wrong numbers. When I finally found NA, I was the only nurse in the group. I thought about seeing a therapist, but I lost my health insurance when I lost my job. There's not much coverage for substance abuse anyway, and those programs are so expensive."

"I went to my pastor," said a nurse named Diana. "He was helpful for a while, but he wanted me to see someone in the church, and I wasn't having any of that. People talk. You know they do."

"I know we're not done with this question yet," said Ella, "but your point leads right into the next one. How important is confidentiality?"

"Confidentiality is absolutely important, and the truth is that it's absolutely a *sham*," said Michael, and several heads nodded in agreement. "People know one way or the other at your work. It's hard enough to accept the fact that you have a problem, and if you know others are looking at you like you're scum, man, that does not help. At all!"

Ella went on, trying to stop her foot from jiggling in anxiety. "If you had a confidential place to go for help, do you think you would have used it before the Board found out? How about someone who hasn't spoken yet. Brenda?"

"Well, I like to think that it would have made a difference, me coming forward early in the game. But I was terrified at first in my practice. I was so afraid I would do something wrong—really hurt someone, rather than help them. I couldn't believe that I had that kind of a reaction once I was out of school. I was top in my class! But then I moved back home and found work in our little community hospital. They didn't have much of an orientation at all, and I was a new grad. There were no young new nurses like me to talk to. I didn't want to lose that job, I worked so hard to get it. Everyone knew me, and my parents were so proud."

Brenda leaned forward and looked directly at Ella. "To reach out early? I don't know. I started using Percodan one day at work because of severe menstrual cramps, but then I found out how relaxed it made me feel. When I'd get all anxious again, I'd look for someone with a Percodan order. I honestly don't know what it would have taken for me to come forth earlier. Maybe if I saw someone like me having the same problem and getting help … maybe I would have paid attention. Maybe if I knew what I know now—how much it would cost, and how my life would be destroyed. Those are pretty negative reasons …."

"But they are reality," Wally countered, "and if just one of us could have gotten that message, wouldn't that be a good thing?"

The conversation lasted another half-hour before the silences grew longer. Ella drew the meeting to a close, and she and Will thanked them again. They promised to personally inform the nurses if and when a program was started. Perhaps some of them would want to help other nurses. Ella shut the door behind her and turned to look at Will. "Well, buddy, what do you think? Is it what you hoped for?"

He stood up, gathering his papers. "We gained lots of support for our ideas, that's for sure. Getting to nurses early, others, too, like their friends and family, coworkers, about help that is available. Maybe presentations in nursing school? By a recovered nurse, with her license back?" He started to tick the ideas off on his fingers. "Transition issues for new nurses, orientation, preceptorships. Specialized nurse support groups, people who have been there. Counselors who are familiar with the issues that the disciplined nurses deal with. Getting to employers of nurses. The list goes on, Ella."

He went quiet, staring off into space.

"Where are you, Will? What are you thinking?" she asked, reaching out her hand to him.

He shook his head to clear it. "Remember when Wally was talking about Viet Nam?" She nodded. "It took me back to my mother, and her life as a POW. I wonder what things would have been like if they had recognized her trauma early and if she could have done something different than resort to alcohol." He continued. "PTSD. It hit me. Again. Maybe we can tie that in to our program somehow." He hesitated, and then spoke more softly. "I dream about making it better for those nurses, so they don't have to lose it all."

Seeing Will's softer edges made something shift within Ella. Goodness knows they had spent lots of time together over the years, and he had shared experiences that touched him deeply. Her, too. But seeing this Will, this more vulnerable side of him, and his passion come full circle, hopeful. His big brown sad eyes. She wanted to reach out and join his softer edges with hers, to be a place of refuge for him. She wanted to help him achieve his dream.

Could his dream become hers?

Giving In

May 1986
Indianapolis, Indiana

Race Day parties were a highlight of the Memorial Day weekend for Indy 500 fans, and although Will did not follow the detail of drivers and cars, he enjoyed being a host. The ritual of cooking for others was a welcome escape from the usual mind-cluttering details of his work life. He had discovered that food was a perfect way to connect with others, even if he wasn't such an extrovert. Ella was helping him be more comfortable in social situations, and after a year and a half of working together on the diversion program, Will realized he wanted more of her time.

Ella had ended her relationship with Dave two months ago when she'd finally admitted to herself that she was thinking of Will as more than a friend. Maybe Dave had been right about what he sensed between them. Whatever it was, she was glad to have cleared the way.

Ella thought that Will's neighborhood party had gone well; it lasted well past 2 a.m. Everyone brought so much food that he had to borrow a second patio table to hold it all. The weather was perfect, something you really couldn't count on in late May. She'd had too much pinot noir, a new wine Will's sister, Sherry, thought she would like. Now she stretched out on one end of his big brown couch, plushly upholstered and always inviting.

Will was in the kitchen, finding refrigerator room for leftover chicken, deciding whether to toss out potato salad, and sampling the baked beans—again. He was a sucker for baked beans at any temperature. And the neighbor's chocolate Bundt cake demanded another sampling, especially the gooey icing.

He filled two glasses with water and carried them to the living room. "Here, Ellie, you need this. I know I do." He claimed the other end of the couch and put his feet up on the big leather bench that served as coffee table and footstool. "Whew. Quite a party."

She opened her eyes and reached for the water, downing it greedily, then sank back down into the soft cushions. "Mm-hm. Thanks …."

Will said, "I want you to stay the night, you're in no condition to drive home."

She nodded. "Good idea, I'm definitely far out."

He laughed. "No kidding! You are … beyond it." "Far out" was their personal slang for "plastered," "shit-faced," or simply "too drunk to drive." *I could offer her the guest room, but she looks so comfortable, I don't want to disturb her.* After a moment with his eyes shut, he gave a big sigh, then hauled himself up out of his cozy spot, and brought back a pillow and blanket. He leaned over and kissed her cheek, "G'nite, my Ellie."

She stirred briefly. "'nite."

By 5:30 a.m. sunlight was spilling onto the bold floral comforter. Will stirred and rolled over to find Ella next to him, asleep. He smiled, dreamily imagining a tantalizing scenario unfolding in his bed. When he returned from the bathroom, his face splashed with cold water and teeth quickly brushed, she was awake and watching him. "Hi, there, buddy. My turn."

"There's extra toothbrushes in the righthand drawer, and I put out a towel for you." She got out of bed and he enjoyed watching this side of her, t-shirt barely covering the lower half of her full, firm bottom. As soon as he heard the shower running, he hopped up to switch on the coffeepot. She returned after a few minutes wearing the towel. Only.

They took their time. With no place to go and nothing they needed to do other than delight in the sensations of each other's skin, the touches, the smells, the tastes—they savored every minute. Will surprised Ella with his deliberateness and control. He was in charge of this, of her, and the sense of being dominated by this gentle man thrilled her. His knowledge of how to please delighted her. She didn't need to ask him to kiss her more gently or touch her there more lightly, as she had with Dave. Will instinctively knew how to electrify her. She had no idea sex could be this … delicious. *Should I thank his prior lovers?* she wondered, *or is Will a natural?*

Now everywhere he looked in his life, Will felt a new lightness and energy that he couldn't explain. His work, the Board of Nursing, his family were all touched by this change, but especially Ella. Besides being his best friend for years, he now saw in her the inviting curves and softness and a vulnerability that stoked tender feelings in him. And a longing, a deep longing, to be in the sanctuary of her.

The summer was a blur. One morning in Will's bed became weekends together at his place since Ella had a roommate. They discussed living together. In August, Ella moved in. They couldn't find enough time to be alone with each other. Ella was amazed at how much she must have been holding back any awareness of her desire for him. The early days of her relationship with Jim had never been this intense or this sweet. Her experiences with Dave and other men were empty dalliances compared with what she felt for Will.

Ella wondered what her mother would think, what would she make of it, this thing with Will. *Am I fooling myself? I've known him so long, why now? What pushed us over the edge?* She didn't want to tell her or ask, afraid of jinxing whatever they had. She wanted to believe it was more than a lustful affair, but neither one said the word "love."

Petra

November 25, 1986
Indianapolis, Indiana

She pushed the shopping cart into the dark, the sudden cold wind pelting horizontal rain and sleet, stinging her face and legs. *Damn,* she thought, *this came a lot sooner than I expected.* The lot was packed two days before Thanksgiving, but she had found one spot out on the periphery. By the time she got to her car, the downpour had soaked the paper bags on top. She quickly loaded the groceries into the backseat, one of the sacks splitting at the last minute. She barely saved the bottle of wine that Gary liked from shattering on the pavement.

What was I thinking, shopping at almost the last minute? Too bad for tomorrow night's shoppers. Maybe they won't have the rain, but they could have icy streets instead. A sudden drop in temperature had arrived, and she reminded herself *water's OK, ice isn't.* Gary could have done the shopping tomorrow, but her schedule was open tonight.

Power had failed at the second intersection, forcing drivers to take turns treating it as a four-way stop. *Double damn,* she thought, *home is just five minutes away!* Two other cars were ahead of her, so she took a moment to unbuckle her seatbelt to wiggle out of her wet jacket. It was her turn to go just as she adjusted the defrost setting and the wipers to high. She had not seen it rain this hard in years. It was so noisy! As she reached over her left shoulder for the seatbelt, she saw the blinding lights of a car barreling through the intersection. *Why is he coming at me so fast?*

Petra's parents, Chick and Jeanette, sat with Gary in the surgery waiting room. They had made the four-hour drive as fast as they could, but it was two in the morning when they arrived. The regional storm had affected all of Indiana.

An hour later Dr. Micaeleus, the orthopedic surgeon on call, came out to greet them. He looked young, as young as Petra, her father thought, distressed that fate had made this important decision for him. Who was this man who was operating on his only daughter? When the doctor removed his surgery cap, Chick was relieved to see gray hair streaking the sides of his head. Dr. Micaeleus looked at both of them. These conversations were never easy, and he understood what the parents were facing.

"Mr. Gillespie?" looking at Chick, "I'm Stephan Micaeleus, your daughter's surgeon." They shook hands, and he sat down with them. He looked as tired as they felt. "For starters, I want you to know Petra's a real fighter. Her vitals were pretty good throughout surgery. But I'm not going to sugarcoat it—" Jeanette took in a sharp breath.

"Her injuries are severe and significant. She has a compound fracture of her left femur, three broken ribs, a broken mandible—uh, that's the jaw bone—and a depressed skull fracture. All left side, the driver's side. We operated on the femur, putting in screws and stabilizing the bone, same with the mandible. Her fractured ribs should heal on their own, although it will be quite painful and take time. The skull fracture, that's what worries us the most. Dr. Patel, the neurosurgeon, is finishing up now and will be out in a moment to explain what's going on."

They sat there, stunned, trying to take in the words. Jeanette spoke first. "Will she recover? How long will she have to be in the hospital?"

Dr. Micaeleus smiled, wearily but kindly. These questions were so common—and always tough. "Mrs. Gillespie, as I said earlier, your daughter is strong, and we will do everything we can to help her recover. A lot depends on her brain function. Bones can heal, especially in a young and healthy person."

As they talked more, "Time will tell" was the answer to almost every question. As Dr. Micaeleus stood to go, Dr. Silvia Patel pushed through the double doors, rubbing her eyes.

A woman? Chick thought. *I hope she's as good as a man.*

December 1, 1986

Ella pulled out the new admit sheet from her stuffed inbox. Since she had taken time off over Thanksgiving, emergency admits outnumbered routine electives. *Petra Gillespie, thirty-three- year-old female. Was that "our" Petra of the focus group? Unusual name, a coincidence? Intensive Care Unit, trauma patient.* She checked her schedule and penciled her in as soon as the Nurse Leadership meeting was over.

She checked in with the third floor ICU and found Joan Kyzocky, Petra's primary nurse, at her bedside, hanging a new IV bag. "Hi, Joan, I'm here to check in on your patient here. How are things going for her?" *She is the Petra of the focus group!* Ella recognized the triple ear piercings, and what remained of her curly blonde hair. Her face was bruised purple-red, and both eyes were swollen shut.

"Well, we're keeping her heavily sedated, and the family—mother, father, husband—have been here on and off. It looks like the brain swelling is being managed, so that's good. She has an intracranial pressure catheter. She's roused a few times and squeezed yes or no with her left hand. She can't see with all that swelling, and her right hand is pretty swollen, too. She has a feeding tube in right now with her broken jaw and all. Poor girl. She's got a long road ahead of her. She'll probably be here a few more days until Dr. Patel's confident about her neuro status. Then on to Stepdown."

Ella nodded. She almost told Joan she knew Petra but held back. *Privacy is paramount. And she might not even want my involvement.* "Joan, would you page me the next time her family comes to visit? I'd like to see how they are doing."

"Sure thing."

"What about her pain?"

"I think we're covering it, but it's really hard to tell through the sedation."

Ella nodded. "When you're done with it, I'd like to spend a little time with her chart. I'll be in the dictation room."

December 5, 1986

Stepdown was busier than the ICU, with the constant shuffle of hospital staff, doctors, visitors, and vendors moving through the hallway. A recent remodel had converted all the patient rooms into private ones. *A good thing for Petra's transition,* thought Ella. *To go from ICU to a double room is often too much of a shock.* Petra was propped up in bed, pillows stuffed behind her. Her arms loosely held one pillow over her chest and stomach. Her eyes were closed, and her mouth might have been slack if her jaw had not been wired shut.

Ella cleared her throat loudly and gently tapped on the doorframe. "Ms. Gillespie, Petra? May I come in?"

With some effort Petra opened her eyes, which were still swollen. Her facial bruising was resolving with just some yellow and green remaining. She nodded. Ella sat down in the guest chair after moving towels off the seat. "Petra, I'm Ella Swensen, a Clinical Nurse Specialist here at the hospital, and I'm here to make sure you're getting all the care you need, your family, too. I—"

Petra interrupted her, speaking carefully and slowly through clenched teeth. "I 'member you ... meeting."

Ella nodded her head. "Yes, that was me."

She scooted the chair closer. "Petra, when patients with your history have had such trauma, it can be harder to manage pain in the usual ways. Are you in pain right now?"

Petra nodded her head.

"You are? OK—" Ella continued, "What is it on the pain scale?" No need to explain to a nurse that one is least, ten is most.

"Eight," she replied tightly.

"Is it time for you to have more medication now?"

Petra shook her head. "Asked. Too soon."

Ella nodded again. "Does your doctor know about your history with narcotics?"

Petra murmured, "No."

"I see." She paused. "Petra, I'm sorry, but I have to ask this. Were you using just before the accident?" Ella tried to make eye contact, but Petra's eyes were squeezed tight. "Petra?"

She was slow to respond. Then she nodded and spoke. "Little."

"I see."

Ella took in a deep breath and put her hand on Petra's. The young woman opened her eyes. "Petra, I can't imagine how hard this is for you. I *know* it takes courage to be honest. The goal of your team is to help you recover, and as smoothly as possible. I'm happy to get involved if you want me to. Dr. Micaeleus and Dr. Patel should know your history because they can adjust your pain meds in the best way."

Ella shifted in her chair. Another page went off in the pocket of her lab coat. "The other thing is that we have a great pain service here at the hospital, and I would be happy to ask for a consult. You're in a tricky place right now; you have acute traumatic injuries that cause a lot of pain. We want to manage that." Ella knew enough about addiction not to say "take away your pain."

"But we also want to monitor your meds over time so that you don't leave here more addicted."

Petra nodded. "S'OK. Tell 'em." A single tear made its way down her right cheek.

"Let's see if we can get you more comfortable right now. How about a back rub, high up, so I don't get near your broken ribs? Or a foot massage?"

Petra nodded, and smiled slightly. "Back. Shoulders so sore."

"Give me a minute to talk with your nurse about what I'm going to do, and take care of this page, then I'll be back." She thought another minute. "Would you like to try some herbal tea, like chamomile? They have it on the unit here, and patients say it helps them relax."

Petra nodded again, and tried to smile, but a grimace was all she could manage. The anticipation of pain relief alone can help reduce the tension and anxiety a lot, Ella knew. And she wanted to see if Petra's pain med orders allowed for something else soon.

Ella learned that Petra and Gary lived close to the hospital, and that she had two part-time jobs, one as a cashier at a Kroger's grocery near where the accident occurred. The other job was waiting tables at McNalley's, a popular locals pub. Although the work was tiring, she could get decent tips with the karaoke crowd, especially on Game Nights. *That could be a problem. There's likely easy access to drugs. I wonder where she gets them.*

"What do you want for Christmas, Ellie? It's getting close." He put down the newspaper and looked at her. They were relaxing on the big brown couch, each in their corner, Ella with her favorite red wine, Will with a mug of hot tea. She had already bought Will a new leather bomber-style jacket and hidden it away in the back of her closet. He was never curious, or a snooper. She knew how much he liked to stay up on the fashion of the moment, but he rarely made time to shop for himself. Recently he was busier than usual with two trips to Lafayette, an hour's drive each way, to check on his dad's deteriorating health.

"I don't know, Will, let me think a moment." She stretched out her right leg to rest on his thigh. "Hmm. I'm thinking … something that starts with a 'D' maybe …." She took another sip. Her heart paced up a little. "How about a new dress, you know, like the red one I saw at Ayre's last week? Or a diamond? Or maybe a dog?" *There, I said it, at least I hinted. Will he pick up on it?*

He looked at her quizzically, then down at the paper in his lap. "Those are interesting choices, Ellie," he hedged. "What kind of dog?"

Is he teasing me? Hard to tell—he can wear such a poker face. Well, I can play along with you, too, buddy. "I was thinking a collie or a German shepherd—you know, big guys. The shepherd especially would be a good guard dog for us. This isn't the best side of town, after all. And most of the neighbors have dogs. I'd rather have a dog than a gun."

"Gun!? who said anything about a gun?"

"Nobody, I was just thinking protection."

"Do we have neighbors with guns?" Will asked, all serious now.

"Didn't you see Robbie last weekend, with his little pals? They were all decked out with guns. Even baby Sheila had one." He smiled at her. *She's deflecting,* he thought. *She must really want a diamond.*

Petra's recovery, like most with traumatic injuries, had its ups and downs, but the doctors and Petra and her family could see encouraging progress every week. She managed to avoid a hospital-acquired infection, but her pain medications provided plenty of struggle and irritation for her and her nurses. Her broken femur was stabilized with medieval-looking external hardware. She was transferred to the rehab unit within the hospital, where she learned to get around safely, first on crutches, then using a walker.

Her jaw wires were removed after six weeks, and after some adjustment, she could begin to talk normally. Dr. Minot, the handsome French neurologist, pronounced her brain function normal with no complications from the head trauma. Although her words came out slower, she could think clearly, and her memories were intact.

Petra only wished she could forget how to be an addict.

The Program

April 6, 1987
Indianapolis, Indiana

"Ready?" Petra nodded. At 10:40 a.m. they slowly made their way past the cafeteria to a hospital conference room. She had just graduated from a walker to a cane. Will and Ella were presenting the Nurse Assistance Program, and Petra would observe, learn, and provide feedback. They needed to keep it short, no more than twenty minutes, because the managers could not be off the floor any longer.

This would be their very first meeting with nurse leaders, the frontline managers who were usually the first to confront a nurse's concerning behaviors. Early identification was key. Will placed two crisp program brochures and a pen advertising their phone number at each seat. On the white board at the head of the table, Ella wrote "1 in 10" and "1 in 4."

"Good morning," Ella began, and introduced Will and Petra. "We're here today to tell you about the Nurse Assistance Program and the help we can offer to you, and to nurses who may have a problem with drugs or alcohol." Some nurses nodded slightly, while others leaned forward, eyebrows raised. Some continued to scribble on staffing worksheets. "These problems that nurses have are no different from the population at large." Ella looked around the room. Nine around the table, two in the back of the room, plus Petra, Will, and her.

"Fourteen," she counted. "There are fourteen of us in this room. Statistics suggest that at least one of us, maybe two, one in ten, has a problem with drugs or alcohol, or both, right now, this minute. And three or four of us has someone close, a loved one, friend, or family member, who is struggling with substance use disorder."

The clipboard scribbling and checking of pagers slowed. She had hit a nerve.

The designated twenty minutes became thirty-five. The questions were precisely the ones they had hoped for.

"What should I do if I suspect a nurse, but I don't have any concrete evidence?"

"If I have a nurse in the program working on my floor, do I need to adjust her workload?"

"What if I suspect a peer of mine here at this table?" Laughter. That was good.

"What does it *really* mean where your brochure says that the call to the program is 'confidential'? Doesn't someone in authority have to know?"

Leaving the room was harder than they expected: both Will and Ella were separately approached by a leader for a side consultation, and Petra was deep in conversation with a nurse she knew from school. The room was scheduled for a noon meeting, and soon people with trays were making their way in.

The three of them, all smiling, headed down the hall to debrief over lunch. Will knew that this experience was unlikely to be repeated every time throughout the program, but he took it as an omen, a very good omen on a special day.

He couldn't wait to share his surprise with Ella.

Dinner that night was a private celebration at home. They ordered take-out from their favorite Chinese restaurant and found a bottle of plum wine they especially liked because it was light and not too sweet. But first Will poured champagne, and held out a plate of brie smothered in orange marmalade with water crackers.

"Ellie, I know that I have had a single-minded focus for a long time, and I also know Christmas was not exactly what you had hoped for."

Her heart thudded. She set the champagne flute back down on the table. He was right, but the tiny diamond earrings she now wore all the time were beautiful. She wanted to protest, but he held up his hand. "Let me go on, I have more to say."

She had not noticed the small box that sat on the counter behind them. "You have been invaluable to me in this work, Ellie, and I want to cement this milestone with you. You are so much more than a friend or a colleague, you know that. You are a true partner. Your commitment to my dream has meant more than I can say … it's like you have attached yourself to my soul. This work is what I have felt called to do, my purpose. And I see us as life partners." He reached back to put the box on the table between them. "Again, Ellie, this might not be what you were expecting; it's certainly not conventional. But to me, it symbolizes more." He slid the box to her. "I love you, Ellie, you know that, don't you?"

She nodded, speechless.

"Open it."

Inside was a delicate silver filigree heart with a stunning diamond suspended in the center. *It's got to be a half-carat at least,* she thought. The chain was so fine that it would seem like the heart was floating on the wearer. It took her breath away. She had never seen anything like it in the jewelry stores. *There's something vaguely familiar about it.* She regarded Will with tears in her eyes. "Oh my gosh, this is gorgeous! What an exquisite piece—it's so elegant! Did you have it made, Will? Where did you get it?"

He smiled and rose to help her fasten it. She stood, and he wrapped his arms around her, kissing her neck, at the very place and in the slow way he knew she loved. She laughed and wiggled. "Wait a minute, I'm hungry!"

"I know," he said, "I'm hungry, too." He kissed her neck slowly and teased her some more. "But OK, we'll have dinner first." He sat down again and looked at her. "I love it on you, Ellie." She walked over to the hall mirror to check her reflection.

"I love it, too, Will, it is absolutely perfect."

She came back to the table to find a second box at her place. He nodded at her questioning look. "Go ahead. Open it." Inside was the pendant he had shown her years ago, the graduation present from his aunt. *That's it!* she thought. *That's why it's familiar.* The shape and size of hers was a replica, minus the button and garnet. Her chain was modern compared to the original.

She sat there, overwhelmed at the meaning of his gesture, this little nondescript button that had been treasured so carefully for more than a century. She couldn't imagine all the thought that he must have put into it … "Are you—giving this one to me?"

He shook his head. "No, Ellie, sorry. I was thinking that together we might have the pendant mounted, and displayed, maybe in our office, in honor of its original owner, Sarah Rule. Her compassion, her commitment, her call. I see them all in you, Ellie, and I love that those qualities connect us together."

She held the pendant in her open palm, and closing her fingers around it, brought it to her heart, as if in prayer. "Me, too, Will. Me, too."

Growing Pains

Ella lay shivering on the couch, propped up on pillows, trying to warm her hands with a mug of tea and wishing the damn headache would stop. The worsening cold had plagued her for four days, and she had called in sick the last two. Now she fretted that it was something more than a flu bug. She just didn't feel right in her chest and her head. Will had insisted that she make an appointment with the doctor. She hoped for the "waiting list cure," but so far her body hadn't gotten the message to heal itself before a doctor had his say.

Four years had flown by. Pressures intensified last year when it was time to renew their contract with the Board of Nursing. Ella wondered if Will was letting his new title of Executive Director go to his head. After all, it was just a title change, no raise; the budget wouldn't allow for it. If she was busy on the phone, Will would pick up the second line. He made copies, dialed his own calls out. He conducted intake assessments, the same as she. *He treats me like a game piece to move around whenever he wants ... consulting me less and less in decisions. Except, of course, at the last minute! I thought we were partners.*

The Nurse Assistance Program, NAP, had three employees: Will, Petra as administrative assistant, and Ella as clinician. She didn't care for the abbreviation, NAP, and thought the title was a little dull. Ella had reluctantly agreed to leave the job she loved at St. Alphonsus. She filled NAP's half-time role, but in reality, she was usually doing something for the program five days a week, her tasks spilling over into much more than half. Will wanted to devote part of the budget, *the part that could pay me for all*

430

my hours, Ella pouted, for another office in the southern part of the state. Their clients were complaining about the travel hardship.

Three years after he gave her the diamond necklace, they had finally found the time to plan a wedding. "It's not the right time," he kept telling her. She insisted they didn't need much time to go down to City Hall, but he pushed back. It would be his first and, he hoped, his only marriage, and he wanted to do it right. He imagined a traditional wedding with attendants and romantic touches, his little niece Chloe as flower girl. Ella thought his grandiose ideas were holding up progress on their plans. Did he really want to get married? She started to doubt it.

And then he had changed his mind. She wasn't sure why—maybe their ages? She was forty, Will forty-two. The biological clock argument that pushed some of her friends was not an issue for Ella. Though she had enjoyed a happy childhood in a house of seven, she was surprised that she never felt the call to motherhood. She and Will had decided against children long ago: too many people populated the planet, and Ella had witnessed the worst of human behavior toward children. She would always remember the Anderson children: Tuesday, March, Monday, and baby July. She wondered if those parents had started out with normal dreams for their children, and if so, what happened to create the tragic end.

"Why now?" she had asked Will several times.

"I have no idea. Something you put in my tea? It's just time, Ellie, really, I'm ready. And, I don't want to lose you." Whatever it was, she was glad. She longed for the security of marriage, even if it was old-fashioned and un-feminist. But she chose to keep her maiden name. They talked about her taking a hyphenated name, or both of them doing it. No way, they concluded, would either one of them be Swensen-Swain, or Swain-Swensen. Too much like clumsy whistling.

Their wedding last September was smaller and simpler than Will's original plan, with their families and just a few friends. They took a week-long trip to Chicago, exploring the city's architecture, neighborhoods, and food. Food was the highlight for Will, shopping and fashion for both of them. He was still as interested in keeping up with the styles as in his younger days.

Now in the waiting room, while Will read the latest copy of the *American Journal of Nursing*, Ella sat with her eyes shut. The bright lights only aggravated the worsening headache, and she wondered if this might be her first migraine. It hurt to breathe. She was more worried now since the Tylenol wasn't touching her headache or her fever.

Two women sat across from them. Will thought the younger woman was probably the patient, the way the older one was being solicitous, as well as doing all the talking. "So yesterday," he heard her say, "I found more of Great Aunt Cora's things from her nursing school days. You know that trunk in the attic from my Mom? With the house up for sale, I finally got the gumption to tackle that stuff. There's a wonderful collection of all her class notes, a little record of what she had to pay each month and what she earned. Heavens, those were long hours they had to work, and for next to nothing! They sure have it easy today compared to way back when."

Will smiled to himself. *Easy? Nah, just different.*

The younger woman nodded. "So all these things you're collecting, what on earth are you going to do with them?"

"They're for my friend Karen. She wants to start a nursing history museum."

March, 1991
Indianapolis, Indiana

Ella handed the mirror back to Lissa, "I do like it, though it will be a different look for me now." Her hair was beginning to grow back and Lissa had convinced her that a short curly asymmetrical style would suit her and her return to health. She had added some darker streaks to the longer side. "This will draw more attention to your face and your eyes. And the freckles, Ella—they're one of your most attractive features."

Ella rolled her eyes. *How can anyone think that?* She had finally made peace with them after all these years. But deep down she still longed for unmarked skin. Three months after the initial diagnosis, the benign brain tumor was gone, and the accompanying fear was fading. While the vast majority of brain tumors are benign, the concerns about a permanent effect on her thinking, balance, and vision had taken time to recede. Overwork and stress had joined forces to weaken her immune system, leading to the pneumonia last winter, which Dr. Patel declared was totally unrelated to her headaches.

After she was pronounced healed, Will surprised her at breakfast one Thursday morning. "Pack your bag, my Ellie, we're getting out of here. You need a break. We need a break. I need some perspective, and we've both earned it. It's been a tough winter in so many ways. We leave tomorrow morning."

What!? she thought, *he's taking off on a Friday?* "Where are we going? Really, we're taking a vacation?"

"It's a surprise, Ellie, you'll see tomorrow. It's just a little time away. But for now, pack enough for three days and the usual clothes for Indy weather. I wish it were Hawaii, but that'll have to be another trip." Gathering his briefcase, keys and jacket, he kissed the top of her head. "Gotta go. See you tonight. I might be late."

I'm not really in the mood for this, but he's right, we both need a change of scene. Maybe we can get back on the same wavelength. It's been hard on him, too, me being sick and then recovering from surgery. Plus finding someone to step into my role. So glad Sheila's working out. Dread clawed at her stomach, as it did each time she thought about returning to work.

Click. He shut the door slowly behind him with a smile on his face as he imagined the afternoon ahead. "Well, sweetheart, what do you think? Enjoying this return to our honeymoon spot?"

Ella stood at the window looking down at the traffic. Lake Michigan sparkled with diamonds, and the usual breeze blew the water into waves. A lovely early spring afternoon. But a heaviness, a sadness she couldn't shake perturbed her.

She took a deep breath in and let it out, but it was so loud it sounded to Will like a sigh. *You're just out of practice,* she thought, *we're both out of practice. Act like you're excited to be here, and the feelings will come back, you'll see.* She heard her own counsel to others echo in her head. She put a smile on her face and turned to look at him.

"That lunch was beyond superb, Will, I loved it. But two Bloody Marys … well, I haven't had that much to drink in a long time." She eyed the inviting king-size bed. "A nap?"

He winked at her. "Sure."

They lay naked between the cool sheets in the darkened room. After a few minutes Ella began to snore lightly. When she started stirring, Will inched close and spooned his body against hers. "Mmmm, that feels good," she murmured as he began to gently kiss her neck. When he breathed into her ear, tugging on her earlobe with his teeth, she turned into his warm arms and they began kissing. At some point, when their deepening kisses usually moved from each other's lips to each other's skin, Ella stopped.

"What is it, Ellie? Something wrong?"

"Um, not sure, honey. Maybe I need some more time." Silence. She frowned. "I guess I'm not really into it."

He let out a sigh. They hadn't made love for nearly four months. *Is it true what they say about marriage? The end of sex? I need to be patient here. She's been sick, and then the surgery. Just because I'm aroused doesn't mean I have to push her.* "OK, why don't we just lie here a while and watch the late afternoon come on." He rearranged the pillows behind his head and pulled her to him. She reached her arm across his chest, listening to his steady heartbeat. "Tell me what's going on inside that tumor-less little head of yours," he said, trying to lighten the mood.

"Will, I'm sad and you … you're making fun of me."

He moved his hand from her shoulder to her head, playing with her short curls. "Sad, Ellie, sad? Wow, I can't believe that, I mean after all this … you've been given a clean bill of health, and you look fantastic. What do you have to be sad about?"

"Looks are the least of my worries, Will, I can't believe you even said that."

Prickly, better back up a little, guy.

"OK, sorry. Let me try again. What's the sadness about, Ellie?"

"Well … I get this sense of heaviness when I think about …."

"About what, Ellie, what is it?"

She sighed out a deep breath. "About returning to work. It feels like such a chore now, and I just can't get excited about it anymore."

Me, too, some days. Better not go there either. "How long have you been feeling like this?"

"Um, maybe a year?"

"A year?" He wanted to explode. "Why didn't you say something about this sooner? That's a long time to be carrying this around."

"I don't really know, Will. For a while I thought you'd surely notice, but you were so preoccupied with all the contract renewal stuff. I just tried to stay out of the way. It really started to get under my skin. And then, you'd have to find someone to replace me. The wedding and our honeymoon distracted me for a while. And then I got sick, and the tumor …." Ella felt tears collect as her vision blurred. One escaped, then another.

"Damn, Ellie, I wish I'd known. But finding someone else these past few weeks was easier than we thought, though, wasn't it? Sheila's worked out great, hasn't she?"

Ella nodded.

"On Monday first thing, we'll start the process of filling the position," he said, careful not to say "your position."

"There's something else," she said, shifting to look at him. She picked up his left hand and toyed with the wide gold band. "Part of me has been holding back because I don't want you to feel like I'm abandoning your dream."

"What!" he said, wanting to explode for the second time. "You're afraid I won't see your support of my dream because you want a change?" He sat up and faced her fully now. "Ellie, you are so much more supportive than I ever could have imagined, or wanted. You were on board from almost the first time I talked about this in grad school. I could see it in your eyes, your interested questions. And our work, your work with the Board and all those presentations you made." He reached back to the nightstand for the glass of water and took a drink. "And the clients, Ellie, they love you!"

He shifted his position, silent for another minute. He then sat up, looking official and formal. "I release you, Ella Swensen, from holding on to my dream and trying to make it yours." They both smiled. "I'm sorry, sweetheart—I was wrong for not seeing it earlier, not checking in with you about how you felt."

She looked at him, trying to see if there really was truth in his words.

"I'm sorry, Ellie, I really am. Let's change things."

Ella moved a little closer to him, their knees touching through the sheets as they sat cross-legged facing each other. She reached out to take both his hands, softly massaging his palms. "Thank you, sweetheart. You can't imagine the relief I feel."

She inhaled deeply and let her breath out, slowly. "OK, here's one more. I think it would be good for us, well, me for sure, to have some distance from each other, but—" she added hastily, "—just in daytime … I want new things, different things, to share with you in the evenings. We spend *so* much time together, and I think new experiences would be good for me, good for us." She looked down at his soft capable hands, the hands she loved to imagine, the hands she wanted to feel move across her body. "I'm afraid you'll feel let down."

"Not let down, Ellie, not at all. Your dreams matter to me, sweetheart, they do."

She put his hands on her breasts and leaned in to kiss him, hard. "Let's see how much they matter, Will. Can you tell what I'm dreaming of now?"

He gave her a big grin and nodded approvingly. "I think I might. Let me show you."

"So many options! It's like a six-page menu for a gourmet meal," she said to Donna Evans, the career counselor across the table. Donna was a tall woman with ebony skin and almond-shaped eyes. She wore a leopard print skirt with a black sleeveless tank top, showing off beautiful arms and a slim silhouette. Practical flats on her feet contrasted with big gold hoops in her ears. *I could learn a thing or two about fashion,* Ella thought. *I'd love to look like her.*

"Your assessment shows you have the aptitude for many nursing roles, Ella, and with your experience and education, the sky's the limit."

"I just know that now is the time for a change. For me, a real change. I have fifteen or twenty years left before retirement, and even if I need to go back to school or get additional training, it's fine. I want to stay in nursing, that's where my heart is …."

"There are two steps to this process, Ella, the role selection piece, and then we look for where those jobs are available. Or we could even work to create something to suit your interests and promote that role to a prospective employer."

After an hour together, Ella left with a list to ponder. Oncology, surgery, hospice, pediatrics, community health, all so different from her work at NAP.

"I can see you in these others," Will replied, stirring the thickening Alfredo sauce as it bubbled and sputtered in the pan, "but surgery? You mean like working in the operating room, passing instruments, all that?"

"Well, yes, maybe. I've always been intrigued with how fascinating the human body is, its ability to repair itself, adjust, fight off 'those foreign invaders.'" They both smiled, remembering their student days and Mrs. Kellogg's favorite expression. "Seeing inside the opened-up chest again or really understanding bones and their attachments … I think that would be really neat, don't you?"

He nodded. "I guess. I can see why you'd consider that, but, Ellie, you'd have such a limited audience for your exquisite communication and caring skills. It'd be just the team around the patient."

"I've thought about that, too. I do want to use my psych background, and on somebody other than a surgeon or anesthesiologist. But God knows, they sure could use it!" she said, shaking the linguine in the colander. She bit into a slippery lightly salted noodle, hoping for the tiniest bit of resistance in the middle. She found it. "Perfectly al dente. The salad's done, too. Let's eat."

Annie

Ella rang the doorbell of the tired little frame house, remembering her public health days. Excitement, or was it anxiety? raised her pulse. *What will I find today?* She heard a yappy barking inside. *You've been here before. Relax.* Before she had time to shift her shoulder bag, a short older woman opened the door, trying to keep the feisty terrier behind her. As she bent to grab the dog's collar, a wide part in the middle of her thinning hair was apparent. The collar of her faded green blouse had frayed, and a rip at the back of her sleeve suggested—what? Inattention, no time, financial strain?

Seeing the lettering on Ella's bag, the woman said, "Oh, you must be the hospice nurse. I've been waiting for you."

Ella nodded. "Yes, that's me. Ella Swensen," she said, handing the woman a business card. "And you're Mrs. Gordon?"

"Yes, Annie Gordon. Please call me Annie. Come on in, and don't mind Bruiser here. He's all bark—never bit a soul in his life. Doubt he'd want to start now, now that he's missing teeth. He's not seeing well these days, either." She pointed Ella in the direction of the living room. A pleasant blend of cinnamon, cloves, and something unidentifiable freshened the air.

"I'm so glad you're here. Do you want to see Dora now? She's sleeping, but I can wake her—"

"Oh, no need, not at all yet ... a little later, once I get some information. And a chance to understand what you are dealing with, with your—granddaughter, is she?" Ella checked her notes.

Annie nodded. "Yes, terrible, isn't it? To outlive a grandchild? A child is bad enough, but a grandchild ... There's no fairness, or justice. It's just fu—obscene," she corrected, worrying the tissue in her hand. "And me her only real living relative. Dora should have a steady boyfriend by now, not this damn cancer." Pointing to the kitchen table cluttered with pill bottles, papers, and the remnants of toast, she nodded for Ella to take a seat. "What a mess," she muttered.

Dora was Ella's third hospice patient, her first as intake nurse. As Annie answered the questions, Ella was grateful that she could keep her reactions from showing. Dora, now twenty, was born with Fetal Alcohol Syndrome and abandoned by her mother when she was seven. The Gordons had cared for her since then, struggling during Dora's adolescence to cope with her erratic and often difficult behavior. "Somehow we got through it," Annie said, shaking her head, "though to this day I don't know how. Her mother basically disappeared. Probably was her teachers … they were good for her." The shrill whistle of the kettle pierced the air as she slowly pushed herself up from the chair. "Plain black tea's all I got, Lipton's, hope that's all right."

Dora had faced many obstacles in her short life. Besides her slow academic progress, classmates teased her for living with her "old granny." "But that was nothing," Annie said, "compared to her being biracial with very dark skin, and wild hair that I finally learned how to take proper care of. She has the bluest of eyes. She was a beautiful child, really, once you got past the shock of those bright blue eyes shining out of her black skin, but nobody paid much attention to that. Her slowness caused lots of people to take advantage of her, in school and after, didn't matter."

Ella sighed. *What a life—and to have it end so cruelly.* "When did you learn about the Fetal Alcohol Syndrome?"

"Around the time she came to us. We got her from Child Protective Services, Herb and me. He was still alive then and would have been a wonderful grandpa for her today, if he was around. Not to mention a help to me." Annie chewed on her lip. "But the last year or so, especially with the pain of her cancer, and all the drugs, Dora hasn't missed him so much." She took in a big breath. "Not so for me. I miss him terribly, I tell you that. I am *so* worn out. If it wasn't for my Bruiser, and the neighbors, I don't know how I'd have gotten this far."

Ella peeked at her watch, trying not to seem hurried. Thirty minutes had passed already, and she still needed to see Dora even if she was sleeping.

"Gram? Gram? I need you—" came a weak voice from the bedroom.

"Oh, my, I got carried away with all the talking. Let's go see to her."

Annie had tended her with care, Ella saw, from the tidy sickroom and organized surroundings. Nothing in Dora's appearance was unusual given her history. But Annie was right. Dora's small eyes demanded notice. Blue and piercing, they sought something from Ella that she couldn't put her finger on.

"Hello, Dora, my name is Ella. I'm going to be your nurse. Did your grandma tell you about me?" Dora nodded. "Good. Are you in pain now?" Dora nodded again. "Annie, why don't you show me the medicine you've been using and what you do when Dora's feeling like this?"

Ella left Annie and Dora with plans to adjust her medication from pills to liquid, order a hospital bed and bedside commode, and talk with the doctor about oxygen. Dora's oxygen saturation level, eighty-eight, clearly showed the result of the cancer spreading to her lungs. Ella knew that if her breathing was eased with a normal saturation level of ninety-six or greater, the bone pain would lessen a little, too. Keeping Dora comfortable and supporting Annie were the priorities now. Annie also needed a break, and Ella had talked with her about getting a sitter for two afternoons a week so she could get out of the house.

When Ella returned the next day, a home health aide had helped Annie move furniture in the living room to accommodate the bed and commode. They used a wheelchair to move Dora to the hospital bed and worked to find the most comfortable position for her. Ella showed Annie how to manage the oxygen and the long cord that attached to the nasal prongs. Dora didn't like having it on her face but as she drifted off to sleep again, she let it alone. Her saturation had risen to ninety-two.

Annie invited her to the kitchen for a cup of tea. "She don't have much time left, does she?" asked Annie. "She's sure gone downhill since I called you all in."

"It's so hard to tell these things, Annie. She can have slumps, and just as suddenly she can have periods that look like she's improving. We've been changing the environment around her a lot. Let's see what the next few hours bring."

Annie pointed to a letter on the table in front of Ella. "This came in yesterday's mail. I don't know what to do about it."

Ella raised her eyebrows in question.

"It's Dora's mom—Marty, my daughter. Somehow she decided that now was the time to get back into Dora's life." Annie looked at the envelope. *Is that disgust on her face? Or sadness, anger—maybe all of the above?*

Ella nodded. "Hmm. What are you thinking, Annie? Are you going to respond?"

"I don't know what to do. I'm just so … shocked, I guess. And it's taken me back to that awful time when we first got Dora. I kept hoping she would get her life together and be a real mother to her, but it never happened. We got three letters in thirteen years, and never a birthday or Christmas card. Forget presents! Dora finally stopped asking about her mother after her thirteenth birthday. She might not have much self-control, but somehow she knew enough not to bring it up again. My heart just breaks for her. And now … I just don't know."

"What does Marty want, Annie?"

"To see Dora, maybe get her to move in with her. *Now* she wants to be the mother!?"

"So she has no idea about the cancer."

"Nope. None."

They sat in silence. "What do *you* want, Annie? What would be best for you?"

She shook her head. "I dunno. As much as I hoped and prayed for this moment to come, I sure don't want it to be now. Dora wouldn't know her probably. Marty would most likely freak out about the situation. I'd be losing a granddaughter, gaining a daughter—maybe—and most likely, saying goodbye to *her* all over again." She shook her head, and wiped at her eyes. "It's just too much. I can't do it."

"Do what, Annie?"

"Let her back in again. That door's shut."

"It's a huge request from Marty."

Annie nodded.

"I need to be going in a few minutes, but I have one thought to leave you with, Annie. If you say 'no' to any contact with Marty, no contact with you or no contact with you and Dora, how do you think you would feel about that choice down the road, say, in a year or two?"

Annie opened her mouth to speak.

Ella held her hand up, gently, toward Annie. "Don't answer me now. Let it sit a little while. I'll be back tomorrow to check on Dora, and we can talk more then. But here's the thing I want you to know. I can help you with this, Annie. I'm here for you, too, not just Dora. And if you decide to say 'yes' to Marty and she comes to see Dora, I can be here with you."

One week later, Annie agreed to allow contact with Marty and asked Ella to sit with her while she phoned her daughter. Annie's side of the conversation was awkward, with lots of silence. Finally she held the phone out to Ella. "Here, you talk to her, will you? I can't say what she needs to hear."

Ella told Marty of her daughter's diagnosis, that hospice was involved, and that Dora didn't have much time left. Marty lived in Louisville, ninety miles away. She said she would come as soon as she could and that her friend Ray would bring her. They settled on the next day.

Ella was relieved that the home health aide would be present in case an extra person was needed to help manage tension or anxiety or … anything. Annie answered the door as the aide was getting Dora situated. The pain meds were doing their magic, and Dora could occasionally be roused from her sleepiness. When she could tell that Annie and Marty were speaking civilly, Ella went to the front hallway and introduced herself. "Marty, let's go visit in the kitchen for a few minutes while Annie helps Dora."

Marty was of medium height and thin. Once she took off her jacket, revealing a tight-fitting turtleneck sweater, Ella could imagine that she was wiry and probably quite strong. Her fingernails were bitten down to the quick, and when they shook hands, Ella felt calluses. Her thin hair was blonde, in need of a touch-up and without much shape. She had recently applied a thick coat of lipstick. Marty had the same bright blue eyes as her daughter. She wore old sneakers, lightly caked with mud. *I wonder if she works outdoors? Probably had a hard life herself.* "Ray will be back to get me in an hour or so," Marty said, "but he'll wait outside longer if I need him to."

Ella nodded. "Marty, I can guess how difficult this must be. Thank you for being brave enough to be here. I don't want to keep you away from seeing Dora, but I'd like to prepare you for what you're going to see." Marty, big-eyed and serious, nodded. Annie joined them in the kitchen, standing in the doorway.

"First of all, Marty, we are managing Dora's pain with morphine, so she'll appear sleepy, off and on. She may not recognize you. It's been what, thirteen years? I'm sure she'll look very different to you—after all, she's an adult now. With the bone cancer she's lost a lot of weight, and the cancer has spread to her lungs now, so it's been harder for her to breathe. That's why she's on oxygen."

"Can I touch her?" From the corner of her eye Ella saw Annie stiffen.

"Are you worried that your touch could cause her pain?"

Marty nodded.

"If it's all right with Annie, it's OK. People at this stage of their lives seem to be comforted by the touch of people who love them." Ella knew this was might be a stretch, possibly hard for Annie to hear. "I have a suggestion. Annie, why don't you go in to Dora and talk with her a little. Tell her that she has a visitor. If she asks who it is, tell her it's her mother. If she doesn't ask, no need to explain. Just let the touch and eye contact be enough for the moment."

Marty took a big drink of water, nearly draining the glass. She put it down carefully, staring down past her hand. Ella asked quietly, "Are you all right, Marty? It's not too late to change your mind." Marty swallowed and nodded slightly.

"Ready?" Marty took in a deep breath and let it out. She nodded again and stood. Annie went into the living room and sat at the edge of Dora's bed. Ella and Marty watched from the doorway.

Ella put her hand on Marty's shoulder. "I can't imagine what's going through your mind right now, or how you're feeling. This is a really hard thing you're doing. But Marty, I see the courage it took for you to get to this point." She took a breath, then continued. "I'm sure you'll get through this. I'll be here with you and Dora, and your mom."

Annie signaled them to the bedside. "She asked," she said. "She knows who you are. She's OK with you here." She slipped off the edge of the bed, making room for Marty to get close.

Dora slowly opened her eyes, dulled from the morphine's effect. "'Zat you, Mom? 'Zat really you?" squinting at Marty.

Marty reached out to touch her daughter's shoulder. "Yes, Dora, I'm here. Your mom's here." Without thinking, she inched herself onto the bedside, occupying the space her own mother had vacated, then took Dora's hand.

"Good," the young woman sighed, "I waited for you a long time. Really long. You finally came." Dora's eyes drifted shut again.

Ella could see Marty wipe her face with the palm of her hand. She bent down low to speak quietly into Dora's ear. "I want you to know, Dora, that I know I was not a good mother to you. I am so sorry, so very sorry, to have missed out on being with you while you were growing up."

Dora opened her eyes, trying to clear them to see her mother better. "You were awful. No visits, no letters, no presents …." She drifted off again.

Marty shifted and swallowed hard, wiping her eyes with the tissue Annie handed her. "I had so many problems, Dora, and I was a mess. But I still thought about you every single day and wondered if I'd ever be able to get you back."

Those piercing blue eyes stabbed at her mother. "You never tried."

Silence. Then, "You're right, Dora, I didn't try. I will carry that regret, that sorrow, with me all my life." She took another breath. "But, baby, I'm here now, and if you and Gram will let me, I'll be right here with you until, until—" She kissed Dora's cheek, then whispered, "I love you." Quiet sobs shook her shoulders as she pulled her hand out of her daughter's. Turning to Annie, she asked, "Bathroom?" and hurried in the direction Annie pointed.

Annie had allowed Marty to stay "until the end", and Dora died two days later. But Ella needed to check on one more patient—the relationship between Annie and her daughter.

The next day all three sat around the kitchen table. Although the living room had been cleared of Dora's equipment and reminders, memories there were too fresh. Ella began. "I want to check in today and see how both of you are doing," purposefully vague. "We have some additional hospice services you should know about; one-on-one grief counseling, and support groups that many people find helpful."

Neither woman spoke.

She decided not to push too hard. "The time after someone dies, especially if it's the place where the person died, everything can seem unreal, strange, awkward, like you don't know what to do anymore. For you, Annie, most of your time for the past two years has been consumed with caregiving. And now?" Ella paused. "Now things are totally different." She stopped, hoping Annie would speak.

Annie nodded. "All that was such a huge responsibility, at the end I was exhausted. I have a lot of sleep to catch up on. Yet, it don't really seem real. And then of course," she angled her head slightly in Marty's direction, "I guess we have to figure out how to get along now. I don't know ...." She shook her head.

"You don't know what, Mom?"

"If it's even possible, or if it's something I even want. I mean, not hearin' from you all those years when Dora wanted you so badly .... I am just so, so—"

"I know, I know," Marty interrupted, "You have every right to be upset with me, every—"

"Upset!?" Annie stood quickly, knocking over the flimsy kitchen chair, "every right to be *upset!?* What do you think I am, a trained monkey or a seal or somethin' that you can treat like shit one day, and the next day, expect me to forget it all?" Annie leaned over the table into Marty's face. "Try *angry*. Try *disgusted*. Try *furious*. What mother treats her daughter like you treated Dora!? When I look at you, I don't see a mother, I see a fuckin' *parasite* I should disown. Just like you disowned Dora all these years!"

Marty's face was white, her big blue eyes wide.

"Oh, ladies," cautioned Ella, "let's breathe a minute here." She gestured that Annie should sit down. "Those are harsh words, Annie. I can't say that they're right or wrong, but they came out of you all of a sudden, like water out of a fire hydrant. You must have been holding in a lot these past few days. And I'm guessing Marty needs a minute to process this all."

Marty nodded, stunned.

"OK, why don't we all take a few deep breaths." The only sound in the kitchen was the clock ticking. Ella began again. "Since Annie spoke last, Marty, I'd like to know how you feel about what she said."

Marty was silent another moment, as tears began to roll down her lined face. "Ashamed. There's no other word for it. Ashamed. I could tell you all the reasons why I was an 'MIA Mom,' that's what they call us in the program, but you didn't ask me for reasons. You asked how I feel. And the answer is I feel lower than low. Like shit. Like a worm. Like I don't deserve to be here with you, Mom—you, who took Dora in with no question at all."

Ella looked at Annie and nodded. "Annie?"

"I dunno. I'm kinda surprised she didn't try to give me all her—"

Ella interrupted. "Talk to her directly, Annie, 'you didn't try to give me all your—'"

"You didn't try to give me all your usual bullshit psychobabble half-baked reasons why you couldn't this or that."

"So, Annie, you're surprised that Marty feels ashamed, is that right?"

Annie nodded.

"Is there anything else that surprises you in what Marty said?"

"Just that she admitted she don't belong here."

Ella nodded. "What do you think, Marty? Did she get it right?"

Marty nodded. "Yeah, she heard me. Ashamed and, well …."

"Lonely?"

"Yes, I guess."

Annie paused, then murmured. "Me, too. Lonely."

Ella took a deep breath. "Marty, what did you hear your mother say when she first began?"

"Hmm, well, she was, I mean, you were really, really angry, and maybe you felt like you didn't have a daughter that … you … were proud of? Like, umm, you wanted to disown me."

"Is Marty right about that, Annie, did she hear what you were saying?"

Annie nodded. She took in a deep breath. "Yeah, that's pretty much it. Lots of water under *that* bridge." Annie looked deflated.

"I know this is intense, and you haven't been talking for very long. But maybe now's a good time to stop for today. Marty, Ray's taking you back to Louisville right away?" She nodded. "He's been doing some errands for me, but he should be along any minute now."

Ella continued. "Annie, do you have a friend you could go out to lunch with? Maybe a neighbor you could visit for a change of scene?"

Annie looked skeptical.

"You've been through a lot, and I'm guessing you really want to sleep. But getting outside for some fresh air and a bite or a cup of tea with a friend is something you haven't enjoyed for a long time. You'll sleep better, I'm sure of it."

Both women shifted in their seats, signaling a change. "Before I go, I want to leave you with one more question. For each of you, what would it take for you to have a mother-daughter relationship again? Would you even want one? That's two questions, really."

Annie and Marty looked at each other.

"If you decide you want to go forward with each other, you can contact me, and I'll help you find someone who can guide you in figuring out how to make that happen. Perhaps our grief counselor can refer you to someone. Indianapolis and Louisville are pretty close. It wouldn't be too hard to see each other more often—that is, of course, *only* if you *both* want it." Ella stood to go and handed her card to Marty.

She left the little house and slid into the driver's seat—and just sat for several minutes, watching blue patches of sky appearing through dirty gray clouds. Except for the pumpkin-spice feel that heralded fall and Thanksgiving, November was her least favorite month. But at that moment

Ella sensed the gentle nod of heaven's blessing. She smiled, pleased and grateful, so grateful that she had found another way to be completed.

Ella wasn't the only one who wanted a change. Two weeks later, Will raised the topic of buying a house. They'd been in the same house he'd rented during their school days, and he thought having their own home would do them good.

For seven years his focus had been on NAP and getting it off the ground. It was time to shift gears and give more attention to another part of his life. Could he even leave NAP, something he had worked so hard for, had dedicated his life to? He was tired of what so many days seemed like an uphill battle, convincing people that nurses with substance use problems were worth saving and deserved second, and, yes, even third, chances. Addiction was a chronic, relapsing brain disease, not a moral failing. His seemed to be a lone voice shouting that message.

The recent scare with Ella's health and the fear of losing her—to cancer, to pneumonia, or any other condition that would separate them— threw him off balance. *What is this restlessness I'm feeling? Could a new home settle it, at least for the moment?*

The realtor suggested they look in Beech Grove, a small neighborhood, technically a city now, on the east side of town. Ella had more flexibility in her schedule for house hunting, but on the first trip out, she could not get excited about any of the five homes Liz Eaton showed her. Two were really rundown, definitely within their budget, but would require too much work and money to bring them up to a level she and Will would consider. One was just a bit over their price range, and it had a little additional building, a "mother-in-law" unit Liz called it, that they didn't need. The fourth was a good possibility, but all the windows needed upgrading, and that was expensive. In the last, a 1930s bungalow, the rooms were chopped up and tiny.

"Don't give up," Liz replied in response to Ella's glum look. "It's always a process. I'll let you know when I have more to show you, now that I have a better idea what you're after."

Annie

Home

"What would a button say if it could talk? 'Hey, I'm in the wrong hole! Get me out of this box with all these others—put me somewhere I can do my job! Are you kidding me? You think that white one works with us ivories?'"

Will advanced the slide. "This old button, at least one hundred thirty-four years old, held carefully in the pendant, would probably tell us about being in the right place, being the right one, wanting to be useful. The button could tell us what it's like to step up to help even though you're not sure you can." He paused to examine his audience. "Maybe you're not ready. Maybe you're afraid. Those are issues that confront all nurses at one time or another."

Three years had passed since Ella had helped Annie and Marty with Dora's death, and Will was invited to address IUPUI's graduating nurses. "Nursing's Future Through the Eyes of a Button" opened with the story of Sarah Dunlap Rule and her desire to serve first, and then to become "a real nurse." He told them about his great-grandmother Suzanne Swain, who had given the pendant to another dreamer, his grandmother, Charlotte Swain. He described Charlotte's frontier nursing life, and the creative and energetic spirit that led her to question what was right, and to be practical and understand what worked.

Will introduced his mother, Estelle, through her imprisonment and courage. He had to stop once and clear his throat. He talked about her short life, its unhappy ending, never seeing her grandchildren. He showed three photos of her, one at her nursing school graduation, one with the other POWs on the day of liberation, and the final one taken a year before her death. He took a sip of water and a deep breath. *This is hard—I've talked about all this before ... but my heart's pounding like crazy!*

"I would be remiss if I didn't remind you that you have chosen to practice in a stressful place. I am sure that you have probably witnessed that for yourselves already. The conditions change all the time. Every single day you will feel pressures, and your mental health, not to mention your physical health, will be challenged. But you are also given a sacred privilege—to share in the extreme joy at the first cry of a newborn, to be in the presence of a person taking their last breath, perhaps to be the last caring face they see. To see the healing that's facilitated by caring physicians and your colleagues. You will see relationships reconciled, and simple acts of kindness, and courage, and love, every day.

"But there is one condition. To be an actor on this stage, and to sustain it, you need to think of yourself as the most important person first. If you have taken care that your health is good, then you will bring your best to enable the healing of others. What does taking care of yourself mean? The list is long, but to me the most important one is this—" He paused, noting that the room was dead silent.

"Is your life in balance?" A ripple of chuckles forced a grin from him. "I know, I know—I have not always been a good role model, as my wife Ella could tell you. But I have made a change, at my 'ripe old age' of forty-eight. For me, having a consuming hobby has helped provide balance. I joined a men's chorus last year, and it has opened up my life in surprising and refreshing ways. So, now I ask: what would that be for you? A painting class? Regular date nights with your spouse or partner? Learning a new language?

"The future of nursing rests on its foundation of compassion for others, knowledge, skill, and discovery. We cannot begin to imagine some of the challenges that will confront us. Some are on our doorstep right now. But one thing is certain, challenges will show up daily. If we hold fast to those underpinnings and use them as our North Star, then the path we have been called to follow will be rewarding, and provide purpose for a lifetime."

Will stopped, and the applause began. It was a good speech, he thought, but he was more excited about what was next. He remained at the lectern. Some people stood to leave. The dean, Dr. Bridger, joined him, leaning in to tap the microphone. "May we have another moment, please?"

Will began to address the group again. "I beg your patience for just a few more minutes. I would like to make an announcement, and to tell you about a new venture for nursing that my wife Ella and I are beginning. Ella, will you join us on stage?" She rose from her seat in the front row and came to stand next to them.

Will continued. "When Ella and I began to look deeper into the rich history of nursing that Sarah's little button symbolizes, and what it represents to us," he smiled at her, "we thought that establishing a place where others' nursing mementoes could live into the future would be an important step. A place where items could be housed, papers could be stored, catalogued and archived, and accessed. A home where the thoughts and experiences of our nursing forbears and leaders could be held and easily referenced as the profession continues to advance."

He motioned Ella forward. She looked around and then spoke into the microphone. "Will and I are thrilled today to announce the opening of the Sarah Dunlap Rule Museum and Library of Nursing History. At this time, we will store items in a little building at the back of our property." Will advanced the slide to show the building and the sign in the window. "Dean Bridger, we want you to have the first honorary key. Of course you will have to get your own library card—and volunteer to answer the phones too!" The audience laughed, and so did the dean.

Ella continued, "As you can imagine, this is the first tiny step toward our new dream. But we have long wished for a proper place for Sarah's button and all that it stands for, and now we can say it has come home."

Twenty Years Later
May 10, 2014
Indianapolis, Indiana

Will glanced at his watch and proclaimed, "Four-thirty on a beautiful Saturday afternoon—what a gorgeous day! Join me here, Ellie?" He patted the cushion beside him. She sat down carefully on the loveseat, juggling appetizers and a glass of wine in each hand, a chardonnay for Will and a cabernet sauvignon for her. They had started a weekly ritual of dreaming for their retirement, just two years away. "Guess what's coming up?" he asked her.

"I don't know ... the race?"

"Nope, that's a still few weeks away ... something closer."

"Hmm." She thought for a moment. "Give me a hint."

"Well, it has to do with nursing." She rolled her eyes.

"Oh, sure, now I got it! May 12, Florence Nightingale's birthday."

He nodded. "I was thinking of how she has changed so many lives. Our lives, Sarah Rule's, Charlotte Swain's. My mom's. And think of all the nurses of today that we know."

She smiled and shifted toward him. "I wonder, Will, what it would be like to have Sarah and Charlotte here with us, right now, on our patio, maybe even Florence herself? Your mother, too, she'd be here. What would they say? Imagine everything they would have to talk about."

He spread Boursin cheese with chives on a Triscuit and studied it. "Well, I'm thinking Charlotte would talk about the development of the American West, and travel. She'd be thinking about all the roles she had as a nurse and the places she could visit just because her skills were needed."

Ella smiled, thinking, sipping. "She'd probably wonder how Woody's life could have been extended if his TB had been treated in the 1950s rather than the 1900s."

Will nodded.

"And certainly both Sarah and Charlotte would be amazed at the progress of women's liberation—and disappointed at how much work still needs to be done. Pay equity, I could go on and on …." Ella shook her head. "I wonder if they'd think of mental health as a foundation. No matter the practice or specialty, everybody a nurse encounters comes with a mind *and* emotions *and* spirit, even if we are caring for them in a most routine non-urgent manner. And how about the huge wall of stigma we have to scale if we're ever going to have a country of healthy Americans?"

Will nodded. "Yeah, and just think of the advances we could make if nurses knew how to immunize *for* a baby's mental health as much as we can *prevent* smallpox or measles."

"Mm-hm. You're so right about that. But prevention's not very sexy, Will. Maybe we should tackle *that* in retirement."

Will winked at her. "Sounds like another job to me."

She smiled back at him. "You never know what we might be called to do. Say, this is a great wine, Will, thanks for finding it."

"Anytime, Ellie, anytime."

She took another sip. "Well, the nurses that come along after us will have their work cut out for them, won't they?"

He nodded and sighed, a deeply contented sigh. "They sure will, Ellie, they will. But one thing's for sure—it will be good work."

ACKNOWLEDGMENTS

While writing may seem like a solo activity, the evolution of *Called to Care* was a team event, and I am deeply grateful to everyone who came along on my journey. My first, and biggest, debt of gratitude is to my husband Neil. Thank you for believing in and supporting my dream, and tolerating the pull of early-morning disappearances into my writing sanctuary.

I value and respect the wisdom and perspective of the nurses who helped me understand aspects of nursing I was less familiar with, and who pointed me to resources and answered my numerous questions about nursing's history and its future: Rhonda Anderson, Dave Hrabe, Amy Steinbinder, Craig Laser, Kathy Malloch, and Alice Sisneros. Shawn Harrell generously shared her detailed three-part history timeline celebrating 100 years of the Arizona Nurses Association. Studying Shawn's display banner was a highlight of researching this book. Carla Rotering, Kathanne Lynch, and Tresha Moreland led me to additional resources about tuberculosis, Cochise County history, and healthcare workforce issues.

Thank you to my generous beta readers for your time and thoughtful critique of the manuscript: Nancy Berg, Maryann Gosling, Barbara Floyd, and Rebecca McElfresh. Your comments and suggestions helped me stay excited and intrigued for the last mile of the marathon.

John Floyd, a first-time author like me, gave unselfishly of his time and shared his knowledge of the world of independent publishing.

This book would not be where it is today without the sharp eye and brilliant suggestions of my editor, Wynne Brown. Wynne's style, humor, enthusiasm, and support for my project were exactly what the doctor ordered. I thank the stars for the recommendation made by my friend, Karen LeMay, who thought I needed to reach out to Wynne. "You'll have a lot in common," she said, "and she's also writing a fascinating book about the botanist for whom Mount Lemmon is named." I admire Wynne's own works tremendously; what an exemplar she is!

I appreciate the work of eagle-eyed proofreader and copyeditor Dave Peterson, guiding me through the final, exciting, stage of polishing. Who knew there were so many versions of apostrophe?

Thank you to all the family and friends who never missed an opportunity to ask, "What's new with the book?" You faithful companions are too numerous to list; you know who you are, and I appreciate every chance you provided to talk about this project. Your interest and enthusiasm helped bring it to life.

Finally, a note about nursing's future. I started writing *Called to Care* three months before COVID-19 was declared a pandemic and the world witnessed the overwhelming impact on nurses in hospitals and other healthcare facilities. At first I struggled, wondering what kind of message I was sending to my potential readers. Was I naively painting a picture of nursing that ignored the reality of COVID, the nursing shortage, and the upheaval of the healthcare system?

Given all these challenges, some say this is a difficult time to become or continue to be a nurse. Difficult, yes—yet I believe it's first and foremost an *exciting* time because the next generation of nurses will benefit from the intensified struggles of the 2000s. I discovered that many people and organizations are working collaboratively to understand the issues and create new approaches to solve them. The future holds many opportunities for meaningful practice with nurses at the helm and with technology's assistance. Nurse innovators will be welcome as nursing's true value is recognized and rewarded.

Nurses have always been problem-solvers. Sarah, untrained though she was, discovered that the need to "make do" with what she had, whether at Pittsburg Landing or in a patient's home, was exciting and challenging and allowed her to bring herself and creativity to the work. Charlotte, fueled by her curiosity and her partnership with Dr. Lyda, recognized their gold mine of valuable information at hand, information that could further the understanding and care of patients with tuberculosis. Will and Ella's pursuit of a program to help nurses with substance use disorder began with the question, "What if…?"

Here's another question: Who, besides a nurse, is better suited to the challenge of reinventing healthcare for the future?

ABOUT THE AUTHOR

JILL BACHMAN'S three-plus decades of experience as a registered nurse inspired her to introduce readers to the vast and fulfilling world of nursing. Her practice arenas have included mental health, nursing education, administration, and healthcare quality. Friends and family say that her superpower is listening. Jill plays the piano, enjoys travel—especially when combined with birdwatching, and she is passionate about the natural world. She lives in Green Valley, Arizona, with her husband and an indoor birdwatching cat, Pita.